BUTTON GIRL

A NOVEL

CLARE BECK

ISBN-13: 979-8-9916879-0-4 (Ebook)

ISBN-13: 979-8-9916879-1-1 (Paperback)

Published by Blue Barn Publishing

Cover design: kahnsdesign

For Grace, the OG button girl

PROLOGUE

GREER

When we were children, my mother's go-to bedtime story went something like this:

"Once upon a time, there lived a handsome prince who fell in love with the most beautiful girl from his village. He promised her that one day, he'd ask her to marry him. For months, they were the *it* couple. They were invited to the best parties and always surrounded by friends who wanted to bask in their energy and glamour. Then, a less beautiful girl moved to town. She was mousey-haired and quiet, with eyes as dull as buttons, but had more wealth than the prince's girlfriend. So the prince's *evil* parents made him reject his sweetheart and ask the new girl to marry him."

My mother always placed her hand over her heart at this point in the story, sighed deeply and shook her glossy gold hair.

"The prince's true love, distraught and cast aside, was then rescued by the prince's best friend, and they *tried* to live happily ever after."

Caroline and I were always sucked in. The ending never ceased to leave my sister feeling cheated. She demanded to know exactly what happened with the prince and mouse girl. Did they live happily ever after? Or did the prince pine for his true love forever?

For me, I wanted to know what happened between the prince and his best friend. Did their friendship endure, or did they become enemies? And not once did I call the prince's wife "mouse girl." She was always "button girl" to me.

Even as a small child, I swore my mother was referring to me when she described the homewrecker. Unlike my mother and Caroline, whose hair was as shiny and blonde as my mother's, I had hair as dark and ashy as a mouse. I was obsessed with sewing even then and collected stray buttons in a mason jar.

My mother dismissed my passion for needles-and-threads as a useless, weird hobby until we needed it to survive. That was after my fourteenth birthday, the day her bedtime story turned into a real-life nightmare for our family and all our fairytale questions were answered.

The prince and button girl, Nicholas and Ana Camillo, were indeed living happily ever after. They owned nearly every commercial development and apartment building in our Virginia hometown. They had three sons, all of whom were smart and handsome – and athletic, which carried more weight in our town than brains and looks combined. As far as I knew, Nicholas Camillo never once glanced in my mother's direction. And his wife was no mouse. She was as beautiful as my mother, but with chestnut hair and bright green eyes.

My father was Jack Scott, Nicholas' best friend growing up. He was incapable of being anyone's enemy. He was kind, easy-going, and generous with everyone in our town. But because of my mother and the broken heart she wore perpetually on her sleeve, his lifelong friendship with Nicholas ended the day he committed himself to her.

My father's love for my mother, though unrequited, was everlasting and true. And he loved my sister and me in the same way. He was happy despite having a wife who coveted someone else, until the day he left us all for good.

The aneurysm exploded in his brain outside the fabric store on my fourteenth birthday. He slumped over on the sidewalk, his fall peaceful and slow. It was the brand-new sewing machine he was carrying that crashed and splintered into a thousand pieces all over the concrete.

The Camillo's black and shiny SUV screeched to a stop, and Nicholas was suddenly there shouting my father's name, fisting his chest and blowing into his slack mouth, while I stood motionless beside them, unable to move or scream like I was trapped in a bad dream. Ana Camillo called 911. Their middle son, Nico, emerged from the side door with tinted windows. Suited for a football game, his cleats clacked on the sidewalk, kicking away pieces of my shattered birthday gift in his path to reach me.

"Greer." That he knew my name surprised me. His voice was gentle as he turned me around, grabbing my hand. The colors of his jersey shined in the bright sunlight. Royal blue with gold numbers one and seven. Seventeen. The stitches were tight and perfect, something the Singer Quantum Stylist 9960 now smashed on the sidewalk – "the supercomputer of sewing machines" as my dad just teased the staff, making all of us giggle – could have performed with ease. Grass stains streaked along Nico's white pants, and his shoes were caked with dirt.

He had his mother's green eyes. They shined despite the black grease striped under his thick lashes, bleeding down his flushed cheeks. He smelled of sweat and freshly mowed lawn, and his hand warmed my chilled skin when he squeezed it. He was being kind, and he wanted me to know he cared. I sensed this immediately and felt the intense urge to lean my head against the numbers on his broad chest and pretend nothing catastrophic was taking place behind me.

Nico Camillo was only a sophomore but the star of our town's high school football team. And he wasn't even the quarterback. The girls in my eighth-grade class were crushing on him even though he was dating a senior – not my sister Caroline, who was actually the quarterback's girlfriend, but one of her pretty blonde friends.

Maybe it was because he was named for his father, the man who ruined my mother's life and made her the insecure, unhappy woman she was. Or that he was trying to shield me from this situation, which I knew intuitively was horrific and final. My beloved father's slack mouth was not coming back to life. He was never going to laugh again with me and Caroline. Or smile adoringly at my mother, which he did all the time, mostly when she wasn't looking at him. His voice, rich and full of advice and constant encouragement for all of our hopes and dreams, was no more.

"I hate you!" I hissed to Nico, yanking my hand away and turning back to my father.

"Come on, Scotty!" Nicholas was whimpering now. My father was Jack; I'd never heard him called Scotty. He was dressed in jeans and the grey concert T-shirt my sister and I gave him, and Nicholas was pumping his clasped hands, bunching the distressed plus, multiply and divide symbols – titles of Ed Sheeran albums – along my father's chest. I reached out to smooth the cotton fabric.

My father was a whiz with numbers. We weren't as wealthy as the Camillos, but the entire town trusted his astute financial advice. Caroline and I admired the irony of the shirt. Our obsession for the pop idol depicted by the math symbols my father revered only second to our mother and us. When he came downstairs this morning, he showed off his shirt. "I'm wearing this for *you* today, Gree."

Then, he made us pancakes and retold the story of the day I was born. I arrived with a headful of black curls, the polar opposite of Caroline's golden strands. When the nurses combed it, it mirrored my father's own thick, dark hair. "You reminded me so much of my mother, I begged Mom to name you Greer Scott. Fortunately, she agreed. You never looked like a Priscilla."

"Prissy Scott." Caroline pointed to me, laughing. "Can you imagine?"

"Priscilla's a beautiful name," my mother defended.

"Priscilla is a girl who wears Lily Pulitzer, carries Kate Spade, and gets pedicures," Caroline said. "Greer is a girl who dresses in black leggings and T-shirts and sews kitsch in her room all day."

"That's our Greer." My mother leaned over and patted my head.

"One day your sister's designs will be famous," my dad said to Caroline. "She made that shirt you're wearing, didn't she?"

Caroline wore a fitted royal-blue shirt with her boyfriend's number hand-sewn on the back. The stitches were neat and close-to-perfect, but not nearly as tight as the machine stitching of Nico's jersey. As the queen bee of all the players' girlfriends, she couldn't wait to show off her unique tee at the season opener. As I straightened the hem of the Ed Sheeran T-shirt, I wondered where she was right now as our father lay dying on the main thoroughfare of our hometown.

The squeal of sirens made me look up, and I saw my father's dead eyes. Wide and glassed over, they looked black and cloudy, no longer violet grey. I stood as the paramedics quickly took over. A mask was placed over his face while uniformed men resumed CPR. On one side of me was Nico, silent and unmoving, but so close I could feel the warmth of his powerful body. On the other was Nicholas, no longer whimpering but sobbing and talking to my father.

"Come back to us, Scotty. I love you so much, Scotty. Jesus, Scotty, don't leave us now. You have so much to live for, man."

From the corner of my eye, I watched Ana Camillo walk over and put her arm around her husband. He hugged her back, clinging to her and crying even harder. In my fourteen years of life, I'd never once seen my own parents comfort one another like this.

A flash of anger, and renewed hatred for the Camillo family, washed over me.

When the back doors of the ambulance closed with my father inside, Ana assured the paramedics they'd take care of me. I stepped away from them. My foot landed on the intact presser foot lodged in a piece of cracked plastic. Minutes earlier, the salesperson had touted the quality of the presser foot, far superior to other models on display, and my father joked, "Nothing but the best presser foot for my Greer." I lost my balance and heard myself gasp.

Nico reached for my flailing arm, but I pulled away and regained my footing before he could assist me. Then I turned my back to the Camillos and ran.

1

GREER

*B*itter was the word that came to mind on my first day of college. Not just due to the chicory coffee, which I had to drink black because my mother and Caroline used up all the cream for their homemade facials late last night, after I'd gone to bed. Remnants of curdled cream and soggy cucumbers littered our worn laminate countertops this morning, which I cleaned up. *Bitterly*, I might add.

At this point, I couldn't see the value of a degree for me. Scotty Designs was busier than ever, and taking classes with kids still living in a bubble, without any real-life experience, seemed like a colossal waste of time.

But my silent partner insisted I needed basic skills if I wanted to take our business to the next level. And she or he was unwilling to keep infusing cash into a company, no matter how profitable, whose chief had difficulty with fundamental marketing, deciphering the complicated language of contracts, and reading a basic balance sheet without asking a dozen questions.

In short, I needed a business degree.

Fortunately, the high school where I enrolled when we moved to this charming Georgia college town allowed me to take online college courses my junior and senior years. Because of that, the local state university already accepted me with twelve credits. If I took courses in the summer in addition to six classes each spring and fall semesters, I hoped to earn this essential piece of parchment within three years.

Three years still seemed too long.

Most kids who went to college never wanted to leave. They stayed for four years, sometimes five, a few even six, to complete their bachelor's and maximize their college experience. Not me. I had no intention of lingering around campus more than I had to. Parties, clubs, sporting events, and Greek life were distractions I couldn't afford. Unlike Caroline, who'd already graduated from Butler University but still stopped by her old sorority house daily to help her *sisters* gear up for the upcoming football season.

"This is *our* year for the SEC championship," she told my mother and me when she moved in with us despite having good job offers in Atlanta and Miami. The promising team was just an excuse. She was hooked on college life. And football players.

I planned to go from class to my studio to work. Orders from the website continued to increase, and the pressure to develop new products was constant. I'd have to make time for homework and studying at some point. Deep down, I hoped the university classes were as easy as high school, when I barely cracked open a book.

I locked the door of our century-old townhouse and waved to my neighbor Nancy already sitting on her front porch, the newspaper spread out before her. In her hand was a pen, so I knew she was already hard at work on her puzzles.

"Good luck on your first day, Greer," she called to me.

"Thanks, Nancy." Her words were comforting. My mother and Caroline still slept soundly inside, oblivious to my trepidations about starting college and managing my business at the same time. The irony was, of course, that Scotty Designs was our family's only source of income right now. My mother refused to work unless she needed Botox money, and Caroline just turned down two entry-level broadcasting positions.

"It's not like I'd be on camera," she'd defended her decision. "They were behind-the-scenes-only jobs. Running errands, writing copy, and sitting inside dark news vans. That is *so* not me. Besides, Tripp Saunders is the starting QB this year, and he's been crushing on me for two years."

I shook my head at her. *You have to start somewhere,* I wanted to say but didn't. Part of me felt enormous relief that, after four years, we were all living under the same roof again. Caroline could now share the burden of dealing with my mother's erratic behavior. Also, she and my mother no longer posed a threat to the financial health of Scotty Designs.

Since entering into a partnership with an anonymous investor, my monthly income was fixed. After our expenses, including phones and cars, we were still able to save a couple of hundred dollars each month. There were never enough funds for my mother's cosmetic procedures. But she was fortunate that her dermatologist allowed her to greet patients in the office a few days every six to ten weeks as payment in kind. In her mind, Dr. Mark Wilson was getting a deal; she was a walking advertisement of his skill.

But I suspected that Dr. Wilson didn't really need my mother's help. It took months to get an appointment with him. Based on the way he picked her up and dropped her home – always holding open the door to his luxury sedan, walking her to the porch – he was half in love with her.

My car was parked more than a block away. I could walk to

campus, but my small studio – another perk from my silent partner – was a few miles outside downtown Butler. Since I had three classes this morning, all back-to-back, I hoped to be in my studio by noon.

The sidewalk of our tree-lined street was old concrete, so I kept my head down and avoided squares made uneven by mature roots. Compared to my childhood home, where I spent the first fifteen years of my life, this neighborhood was urban, less pristine, but safe. While I now considered those years idyllic, because my father was alive to love and care for us so completely, I tucked them deeply in the back of my mind. Instead, I learned to embrace the grittiness of this world.

We were surrounded by people who worked hard to make ends meet. A mix of blue- and white-collar professionals. But nearly everyone was friendly and unflashy. Nancy, whose house connected to ours, was a retired schoolteacher. Superficial people, families like the Camillos back home, would never choose to live here.

For that, I was grateful.

The car I drove was my family's old minivan. My mother almost succeeded in trading it in after my father died, but I begged her to keep it for when I turned sixteen. When her Mercedes G-wagon was repossessed, we were fortunate to still have the minivan in the garage.

Practicality was the bedrock of living well, my dad used to say, and the minivan with its sliding side doors and deep rear well was "car engineering at its finest." From trips to the grocery store to week-long vacations at the beach, this was his preferred mode of transportation.

And now that Scotty Designs was making more than wallets, phone cases, and bags, the square footage came in handy. Garment racks filled with samples fit snugly in the back. The Georgia heat and our lack of a garage had bleached the black exterior, but inside, the car still carried my father's scent. I never shared that detail with my family though. They already thought I was a freak.

Besides, they were both afraid to be seen driving this old van, I thought to myself as I carefully extracted the boxy car from its tight city parking spot. Instead, they shared a Mini Cooper. Used when we bought it but with low mileage. Something my silent partner – otherwise known as my *fairy partner* – found for us.

Though I didn't know for sure, I suspected my silent partner was a woman. My original Etsy storefront, which went live shortly after my father died, sold cute accessories for girls and women, all with a decorative, but sometimes functional, signature violet button. My early clients were my classmates in Virginia and their moms, but within a few months, I'd started receiving orders from all over the country.

The sales were empowering, and validating, but my work was soon all-consuming. My grief was buried. Caroline graduated high school and moved here, while my mother exhausted my father's estate and life insurance money in her quest to win back Nicholas Camillo. I was too busy in my bedroom with my Singer Quantum Stylist 9960 – replaced and delivered by the fabric store the night my father died – to notice just how reckless she'd become.

In less than two years, what she hadn't squandered an incompetent investor lost for her. Nicholas Camillo still never glanced her way. The only thing of value not taken by the bank was her hourglass figure, constructed by one of the world's top plastic surgeons. So we loaded whatever personal items we could into our practical and dependable van, including my sewing machine, and followed Caroline here.

. . .

THIS MORNING'S drive to campus took only minutes. I parked the van in the commuter lot closest to the business school. Caroline was helpful in this respect. She knew the university like the back of her manicured hand and told me where to park so my walk to and from classes was brief.

I only registered for early morning classes, knowing they wouldn't be as full as the afternoon sessions. Today I had international marketing, social media for business, and the history of capitalism, which was an elective for the entrepreneurship program I'd been accepted to. While the first two courses promised real-world applications for Scotty Designs now, it was the third class I was most looking forward to. History had always been one of my favorite subjects, and skimming the books assigned by this professor made me feel slightly excited.

As I walked through the quad, in a Scotty sundress and my Doc Martens, I took a few deep breaths. Most kids wore shorts, T-shirts, and flip-flops. But I wasn't the only one in a dress. Southern girls were known for glamming it up. Spotting a few sorority girls now, primped like my sister in designer skirts and dresses, wedge sandals, and with perfect loose waves in their hair, made me feel more comfortable about my outfit. Showing up at my studio in shorts and a T-shirt was something I avoided, but I also didn't want to call attention to myself on campus. Like Caroline. My boots might be slightly goth, but operating commercial sewing machines required steel-toed shoes.

At fifty minutes each, the first two classes flew by. Both took place in lecture halls, surprisingly full. The professors were joined by a handful of teaching assistants. Each professor went over the syllabus and what was expected of students. The social media class also listed the most important platforms for businesses and how we'd be studying them over the next three months. Scotty Designs had Instagram, which we used, but our other accounts like TikTok were weak. And even our Instagram could be better. I was the last to leave the lecture hall, jotting down notes about each site and taking pictures of the overhead slides.

Because of this, and getting lost on my way to Smythe Hall, I was late to history of capitalism, the one I'd been looking forward to. Unlike the first two lectures, which took place in dimly lit theaters, this was held in a traditional classroom. Every face turned to me when I opened the door and stepped inside. Professor Helene Simmons, salt-and-pepper hair slicked back in a tight bun and dressed in a navy-blue-and-white gingham pantsuit, was propped on a stool in the center, a podium beside her.

I stood, frozen, too embarrassed to move.

She studied me over the tortoise-shell reading glasses perched on her dainty nose. She was older than my retired neighbor Nancy, but her glare was laser sharp.

"Greer Scott, I presume," she finally said, her Southern drawl light and refined.

"Yes," I answered. "I'm sorry I'm late."

She didn't reply, but her scrutiny of me from head to toe kept me immobile. No sounds came from the other students, who continued to stare at me. Judging by the tension in the room, I realized right away that I'd already committed a sin by arriving late. A pencil dropping to the floor echoed in the distance, breaking her silence.

"Please take your seat." Her hand pointed to the only vacant wooden desk in the room, in the front row, directly under her intense expression. No wonder no one else had claimed it.

My own eyes were now too distracted by the leopard-print kitten heels she was wearing, shoes my own mother would covet but paired poorly with her patterned suit, to notice anyone else as I took my seat. Prior to arriving, I had been curious. As chair of the entrepreneurship program, Professor Simmons signed the letter inviting me into this selective major. My academic advisor warned me that this class would be all upperclassmen due to its rigor, but that Simmons made an exception for me because of my business experience.

"Everyone's here at last," she stated as I sat down. "And I commend all of you who arrived *early* for this most important first day of class." She went on to explain that only twenty-five percent of the final grade would be the midterm and final; the remaining seventy-five percent would come from our partnership projects. As she spoke, her eyes kept boring into my own, holding me captive. Next class, I promised myself, I'd arrive on time and grab a seat in the back of the room.

"Historically speaking, partnerships are important when studying capitalism," she said. "One could argue that capitalism wouldn't exist without people working together and joining forces." As she spoke, I couldn't help but admit she was right; without my silent partner, my family's circumstances could have been dire. "Growth and profits suffer without teamwork. And you will learn that firsthand here." She glanced around the room then, a smile on her face.

"Now for the moment you've all been waiting for," she announced excitedly. I had no idea what she was talking about, but I couldn't turn to another student for help because I was afraid to break eye contact and risk annoying her again. She described how there were twenty students in the class divided into four rows with five chairs each. As such, I was seated in row two, chair one.

"The seat you occupy now will be yours for the duration of this semester." She smiled. Inside, I winced. Five minutes under her watchful gaze was torturous already. "Remember I have chosen partnerships *carefully*, and I have a proven track record for creating successful teams. Rows one and two will be working together," she pointed at our ten chairs, "as will rows three and four. So the person seated next to you is your partner." Her hands snapped together, pleased with herself.

I turned to my left. Seated in row one, chair one was a guy who looked uncomfortable in the wooden desk. He was tall and muscular with a mass of thick hair, damp from a recent shower. Like most guys on campus, he wore khaki shorts, a faded T-shirt, and leather flip-flops. He looked like he just stepped off the beach, with tanned skin and hair kissed by the sun. When my eyes finally met his, I felt my blood turn to ice.

Familiar green eyes. Shining brightly under the fluorescent lights.

Nico Camillo.

2

NICO

My first class and *she* walked in?

It had been almost four years since I last saw Greer Scott. She was a high school freshman when she and her mother skipped town, in the dead of night, abandoning her family's foreclosed home, the pool house still under construction. When the news of their departure flew through our small Virginia town, my mother exhaled for what seemed like the first time in her adult life. Sophia Scott was a menace to our family, more so after her husband Jack, who my dad considered a brother even now, died suddenly.

Her sister Caroline had already graduated from BU, and the rumor at home was that Greer was going to some fashion institute in New York or London. That's where she belonged, not some university in the south where football mattered more than academics. That's why I transferred to Butler after all.

When the bribery scandal hit the sports program at Michigan College this spring, during my sophomore year, there was only one team that had a shot at a championship and needed a tight end. This school. I knew running into Caroline or Sophia Scott was a risk, but a small one. Caroline was probably working in Atlanta by now, and there was no good reason for Sophia to be on campus. Even so, Caroline and Sophia were two sides of the same coin. I knew what they were after – money, power, and fame, mostly in that order. Thanks to bad experiences, I avoided that type of woman like a nasty infectious disease.

Greer was different though. Which made this situation worse for me. I liked her. I'd always liked her. Not in a romantic way although she did look awfully pretty right now. But she was cool. Interesting. According to my father, Jack Scott was the same way. A guy that everyone adored and respected, and cheered for. Despite what happened between him and Sophia, my dad never stopped caring about his best friend.

To this day, my dad's biggest regret in life was losing his friendship with Jack Scott. He also regretted that Jack never got to know my brothers and me. "He would have loved you guys," my dad would say, "and you'd have loved him."

Then, my dad would start crying. When it came to Jack Scott, my dad *still* got emotional.

Greer looked like a deer caught in the headlights when she entered the classroom. The professor was hard-nosed, I could tell from the way she took attendance and assigned us seats. She was angry at Greer before she even arrived because of her *tardiness*. But as soon as she said her name in her Southern intonation – "Gree-ier" as if there was an extra syllable in it – I had a premonition that this was the same girl from back home.

And then she walked in. All grown up. I swear my heart stopped beating.

She was the opposite of Caroline, a pretty blonde but totally generic if you asked me. Greer's hair was dark brown, almost black, and shiny like in those shampoo commercials. Her eyes were an unusual color. Grey or hazel, but they looked like purple diamonds when they focused on you.

I still remember how she'd glare at me in high school.

She and I had an unspoken connection. I was there when her dad died. My parents were too, and my dad tried his best to save Jack Scott's life when he saw him go down on the sidewalk on Main Street. Greer was with him. You could tell she was in shock, grabbing at her father's T-shirt while my dad administered CPR. She even told me she hated me, and then she ran away from us.

I tried not to take her words personally. They stung though. I convinced myself that she didn't know what she was saying, and since she was likely in shock, she'd never remember them anyway.

But I was wrong.

Next time I ran into her was the high school cafeteria. She was a freshman, and I was a junior. I felt her almost as soon as I entered the room. I turned my head and found her seated at the end of a tableful of other freshman girls, smiling and chatting. She wore black leggings and a lavender sweatshirt. The girls at the table, all carrying phone cases made by Greer, started talking about me. Obvious, because all heads turned towards me and they soon started giggling nervously. Except Greer of course, whose violet eyes shot me such a look of distain, pure hatred, that I almost walked into a steel joist.

And that's how the rest of that school year went. She'd give me the stink eye whenever we crossed paths. In the spring, I'd reached my breaking point. Despite my family warning me to stay away from the Scotts, I'd worked up the courage to confront her. On one hand, I wanted her to know how sorry I was about her dad dying. But, I also needed to find out exactly what I ever did to her to warrant such treatment. I mean, Nico

Camillo was a god at that school. Just like my father and older brother Matteo were before me. And just like my younger brother Enzo was now.

We were also good guys. My mother was determined that her sons be gentlemen – sportsmanlike on the field, respectful of teachers and coaches, and chivalrous to girls – always. If we went to the store and didn't hold the door for the person behind us, or help someone in need load their groceries in their car, we heard about it.

But I never got the chance to confront her. They left town. The school year ended. And I never saw her again.

Until now.

Dr. Simmons, as she just insisted we call her, pointed to the seat next to mine for Greer. It was the last available wooden desk in the room. I was torn. Part of me didn't want to start off my junior year at a new college feeling uncomfortable and awkward. On the other hand, I didn't know a soul at this school. This morning was the first time I'd even worked out with my new teammates, and they weren't exactly happy to see me.

I'd be taking one of the starting tight end spots away from someone. Either Ryan Edwards or Beau Meyers, both of whom told me they'd be kicking the shit out of me later. I knew it was Tripp Saunders, the idiot ringleader, who put them up to it. The QB decided from the moment he met me that I wasn't welcome.

Maybe Greer Scott would be my first friend here?

When she sat beside me, her scent of sunshine and fresh honeysuckle – pure Virginia summer – smacked me in the face. Her short dress was sweet and showed off her toned legs. She wore clunky black boots. Impractical in this heat, and ugly. But badass. And unlike every single sorority girl I'd already encountered decked out in three-inch heels. The camo-green backpack at her feet was one of her original designs. I'd recognize it anywhere given that my own mother had a few of Greer's bags hanging in our mudroom.

My dad was always happy to support the girl who hated my guts. "Jack would be so proud of Greer," he'd say to my mom. "Order whatever you want from her website. That girl's got talent!"

But then the professor announced that we'd be partners. For the entire semester. No requests for changes. And Greer turned to me, recognition that I was Nico Camillo slowly dawning on her heart-shaped face. A small beauty mark dotted her blanched cheek, and a slight cleft dimpled her chin. Her lips, full and pink and shaped like a bow, remained locked. Despite her dismay, she really was beautiful.

Even down to her purple diamond eyes, which now sliced daggers through my entire body still burning from today's workout.

Then Dr. Simmons told us to get to know our partners while she studied something on the podium beside her. The room erupted into the buzz of voices chatting. Like Greer and me, these students were just finding out who their partners were but seemed familiar with each other. Perhaps Greer and I, both new to this school, were destined to be partners?

Greer suddenly took her eyes away from me to process what was going on around her. Desks started scraping against the polished floor as the others began to huddle closer as they talked animatedly. She was thinking the same thing as me. Even if she wanted to get out of this assigned partnership, what other set of two would be willing to make a trade? The rest of the class was, simply, hand in glove already.

When she turned my way again, I said, "Hey Greer."

She blushed before her expression turned fixed once again. She didn't say anything at first, just stared at me. Then she looked to the front of the room and said quietly, "Why are you here?"

As soon as I heard her voice, though hushed, something inside me stirred. As though a butterfly was released in my stomach. Her voice was pretty, like the rest of her, and suddenly I wanted her to keep talking.

"I just transferred from a school in Michigan," I answered her. "For football. Why are *you* here?" My tone wasn't gentlemanly – Mom wouldn't have approved – but my being here for football made way more sense than Greer, who was creative and pretty darn successful already, being here. The only reason Dr. Simmons accepted me into this program was because of the landscaping company my brothers and I started in high school. Our "clients" were our parents, cutting grass and weed whacking their properties. All the sudden, I felt sorry that she had to go to this huge state university when she should be following her passion in a more fashion-forward part of the world.

Deep down, I knew her toxic mother was to blame.

Greer didn't answer me, but I did notice her roll her glittery eyes and shake her head. She was about to say something, but Dr. Simmons interrupted and called for the class to be silent and return desks to their rightful places. For the rest of the period, the professor reviewed the syllabus and started in on the first chapter of the major textbook which most of us, myself included, didn't have yet. Greer certainly wasn't sharing her copy with me though.

I wasn't the only person in the room who noticed that Greer was not being very neighborly. Dr. Simmons watched the girl like a hawk, perched from her stool in front of her.

When class concluded, I followed Greer out of Smythe Hall. She hurried across the quad. You'd have thought she wore running shoes instead of heavy boots. But my legs were longer and stronger, and I quickly caught up to her.

"Greer." My voice stopped her.

"Are you following me?" she asked. Her face flushed. She was angry. It was late morning, but the sun blazed overhead.

"No," I said at first. "Well, yes, I guess I am. But we are *partners* now."

"We can't be partners. I'm emailing her today," she said. "And if we have to be partners, then I'll just drop the class."

I stared at her, taken aback. Was she serious? Just like home, I had done nothing to this girl. "That's extreme." I smiled, hoping to diffuse her anger.

"Yes." She hitched her bag on her shoulder and folded her arms. "But necessary I think."

"Why are you so hostile?"

She laughed. "Are you for real?"

"Yes!" I raised my voice. "We're from the same hometown. I don't know anyone here. And I've never done anything to you, Greer. Why are you treating me as though I've harmed you in some way?"

She closed her eyes and exhaled. She started shaking her head, the same as before in class. As though there was something between us, something obvious, but that I was too ignorant to see it. She was being condescending, and I didn't like it. Even a little bit.

"Is this about the restraining order after Charleston?" I asked her. My parents had no choice but to file one after Sophia showed up on their anniversary weekend getaway and then confronted them in their bed-and-breakfast. She was unhinged, her behavior criminal, and my mother suffered PTSD for months afterwards. Unlike the other episodes, once in Turks and Caicos and then again in Italy, this took place on American soil. The law was on my parents' side.

That question got her attention. I'd surprised her, and then suddenly regretted my words. Even I wasn't supposed to know about the restraining order. I'd overheard my parents talking late one night when Greer still lived in Virginia. It wasn't until a few months after the Scotts left our town for good that I'd asked my parents about what I'd overheard. And they told Matteo and me the entire, frightening story. But they also asked us to keep it to ourselves because they didn't want Jack's daughters being punished for their mother's poor decisions.

On the grassy lawn, I watched Greer as her mind rapidly went from surprise to acceptance. As though I'd suddenly put the last puzzle piece in place, and she understood why her mother uprooted her all those years ago. What she would do with this information was another story. I'd let the cat out of the bag unfortunately.

Sophia would now know I was here and that I'd unleashed the secret she was obviously keeping from Greer and possibly Caroline. No one from home knew about Charleston. Maybe it was time to get the truth out in the open. Because of Sophia, my parents were furious I'd reached out to the coaches at Butler. They understood why I had to transfer out of Michigan; they just didn't want me here. My father, especially.

And then when I chose Butler over other good offers, he was devastated.

"Sophia Scott threatened your mother's life!" he'd raised his voice. "You can play football anywhere. Why would you do this to us?"

When I explained why – that this was the only team in my estimation that had a legitimate shot at a national championship – my dad still wasn't satisfied. Then he told me that he, my mother, and my brothers would never set foot in Butler, attend my games, and support me.

It was a direct cut and hurt badly. But after what went down in Michigan, I decided I was better off going it alone. I'd never accepted a bribe to throw a game. In fact, none was ever offered to me. But that didn't stop people from believing I had. It was my parents' wealth that gave that impression.

Greer was clearly upset. I watched her swallow a deep breath. It wasn't my fault though. Her mother did this to her. Perhaps I'd done all of us a service by getting the secret out in the open, on day one.

"Just stay away from me." Greer's voice cracked slightly, and I wondered if she was about to cry. "Please."

"Greer, wait—"

She took off across the lawn. Walking fast, occasionally running in her black boots. I gave her a head start, and then quickly closed the distance between us. I wasn't going to confront her again, but I wanted to know where she was headed. Stopping short of the commuter parking lot, I watched her step into her family's old minivan. Our high school's decal, faded, was on the back window.

I didn't live on campus either, but at least now I knew where to park.

3

GREER

I parked the van outside the nondescript, brick office building that housed my studio. My brain was on autopilot getting here. Most traffic in this town revolved around the university so the drive to work was brief as usual. The clock on my dash read 12:06 p.m.

About an hour had passed since Nico Camillo rocked my world by showing up on campus. But then he absolutely crushed me after class.

Everything clicked into place after he said "Charleston."

To my mother, my father's death was a windfall. The flashy car. Never-ending cosmetic procedures. Blonder, ever longer extensions. Even our house, which my parents had renovated before my father died. She had it gutted for top-of-the-line flooring, furniture and appliances. A two-story addition went up, even though my sister had left for college. A kidney-shaped pool was carved out of the yard and garden my father loved to maintain, and a pool house with an efficiency apartment was erected. She even hired a pool service, which she obnoxiously referred to as her "pool boys."

Then there were exotic vacations. She renewed her passport and disappeared for weeks at a time. Caribbean resorts and European chateaus. The Charleston trip to a romantic hotel seemed to come out of the blue since she wasn't dating anyone, but everything changed when she returned home early. Certified mail began to arrive for her signature. And, soon afterwards, we packed up the van and left.

I should have known the Camillos were behind it.

Yes, my mother was out of control while my sister and I were wrapped up in our own worlds. Caroline loved college life so much she refused to come home. And my days flew by with school and fulfilling Scotty orders. I used to joke that the Singer Quantum Stylist 9960 was my only friend.

But why did our family's sorrow always revolve around that family?

I told myself then that my mother's behavior was due to my father's death. Like Caroline and me, she was grieving in her own way. Everyone who knew my dad loved him. Nicholas Camillo couldn't hold a candle to Jack Scott. And my mother didn't realize how good her life was until he was gone.

But her obsession over Nico's dad must have increased exponentially, and Caroline and I were too preoccupied to notice. What had she done in Charleston to result in a restraining order? The best-case scenario was that she stalked from a distance. But could she have also threatened Ana Camillo?

I had no way of knowing unless I asked Nico directly, and that wasn't going to happen. My mother wasn't trustworthy either. She was a master manipulator. Besides, I'd be crazy to confront her with this. Her takeaway would be that Nico Camillo was in her backyard, which meant that Nicholas Camillo would also be here one day soon.

I promised myself to never tell my mother and Caroline that Nico Camillo was here in Georgia.

My studio was about seven hundred square feet, comfortable for the various industrial machines I'd acquired, most of them secondhand. We had a private bathroom and small kitchen area too, something my partner suggested considering I spent more time here than home. Once inside, I printed out the new website orders. Just like every day this month, when back-to-school shopping was at its height, there were too many for me to handle within three days. I called Melanie, a local seamstress whose work was excellent, to see if she could help out. She agreed, thankfully, but reminded me that she was going on vacation the following week. No matter how much we got done in the next few days, I'd be here all weekend filling orders.

My partner had been encouraging me to outsource some of our most popular products now that my semester had begun. Scotty bags and phone cases still sold very well. And I did have a large amount in stock. It was the custom finishes that held up shipments – choice of fabric lining, embroidery, buttons or zippers – finishes that I liked to do personally. I wasn't ready to let go of designing and creating each item that was mailed from this studio.

My clothing inventory was a different story. Scotty dresses, shirts, and skirts were becoming increasingly popular, and these were harder to keep stocked. When I first started sewing as a little girl, it was to make doll clothes. In middle school, my friends wanted new phone cases for each day of the week. So I constructed durable polyester phone case covers with button-hole clasps, and from there, moved on to bags and wallets. But designing clothes for women of all shapes and sizes was as fun as it was challenging. Like the accessories, I wanted to touch each product myself.

I was a control freak. Plain and simple.

Before I allowed myself to get blissfully lost in work, my mind removed from Nico Camillo and his picture-perfect family, I had to email Professor Simmons to tell her I needed a new partner or would drop the class. Even though I'd been looking forward to her class, there were other electives I could take and still graduate according to my ambitious schedule. My note to her was concise and firm. And once it was done, I breathed easier.

But freeing my mind of Nico Camillo wasn't as simple as I'd hoped. I still hated him, but my body also reacted to him in unexpected ways. I'd wanted to move my desk closer to his when the other students were doing the same. And then in the quad, as he stood before me, I couldn't help but admit that he had the ideal body for a guy. Tall with plenty of lean muscle, and a face that was handsome and intelligent. His focus was sharp even with the sun high above, shining in his eyes. Scotty Designs had yet to create clothing for men, but if we did, he would be the perfect model. Years ago, if Nicholas Camillo looked anything like Nico, no wonder my mother was still infatuated.

Thankfully my mind and heart were steeled. Never would I be weak like my mother. But keeping him a secret from my family would be impossible. Soon, he'd be sought after, no matter how well or poorly he played football.

After ten mistakes, which were not easy to fix on my commercial machine, I forced myself to take a break. I changed into running clothes and ran the perimeter of the industrial complex for thirty minutes. Then I ate my lunch, peanut butter on bread and an apple, and coached myself into focusing for the rest of the afternoon. TV helped dull my mind still spinning from this morning. And by the time the sun was low, I had made a significant dent in the orders.

I locked my studio and followed a few stragglers, two men and a woman dressed in business attire, out of the building. There were trendier parts of town, where a studio like Scotty Designs would likely do well if we added a storefront, but my partner and I decided against that, for now. I could barely keep up with the online orders as it was, and the rent here for the amount of space was cheap, especially two years ago when we signed the lease.

In January of next year, when the lease was up for renewal, we'd have to reevaluate. November and December were every retailer's busiest months, and Scotty Designs was no exception. This year, I'd also have finals and projects due. *One deep breath does wonders, Greer,* my father used to say whenever I felt stressed.

But he wasn't here to help me, and my mother and Caroline were not reliable. They *were* reliable to make demands at the end of the day, asking if I could pick up takeout on my way home from the studio. My phone had three texts from Caroline, and four from my mother, asking for sushi rolls and edamame from a restaurant close to the studio. Because the place was off-the-beaten-path from campus, and inexpensive, I texted them back that I'd grab dinner.

I realized it made zero sense why I let my family do absolutely nothing all day long yet was willing to stop for groceries, or takeout, or anything really on my way home from work. My dad was the same. Whatever I needed as a kid, whether a new sketch pad from the pharmacy or Green 3268c thread the fabric store could not seem to keep in stock, he stopped. My sister and mother were as needy as me too. But he never complained about it. He always seemed happy to run errands for us.

I wasn't quite that noble though.

. . .

"Is there a reason one of you couldn't take care of dinner tonight?"

My scalp was sweating and my clothes damp by the time I arrived at our townhouse. Because university was now in session, finding a spot for the van took fifteen minutes. There was no parking left in our neighborhood. I ended up so close to campus, I could just walk there for my morning classes.

My mother met me in the front room and took the food bags from me. She wore a bikini top and a sheer sarong. "Oh Greer!" Her face was thick with sunblock, which made the tan on her body darker. She still loved to sun, and usually did so in the afternoon on her bedroom deck that faced west or outside in our small backyard when Caroline was home. "You know how hard it is to find a parking spot when school is in session."

"The Mini has a parking pad out back!" I said, frustrated. The pad was too small for the van, which at least saved my mother and me from fighting over it.

"But the alley is always blocked, and it's a pain getting out," she argued. "Besides, you work right around the corner from Sushi Hana."

Caroline walked in from the backyard. She too was in a bikini, a wine glass in her hand. Like my mother, she protected her face from the sun. A pink trucker hat emblazoned with her sorority's letters was pulled low on her face. I couldn't see her eyes, but my guess was that she was buzzed. Since moving home, she tended to have a few glasses of wine each night. Something, thankfully, my mother didn't do with her. My mother had a slew of problems, but alcohol wasn't one of them.

"Gree," she said, "you are *not* going to believe what I'm about to tell you!"

I froze. Did she already know about Nico Camillo? I glanced

at my mother. She was smiling at Caroline and then at me, but it wasn't her schizo look.

"Let's sit down and you can tell her over dinner." My mother smiled at me.

I exhaled. If Caroline's news had anything to do with the Camillos, my mother wouldn't have smiled. She'd be frantic and pacing, like a caged lioness, certainly not acting happy with sunblock smeared all over her face.

Though Caroline needed to enter into the workforce now that she'd graduated, home life was better for my mom and me with my sister around. She was a buffer. I was head of the household after all, and even though my mother didn't do anything to change that, she held it against me. In Caroline, my mother had a friend rather than the reverse mother-daughter role she had with me. They talked about clothes and makeup, gossiped about my sister's friends, and followed the same TV shows.

Caroline was also full of energy. She talked animatedly and moved from place to place to keep herself from boredom. Growing up with her, she could be exhausting at times. But since my father died and our circumstances changed, she was a ray of light in a dark house.

"I stopped by the Delta Gamma house today." Caroline sipped her wine. "And Lila told me that the sorority board has *approved* hiring Scotty Designs to make the homecoming dresses!"

My mother clapped excitedly. I stopped eating my salmon and avocado roll. I'd met Lila in June to discuss designing pink dresses for the sorority's homecoming dance at the Butler Hotel this fall. The sorority was co-hosting with the football team, and the groups were fundraising for breast cancer. But I never thought she was seriously considering Scotty Designs. During the meeting, she mentioned that she'd already interviewed Stacey Bendet and that Alice + Olivia was bidding on the event.

How could Scotty compete with her brand? My partner and I lowballed her, hoping the exposure and hype would make up for the loss. But my partner was concerned because the sorority was also expecting a hefty donation from whatever designer got the job.

"I didn't realize Delta Gamma hadn't already made their decision," I said. "I mean the dance is only six weeks away."

"*Eight* weeks," corrected Caroline. "And I can't believe you're not excited, Greer. I mean, Delta Gamma could have hired anyone. But Lila wanted to give the *local girl* a chance. You are so weird."

"I am excited. It's a huge job, and I'm honored that Delta Gamma chose us—"

"Chose *me*," interrupted Caroline. "They would have never given you this job if it wasn't for me, Greer."

When I met Lila this summer, she didn't realize that Caroline was my sister. She found Scotty from promotional materials my partner mailed to local businesses near the university. But it wasn't worth mentioning this now. Besides, maybe Caroline did sway the board's decision in Scotty's favor?

The reason I wasn't as excited as Caroline and my mother was because this job might derail my budding college career. Lila wanted custom dresses for each of her sorority sisters, which amounted to over fifty dresses.

"I can't wait for the dance." Caroline clapped like a seal. "It's going to be epic!"

"I thought it was limited to current students and donors. Lila said the venue is too small to open it up to all the alums."

"You are such a downer, Greer. I can't get my own ticket, but I *can* go as the guest of the football team. Tripp Saunders broke up with his girlfriend. I made sure that he knows I'm available."

I took another bite of my dinner. At least the Camillo news hadn't reached them. If Caroline knew about Nico, she'd have said his name first. I also knew my sister. If she wanted to go to the dance, she would. If it wasn't Tripp, it would be another football player.

Would she pursue Nico?

I liked to think that Caroline would choose her family over Nico. But deep down, I knew she'd choose going to the dance over us. When I thought about her and Nico together, I wanted to spit out my salmon roll.

Creating so many dresses was also a problem, with Melanie leaving for vacation. I needed to hire a seamstress, fast. An experienced one.

"I think you should make all the girls look like pink fairies," my mother said. "For Halloween."

"This is early October and the Butler Hotel," my sister said. "The guys are going to be in tuxes, Mom. They have to be black-tie caliber dresses."

"My Elsa costume is gorgeous! People still ask me about that."

My mother's sheer Elsa costume frightened the trick-or-treaters and made all the dads blush when my mother handed out candy. While they started to argue about sexy Halloween costumes, I finished eating so I could write to my partner and start homework. Professor Simmons had also emailed me back asking me to stop by her office the next day, so I wanted to study the course catalog before our meeting.

"I have some reading to do for school." I stood up.

"But Greer," Caroline said, "you haven't even heard the best part!"

I sat back down.

"I told Lila that I'm going to be leading this project."

"What project?"

"The dresses for the dance," she said. "I'm going to be in charge."

I stared at her. Once my sister left for college, she viewed my Etsy storefront as a joke. According to my sister, nothing I created or sold no matter how popular was ever as good as designer goods from department stores or boutiques in downtown Butler. "In charge of what?"

"The design of the dresses." Caroline counted on her fingers. "Collecting credit card payments. Making sure they are finished on time. Keeping the sorority girls happy. There's a lot involved."

"It's the least you can do, Greer." My mother pouted. "Caroline got you this work, and she could use the extra money. She'd be a fabulous partner for you."

"I already have a partner."

"We should talk about changing that," said my mother. "Caroline would be fantastic for the studio. She can model the clothes." My mother beamed at my sister.

"Caroline majored in broadcast journalism," I said. "And she *despises Scotty Designs.* Her words."

"You are so immature," Caroline spit at me.

I took a deep, steadying breath. This was a conversation that would turn nuclear if I didn't end this and walk away.

"It is not possible for Caroline to be in charge of this. There is no budget for an additional person. My partner and I already agreed that for us to do this for Delta Gamma, we would be donating my time and our profits back to the sorority. There is no extra money. Only expenses. And to complete more than fifty dresses, we have to hire a seamstress."

"Sewing is all you do, Greer! You don't need another seamstress."

"You already turned down two broadcasting jobs," I said,

changing the subject. "Why don't you send out resumes again and go for a real job?"

"Oh my god!" My sister stood up. "You are so selfish, Greer! Lila should have gone with another company. This is the last time I ever try to help you." Then she stormed upstairs.

My mother stood next. "Your sister got you this opportunity, Greer. You should learn to be more appreciative of her efforts." Then she walked out of the kitchen. In anger.

I couldn't even disappear to my room until I cleaned up all of the containers.

4

───────

NICO

In my hometown, people used to ask me why I wasn't a quarterback like the rest of the Camillos. Simple. I grew up protecting my older brother Matteo on the field. Few defenders got past me, and when our team needed the first down, or a score from the red zone, I was his go-to receiver.

He was named one of the best high school quarterbacks on the East Coast his senior year. But when he went on to play college ball two years ahead of me, his stats plummeted except sacks. He'd recovered eventually and finished with a respectable record, but Matteo's dream was never the NFL. He was smart like my mother, and was now happily enrolled in an MBA program in Philadelphia.

His first college season was his toughest because, as he said, he didn't have me with him. He also couldn't imagine his tight end was me, the way I always imagined my quarterback was Matteo. When it came to football, that was my only strategy. Pretend the guy behind me was my older brother, the guy I'd looked up to forever and would give my life for.

That strategy wasn't going to work for me here.

Right now, I wanted the defensive line to pummel Tripp Saunders, easily one of the most arrogant guys in the league. Like his buddies Ryan Edwards and Beau Meyers, Tripp didn't want me here. He wouldn't pass the ball to me during drills, or he'd overthrow or underthrow the ball depending on the call. I'd memorized the plays and knew *exactly* where I was supposed to be, yet magically, the ball wasn't there and I looked like a fool in front of the head coach.

Deep breaths, that was all I could do to release the anger and frustration building inside me. Exploding on Tripp Saunders, whose jersey outsold every other jersey in the SEC, would get me nowhere. The offensive coordinator should have known what was going on, but he was too busy flirting with the cheerleading coaches. So I kept my mouth shut and jogged back to the line where Tripp would have some snide comment.

"Sorry, Nicole, I guess you just aren't as good as the hype." Or, "That Michigan money must have made you soft, man."

Keep your head down, I told myself. Next play, Saunders actually threw it to my numbers, but I was taken down just as my hands clutched the ball by one of Tripp's minions who wasn't even supposed to be on the field.

That got the coach's attention.

"Jesus Christ, Beech!" Jon Hampton finally spoke up. "What the fuck are you doing on the field?"

Of course, the cornerback Malik Beech was blamed for the star QB's douchebag antics. But the hit was solid, I had the wind knocked out of me, and was now forced to sit out until I recovered. Watching from the sidelines as Ryan and Beau caught every single ball for the next fifteen minutes was the bullshit I had to swallow until Coach Phillips got his head back into this practice.

Practice was called before he returned. Tripp ran off the

field and patted my shoulder in front of Hampton. "Welcome to the SEC, Yankee!"

As a Virginian, I wasn't a Yankee, but Tripp hit his mark in front of the coach with his cheap shot. I knew I'd get my revenge without having to do anything but watch from the bench. Films don't lie, and Ryan and Beau were both weak links on the offensive line. If Coach didn't play me, Tripp would be sacked plenty this season.

Beech's hit was hard, so I was the last to leave the locker room this morning. The athletic trainer wanted to take a look. Bruising around my ribs had already begun, but I'd experienced worse. She told me I'd need to arrive early for afternoon practice for taping. Hopefully my appointment with Professor Simmons wouldn't run too long. It was odd to be called to a professor's office so early in the semester. I'm sure this had something to do with Greer Scott. She most likely got her way, and now I'd be matched with someone else in history of capitalism.

This was for the best. My parents had called me last night, but I was already sound asleep from a grueling afternoon practice yesterday. I'd yet to tell them about my run-in with Sophia's daughter. Maybe, now, her name would never come up.

"Hey, Camillo, wait up!"

I was surprised that Dylan Ryder knew who I was. Tripp Saunders was arguably this year's NCAA golden boy, but any football analyst understood that his success wouldn't be possible without his left tackle. And, if I ever made it onto the field after this morning's shitty performance, Dylan would be the guy to have my back when I was the intended receiver.

"How the ribs?" he asked me when he caught up to me. "Beech got you good."

"Bruised." Unlike some ballers, I was never the type to talk bravado. My dad and brothers were the same. Being truthful was the easiest path to confidence, my dad always reasoned, particularly when it came to football. "They need taping for this afternoon."

"Well, I guess I don't need to warn you who the assholes on the team are, do I?" He smiled at me. Dylan was a sophomore and one of the reasons I chose this team. Tripp only became a superstar last year, which was Dylan's first. This team would be competitive for as long as Dylan was here and healthy.

I gave no reply. For all I knew, Dylan was another one of Tripp's cronies trying to stir the pot. Instead, I noticed his full backpack and said, "You got class this morning?"

"Yep," he answered. "Headed to Smythe Hall. Food marketing."

"Oh yeah. Business major?"

"I am," he answered. "But I should be in culinary school. Cooking's what I'm really good at. My family owns a restaurant and café."

"I guess culinary schools don't have D-I football programs?"

He laughed. His family's restaurant was on Amelia Island in Florida, a place my parents once took us to as kids. The more we talked, the less I suspected he was one of Tripp's followers. Dylan was definitely his own man. He knew what he wanted, a restaurant of his own back in Florida, and football was a means to get him there.

"My girlfriend's a Delta Gamma," he said. "I'm cooking for the sorority house tonight. A few guys from the team are coming over. Do you want to join us?"

When I didn't answer right away, he added, "Tripp may be there with his gang. A lot of the Delta Gammas date football players, but the cool girls stay away from him even though he's QB. He's a total whore."

"Sure, I'll come." For better or worse, Nico Camillo was a team player. The sooner Tripp and I settled our differences however one-sided, the better off the team would be. "I'm warning you though. I've never tasted anything better than my mom's cooking."

He laughed. "Neither have I."

JUST LIKE THE DAY BEFORE, I was seated before Professor Simmons waiting for Greer Scott to make her entrance. My two classes finished by noon. I grabbed lunch on campus and arrived to this office fifteen minutes early. Why? Because I had to get to the stadium early to tape up my ribs and be ready for this afternoon's workout.

Greer wasn't late. Yet.

Dr. Simmons didn't explain why she called me to her office, only that we were waiting for Greer. And I was suddenly annoyed. This was Greer's problem, not mine. I'd made it perfectly clear to her that I didn't mind being her partner. She'd followed through and emailed the teacher about making a switch. *She* was the one with the issue, not me.

The office door was ajar. Dozens of noisy students passed by the sun-filled corridor. The Adams Center, where most of the faculty offices for the business school were located, was a glass-paneled building, modern and open. Except this office, which was dimly lit with hundreds of musty books lining the shelves. Whatever space wasn't cluttered with books, paintings of European cities and iconic towers filled the walls. Italian classical music played softly in the background. Dr. Simmons was scrolling through her computer, but I still felt like I was sitting in Great-Grandma Camillo's parlor as a kid. There, my brothers and I had to sit, with our hands folded in our laps, and not touch anything. It was torture.

Then I saw her. She was exchanging numbers with another girl, but I couldn't take my eyes away from Greer. Today, she wore a white top that stopped right above her belly button, a short skirt, and black combat boots. The army-green bag was strapped to her back. Other than the punk boots, which were ugly and goth, she looked really cute. Her smile against her dark hair made her face more beautiful, if that was even possible. And I realized that I'd never seen her smile before now.

Like the day before, when I wanted to hear the sound of her voice, I had a strong desire to make her face light up. I wanted to be the person to make her happy.

The moment was ruined when she stepped through the door and realized, once her eyes adjusted to the dim light, that I was also here. Her smile quickly turned to a scowl.

"Please close the door and have a seat, Miss Scott." Dr. Simmons shut her computer, giving us her full attention. Her hair was less severe than the day before, and she wore a cardigan rather than a suit. But she still reminded me of a hawk. I was nervous for Jack Scott's daughter. Sort of.

Greer did as she was told, and her honeysuckle scent hit me as soon as she was seated.

"Thank you both for meeting me today," she started. "Mr. Camillo, are you aware that Miss Scott wrote to me and asked to sever your partnership?"

I glanced at Greer, whose skin was ghostlike. She didn't realize I'd be here with her today. "She told me she was going to write to you, Dr. Simmons."

"So do you also want a new partner?" she asked.

I wasn't going to lie, not for Greer. "No," I said. "I have no issue working with Greer this semester."

Greer's gasp was quiet but audible. "Dr. Simm—"

"I want to hear what you have to say." The professor held up her hand to Greer. "But first I'd like to talk. Is that acceptable to you, Miss Scott?"

Greer nodded.

"I have been teaching at this school for forty years," she said. "Keep that number in mind. When you were born, I'd already been here at this university for twenty years give or take. Fully tenured. Not bad for a Georgia debutante."

Vivaldi's *Four Seasons* continued to sound. Neither one of us spoke. I for one had no idea where she was going, but she needed to wrap this up soon or I'd be late for the athletic trainer.

"My point being that, in my time here, I have *never* severed a partnership. Moreover, no student has ever had the *audacity* to request a new partnership." She studied both of our faces. "Both of you are new to this university, and obviously unaware of my reputation on this campus. I will not be granting your request, Miss Scott, nor will I allow you to withdraw from my class."

Greer was about to object, but Professor Simmons held up her hand. "I also found your request *ironic*, Miss Scott. Capitalism was built upon partnerships. Tribes, towns, and countries throughout history were not always *friends*, but these groups needed to trade to survive. Money is the great equalizer, as you both shall see." Her hawkish eyes moved from Greer to me. "Your partnership is exciting because we have a fashion designer married to a landscape architect. You each bring entirely different skill sets into this partnership, which should be inspiring and empowering."

I shifted in my chair because my ribs were sore, not because this elderly professor just compared our partnership to marriage while also inflating my skill set. I was a grass cutter and weed puller, not an architect of any kind. I didn't know the girl next to me well enough to predict how she'd react to this dressing-down. But curiosity got the best of me. So far, Greer wasn't responding, but I'd risk missing practice entirely to witness how she was going to handle this formidable woman.

"May I speak now?" Greer asked confidently.

"My decision is final," Professor Simmons said. "But, please, feel free to say what you like."

"I'm speaking on behalf of myself only," Greer said. "Not *him*." She pointed to me.

"Understood."

"This is one of several electives in the entrepreneurship program." She spoke quickly, like her mind was on rapid-fire. "Nowhere in the course catalog does it state that students pair off for the duration of the semester. And it definitely doesn't explain that what happens within the first few minutes of the first class cannot be reversed."

"This is an upper-level elective, Miss Scott," she replied. "All courses require teamwork. Every single business major here knows exactly what happens in my class on day one."

"But you just admitted that Nico and I didn't realize how the class was run."

Greer wasn't speaking on my behalf, but I felt a little rush when she said my name.

"No one has ever complained before," she countered. "This class is the most sought-after in the business school, and probably the entire university."

"So, someone would take my spot?"

"Tread carefully, Miss Scott." Dr. Simmons touched her glasses. "You are in dangerous territory."

"If this class is so popular, you can easily find a replacement for me," Greer said. "Nico Camillo *won't* care. I promise you."

That wasn't entirely true, but I kept my mouth shut. Greer and Professor Simmons were locked in a staring contest.

"I hand select each pupil in my classroom," Dr. Simmons said calmly. "Simply put, it's an honor for you to be here. If you withdraw from my class, Miss Scott, you might as well with-draw from the university and start over someplace else."

Whoa! I glanced at Greer, who looked as confused and surprised as me. She was silent, but she didn't look over to me as much as I wanted her to.

"Were you two lovers perhaps?" she asked.

"No," I said.

Greer's "No!" was louder and accompanied by a head shake.

"I have had exes in class before." She raised her eyebrows. "Even the most difficult circumstances have created wonderful partnerships."

Professor Simmons stood up. "Thank you for meeting me this afternoon. I look forward to seeing both of you in class tomorrow morning at eleven a.m." She looked over at Greer. "Sharp, Miss Scott."

Greer nodded but said nothing. Instead, she lunged for the door, opened it wide and rushed out, her heavy boots stomping all over Vivaldi. She forgot her army-green Scotty bag. I hitched my backpack over my shoulder carefully – my ribs would get worse before they felt better – and then grabbed Greer's off the floor. I'd most likely be late for the trainer, and then practice. But it had to be done. As my mother always taught me, a woman's life was in her purse. Chasing down Greer, the girl who hated me, to return her bag was the right thing to do.

Professor Simmons, watching me, smiled when I turned to thank her for her time. Even though I didn't request this meeting and had other, more important places to be.

"Thank *you* for coming, Mr. Camillo." She laughed, nodding to Greer's bag. "Looks like you two are well on your way to being the best of partners."

5

GREER

*J*raced to the main entrance of the Adams Center in search of fresh air. In addition to being a horrible dresser, Professor Simmons was a tyrant. Nico was smug. And my whole body was pulsing with anger. Outside was no relief though. Late summer in Georgia meant thick afternoon heat. Deep breaths weren't cleansing or refreshing. I felt like I was sucking down warm butter. Splashing cold water on my face from one of the restrooms in Adams would have been a better escape.

Closing my eyes to the afternoon sun and exhaling through my nose, I tried to slow down my heart rate. The cicadas sounded like a sawmill in the sky. But then I felt a shift in the air. It wasn't a breeze unfortunately. Someone tall and bulky, with the earthy but pleasing smell of a grassy field, shielded me from the sun. With my eyes still shut, I knew Nico Camillo was standing beside me.

I opened my eyes. In his hand was my backpack, which I'd left in Dr. Simmons' office when I fled. I took it from him when he held it out, his expression difficult to interpret. He wasn't happy, but he wasn't mad either. His jaw was firm but relaxed. His green eyes shined brightly, like this amused him. If the situation was reversed, and he had me called to a meeting to be reprimanded for no reason, I would not be a good sport about it. His fingers brushed mine when he let go of the bag, afraid I might drop it. The touch sent a cool shiver up my spine, and I sighed, frustrated with myself that I was in this position in the first place.

"You didn't have to bring me this. I would have gone back for it."

"And face Dr. Hawk again?" he teased.

I smiled. She did resemble a hawk with her yellow eyes, magnified by her reading classes fixed on her nose. Why would she choose to wear a navy-blue sweater over a royal-blue shell? For a Georgia debutante, Dr. Simmons missed the lesson on what colors *not* to wear together. Unless, of course, she was color-blind, which made me feel sympathy for her even though, right now, I despised her.

"Thank you," I said. "I'm sorry she made you come today. I had no idea she'd do that." Something of value I *had* learned as a small-business owner was that it really was best to be honest with clients. And if you did something wrong, like mess up an order, you apologized first and then rectified the problem. I wasn't sure how to fix this partnership, but at the very least, I could apologize to Nico for making him be here.

Until now, I'd had a good day. Today's classes were prerequisites, literature, philosophy, and phys ed, and I'd made a new friend named Emma. She was a fellow freshman, from Maryland, and happened to be in every one of today's classes. We made plans to study together on Sundays. I'd also had lunch with Lila, the Delta Gamma president, and we'd agreed that I could design a few dresses and vary them with fabric and finishes. I'd sketched a few basic patterns to suit most female body types, and she seemed pleased. Which meant that Caroline would also be pleased. Fifty-two dresses were still daunting, but Melanie and I could probably assemble most of each dress the week after she returned from vacation. We'd then have about three weeks for finishing touches.

"If it makes you feel better," he said, "my name could have been Montague, yours Capulet, and she'd *still* make us be partners."

I nodded. He was right. She was doubling down almost as soon as she started speaking. When she said *married*, I cringed inside.

"Professor Simmons does have a point though," he said.

"What's that?"

"This partnership doesn't have to be personal." He bent down to look into my eyes. "We're not our parents."

True, but suddenly I didn't like his tone. "What's that supposed to mean?"

"Isn't it obvious? You're not your mother. And, well, I'm not my father. Though my dad's a good—"

He didn't finish his statement but he didn't have to. I glared at him. "Are you for real?" I asked, my anger reemerging. "This is exactly why I don't want to be your partner! You think your dad is better than my mom. Admit it."

"That's not what I was going to say."

"You said your dad is *good*." My voice was raised. "Which must mean that my mom is *bad*."

He looked away from me. We were standing on the landing of the Adams Center. Several feet below us was a wide brick walkway that sloped downhill to the lower campus. Guys passing by started calling his name. Definitely teammates, most likely heading to the stadium. Sorority groupies, blonde and pretty just like Caroline, trailed close behind.

"Greer," his voice was soft, "my dad isn't who you think he is."

"Your dad led my mom on," I said, "and dropped my dad."

"No, he didn't." His green eyes darkened. He was angry with me. *Truth hurts*, I wanted to say to him. But I stopped myself because deep down, I knew my mother was no angel in all of this.

This conversation needed to change direction. I took a deep breath. "When the time comes, I think we should divide up the work, complete our parts individually, and then piece it all together. We don't even have to meet." Staying far away from one another was the only way we could avoid fate. Just like Romeo and Juliet, we were destined to meet with disaster. I opened the front pocket of my bag and handed him a Scotty business card. "This has my email and cell phone."

He stuffed the card in the front pocket of his shorts, never glancing at it. *Oh well.* He probably thought the business card was high-handed, but I didn't want to waste more time exchanging contact information. Caroline could also show up at any moment, making this encounter with him even more uncomfortable.

"Seems you have this all figured out." His words were stiff. "Anything else?"

"There is one thing," I said, surprising myself. "My mother and Caroline are going to find out about you being here. They won't hear the news from me, but it's only a matter of time. I will *not* be telling them that we are partners for Dr. Simmons' class."

"You afraid they're going to invite me to dinner, Greer." He smiled.

"Actually, yes." I turned my back to him and walked away.

. . .

BEFORE I LEFT for the studio, I stopped at the grocery store for the basics and then went home. It was already mid-afternoon, so I'd be working late and not returning for dinner. Caroline and my mom were sipping iced tea on the porch, talking with Nancy. Their rolled-up yoga mats were leaning against the house, which meant they'd just returned from the gym.

"Lila texted me and said your meeting went *really* well," Caroline gushed.

"I hope you thanked Caroline for helping you get such a big order, Gree," my mother added.

"The meeting went well. Thank you, Caroline." I kicked the screen door open with my boot since my hands were full of shopping bags. "Hi Nancy," I called out before disappearing inside.

I caved in when Lila invited me to lunch and formally asked me to design gowns for the sorority's benefit. Partly because Lila was nothing like my sister. She was apologetic about how much they were asking me to do and completely understanding if I had to decline. Another reason for taking the job was to keep the peace in this house. Never again did I want to relive the drama that forced us to leave Virginia. If my sister was happy, my mother was happy. Life was calm.

News of Nico Camillo was a ticking time bomb, but at least I could mitigate the damage by keeping my own Nico news a secret. If he and I never had to meet, never had to interact outside class, there would be less chance my mother and sister would interfere in his life.

Caroline would soon get bored hanging out with our mother all day. She'd eventually get a job and leave this town. *Right?*

After I put the groceries away, I packed myself a salad and sandwich for later and gathered my homework for tomorrow. My plan was to multitask work and school at the studio so that I wasn't up too late tonight. Though I was already dreading history of capitalism tomorrow. Even without the Nico situation, Professor Simmons' syllabus was the most demanding. And she made it clear this afternoon that she was no fan of mine.

The van was double-parked out front, so I hurried. "I'll be at the studio late tonight," I announced, "so I won't be here for dinner."

"I'm having dinner at Delta Gamma," Caroline announced

"What about me?" my mom asked. "I hate eating alone."

"Have dinner with me, Sophia," Nancy called out. "I made seafood gumbo."

"Thank you, Nancy," my mother said. "At least someone around here cares about me."

I headed down the front steps, rolling my eyes. My mother could be so dramatic.

The motors of several machines were humming upon my arrival to work. Melanie already had a dozen bags, wallets, and phone cases waiting for me and had moved on to Scotty clothes. Her family owned a dry-cleaning and alteration business in Butler, and Melanie handled alterations. Her stitching skills were amazing, having learned to sew as a little girl from her Filipino relatives. As much as she loved working for Scotty, she told me that she could never quit her family's business. When we were really busy, like now, she brought her alteration work with her and spent her days here.

Sometimes, her four-year-old twins, Sam and Beatrice, tagged along with her.

"Greer," she said when I walked inside. "You will not believe the number of orders that came in!"

Typically this news was exciting, but right now, it stressed me out and I told her. Then I showed her the sketches I shared with Lila earlier. Unlike me, though, she wasn't worried.

"This is a smart strategy, Greer," she said. "These designs are very basic, fitting with the Scotty brand. Before I leave today, let's create some rough patterns. Tomorrow I'll bring in some fabric from the shop and we'll piece together some samples. This will be fun!" She hugged me. "I told my parents that you needed my help, so my aunt from the Philippines extended her visit."

"Really? I hope she doesn't mind."

"Not at all," she said. "She was already coming here so that we could go on vacation. My parents are over the moon to keep her here. She's my father's only sister, and they miss each other very much. She's also an excellent seamstress."

"I don't know how to thank you, Melanie. College is not going to be as easy as high school. Once this dress order is finished, the holiday season will be here. I just hope we can manage everything."

"I will help you as much as I can, Greer. You know that," she said. "But I don't think it's a bad idea to outsource the accessories, like your partner suggested. Or hire another seamstress. Although this space may not hold three of us." She laughed. "But do *not* quit college. Please."

Melanie returned to work, and I powered up my straight-stitch machine. Melanie had always been honest about her regret of not attending the university. She had been practical then. Why go to college when she knew her future was the family business? She married and had children young, and now felt like she couldn't go back until the twins were eighteen. When she revealed this to me, she admitted that she wished she hadn't been in such a hurry to grow up.

Our circumstances were different though. She had the safety net of her family. My mother and sister depended on me for everything.

Melanie left with the promise she'd meet me here with yards of fabric tomorrow around noon. Something to look forward to while I suffered through history of capitalism, under Dr. Simmons' hawkish eyes and next to Nico. He was handsome and, if I was honest with myself, sweet. He didn't have to carry out my bag. Once those sorority girls realized who he was, they'd be following him all over campus. I wouldn't even blame them. But it still didn't mean I liked him. Far from it.

I put on my headphones and picked up where Melanie left off. No matter how long it took tonight, I'd finish all of our current orders. There'd be more tomorrow, and we had sample dresses to construct for Delta Gamma. Security knew I'd be here past business hours and planned to escort me to my van like they normally did when I worked late. It was a safe neighborhood, but I spooked easily. And I hated being in an empty office building alone.

In between each finished product, I jotted down notes from my reading assignments due tomorrow. Today, Emma suggested getting the Audible app for my phone and listening to reading assignments while I sewed. Such a simple solution that allowed me to work and study at the same time.

For the social media class, the professor asked us to create a new post based on what we learned our first day. That too was easy with Emma's help. She took a picture of my outfit earlier. My hair blocked my face, but the fitted white tee and black skirt – both new Scotty items – photographed well, the basic colors sharp, on the university's lush quad. The point of the assignment was to target a specific audience, and one of Scotty's goals was to break into the college market. Perhaps the post would generate new orders?

By the time security escorted me to my van, I'd completed yesterday's and today's orders and no longer felt so overwhelmed by school. Granted, projects hadn't started yet, especially those with Nico. But for now, I could sleep well.

Today was a sixteen-hour day. When I pulled the van onto

our street, there was a rare open spot a few doors down from ours. I wouldn't have to park a half-mile away. This day was finishing almost as well as it started when I sat down beside Emma in my eight-a.m. class, and she told me she liked my outfit. Even the low point of the day, meeting with Dr. Simmons and Nico, had a positive outcome. We now had a plan to make it through this semester as partners who never worked alongside each other. With the Delta Gamma formal and the holiday season looming, the next four months should fly by. *Before you know it, Nico Camillo will be just another jock on campus*, I told myself.

I grabbed my bag and locked the car. All of the sudden, Nancy appeared on the sidewalk in front of our house in a pink nightgown and slippers.

"Thank God, you're home," she said. "I was going to call but I didn't want to disturb you at work. Your mother's acting strange."

I glanced at our house. Through the porch window, I watched my mother pacing the downstairs rooms. Her makeup was immaculate, her hair in perfect waves. I could tell she wore a skimpy dress and, by her gait, strappy high heels. It was now midnight, when she was usually tucked in her bed watching reality TV.

"Is Caroline home?" I asked.

"I haven't seen her yet."

"Did something happen?"

"We were sitting at my dining room table having a cup of tea. Sophia and I had just done the dishes. She helped me clean my gumbo pot because of my arthritis." Nancy held out her swollen hands. "Your mom's phone beeped a few times, and then she stood up and left without saying anything. She's been in this *state* ever since, Greer."

I thought I'd prepared myself for this, but my entire body

suddenly felt limp. It was happening again. There was only one person, one family, who made my mother like this.

"Thank you, Nancy. I'll take care of this from here. I'm sorry my mom kept you up tonight."

"You sure, honey?" she asked. "Do you want me to call someone?"

I thought of Caroline, but a flash of raging anger at my sister ripped through me. *She* did this to my mother. "No, I'll take care of her."

"Knock if you need me." I watched Nancy disappear into her house before I entered ours.

"Greer!" My mother ran in her heels from the kitchen to the front door to greet me. The house, for once, was picked up, the surfaces of our cheap furniture gleaming. Her phone was in her hand, and she held it out to me. "He's here. I just know he's here for me."

My sister had texted her a picture of Nico Camillo, beside Lila and some guy I didn't know but who had to be another football player. The three of them were standing at a kitchen island, all wearing aprons, plating chicken and biscuits. None of them looked at the camera, but they were all laughing.

Below the picture, my sister had written, "Look who just transferred here!"

My mother's glassy eyes met mine. Her taut, wrinkle-free skin, attempted to stretch when she smiled. There was only one word to adequately describe her right now: crazed.

I wanted to murder my sister.

6

NICO

Perched on her stool, Professor Simmons smiled and said, "Hello, Mr. Camillo," when I walked through her classroom door. I returned her greeting and then took my assigned seat. The bruising from yesterday's hit was worse today, and this morning's drills compounded it, so I had to slowly lower myself into the small chair. No one else had arrived yet. But within minutes, the other students began to trickle in. My eyes watched the clock more than the door, hoping for Greer's sake that she wasn't *tardy* again.

I was apprehensive about seeing her today. By now, Caroline Scott would have told her family about my arrival in Georgia. Granted, Caroline's presence at the sorority house dinner took me by surprise last night. But unlike Greer, I was relieved the entire Scott family knew that I transferred here and had a spot on the football team. News like this was always best out in the open.

The threat to my parents' safety, especially my mother's, had always been real. It was why my parents vowed to never support me here in Butler. I was on my own, they said. But if

Sophia Scott ever tried to hurt me, I wouldn't hesitate to involve law enforcement like my parents had in Charleston. As much as that might pain her daughters.

Greer had me conflicted. She infuriated me yesterday when she dictated the terms of our partnership. Who made her the boss? Yet then I went to practice, and Tripp Saunders asked me who the cute girl with the butch shoes outside Adams was, and I wanted to sack him myself. Greer was more than cute. When emotion took hold of her, like yesterday, and her face was flushed and her violet eyes focused on mine, she was totally hot.

She was different than other girls. At the sorority house last night, all the Delta Gammas were attractive and friendly on the surface. Many looked like Caroline Scott, highlighted blonde hair, tanned skin, sexy clothes. They were predictable in behavior too. Flirtatious smiles, bodies not-so-subtly brushing up against you, high-pitched demands to commandeer your phone and enter their contact information. Even Caroline still played those games.

She squealed when she recognized me and hugged me a little too long, her breasts pressed against my chest. Then she introduced me as one of her *best* friends back home, which simply wasn't true. Sure, I dated her friend Lucy for a few weeks, but I was sixteen and way too inexperienced. Lucy dumped me right after homecoming weekend, which at the time, came as a huge relief.

When I asked Caroline what she was up to since graduation, she told me she was a dress designer.

"Isn't that what your sister does?" I asked.

"Sort of," she answered. "But I'm the one who's going to take the family business to the next level."

Dylan asked me to help him with the biscuit dough, so I turned away from her. But I could still overhear Caroline talking.

"Greer didn't tell me that you were working for her!" Dylan's girlfriend Lila said to Caroline. "And I had no idea you were designing dresses. Here I thought you were looking for a broadcasting job! Those sketches she showed me today were *amazing*."

"I know, right?" Caroline laughed. "I'm not sure what she quoted you, but vintage Scotty is selling for a *ton* right now. We're going to have to increase the price."

"Well, I was expecting the gowns to be double what she quoted me," Lila said. "I can check with the board, but I don't think an increase will be a problem at all."

Something was odd about their conversation. I only knew the Scott family from the outside, but Greer didn't seem like the type of person who would put Caroline in charge of anything. Based on yesterday's events, Greer fled or got angry when she lost control. But Scotty Designs had been her family's only income source since they left Virginia. Maybe she relied on her big sister more than our hometown gave her credit for?

Back then, most felt Caroline left Greer in charge of their crazy mother and never looked back.

Greer was the last student to arrive, but she wasn't late. She looked awful though. Not just because her shiny dark hair was hidden from me, pulled into a tight knot. The style exposed the shadowy circles under her eyes, which were dull grey and devoid of any violet spark. Worst of all, she looked like all the other college girls in denim shorts and a T-shirt. I was enjoying her dressy clothes. At least she had on her combat boots, which were growing on me.

I deliberately pocketed her business card yesterday, pretending it meant nothing to me. But I stalked Scotty Designs last night before I went to bed. It was a well-designed website with a ton of products. My mom only ever owned the bags. But they had pages of clothing too, all for women. Even though her face was hidden in the most recent Instagram post, it was clearly Greer on the quad yesterday, dressed in her own label.

With her badass boots, she looked like the cool chick that everyone wished they were friends with.

Part of me was a little jealous witnessing all that she'd done since leaving Virginia. She was two years younger than me too. My parents made my brothers and me work hard, but none of us had ever created anything. Instead, we managed what other, smarter people created. Like energy-efficient buildings and businesses that succeeded under stressful market conditions. Food and medical equipment suppliers were typical Camillo investments, especially those that partnered with government agencies to help countries afflicted with natural disasters. As my dad always said, "We make money in good times and in bad."

All I had to do was steer a commercial mower around grass and pull out the weeds and Canada thistle that sprouted on mulch beds.

Professor Simmons must have noticed the difference in Greer because she didn't put her on the spot like she did most everyone else throughout class. Instead, she gave her a pass. The girl looked rattled anyway. At last, we broke into our partnerships, and Dr. Simmons announced she'd be spending time with each pair, frequently, throughout the semester.

Of course, she pulled a small chair up to Greer and me first.

The first assignment was a research paper, nothing too complicated. Our topic was the rise of mercantilism during the Renaissance era. Greer said nothing, which after yesterday, appeared out of character for her. Instead, she stared at the professor's feet. Dr. Simmons started us off by asking if we'd considered what we might focus on.

I'd done some reading the night before since the textbooks finally arrived to my place. Italy was the hotbed of mercantilism, precursor to capitalism, so I suggested that country as a starting point.

"Because you're Italian?" Greer looked at me. Her face suddenly looked young and vulnerable, but I wasn't about to let her get away with being a total bitch to me in front of Dr. Simmons.

"No," I replied in a calm voice, smiling at Greer and the professor. "I actually thought the topic would be of interest to you, Greer. The demand for textiles from Florence and Pisa from other European countries was, arguably, what started mercantilism. Which, of course, eventually led to capitalism."

"*Excellent* point," Dr. Simmons said. "I'm very impressed, Mr. Camillo. Football players are so underestimated on this campus, don't you think?"

I laughed. "Some deserve to be. Quarterbacks especially."

Dr. Simmons legit giggled before she stood up, lifted her chair and moved on to the next group. "Sounds like you two can figure this one out on your own. I look forward to your final paper."

From Greer I'd expected a strong eye roll when the professor wasn't looking, but instead she gazed at the desk, the fire in her extinguished. Something was wrong. We only had a few minutes left of class, so I asked her what her problem was.

She responded with an eye roll. Perfect. At least it was a spark.

"When do you want to get together to work on this paper?" I asked.

"I told you I'm not getting together with you," she replied. "We can email it back and forth."

"What if I don't want to work that way?"

"Even if I *wanted* to meet you outside of class and discuss mercantilism in Italy, which I don't," she glanced at me, "my time is limited."

"Same with me. Football comes first. But I'm sure we can find some free time in our schedules. You have to eat, don't you?" I opened the calendar on my phone. "How about dinner at my place? Any night except Friday. Mandatory team dinner before game day."

Greer wasn't repulsed by me. She'd slid her desk closer to mine when we broke into groups, saving my bruised torso from what would have been a painful task of moving my desk to hers. But the expression she gave me now could only be described as fearful. Her face blanched, deepening the shadows under her eyes.

"What is it?" I asked her quietly. "I'm not going to bite you." *Dinner at my place* wasn't something I'd planned earlier. The words came out of my mouth because the girl looked sickly, and well, I *was* Italian. Food was restorative. But her look to me right now hit hard and bruised my ego.

Unlike Tripp Saunders, I wasn't a player and never took advantage of girls. At the same time, what female on this campus wouldn't jump at the chance to have dinner at my place? Girls like Caroline Scott would rejoice over the invitation.

She exhaled and then spoke, matching my tone. "I just can't." She stood and was about to move her desk back into place. Class was ending. "Email works best."

"Let me put my information in your phone," I said, surprising myself by behaving just like a sorority girl. Greer's total contempt was forcing me to act out of character.

"Can you text it to me? I have to check in on my—" she paused.

"What?" I asked when she didn't finish.

"I have to get to work."

"Fine," I said, giving in. "If we're not meeting, I'll feel better knowing you have a way to get in touch with me. Besides what if I misplaced your business card?" I lied. Her card was on my nightstand at home, her contact information already stored on my phone.

"Are you always this bossy?" she asked, unlocking her phone and handing it to me.

I laughed at her. Me? Bossy? *She* was the controlling one. But I kept that to myself since she did give up her phone. I opened her contacts and added my name, mobile and email. Because Dr. Simmons happened to pass by my desk just then, I stood slowly and took a selfie with the willing professor from Greer's phone and added it to my contact. I overheard Greer whisper, "Oh my god," but she was laughing along with a few of the other students who witnessed me having fun with the professor, who was *clearly* a fangirl.

Like her book bag, Greer's phone case was her own design. I closed the cover and buttoned the clasp, handing it back to her. "Thank you."

When we left the classroom, Greer said, "Since you already *decided* on our thesis, would you like to write the rough outline? We can split the sections. It's due next week, so I'd like to have my portion done over the weekend."

"Sure." I walked alongside her and the rest of the students steering out of Smythe Hall at the same time. She hadn't run from me yet, and I wanted to ask about her family. Though we were surrounded by people when we walked outside the doors, I could still detect Greer's light but sweet scent. It was like a gulp of fresh air in the sticky Georgia heat.

Just as on Monday, Greer headed across the quad to the business school commuter lot. Same place where my car was now parked. I still had another class but I wanted to keep walking beside her. Having her next to me was comfortable in a way I didn't fully understand. She reminded me of home. Caroline did too, but my body had the opposite reaction to her. Last night, I felt stiff when she hugged me.

As we approached the walkway to the parking lot, I broke our relaxed silence. "Did Caroline tell you I bumped into her last night?"

Greer froze and glanced up at me. Her cheeks were now pink but her eyes were still sunken, as though she hadn't slept the night before. "She didn't. But she didn't come home last night either."

I nodded, not realizing that there was a chance Sophia Scott still didn't know I was here.

"My mom knows if that's what you're asking." She exhaled.

"Good." I smiled. "How'd she take the news?"

"*Exactly* as I expected." Then Greer turned and walked away.

7

GREER

ortunately, my mother was sound asleep when I double-parked the van outside the house. Passed out was more like it. Her manic episode caused us both a sleepless night. She scrubbed the house, exfoliated her skin, tried on sexy outfits that would entice her *Nicky*, and then repeated the sick cycle.

All. Night. Long.

Caroline was likewise passed out in her bedroom. Unlike my mother, hers was surely due to alcohol and partying until dawn. On a Tuesday night at a sorority house where she no longer paid room and board. With carefree guys like Nico who had professors like Dr. Simmons wrapped around their fingers. I laughed along with the other kids when he got her to snap a goofy picture with him. But there were casualties for their reckless behavior.

I hadn't talked to Caroline yet, but I'd prepared myself for what was next. Nico Camillo wasn't surprised when I told him Caroline never came home last night. Was she with him? He was just her type. A good-looking football player with a shot at the NFL. The only strike against him was that he wasn't QB. After all, her dream was to be the wife of a franchise quarterback. But now that she was no longer an undergraduate, time was running out. Nico had a history of dating girls who were older than him. He ticked off enough boxes for her that I'm sure one blank box wouldn't deter her.

Nico was exactly like his father. He'd never choose Caroline. She was beneath him, just as my mother was for his father before him. So in addition to having to care for an unhinged mother, I would soon have a psycho sister on my hands. Scotty Designs would suffer. My silent partner would quit on me. We'd lose the house along with everything else. And then I might have a nervous breakdown.

My only hope was to convince Caroline not to fall for Nico.

"Get up, Caroline." I shook her awake.

"What the hell, Greer!" she shouted. "I slept for like *two hours* last night. Leave me alone!"

"I have to go to work. We are cutting out the Delta Gamma sample dresses today, and I can't be late. But you have to wake up and watch Mom. Thanks to you being thoughtless and selfish, she thinks Nicholas Camillo is leaving his wife for her."

"She always thinks that way," my sister snuggled deeper into her covers, "maybe she's right this time."

"She's *wrong* about this, Caroline. You never should have sent her a picture of Nico Camillo."

"Nico is awesome, Gree. You don't know him like I do. He was one of my *best* friends in high school."

"No, he wasn't." I rolled my eyes. "Just go lay down in the living room. Mom's asleep but someone has to keep an eye on her. It can't be me, and it can't be Nancy again."

"You are worrying over nothing." She stood up and grabbed her pillow. "But since I think Nico might ask me to the Delta Gamma formal, I will sleep on the couch for you."

"You're as crazy as she is, Caroline." I spoke quietly. "The Camillos don't like us. Nico will never ask you to the dance! Wasn't your heart set on Tripp Saunders?"

She laughed. "You weren't there when Nico hugged me last night. He didn't want to let go. Tripp's still interested in me, especially after Nico's hug. There is nothing like being in a football player's arms."

I couldn't speak because I truly thought I was going to throw up.

"Nico is seriously hot," Caroline continued. "Wait until you see him on campus."

ONCE MY EYES witnessed Caroline curl up on the couch, I fled the house, not stopping in my bedroom to change out of my casual clothes. Projecting a professional image was important to me, and I hated showing up to the studio among other business-people in ripped denim.

But Nico and Caroline? *Dinner at my place*, my brain replayed. Why the hell would he ask me to dinner when he was coming on to my sister? What a sicko!

Revenge for Charleston was the only logical explanation. He wanted Caroline and me to suffer the way his parents suffered at the hands of our mother.

Melanie and her children saved me the moment I walked through the studio door. She brought Sam and Beatrice with her because her parents were in Atlanta, picking up Melanie's aunt from the airport. Giant pieces of scrap fabric were scattered along the hardwood floor. The twins were rolling themselves in individual pieces, as entertained and giddy as if they were rolling down a hill.

I pushed my worries and fears, and anger toward both Nico and Caroline, aside for the afternoon. I had to, or the patterns would never get cut. Today's orders were similar to the prior two days with the exception of tops and skirts. The Instagram post from yesterday, taken on the quad, did convert to new orders. Before we even touched the Delta Gamma dresses, we ate peanut butter sandwiches with the kids and took inventory.

My social media professor required data, so I pulled all the sales reports from our website and saved them in Excel. Once I had a week's worth of figures, I planned to create some visuals for class. Sending these to my silent partner would also be cool, I thought with a smile. She or he would be happy to see evidence that college was concretely benefiting Scotty Designs.

Then, the fun began.

We pulled out the dressmaker dummies from the closet and started to construct the sample dresses we'd patterned from my original sketches. Though the final dresses would all be in shades of pink for breast cancer awareness, Sam and Beatrice were in charge with picking out whatever fabrics they wanted for each different style.

The goal of each dress was to draw attention to one aspect of the female form. A sleeveless full-length gown that had a plunging neckline, a backless halter dress paired with a straight long skirt, a bodycon mini dress, and a strapless gown. Each one allowed the wearer to show off whatever trait they were most confident of, whether it be their breasts, their back, their legs, or shoulders.

The mistake women made, in my opinion, was to reveal too much. Full cleavage *and* a lot of leg, dresses my mother insisted upon, failed because they tried too hard. They overwhelmed the person, usually a guy, who the wearer was trying to impress. Better to leave more of yourself covered so that the same guy had to use his imagination. A well-designed dress *teased* rather than let it all hang out.

The pieces were also basic enough that we could allow for

slight variations. The bodice of the strapless dress could become one-shoulder. The halter dress's skirt could be made as wide-legged pants that were trending right now. And the plunge of the neckline could always be adjusted depending on cup size. What had to happen quickly was to take the samples to the Delta Gamma house for each of the girls to try on and order. Then we'd construct them, followed by a round of fittings. It was a lot of work with very little profit given our promised donation. But as I stated to my silent partner, these fifty-two dresses had the potential to open a new market for Scotty Designs. So she released funds for me to order the high-end natural and synthetic fabrics and make this happen.

Later today, I would send another request. One that would make my silent partner rejoice. I planned to ask for reserves to hire a part-time seamstress through the end of the year and a list of manufacturers to outsource some of the Scotty orders. As fast as I sewed, and as much as Melanie pitched in, there was too much work to handle in this studio. Caroline made it clear she would encourage my mother in her crazy quest to steal Nicholas Camillo from his wife. At the same time, my sister was hell-bent to stay the course on her own destructive path.

Relinquishing control of Scotty was, ironically, the only way I may be able to save the company and my family from ruin.

"These dresses are so pretty." Beatrice patted a gauzy skirt.

"They are." Melanie smiled at her daughter. "Greer, you keep outdoing yourself. Classic with a twist. One day, Beatrice, you will wear one of Greer's dresses!"

Beatrice smiled back at her mother. Melanie was amazing with her twins, always calm and encouraging even when they were boisterous or cranky, stuck at work with their mom. There was a time when my father was alive that my mother was patient and loving, when she took care of us. She made meals for us, styled our hair and took us shopping, reprimanded us softly when Caroline and I argued. She cared about our feelings. So much had happened since my father died and Caroline left for college without a glance back, that those memories were fading – and fast.

"Melanie, do you know any seamstresses looking for part-time work? I'm going to ask my partner for additional funding." Maybe if I spent more time at home with my family, helped Caroline look for a job and my mother to focus on something other than Nicholas Camillo, our lives wouldn't feel so out of control.

"Once I get back from vacation," she said, "you'll have me and my aunt. We will help you, Greer."

"What about your family business?"

"We'll work in shifts. And with your permission, we can bring some of the dresses to our shop and use the straight-stitch machines there, when the time comes of course."

"That would be awesome." I hugged Melanie. "You have no idea what this means to me."

"Because of you," Melanie held my shoulders, "my husband and I are taking the twins on a family vacation. And we've had the extra income to enroll them in private preschool. The dry-cleaning business is slow this time of year. So, this is the least my family can do for you."

I returned to my machine because I was about to cry. Melanie and her family might just get me through this until we could outsource work. It was positive news after my encounter with Caroline.

At that moment, Melanie's graciousness reminded me of my father.

How did *he* manage to handle my mother when we were young? She was never shy about how Nicholas chose Ana over her when they were in high school and how she never got over it. But she didn't act psychotic when my dad was alive. Why?

What did he give to her emotionally that allowed her to live her life without going off the deep end?

This morning after class, I'd considered confiding in Nico and begging him to stay away from Caroline. To protect not only himself but his entire family. Little did I know, I was too late. She'd already had him in her clutches, and he was a willing participant. Was Caroline the reason he was in such a good mood this morning?

Stop worrying about what you can't control. More advice from my father when I got upset. I had no control over Nico. And hardly any over my sister and mother. I controlled their purse strings, but after expenses, there wasn't much left over anyway. The only thing I really had control over was Scotty Designs.

We finished all four dresses, two in size eight and two in size ten. Knowing Delta Gammas, they'd probably all be size two or zero. But it was important to be able to give girls of all sizes an idea of what looked best. I placed them all on hangers, packed them with tissue, and the four of us loaded them into the van along with all of the fabric choices. Tomorrow evening I'd be meeting with the sorority to get custom orders.

I hugged Melanie and the kids goodbye, then returned to the studio and finished as many website orders as possible before fatigue took over and I went home.

My mother and Caroline were watching TV when I walked in. Like me, they both looked exhausted. My sister said hello while my mother ignored me. Obviously, she was still upset with me for challenging her the night before over Nico Camillo's true reasons for being at Butler. At least she was no longer manic. For now.

"I'm going to bed," I told them. "And I'll be leaving early for school." My first class wasn't until nine, but I planned to get to campus to do homework and start my research paper. "Will you be here tomorrow, Caroline?"

"Mom and I are going to yoga in the morning," she said, "and then we're hanging out, right Mom? We'll start prepping for the game on Saturday."

"But you'll stay with Mom all day?"

"Stop treating me like a child, Greer!" My mother sighed.

"I'll be here." My sister squeezed my mother's hand. "Not because I *have* to but because I *want* to."

Because you have nothing else to do, I told myself as I walked upstairs.

I showered and climbed into bed, my bones weary. Before I fell asleep, I checked my email. Surprisingly, Nico Camillo had written to me already.

Hey Greer.

Here's my attempt of an outline for mercantilism during the Renaissance. I wasn't trying to strong arm you into focusing on Italy. Textiles seems like something you'd enjoy researching. I still would rather we meet in person to work on this paper and the rest of Professor Hawk's partnership projects. My dinner offer was legit. The only nights that don't work are Fridays. And Saturdays if the team is away.

Attached is our football schedule so that you know when I'm away. If you misplace this attachment, the schedule is posted every five to ten feet on all 750 acres of campus.

Nico

I must have read his note a dozen times. Each time, his words came across as thoughtful, considerate, kind, and even funny. Yet all I kept telling myself was that his motives were sinister. This was not someone I could trust, or ever confide in. Meeting him for dinner at his place was out of the question. My response had to be prompt, and brief, so that I could get some quality sleep.

Dear Nico,

Thank you for the outline. I hope to have my sections of the paper completed by this weekend and will email them to you as previously agreed upon. Since there are RVs parked every five to ten feet of campus, Saturday's game must be home. You should have my portion on Saturday afternoon. Perhaps you can read it over dinner?

Meeting you outside class is not possible.

Greer

Imagining him reading a term paper over dinner after the season opener, one of the biggest games of the year, did make me smile before I fell asleep.

8

NICO

When I pulled my car into the business school commuter lot on Thursday morning, I was surprised to find Greer's van already there. It was six-thirty. The thin sunlight was still pink. On my fifteen-minute walk to the stadium, which helped loosen up my torso before practice, I kept a lookout for Greer but there was not a soul on campus yet. Where could she be, and why was she here so early?

I wasn't surprised she turned down my dinner invitation again. But she did it with humor, and that was progress. At least she didn't shut me out.

My phone buzzed. My dad, probably sitting next to my mom in our house in Virginia, having coffee at the breakfast table.

"Hey," I said.

"Nico. Mom thought we might catch you before practice."

"I'm walking to the stadium right now."

So my dad put me on speaker, and I heard my parents' voices for the first time since I moved to Butler. They'd hugged me goodbye, but things were still weird between us. Had I gone to

72

any other school, my parents would be on their way to watch me play this weekend.

"Are you ready for your first game?" my mom asked.

"I'm ready, but I won't get in."

"Why?" asked my dad. He was on the call when Coach Phillips recruited me. Even though Butler was a hard pass for my dad, he heard Phillips say that I was his guy and would be in the starting lineup.

"I had a bad hit a couple of days ago. My ribs are still bruised. The athletic trainer said I'll be eligible to play but there's no way I'm starting. I'm practicing full speed, with tape, and icing afterwards, but they don't like the size of the bruise." I never lied about injuries, but I wasn't going to tell my parents that the bad hit was orchestrated by the star QB, my own teammate.

"Why didn't you tell us?" my mom asked. "Do you need us to come down?"

"We're not going to Butler, Ana," my dad said. "Nico's just going to have to manage this on his own."

"Can we *not* do this right now?" I was suddenly annoyed. "Besides I'm fine. I don't *need* you guys here."

My dad sighed. He was pissed, I could tell. "Nico, don't upset your mother."

My dad was an expert at making me feel guilty. Since I knew exactly what Sophia Scott did to my mother and why coming to Butler terrified her, I had to end this.

"I'm not trying to upset anyone, especially not Mom. But we've been through this. I'm in Butler. That's not changing. The coaching staff here is the best in the NCAA. Butler is going to the championship with or without me. But I *know* I can contribute here and possibly make it to the NFL. I want to give it a shot." I exhaled. "Sophia Scott is a danger to you guys. But she and her daughters are not a threat to me." I even grinned thinking about how Greer was repulsed by me that first day of class. "Her one daughter can't even stand me."

"Who?" asked my dad.

"Greer," I answered truthfully. "I have a class with her."

I waited for my parents to respond. When they didn't, I explained to them that I was almost at the stadium.

"I thought Greer was going to school in New York," my dad said. "She's probably still taking care of her mother. What an unfortunate situation."

"Why can't she stand you, Nico?" asked my mother.

"Does it matter?" I didn't want to reveal that Greer blamed my dad for leading Sophia on and for ditching her dad. "She doesn't want anything to do with me. She wasn't happy to see me here, and she didn't want her mother and sister knowing I transferred."

"I wonder why," my mom said. "Are you sure you're okay, Nico?"

"I'm fine, Mom. I promise. But I need to meet with the trainer before practice to get taped up." I glanced at the sky before heading to the locker room. The light was still pink. Dawn would soon be replaced by bright sunlight laced with Georgia heat. Just in time for morning drills. "I love you guys."

My parents repeated the words back to me before hanging up. My mother's voice sounded like it was about to break, and I was sorry for causing her so much pain by being here. They weren't used to watching me play from a distance. They'd never missed a game in Michigan, or high school, or any sporting event in my childhood. They were always present for me, and the first people I turned to when something good or bad happened. Since committing to Butler, I'd prepared myself for not having them constantly by my side.

But I never put myself in their shoes. Not being here, not cheering for me, was hard for them.

. . .

LIKE THIS MORNING, Thursday's afternoon practice was tough. The coaches didn't just want a win this Saturday against Florida, they wanted to dominate. Dylan Ryder and I both had to spend time with the trainer afterwards, so we were the last two guys to leave the stadium. It hadn't taken me long to figure out that Dylan was one of the good guys. He was religious, the type of guy who would thank Jesus Christ before anyone else when a reporter interviewed him on camera after a big game. But he took his God-given talent seriously. He put his head down, worked hard, and made big plays.

Unlike Tripp and his sidekicks Ryan and Beau, Dylan wasn't a partier or a player. Drugs, alcohol, and girls throwing themselves at his feet didn't distract him. His girl Lila would be his wife one day, and he couldn't wait to be married to her.

He was intense for sure, but you had to respect him for it. He'd never intentionally hurt anyone, and deep down, he really did want the best for other people.

"Where you headed?" he asked me as we started walking uphill to the main campus.

"Just home," I said. "My car's parked in the business school lot."

"Cool. You can walk me to Lila's. We're having dinner at Delta Gamma. You're welcome to join."

"Big party like the other night?"

"Nope." He laughed. "Girls only. They're trying on dresses. Lila said they all just want green salad for dinner."

"I might need a little more than green salad," I joked.

"You're covered, man," he said. "I got filet and potato salad in her fridge too. The potato salad is my family's recipe. It hits the spot after a tough practice."

"Thanks, but I'm beat. I'll walk that way but will just head home."

"How you feeling about Saturday?" he asked.

"My bruising's a lot better. When I'm taped, I don't even feel pain. But I doubt I'll get in the game."

"Don't be so sure," he said. "Ryan played like shit today. He hit the bars last night. If Phillips and Hampton find out, he's done. They may pull him anyway because he's a weak link on that line. I told him today that he's making all of us look bad."

"If I don't get in, I'll be fresh for next week. Tripp won't get the best of me again."

"Praise Jesus."

The Delta Gamma sorority was an antebellum house near campus, not too far from where my car was parked, so I didn't mind walking a little out of my way with Dylan. The air had cooled some, and it felt good to loosen up after being submerged in an ice bath. When we turned onto Midvale Avenue, Lila was outside with Greer Scott and what looked like a closet on wheels.

"Dylan! Nico!" Lila called out to us. "Can you help us?"

Dylan walked a little faster, reminding me of my dad when my mom asked him for help. "Sure, babe. What do you need?"

Lila started to speak, but my eyes locked on Greer's. My presence was a surprise to her, and she blushed when I smiled at her. The pink light from the setting sun shined on her dark hair. Her day started as early as mine, but she appeared better rested than she had in class the day before. This relieved me. I was worried about her today despite her email rejecting my dinner offer. She had on another one of her cute dresses, this one navy blue and white, but instead of her heavy boots, she wore tan sandals with a heel that showed off pink painted toenails.

She looked professional yet sweet and beautiful. And she

smelled like a honeysuckle hedge. She did not like me, at all, yet I could not help myself but feel drawn to her.

Instead of her army-green backpack, Greer carried a light brown canvas tote bag over her shoulder. I recognized it as another Scotty because my mom had the exact same one. She said it was the best bag for carrying everything from her laptop to a half-gallon of milk. Greer, I noticed, had a thick black binder and a computer tucked away in hers.

"Can you guys carry this into the empty cloakroom across the hallway from the kitchen?" Lila asked. "But be careful and don't crush anything. And no peeking."

"We got it," Dylan said.

Before I lifted my end, I asked Greer if I could carry her bag.

"It's fine." She shook her head.

"Thank you for asking, Nico," Lila said. "I feel bad Greer had to wheel this thing down from the campus parking lot. Here," she took the tote from Greer's arms and handed it to me, "let him give your shoulder a break."

Greer said nothing but I watched her blush darken. She did not like having to be helped like this. My mother would be very pleased with me right now as I carefully placed the bag on my arm before lifting the metal rack and carrying it up the steps and into the front entrance while a group of girls, now giggling, held open the double wooden doors. Dylan led from his end while I was careful not to outpace him. Though the rack wasn't ridiculously heavy, I didn't want to walk faster than him and risk crushing him and Greer's garment bags.

We put the rack down where Lila directed us to. Then she asked Greer what she needed to set up.

"I can take it from here," she said.

"Let us help you, Greer," Lila insisted. "You mentioned that you wanted to brighten up the room. Dylan's making dinner for the house. He'll be here for a while."

"You guys can go ahead and do what you have to do," I said to Dylan and Lila. "I'll stay and help Greer."

"That is so sweet of you," Lila drawled in her refined Southern accent. "You know where to find us if you need anything." She pulled Dylan out of the room, leaving me alone with Greer.

The feisty girl from history of capitalism was not here tonight. In her place was Quiet Greer, and I could tell there was a storm inside her. Whatever emotion was brewing was not directed at me for once. She was nervous. Obviously she was here on Scotty business, but visiting this sorority house wasn't something she did every day. I wanted to ease her mind.

"Tell me what you need me to do." My voice was quiet but sincere. I wanted her to know that I was serious about helping her.

Greer's eyes held mine for a beat. Then she glanced at her watch, and the garment rack, and the small cloakroom. "I need to create two dressing rooms and maybe a workspace for taking orders," she exhaled, "within thirty minutes."

I nodded at her, smiling. "Let's get to it then."

For the next half-hour, I took direction from Greer. We unpacked mirrors and screens and created two dressing rooms. Greer removed a large crate covered in carpeting and flipped it over, propping mirrors around it. From the dining room, we borrowed a small table and chairs.

Then she pulled out her light fixtures, banged-up aluminum lamps with clamps and tangled cords. I saw her confidence break for a moment. "I hope these work." Her voice was quiet. "They're secondhand. I've never used them before."

"These look solid." I took the lamps from her. "Do you want them above the mirrors."

She nodded, and I busied myself. My parents were landlords. Though they had companies that managed their properties, we were often called out to fix problems like leaky faucets, broken windows, and electrical issues. The spotlights weren't complicated. If they didn't turn on, that would be a different kind of problem. But for now, I started by untangling the cords.

Greer's violet eyes showed vulnerability when they looked up and met mine.

"I got this," I said to her. "You must have your office in that bag of yours. Why don't you set up whatever you need so you're good to go."

As much as I disliked seeing Greer insecure – I preferred the girl who was always ready for battle – I was glad that I was the one helping her. Not Lila. And not Dylan, the guy who was always the perfect boyfriend. And it had nothing to do with my mother's constant drilling into our heads to be of service to others. I wanted Greer to need me and to trust me. And I had no idea where that desire came from.

Though I'd always *known* her, I'd also just met the girl. And I'd never felt this way before. Professor Simmons and her talk of partnership must have been messing with my head.

The lamp covers might be dented, but they worked, and it wasn't long before I had them fastened on the mirrors, hooked up to extension cords tucked along the floorboards, and plugged into outlets. Soon, the small room was lit up like a department store.

Greer, for the first time all evening, smiled.

"Thank you, Nico."

"You need anything else?"

"I don't think so."

There were already a few girls lined up outside the room. My mom loved clothes and always asked us for our opinions if she wasn't sure about her outfits. Like my dad, I always said she looked great no matter what she put on. So I wasn't an expert on women's fashion. But I didn't want to leave the cloakroom until I saw what was inside those garment bags. Because I knew whatever they carried, Greer created. Not her sister Caroline, or she'd be here right now bossing everyone around. But I also knew that wasn't my place. These girls needed privacy.

"Holler if you do." Then I left to join Dylan. Greer would need me again. Not right now, but later when she had to wheel this boutique back to her van. And I wanted to be the person to help her.

WHILE I HUNG out with Dylan in the kitchen, he explained to me that Delta Gamma was having a homecoming formal in October with the football team and each girl was having a custom dress made by Greer's company. Each of the football players was expected to attend to help the sorority raise money for breast cancer.

"Lila already found a date for you," he said. "That girl who was here the other night. From your hometown. She's graduated but she really wants to come and support the house."

Caroline Scott. There wasn't a chance in hell I'd be going anywhere with Greer's sister. But I didn't want to advertise this either. I had to nip this in the bud.

"There's someone else I'm interested in," I lied to Dylan. "She's not in this sorority. I'll just come alone. It's no big deal."

"No man! That's cool. Just bring your girl. The sorority is hosting the event, but you're free to bring whoever you want."

That wasn't the response I was expecting, but I supposed it wouldn't be difficult to find a date for this formal outside the sorority. So far, Greer was the only female on this campus who treated me with contempt. Plenty of women, including Professor Simmons, flirted with me everywhere I went. Homecoming was weeks away, but at least now, I no longer had to be worried about being set up with Caroline Scott.

The girls started to come into the kitchen in small groups. Dylan knew a lot of them by name. They didn't pay us much attention because they were excited about what was taking place in the cloakroom.

"I absolutely love the backless dress," said one of them. "I ordered pants instead of a skirt. Dancing will be so much fun!"

"Did you see that floral chiffon?" another one asked. "It is going to be amazing with the sleeveless dress. I'm definitely wearing my hair in beach waves."

"That will be *perfect* with that dress. Greer said the strapless one will go best with my clavicle bones. I hope she's right."

"That girl *knows* what she's talking about," the beach waves girl said. "Trust her. I can't believe she and Caroline Scott are sisters," she added in a low voice. "They are so different from each other."

And that's how the next two hours went. Sorority girls came through the kitchen, each group happier and louder than the prior one with their choice of dress. Only a few were brave enough to sample Dylan's potato salad, which tasted like a loaded baked potato. I had two servings along with my steak and salad. This evening was unexpected, and I was glad to be here, not just for the awesome meal.

"I'm going to have to make my mother's spaghetti and meatballs for you," I joked, "and see if I can outdo you, Ryder."

"Anytime! I'd love to learn how to cook Italian."

Lila walked in while we were cleaning up and asked Dylan to make a plate for Greer. "She said she's not hungry, but let's give her something anyway." Because his arms were buried in a sink of sudsy water, I made up Greer's plate with a little bit of everything.

"Football player portions." Lila laughed at the plate piled with food. "Thanks Nico. I'll bring it to her. We're almost done by the way."

Before long, Lila called us into the cloakroom to help Greer break down her portable studio. The dresses she'd brought were already zipped into their bags before we entered the room. Greer's plate was not untouched. Half her meal was gone, which meant she ate at least twice as much food as the other girls.

"Thank you for dinner," she said to Dylan. Her voice was relaxed and cheerful. Whatever happened in this room tonight, she was pleased with the outcome. "The potato salad was delicious."

"That's my mother's recipe." He winked at me. "She'll be glad to know you liked it."

The cleanup went smoother than the setup, and within a short time, Greer was ready for us to carry her closet back outside. Once Dylan and I placed the rack on the sidewalk, Greer insisted she could take it from here, that her van was only a block away in the commuter lot.

My car, I told the group, was in the same lot.

"That's perfect!" Lila hugged Greer and then me. "Thank you so much for tonight. We're all so excited for homecoming. Oh, and Nico, Caroline can't wait for you to invite her. Greer can give you her number if you didn't get it the other night."

Dylan shrugged at me, then Lila pulled him back inside the sorority house. Greer and I were alone, but the sudden change in her was easy to detect. Her skin blanched, her expression steely like before.

She glanced down at her feet and sighed. Then she said, "This is easier to wheel on the street."

9

GREER

Until the end, tonight exceeded my wildest expectations. I was so nervous bringing the dresses to the sorority house. I spent the last four years criticizing Delta Gamma and its members as shallow and irrelevant. But this was always because of Caroline. In my sister's mind, Caroline came first, Delta Gamma second, and everyone and everything else in her life, my mother and me included, were all tied for last.

But Lila was not like Caroline. Her energy was infectious, and she had a kind spirit. For her, breast cancer was personal since it took her mother away from her. She was determined to raise thousands of dollars for research at the homecoming formal. She and her sisters were dressing in pink no matter what. But she gave Scotty Designs and me a chance to shine because Caroline was her sorority sister.

If Scotty could succeed with dressing the highly fashionable Delta Gammas, the most sought-after sorority on campus, we could succeed anywhere.

Then I let Nico save me when my guard was down.

I was fighting so hard for calm when he appeared with Lila's boyfriend Dylan. Like every day this week, I felt overwhelmed with school and work and trying to keep my family stable. The only reason Caroline even stayed behind tonight and agreed to keep an eye on our mom was because I gave her cash to go to the hairdresser tomorrow. Nothing could stop me from showing up here, on time, and appearing like I had my shit together.

It was one thing for Lila to like my sketches. But if she and her sisters didn't like the sample dresses, there was nothing for me to do but apologize for wasting their time.

Hopefully Nico didn't realize how stressed out I was, or how much his presence and thoughtfulness affected me. All I could think about was how terrible it would be for me and my family if even one of the fifty-two girls hated my dresses. I literally almost fell into his arms and hugged him when he assembled those ancient spotlights, just after he brought me a table and chairs to set up my computer. At that moment, I'd wanted to be held by him too.

Just as I did on my fourteenth birthday.

But the constant stream of Delta Gammas and squeals of delight over what Melanie and I pieced together the day before pushed those dark memories away. Soon, I was in my zone. Pinning samples, helping girls decide on their dress, deliberating over fabrics. Some ran back to their rooms and retrieved heels, jewelry and wraps, to either help them decide on a fabric or assist a friend. The entire night felt like a dream. And then Lila carried in a plate of food, and I sat on the floor and devoured it while she and a few of her friends had the chance to try on the samples.

Lila wanted to wow Dylan but at the same time honor her mom. For someone like her, who was slender but had toned arms and curves in all the right places, the gown with the plunging neckline was ideal. And the pale pink fabric we chose was the perfect shade for her olive skin and brown hair, the cool tone allowing her warmth to shine.

"But seriously Lila," I said to her. "I think you could show up in a trash can liner, and Dylan would be happy."

"Isn't that the truth, Greer," added Megan, another one of the board members. "Eight makes all guys look bad." The sorority sisters referred to most football players by their numbers so Dylan was just Eight. "By the way, I was shocked to learn that your sister is Caroline Scott. I mean she never even told us about you!"

I got up from my spot on the floor before anyone noticed my face redden. *This was Caroline's safe place*, I told myself. *Where she could be whoever she wanted. And she didn't want to be a big sister to a sewing freak and a crazy mother, who lived in a house much smaller than this one in a less desirable part of town.*

So when Lila announced a moment ago that Caroline couldn't wait for Nico to ask her to the formal, how should I have reacted? As dangerous as I thought a relationship was between them, due to my mother and her sick obsession over Nico's father, I understood her attraction to him. And Nico was being nice to me because he felt the same about Caroline.

Maybe his motives weren't sinister? Maybe I had to stop interfering?

So we wheeled my garment rack up Midvale Avenue and into the commuter parking lot without talking, the steel wheels rattling on the asphalt like a squeaky shopping cart. He must have recognized our old van since he led the way and stopped behind it and asked me for the keys. I handed them over because he seemed to enjoy being helpful. We had to lower the rack about a foot, and we both had to lift the rack in order to get it to fit snugly in the van.

"Did you get this out of the van all by yourself?" he asked.

"I have a method," I confessed. "I take the rack out first and then load each garment bag or box on. But it's much easier if there's a second person." When he didn't answer, I said, "Thank you for tonight."

He stared at me. The streetlamp shined on his face, so I saw his mind struggling for something to say to me. Most likely, he wanted to rescind his dinner offer to me now that I knew about Caroline. I wanted him to know it was okay and that I never took him seriously in the first place, but I didn't want to argue again about Professor Simmons' class.

"See you tomorrow in class then?" I held out my hands for my keys.

"Right." He handed them over. Before he let them go, his hand hovering over mine, he said, "You did good tonight, Greer."

I smiled and turned my back to him, walking to the driver's side. He was parked only a few spots away from me, in a newer and sporty SUV, the kind of car that Caroline and my mom would know the sticker price of without searching Google. Of course, he waited for me to back out before him, like a gentleman, then followed me out of the lot, tapping his horn with a wave when he went in the opposite direction.

If Caroline and Nico wanted to be together, I wouldn't try to stop them anymore. I could still do everything in my power to prevent my mother from chasing Nicholas Camillo and terrorizing his wife. I'd also stay the course in history of capitalism. I preferred working independently anyway, and I couldn't allow myself to feel anything for Nico. Like I did tonight when I wanted so badly for him to wrap his arms around me and take my anxiety away.

A partnership via email was the only way to go. Just like my arrangement with my Scotty Designs partner. Nico wasn't anonymous to me, but pretending he was another nameless face amidst thousands of college students would keep my heart intact and my mind focused.

GAME DAY at the Scott house was the most relaxed I'd been in months. My sister was due at the sorority house early, having somehow acquired a student ticket for the season opener. My mother also left the house to meet up with her medical office colleagues. Since the Camillos were likely in town for the game, her face was taut and intense, devoid of expression. Dr. Mark Wilson himself picked her up, so she'd have to behave in order to get into the stadium with the spare ticket he'd purchased for her.

Despite the psychotic look in her eyes, I wasn't worried about her today. What kind of trouble could she get herself into surrounded by one hundred thousand fans?

Nancy and I sat together on our front porches and watched the two of them go their separate ways. They were twinning in their fitted football T-shirts, cutoff denim shorts, and wedge sandals. Even their newly touched-up blonde hair was similarly styled in loose curls. As if that wasn't cringy enough, they both had glittery temporary tattoos on their faces. The team's red wolf mascot on one cheek, and red number seventeen on the other. For Nico.

When the street was quiet again, Nancy asked, "Greer, why aren't you going to the game? You're a student now."

The excitement on campus yesterday did make me feel like I was missing out. Even Emma got the memo to dress cute, in a red romper, and support the team. Professor Simmons' midi skirt and blouse actually matched well and showed off her school spirit, but her designer shoes were again all wrong. I wore a Scotty dress but in the wrong colors. Nico, who like all the football players was suited in a shirt, tie, and khakis, asked me if I was going to the game.

"No," I said, "but I'll watch it on TV." My dad loved football and passed that on to Caroline and me.

"Would you like a ticket?" he asked me quietly. "I have two extras. The seats are pretty good."

Is he joking? I asked myself. "Thanks, but I have my research paper to finish." That, and orientation with Melanie's aunt at the studio around kickoff.

"Why don't you work on that after the game on Saturday," he said, "over dinner at my place?"

My face suddenly felt hot, and he started to laugh. Dr. Simmons was all business that day. She had several chapters' worth of material to cover so that we could devote all of our time outside the classroom to our partnership term papers due next week. I glanced at Nico when she said that, and he raised his eyebrows at me, his green eyes shined and he smiled.

He was teasing me, the little sister of his new girlfriend. I didn't like it and kept my focus on the professor and her black Jimmy Choo loafers, which overwhelmed her. Had I been with her when she purchased them, I'd have made her buy the ballet flats. Those would look awesome with her midi skirt.

The memory of the professor's outfit made me turn back to Nancy. "Scotty Designs has a huge order to fill within the next few weeks." I finished my coffee and stood up. "Today I'm training a part-time seamstress and won't be back home until late. Hopefully nothing crazy happens here again. But call me if you need to?"

"I will," Nancy said. "It's such a nice day out. I may walk up to the tailgate and see if I know anyone."

"Here," I joked, handing her a strip of my sister's tattoos. "Make sure you attach these to your face so you blend in."

.   .   .

AUNT ISABEL, as she insisted I call her, and I worked throughout the day. We caught up on the website orders and started on the gowns. Melanie had learned from the best since her aunt required very little guidance. The finishing touches on Scotty accessories were still done by me, but Aunt Isabel observed me carefully and even had a few suggestions on how to improve some of the products or add new features. Subtle differences, like patterned, reinforced lining for our laptop cases, something new she saw back in the Philippines. Colored metallic hardware was also gaining momentum in Asia. While I didn't love most of the materials she showed me online right away, the violet zipper and magnet closures would fit the Scotty brand well. So I ordered some for us to experiment with.

I also placed an order for a dozen new fabrics. Given the sea of red-and-white sundresses yesterday on campus, it was stupid for Scotty not to offer our shift dress, skirts, tees and tanks in university colors. It was something that we should have been doing for years. And I felt so foolish for not paying better attention to the demand for it.

Aunt Isabel's real talent, however, was as a dress seamstress. Her straight-stitch skills were efficient and masterful. She handled the Juki like a pro, and had most of five dresses constructed within an hour.

My sewing, on the other hand, was slower than usual. Kickoff was one o'clock, so I put the television on while we worked. The cheerleader uniforms for Butler drove me crazy. They were stiff polyester, totally outdated, and what was up with the fake boots? The girls were athletic and attractive, yet these did nothing to show off their figures. And the glittery logo lost its trendiness decades ago.

When the announcers mentioned that Nico Camillo, one of

the most promising new tight ends in the SEC, would likely sit the entire game out due to an injury, I felt my blood run cold. *What happened?* I stopped working, turned the sound up, and stood in front of the flat screen until the camera found him on the sidelines.

His helmet was off, yet he looked totally fine. In fact, he looked better than fine. As handsome as ever in his crisp white uniform with the bright scarlet seventeen emblazoned on his padded chest. His cheeks were ruddy, and his dark blond hair was damp and messy and shielded his eyes from the blazing sun. The coach next to him said something to make him smile. And the announcers explained that Nico suffered a bruised torso earlier in the week at practice.

I must have gasped because Aunt Isabel asked me if there was anything wrong.

"No." I recovered quickly. But how was he able to carry the wardrobe rack, leaden with heavy wooden screens and floor-length mirrors, with such ease? I hoped the effort he made on my behalf didn't cost him today's game.

We worked quietly throughout the game. Our team was winning, but Florida was never more than one score behind. Late in the third quarter, though, Tripp Saunders got sacked for a fourth time. Coach Hampton started going bonkers on the sidelines at the coach who'd made Nico smile on the sidelines before the game started.

I stopped what I was working on to see what would happen next. Butler needed a first down, which was now thirty yards away. On the sidelines, I watched Nico put on his helmet, and the same coach bracing his shoulders, talking sternly to him. The camera didn't show him running onto the field, but I noticed number seventeen on the line beside number eight, Dylan.

The play started and all we could see was the quarterback

pass the ball to a receiver and get the first down. The camera panned to Nico's coach, shaking his fist in praise and shouting to the players. But in the replay, the announcers showed clearly how Nico and Dylan succeeded in blocking the rush on the left side, allowing the quarterback to get the pass off.

From there, the lead for Butler expanded. Nico had eight receptions and two touchdowns before the clock ran out. Impressive statistics for someone who played only one quarter, and the announcers were not shy about praising him. It was Nico who turned the game around. When he and Dylan were interviewed together after the game, Nico had his arm around Dylan as he thanked his Lord and Savior.

The reporter, a petite bombshell, then turned to Nico and asked him what he thought of his performance after enduring bruised ribs all week. He bent his head down so that she didn't have to shout, a flare of jealousy instantly heating my skin. Which made no sense; he was just being considerate.

"The bruising was unfortunate, but I'm lucky to have such a great coaching and training staff here to support me," he said. "And Tripp Saunders played awesome today. I'm happy that Dylan and I were able to make a few good plays so that he could do what he's best at, and that's throw the football."

"You're also a transfer student," the beautiful brunette said. "How has the transition from Michigan College to Butler been for you?"

The question surprised him because he didn't have a ready answer. I watched his face deliberate for a few seconds. "The campus has been very welcoming." He smiled. "My classes rely on teamwork. And just like with football, I've made some great partners already. So I'm excited for the next two years. This place feels like home."

Partners? Did he really just use that word? The reporter ended the interview and Dylan and Nico ran off to the sidelines.

I tried to pause and then rewind the television, but the service here was basic; I couldn't analyze what he said.

"Do you know that kid?" Aunt Isabel asked. "He's cute. And he was so polite to that reporter."

"My sister is trying to be his girlfriend."

"Smart girl," she replied. "But what girl on campus *isn't* trying to be his girlfriend?"

WHEN I WOKE up on Sunday morning, my sister and mother were still sound asleep. I was the first to arrive home last night after locking up the studio around eight o'clock. My mother came in after me, her psycho mask slipping a little. She confessed that she was tired from the long day in the sun and didn't want to be disturbed this morning. Caroline came home just before six a.m., which meant she wouldn't surface for at least twelve hours.

I texted Emma to ask her if our study session was still happening. She replied right away.

definitely syl :))

This would work out perfectly. I could finish my homework and study at the library, and still make it home in time to keep an eye on my mother and let Caroline sleep. The studio could wait until tomorrow, for once, despite Scotty being so busy. Aunt Isabel's skill and speed got us ahead of schedule for once.

After having breakfast on the porch and chatting with Nancy, I packed my bag and walked to campus for the first time since starting school. The twenty-minute exercise felt rejuvenating. The entire town was peaceful, due to the decisive win for the football team. Traffic was light, the sky was clear and blue, even the air felt almost crisp. The walk home would undoubtedly feel different since today promised to be hot and humid, but for now, my body and mind were content. Almost happy.

My guess was that Caroline met up with Nico and the rest of the players the night before. Though she was no longer a student, my sister was just like another undergraduate Delta Gamma here in town. But what she and he did was not my concern, and I pushed thoughts of the two of them together aside so that I could enjoy the final few hundred yards to the library.

Inside, I was the first to arrive to our designated meeting spot. The first floor of the campus library was a gathering area where talking was allowed. The open floor plan looked more like the student center than a library. For Emma and me, the goal of getting to campus early was to secure one of the study spaces on the end, by the window.

I powered up my laptop to see if Nico responded to my paper yet. As promised, my sections on the Florentine and Pisan textile trades during the Renaissance were completed and emailed yesterday morning, before I left for the studio. Even though I knew he'd never see them since he'd be consumed by the game and its aftermath, I really wanted him to have them in time for dinner.

Researching and writing my portions were enjoyable and made Friday night pass quickly. Nico was right. Learning about the wool and silk textile market, how skilled the cloth makers were, and how the industry depended upon materials from the rest of Europe and Asia even then was absolutely fascinating. One of my favorite facts I included in the paper was the importance of purple dye, discovered in Florence in the twelfth century. The color violet was integral to Scotty Designs, but Nico didn't know that when he decided upon this topic.

There was no response from Nico, however. My race to

finish my segments of Nico's outline was for naught. This shouldn't have been surprising after his incredible performance yesterday, but I still felt disappointed.

Emma arrived, and introduced me to her boyfriend Blake. I recognized him right away. He took history of capitalism with Professor Simmons. Both were sunburnt from the game the day before, and they spent fifteen minutes rehashing stories from the tailgate and the game itself. For Emma, yesterday was her first college game. Blake, a junior, was a die-hard fan and came to this school for the football team.

Blake was here to meet his partner for Dr. Simmons' class to work on their term paper together. They chose feudalism in Great Britain and still had the majority of work ahead of them, unlike Nico and me. Blake mentioned that his partner Liam was one of his best friends but a total procrastinator.

Nico and I were probably better off not being partners, but I was grateful he wasn't a procrastinator. That would make me mental.

Once Liam arrived, Emma and I went through our literature and philosophy homework and exchanged notes. Both classes required individual term papers during the semester, but the topics were already listed; getting a jump start on these would be easy. The phys ed professor didn't expect much outside of class with the exception of the culminating project at the end. The course was a requirement for every student but tailored to education majors, so each one of us had to create a program for a specific group. Emma, a yoga enthusiast, already decided to create a yoga program for elementary-aged students.

What could I offer anyone besides sewing? Thankfully I still had time to think about what my project would be. Caroline would have taken this class and might be able to help me choose a good topic.

My computer notified me of a new email. From Nico. The

tables around us continued to fill, and kids who knew either Emma, Blake, or Liam stopped by to reminisce about how crazy and fun the season opener had been for them. While they were distracted, I opened his note:

Hi Greer.

I read your report over dinner as you suggested. (Dinner was pretty good. I made my mother's chicken piccata over linguine with a side of leafy greens. I'm sorry you weren't here to eat it with me.) Call me crazy, but it seems to me you had a lot of fun writing about the Italian textile industry and its economic impact during the Renaissance. At first, I was curious about the section on the significance of Florentine purple dye, but then I looked at your business card with your button logo, and I understood. Purple is personal to you. So I'm cool including it in the report, even though it deviates slightly from our main thesis statement.

What may improve the section is to better connect Florentine purple dye to the overall demand for luxury textiles and clothes during that era.

Here is a draft of the completed paper with our sections combined. I'm sorry I couldn't finish it last night for you. I had to verify all references at the library this morning.

Meeting in person to finalize this would still be preferable to me. I have some chicken leftover but based on how much food you put away the other night at Delta Gamma, it won't be enough. Are you a fan of barbecue? There's a local recipe I'd like to try. Let me know if tonight or tomorrow night works for you. The paper is due on Wednesday, and knowing you only a little, waiting until Tuesday night may stress you out.

Nico

The first floor of the library suddenly erupted in loud voices and cheering, but I was so engrossed in Nico's reply to find out what was happening behind me. I mean, who was this guy? Even if my sections were terrible, which they weren't, why would he even care that a small paragraph on purple dye from Florence in a paper about mercantilism during the Renaissance was even included? His future was the NFL. He could probably write fifteen hundred words about his love of Italy, and Professor Simmons would give him a passing grade.

I glanced down at my flannel shirt, which happened to have purple as its base color. Ugh! Shades of purple *were* personal to me, but why would a guy, a jock no less, even notice that?

And then his insult about the amount of food I ate the other night! Seriously? What he didn't know was that I'd been too nervous to eat that day, worried as I was about the reaction to my dresses. But what kind of person would even mention such a detail?

Caroline may be blinded by Nico's looks and ability to play football. But once she experienced *this* side of him – persnickety, intense, and overly critical – she'd flee. *This* was not his fun side, and Caroline only liked fun. Or was he messing around with me, trying to drive me crazy and make me work harder than any of us needed? Blake and Liam hadn't even started their term paper, and they weren't worried. We were as good as finished, yet Nico wanted me to *better connect* my portions to the *main thesis statement*.

Now I had to read his contribution. This passive-aggressive email deserved a snarky response. But I heard my name being called. And Emma, across from me, reached over and pushed down my laptop screen.

"I'm in the middle of something," I said.

"Greer!" With her eyes, she told me to look up and to my right.

Standing above me was Nico Camillo. And he looked pissed.

10

NICO

There were perks to being a football player. I tried to never take advantage of these. Hooking up with groupies, getting a pass at schoolwork, or taking bribes to throw games, which was what most of my Michigan teammates got caught doing. But I was perfectly fine using my height and strength to intimidate assholes. The two guys now at Greer's table sat in rows three and four, seats five, in Professor Simmons' class. They were partners like Greer and me, and I didn't like her being around them.

"Could I have a word with you, Greer?" I spoke in a calm voice. My eyes shifted from one guy to the other. Ironically, both of them had just congratulated me on yesterday's game before I noticed my raven-haired partner at their table.

Her eyes, brilliant purple diamonds reflecting the light from the window, found mine. She blushed, but she almost looked as angry as I felt right now.

"*Of course,*" her girlfriend answered for her. "We were finishing up. You guys want to grab lunch at the cafeteria?" she asked the assholes.

As soon as they stood up, a group of students swooped in to claim the table. Greer, who still hadn't said anything to me, got up from her chair and started cramming stuff into her army-green backpack. This was better because what I had to say to her wasn't going to be pleasant. We needed privacy, and that wasn't to be found on the first floor of the library.

She cinched her bag and looked around the table, making sure she hadn't left anything behind. Or stalling. Her phone was tucked in the back pocket of her cute denim shorts, and she checked her screen for any recent texts or calls. So I grabbed her bag for her and, with my free hand, invited her to lead the way. Her angry expression was now mixed with annoyance but she still didn't speak. I followed closely behind, her distinctive summery honey smell coming from her long, shiny hair. Once we were away from the tables and most of the people, she turned to me and asked, "What is it?"

A sorority girl stopped just then. "Nice job, Seventeen! I ordered your jersey last night."

"That's really sweet." I smiled. "Thank you."

Believe it or not, Greer didn't roll her eyes at me. But her cheeks were still flushed. When the girl waved goodbye, I said, "It's much quieter upstairs." I pointed to the exit door. "Do you mind if we find a room?"

The color drained from her face, and I realized my question didn't come out exactly as I intended. Many girls on this campus, like the sorority girl who just bought my jersey, would call me out for that. Turn it into an opportunity to flirt. Not Greer. She was terrified of me. Hopefully we'd address that today, also.

I pushed open the door and then led the way upstairs. In her white tennis shoes, she had no trouble keeping up with me, but I slowed down when I realized I was taking two steps at a time. Sucking in a deep breath, I tried to release some of the anger inside. I wanted those assholes, not Greer, scared of me.

There were plenty of small rooms available to students on the second floor. I picked one with a glass door so Greer wouldn't feel trapped. We could be seen but not heard.

The room was sparse, a table and a few chairs. I placed her bag on the table and held out a chair for her just like I'd have done if we were in a restaurant. She sat down reluctantly and I took the seat across from her.

Greer was waiting for me to start this conversation. I studied her. She was annoyed and nervous, but no emotion could mask how pretty she was. Her heart shaped face, perfect nose, and pouty lips were easy to get lost in. Her eyes, when they focused on you, revealed her intelligence and strength. And when she smiled, which was rare, it was like she was giving you a gift.

The Scotts were pretty people, there was no denying that. But Greer's beauty was unique. Her almost-black hair and her smooth, fair skin were so different than Sophia and Caroline who, based on what I saw yesterday, looked like they shared everything from their wardrobe to their tanning bed. Most guys I knew preferred that bombshell look. They wanted a brassy blonde-haired and busty trophy by their side. Not me.

As much as I fought it, I was attracted to Greer. I think she liked me too. But she was completely off-limits. She had to be. Family meant everything to me. And even though my parents admired and supported Greer because she was Jack Scott's daughter and was surviving despite her mother and sister constantly dragging her down, they'd never sanction a relationship between us. Of course, I was an adult and could make my own decisions, but I didn't want to ever be in a position to have to choose between them and a woman.

Just like Michigan, this campus offered plenty of girls for me to choose from. Not all of them were like Caroline Scott. Dylan found Lila after all. She may have the cookie-cutter sorority girl look about her, but she was nice. Maybe the formal would be an opportunity for me to test the Butler waters.

But I could still be a friend to Greer.

"Can I ask you a personal question?" I started.

She hesitated. "I guess."

"What brought you here today?"

She exhaled. "I met my friend Emma."

"You guys have class together?"

"Yes," she answered. "Actually, we have three classes together. So we picked today for a study day."

"That's great, Greer. You guys do homework and stuff?"

"Well, yeah." Her tone was biting, as though my question was really, really stupid. "I mean, we don't have a lot of homework yet, but we exchanged notes and brainstormed term-paper topics for later in the semester."

"Smart to work ahead," I quipped. "And who are the guys?"

"I met them this morning." She was relaxing, which is exactly where I wanted her. "Blake is Emma's boyfriend, and Liam is his friend. They're also in history of capitalism."

"I thought they looked familiar," I lied. "What were they doing?"

"They were just starting on their paper." After she said this, she blushed. As though a lightbulb went off in her pretty little head. My hope was that it went off in the part of her brain that felt emotions like *guilt*.

I nodded, staring at her. My anger was just under the surface of my heated skin. "Explain this to me, Greer. You have time to meet your friends at the library on Sunday morning to bounce ideas back and forth. For term papers due *later* in the semester. You also have no problem meeting with partners who *aren't even yours* for Professor Simmons' class."

"I wasn't *meeting* with them." Her tone was defensive. "They came with Emma."

"But *you* still had time to sit at the same table as them while *they* worked on their paper?"

"What's the big deal?" she asked.

"I'm your partner!" I raised my voice, slightly. "You told me your time was limited. Your words, Greer. I assumed this was because of your business, so I respected *your* rules."

"It's Sunday morning!" she said. "I would never have waited until Sunday morning to work on a project due on Wednesday. Why does this even matter? We're practically done our paper. Besides my *disconnected* section on purple dye, of course."

"Why couldn't you have dinner with me last night?"

"I was working!" she said. "If you don't believe me, you can call Isabel Flores. She just started part-time, and I was training her."

"On Saturday night?"

"Yes!" She stood up. "We were there all day sewing dresses. We watched the game together. She even called you *polite* when you talked to the reporter. I wish she was here right now to see what you're like off camera."

Inside, I smiled at her insult. She cared enough to watch the game and my interview where I heaped praise on douchebag Tripp Saunders because I *had* to.

"Can you tell me why you don't want to be seen with me, Greer?" I exhaled. "I mean, I would have met you here if you'd asked. Our paper still isn't finished."

Greer's expression turned into one of exasperation. She started to pace behind her chair. She tugged at a thick strand of her polished hair. Then, she stopped and faced me. "Nico," she said. "Your family—"

"My family has done nothing to yours, Greer."

"Are you going to let me speak?" she asked. "This is hard."

"You're right." I nodded. "I shouldn't have interrupted you."

She sighed. "*My* family and your family just don't mesh well," she said. "And I think the less interaction we have, the better off we'll both be."

"What do our families have to do with writing term papers?" I stood up because Greer wasn't about to sit down. "Are your mom and sister friends with Emma's parents? And Blake's? And Liam's?"

"Of course not."

"Then how does your family factor into our partnership?"

Her face, struggling for words, was still adorable to me.

She shook her head. "I think I know what you're doing."

Now I was confused, and I told her so.

"You're trying to get me to admit that my family is obsessed with yours." Greer was angry. "That we're the ones with the problem. My mother and sister may have a *slight* fixation on you, but trust me, I don't think about you and your family. Ever."

Now we were getting somewhere. Though I don't think I'd call her mother's and sister's fixation on us *slight* given what happened after the game yesterday, but at least she was aware of what the problem between our families really was. But I did think about Greer. A lot. And her words stung a little. "This still doesn't explain why you can't meet me for Dr. Simmons' class."

"Because it would turn out disastrous," she replied. "If I went to dinner at your house, or met you at the library, my mother and sister would insist on coming with me. They'd both be wearing Camillo jerseys with the number seventeen tattooed all over their faces. Caroline would probably jump you. And my mom might too. In her mind, she'd think you were Nicholas Camillo coming back to her at last."

I laughed. I didn't mean to. It was not out of humor. Greer grabbed her bag and went for the door. I blocked her. "I'm sorry." I held onto her arms and stared into her face. She was about to cry. "I didn't mean to laugh." My voice was low. "It's just that your mom and sister were waiting for me outside the stadium yesterday. And I noticed their tattoos." *And your mom jumped me.* But I didn't say that aloud.

Her eyes did start to tear, so I let go of her. She wiped them with her purple sleeve, and I apologized to her again.

"Are we done now?" she asked. "Do you understand why this won't work?"

I didn't respond.

"Unless you're madly in love with Caroline," she said quietly, "then you shouldn't lead her on, Nico."

"Wait," I said. "What?"

"Caroline." She shrugged. "You guys hooked up the other night."

"Before yesterday, I saw your sister once at Delta Gamma." I held Greer's hands and looked into her eyes so she'd believe me. "We did not hook up, Greer. I wouldn't do that."

She took a deep breath and nodded. She believed me. "This proves my point, Nico," she said. "My family is safer – you're safer – if we maintain a distant partnership. If I met you in person, they'd find out about it. And they'd never leave you alone."

I made a mistake bringing Greer here. All I wanted to do was wrap her in my arms and kiss her full lips, and make her forget about her family. Right now. Security pulled Sophia off me yesterday and gave her a discreet, but firm, warning. She was there with a middle-aged guy, who seemed reasonable and normal but unaware of how unhinged she was. Greer definitely had her hands full, and she didn't need me acting like a demanding son of a bitch.

Why did I bring her up here? To prove that she was disloyal to our partnership, which was not cool. But I also wanted us to be friends. Jack Scott was a legend in our house. He was my dad's best friend and had the pictures to prove it. Greer seemed more like him than her crazy mother, and I wanted to get to know her better.

My body didn't want to be just friends with her.

She was right though. My family, and hers, were better off staying as far away from each other as possible.

"Where are your sister and mother now?" I asked.

She looked down, at my hands holding hers. "They're asleep," she said. "I think."

"Do you want to grab lunch?" I asked. "And talk about the paper?"

"We just agreed that's not a good idea." She smiled anyway.

"I didn't agree." I smiled back. "We'll find someplace off campus. Where no one will even notice us."

She didn't respond, but her eyes were still locked with mine. And, for a moment, I sensed she wanted me to kiss her too.

"I think if we improve it just a little, we can get an A on this," I said. "And from what I've heard, Professor Hawk never gives out A's."

She closed her eyes. "Okay."

I grabbed my backpack and her hand and pulled her out of the room and downstairs. The first floor seemed as packed at the stadium on game day so I didn't let her go, afraid she'd reconsider lunch and run away. Her hand also felt perfect entwined with mine. People were shouting "Nico" or "Seventeen," reminding me of Michigan before the bribery scandal hit and athletes became pariahs.

The fans were incredible here, so I tried not to ignore anyone who stopped to congratulate me. I tightened my hold on Greer and kept moving us towards the entrance. Dylan and I, together, dominated the offensive line yesterday. Florida's defense could not get inside on the left, allowing Tripp to look good. Early in the fourth quarter, the QB knew he couldn't fuck around with me anymore. He had no choice but to execute the play calls. And I did my job and completed his mediocre passes. Coaches Phillips and Hampton were extremely happy, Ryan Edwards was definitely not starting anytime soon, and our team now had our work cut out for us to take on Carolina next Saturday.

But, for now, I planned to enjoy whatever time Greer was willing to give me.

My first week of being a regular student was over.

"Nico, wait!" Greer said, laughing.

I glanced her way, and her smile did stop me. It was powerful, transforming her pretty face into something that could stop a man from breathing. We were outside the library, the sun shining on her hair, the sky a deep blue. She was a vision.

"Our hands!" She laughed. "*Everyone's* going to notice you holding my hand! You should let go now."

"Sorry," I said. "I wasn't thinking." *With my head.* Another part of me had hijacked my brain, wanting to drag her back to my apartment most likely. That, or the Georgia heat was finally getting to me. She just asked me to keep my distance, and instead, I pulled her closer in front of hundreds of students.

Then she took off the purple flannel shirt she was wearing in the library and wrapped it around her waist. Underneath she wore a white tank top that stopped at her belly button, which had to be one of the most perfect belly buttons I'd ever seen. If that wasn't enough to cloud my judgement, I noticed that she was a Scott woman after all. Her breasts were perfect. Full and sweet. My eyes quickly returned to her face before she thought I was a pervert.

"Where's your van?" I asked her.

"I walked today."

"Perfect." I reached for her hand again. "I'll drive."

"We can't hold hands!" She smiled at me.

"My bad." I held up my hand. "Let me at least carry your bag. I'm afraid you're going to change your mind."

"So you're going to hold my bag as hostage?"

"Yes."

"You have to learn to trust me. I said I'd go, even though I think this is a bad idea. But I won't back out on you."

I watched her eyes as she spoke, and I gave in. We walked side by side to my car, parked in the business lot, and we each carried our own backpacks. She asked me about my bruise, which told me she cared, so I lifted my T-shirt to show her how faint it had become. Her eyes still widened.

"Did carrying the wardrobe rack the other night make it worse?" she asked.

At first, her question confused me. Carrying that rack was nothing compared to running drills or a weight-room workout. But she couldn't know that. Instead, she was worried that she harmed me in some way.

"Not at all." I smiled at her. "But *nothing* would have stopped me from helping you the other night, Greer."

My words caused her face to redden again, and she looked away from me. She was so easy to tease. Even though I missed holding her hand, having her beside me was comfortable. Her head barely scaled my shoulder, but we fit well together. And even though my goal was to be just friends, I was secretly pleased that people in the library might now be assuming more was going on between us.

What guy wouldn't? Greer was beautiful, smart, and successful already. She was a total catch.

Greer filled my car immediately with her scent, and I smiled to myself. Since I didn't know this town well at all, given that I'd only been here a short time, I asked her where we should go.

"What do you want to eat?" she asked.

"I'll eat anything," I said. "What are you in the mood for?"

"I can eat anything too." She laughed. "And I'm terrible at these decisions."

"Where's the best off-campus dining?" I asked.

She considered this. "I only know the area where my studio is. There're a few places over there, but most are takeout. And I don't think they have wifi in case we need to look anything up."

"Does your studio have wifi?" I asked.

She nodded, a look of alarm on her face.

"Let's get takeout and eat there." I glanced at her bag. "I'd love to see your studio, Greer."

Her mood changed. I think she was nervous about having me on her turf. But I suddenly didn't care about food or our term paper. I wanted to see Scotty Designs. The place where she was always rushing off to after class and where she watched yesterday's game. Where she created things that made customers like my mom so happy. The place where Greer found refuge from her mother and sister.

We grabbed fish tacos at a cool takeout place she recommended. It was next to an Italian ice stand, so I asked her if she happened to have a freezer in her studio. When she said that she did, I was sure she was joking. I picked up ices for dessert. She tried to give me cash for both lunch and then again for the ices, and I had to set her straight.

"I invited you out to eat, and I'm paying," I said. "That's the only part of this partnership that's not fifty-fifty, okay?"

"You're very bossy."

"I'm a good guy," I explained. "Good guys don't take money from girls."

She gasped.

"What's wrong?"

"Nothing," she said, recovering. "You just reminded me of someone."

WHEN WE PULLED into the parking lot of a business park with brick buildings, I was surprised. I expected her studio to have a storefront. She must have read my mind.

"My partner and I picked this building because space was cheap," she said. "The lease is up in January, so we're considering moving closer to campus and having a real storefront. We don't know if it will be worth the additional cost and effort, or if we should stay focused on the online store only."

"When the time comes, I'm happy to help you," I offered. "I know a thing or two about commercial real estate."

Her face blanched. Too soon, probably, to be reminded of the Camillo family business.

"Who's your partner?" I changed the subject. Until now, I thought Scotty Designs was all Greer.

"I don't know. It's a silent partnership."

"You're joking. How is that even possible? You're telling me that you don't know who your partner is?"

"I think she's a woman, but then sometimes my partner's decisions are so black-and-white, I wonder if it's a man."

"How do you communicate?"

"Through a third party," she said. "It works. And I trust her. Or him. Scotty Designs would be limited to Etsy, and my family and I would not have made it here without my partner."

Greer was straightforward with something very personal. I wasn't sure how to respond. "Wow," I eventually said. "Thank you for sharing that with me."

"The ices are melting. Do you want to go inside?"

She unlocked the building door, and I followed her down a

hallway that opened up to a two-story atrium. Skylight filtered through, landing on a small gathering area that was full of Southern charm, rustic chairs and tables. I could picture Greer seated here, chatting with her customers in her Scotty sundresses and combat boots. She and her silent partner did well choosing this space. Then I noticed the glass door with Greer's violet button logo off the atrium. She unlocked the door and held it open for me. In her hand were the melting ices.

"I'm going to put these in the freezer," she said. "Come in."

Her studio was a decent size. She had sewing machines along one wall and a farm table with chairs in the center of the room, a flat-screen TV hanging above. I followed her around the corner and found her putting the ices into the freezer drawer of a stainless-steel Whirlpool unit. It was an appliance I knew well because they fit perfectly in our studio apartment units back home. Greer didn't just have a small kitchen, she had a full bathroom too. I was amazed by the space.

"Do you sleep here, Greer?"

She laughed. "No! But I do spend more time here than at home."

Before we sat to eat, I wandered back into the main space and saw several pink gowns on cloth dummies. I was no expert, but they seemed unfinished. Greer caught me looking at them.

"You're not supposed to see them!" She grabbed a drop cloth to drape over the dresses.

"Why?" I grabbed her wrists to stop her from covering them up. "Last I checked, I'm not a Delta Gamma. I'm interested in how you make stuff."

"You *are* a football player though," she said, "which is even worse. It's like showing the groom the bride's dress before the wedding. It's bad luck."

I let go of her so she could hide her work. As a member of the team, I was obligated to go to the formal but I had no intention of taking a Delta Gamma. But I also didn't want to get into it with Greer and risk having to talk about Caroline. And I wanted to bring her sister up again but only because I was curious about something. Caroline told Lila she was designing dresses, but based on everything I'd seen so far, Greer's sister had nothing to do with Scotty Designs. But that was a conversation for another time.

"You win," I said. "But I would like you to show me how this sweatshop operates."

She shook her head and laughed. And I got to see her smile. Again.

11

GREER

This Sunday kept getting stranger. My emotions went from relief my sister and mother were home safely, anger with Nico for being overbearing about a three thousand-word term paper, crying about the stress my family's inappropriate behavior caused, to what could only be described as joy. Since leaving Virginia at fifteen, I stopped having friends. I had my family, Nancy, and Melanie. But there was no time to hang out and have fun with kids my own age.

My sister and mother did consider me a freak because of my sewing, but I was never a social outcast. When we moved here, Scotty Designs became more important than education. So I maxed out on online classes rather than having to attend the brick-and-mortar high school.

Until this morning, when Emma, Blake, and Liam met me at the library, I forgot how enjoyable friends could be. And then Nico showed up and had me in a tizzy until the very end of our private meeting on the second floor when it finally hit me. Nico was starved for friends too. He'd never tried to hook up with Caroline, whose version of that night at Delta Gamma I was foolish to believe in the first place. Throughout her time at college, my sister was convinced half the guys on campus, and all of the football players, were madly in love with her. Even if Nico wanted a fling with her, I trusted that he wasn't ever going to do that.

Was it because he was holding my hands and staring into my eyes when he said so? Maybe. But I also had a new theory. Nico Camillo, at heart, was not a jock. He wanted an A from Professor Simmons. His critique of my portion of the term paper was heavy-handed but it was also spot on. A minor detail most professors would overlook, not Professor Hawk.

If yesterday's game was any indication, Nico was headed to the NFL. He could just play ball, do the bare minimum to pass classes, and still get a diploma. But he wanted to do well. Torturing me about my portion of the paper wasn't his true purpose. He wanted perfect. And, apparently, someone to eat with.

"I was waiting for the sweatshop line," I said to him.

"You get that a lot?"

"Not until you." I laughed. "But the HVAC system has never let us down." I knocked on the table.

He was still examining the space and the equipment, touching the machines, studying our fabric-cutting and mail stations. Asking questions here and there. He was curious about everything, but I sensed this was how his mind worked. This studio, like the topic of our term paper, was something to learn about. So I placed our food containers on the large table and then pulled out my laptop.

"You interrupted our study session just as I was about to download the term paper." I powered up my computer. "I never had the chance to read it."

He put down one of the brown Scotty shipping envelopes he was examining and said, "Let's get to it." He took the seat next to mine and pulled the chair even closer so that we were both looking at my screen. Nico was not shy about invading personal space. The way he held my hand today, walked beside me to his car, and now this. I remembered how his parents clutched each other the day my father died. Was this touchy-feely side a Camillo trait, learned behavior from a happy Italian family? Or was it from playing football where there was no such thing as social distancing? Either way, he wasn't flirting with me.

Part of me wished that he *was* flirting with me. What was there not to admire about Nico? He was gorgeous, funny, and intelligent. He smelled as good as his sculpted muscles looked beneath another faded T-shirt and khaki shorts. Like a clean, sunny beach. When he showed me his bruise, I had the sudden urge to trace his torso with my fingertips.

Also, his actions had such confidence about them, like pulling me, Greer Scott the sewing weirdo, through the library for all to see. Or insisting on paying for our meal. *Good guys don't take money from girls.* A phrase my father used to tell Caroline and me, whenever we offered to pay for something special that we wanted, with our own money.

But he knew the Scott girls and Camillo boys were dangerous together. When he swore to never date Caroline, I wanted to hug him I was so relieved. Also, he was promised to one of the Delta Gammas. I hoped he chose well. They weren't all like my sister. Maybe Lila could find him someone as nice as she was?

"I'll just read through this while we're eating?" I asked.

"We can read it together," he said. "I only went through it once."

So we sat side by side, quietly reading the paper Nico pieced together last night, eating our fish tacos. I reserved saying anything until we both finished. The tight end for the football team had a well-wired mind. He understood the research better than I did, and wrote exceptionally well. Economics in general came naturally to him. Somehow, he managed to weave together the role of imports and exports, domestic and foreign currencies, and raw materials vs. finished goods in mercantilism to my segments on Italy's textile trade seamlessly. He dealt with the big concepts while my portions were illustrative, specifics that supported his main ideas. Now I understood why he wanted Florence's purple dye tied into the overall demand of luxury goods throughout Europe during that time period.

When I finished, I faced him. "Do your teammates know this side of you?"

His look to me was one of slight confusion. "What side is that?"

"You're *really* smart, Nico!" I pointed to the screen. "I mean, I thought you were making fun of me this morning when you emailed me about Florentine purple dye, but now I see you weren't."

"I would never make fun of you, Greer." His eyes met mine, just like they did earlier when he told me that he would never date Caroline.

"Fine," I said. "You do have the word 'to' spelled wrong here." I pointed to a part in the paper where Nico had "too" instead of "to."

"Now who's the smarty pants?" he joked, fixing it.

Then we went over my sections, and I pulled up the original sources of Florence's purple dye, and with Nico's help, explained why there was such demand for it across Europe and how this illustrated successful mercantilism during the Renaissance. We could have easily pulled out the section on purple since it was extraneous material and we were already over the word count. But Nico wanted to keep it in there, and I sensed this was because purple *was* personal to me.

I printed the final copy. Nico offered to get a cover at the bookstore. "Do you think that's necessary?" I asked.

"Probably not," he said. "But I think Dr. Simmons will be pretty impressed if we include one. She's old school."

"I wonder if Blake and Liam finished their paper." I placed the copy on the table.

"Doubtful," he said. "They'll be up all night on Tuesday or they'll ask her for an extension. And they'll definitely email it to her. Deep down, she'll hate that. But that's to be expected from guys like that."

"You don't like them?" I asked, thinking of Emma. She'd just started dating Blake but he seemed nice enough.

Nico was studying me, hesitating on what to say. "It's not that. They were fans after all." He stood and stepped closer. He was now in my personal space, which was taking some getting used to even though he'd been doing it since the library. "Let's just say I'm glad that neither one of those two is my partner," he said quietly.

I knew he wasn't flirting with me but I felt myself blushing anyway. I kept my eyes focused on his green ones because I didn't want him to think his words affected me. But perceptive Nico noticed. I saw it in his slight smile.

"You ready for dessert?" he asked.

So we pulled out the Italian ice. The stand had only two flavors left when we got there, lemon and mango. He'd ordered the mango. As we each dug into our cups, Nico asked to sample the lemon. So I held it out to him and he took a bite with his spoon.

"Want to try mine?" he asked. "Mango is *much* better."

"Sure." I laughed. But when I reached over, utensil in hand, he held out his plastic spoon already filled with a scoop of slushy mango ice for me to taste. His green eyes smiled as he spoon-fed me. He was enjoying himself, and despite the frozen treat, I felt my face flame once again.

"You won't let me see the pink dresses," his words broke the tension, "but can you show me some of your designs?"

"You really want to see them?" I asked.

"Absolutely," he said. "I want to know everything about Greer Scott."

I smiled at him. He was so different than I expected. But I was also grateful for something to do besides awkwardly eat Italian ice off Nico Camillo's spoon. I walked over to a cabinet and pulled out samples of every single item and pattern offered on the website. This was meticulously organized, at the insistence of my silent partner. It was one of those if-anything-happens-to-you-Greer emails that was necessary with any business partnership but still made me shudder. If anything happened to me, my partner could have another seamstress walk in and recreate all of our products. But what would come of my mother and Caroline?

Now that I had a glimpse into Nico's brain and how perceptive he was, I knew there was a lot going through his mind when he sat at the table and opened every single Scotty bag and phone case, tested the security of each zipper and button, and felt the texture of all the fabrics. He wouldn't examine the clothing but he asked about what materials I used. The tank top I was wearing was a Scotty. When I ran my hand down my shirt and said, "Supima cotton, modal, and spandex," I swore that Nico blushed.

I started to put everything away then. Nico was a straight guy, and women's clothing was definitely not exciting to him.

He helped me restock the cabinet, and then we packed up our stuff and locked the studio door behind us. We sat in the car, waiting for the engine to warm up and cool off the leather interior before pulling out onto the road that would take us back to campus.

"Thank you for today," he said. "I really enjoyed spending time with you and seeing your studio. You should be proud of yourself, Greer."

"Well," I looked into his green eyes, "thank you for making our paper better and including the fun fact about purple dye. And for lunch."

I was conflicted driving back to campus. Half of me didn't want the time with Nico to end, the other half was anxious to get home.

"Where do you live?" he asked.

"Just drop me off at campus."

"Greer, I'm taking you home."

"We talked about this. I don't want my mother and Caroline knowing about this partnership. It will only cause problems."

"*You* talked about it," he said. "I never agreed to keeping us a secret. It's always better to have things like this out in the open."

I turned to him, my heart rate increasing. I was trying not to freak out. "Nico, this partnership is only for a few months. But if my mom and Caroline get involved, the craziness will be everlasting. I'm begging you to just take me back to campus."

"How about I drop you off *near* your house?" he asked. "I'm a good guy, remember? Good guys don't let beautiful girls walk home alone."

Oh my god. He was being unreasonable. And stubborn. *Did he just call me beautiful?* I must have misheard him given the pace of my beating heart. Caroline and my mother would smell the leather of this luxury car within a mile of our house. The only chance I had was if the two of them were still asleep, which *was* a possibility. Nico's clock read half past four.

"Fine," I said. "You win." I gave him the general direction of our townhouse and told him the street but not the number.

When we drove through the neighborhood, we passed my van on a cross street. "There's my car. Drop me off here."

"But that's not the street you gave me." He smiled.

"It's close enough."

"Greer," he said. "This is going to be okay. Do you trust me?"

"Not right now. You don't know my family."

Our street was one way, so he had no choice but to make a right. "We're close, I promise. Just stop the car."

But Nico must have spotted the shining blonde hair up ahead. My mother and Caroline were sitting on the porch, chatting with my neighbor Nancy. "I found your house," he teased. "These front porches are great by the way. Shall I walk you to your door?"

He parked out front. I grabbed my bag off the floor and opened the door. "I hate you, Nico."

"No, you don't." He smiled at me. "Have a good night and see you tomorrow in class."

He had the sense not to walk me to my door. But when I climbed up the front steps, Caroline and my mother looked stunned sitting in their porch chairs, staring at the fancy SUV and Nico, not able to speak. When I turned back to the street, Nico waved to me and then pulled away smoothly, as if he didn't have a care in the world.

"Was that my Nicky, Caroline?" my mother said, her eyes suddenly glazed.

"You are such a bitch," Caroline hissed at me.

"Hi Greer," said Nancy. "How was your day?"

CAROLINE JUMPED up from her chair and disappeared into the house, letting the storm door slap onto its frame. I took her seat. My mom was frozen in place. Nancy suddenly got up from her own porch seat and excused herself, saying she needed to start making dinner.

"Who was that, Greer?" my mom asked.

"That was Nico Camillo," I said. "Nicholas Camillo's son."

"Caroline and I ran into him after the game. He looks so much like my Nicky that my mind plays tricks on me. Why did he drive you here?"

"He's my study partner for one of my classes," I explained. "We have a term paper due on Wednesday, and he drove me home because I walked to campus this morning."

She looked over at me, and her eyes were clear and lucid. "Was Nicholas with him?"

Suddenly, I realized that I'd never asked Nico if his parents were in town for the game. I assumed they were, but he had dinner by himself last night and was at the library before me this morning. They must have stayed away.

"No," I said calmly. "His *parents* were not with him."

My mother processed this and then mused, "I wonder why Nicholas didn't find me yesterday."

"Mom." I grabbed her hand and squeezed it gently. "I don't think he was in town. But even if he was, he's married now. Happily. He's not going to come for you."

She pulled her hand away. "Don't say that, Greer."

I didn't want to argue with her. She was not a rational person, and Nicholas Camillo made her completely nonsensical. I also had to speak with Caroline before she blew this situation out of proportion.

"I was going to make pasta salad tonight," I said, changing the subject. "Are you hungry?"

She didn't answer. "I want to be by myself right now, Greer."

I exhaled. My mother needed professional help. She'd always refused. Once I considered confiding in her dermatologist friend but decided against it. Dr. Wilson was her boss, and I didn't want to risk jeopardizing the only job she had. Maybe my friend Emma, an aspiring psychologist, could help me.

"You're not going to leave the porch, are you?" I asked.

"Greer," she said. "My shoes are inside, and I'm still in my pajamas. I'm not leaving the porch. Please stop treating me like a child."

I left her and found Caroline in her room, awake but lying in her bed. I sat down next to her and waited for her to speak.

"Are you trying to steal Nico away from me?" she asked. "It's bad enough the Delta Gammas are fighting over him, but now my own *sister* is squirming her way in!"

"Caroline." I rubbed my temples, unsure where to start. "Nico is my partner for history of capitalism with Professor Simmons. She matched us on the first day, and now we have to do term papers and projects together. I walked to campus this morning, we finished our term paper, and he drove me home. That is all."

"Why didn't you tell me beforehand then?" she asked. "You were trying to hide him from me."

"Of course, I was!" I shouted. "For this exact reason. You think I'm trying to make him my boyfriend, and Mom thinks he's Nicholas Camillo coming back for her!" I exhaled. "None of those things is true. I am not like you. And I am not like Mom."

She laughed. "You can say that again."

"Shut up, Caroline. You don't have to be so mean all the time. I'm trying to be honest with you. He and I have to work together for a class. That's all. But you are making a huge mistake trying to be with him, Caroline. It's cruel to do that to Mom, and you know it!"

She changed the subject. "I'm shocked Nico Camillo is even taking Professor Simmons' class. That's like one of the hardest classes at school. I've never heard of a football player getting into it."

Because he's ridiculously smart, I wanted to tell her. But that detail wouldn't matter to her.

Like my mother, Caroline was still in her pajamas. Granted, it was Sunday. But still. Her idleness was not sustainable.

"You have to get a job, Caroline," I said quietly.

"Relax," she said. "I will get one. But not until *after* the homecoming formal."

I exhaled. "I don't think you can go if you're not invited."

"You think Nico's the only football player who's single?" She laughed. "Tripp Saunders was checking me out last night and has been texting me all day. Knowing how uptight you are about Mom, you probably told Nico *not* to ask me. If Tripp or one of the starters doesn't ask me, I know I can get one of the freshman or sophomore players to take me. I'll just steal Nico away from his date at the dance."

"You are so selfish, Caroline," I said to her. "What would Dad think of you right now?"

I walked out of the room before she could respond. It was the only bomb in my arsenal when it came to my sister, and I was hoping it hit its mark.

12

NICO

The offensive coordinator was the reason this team took me from Michigan College. I proved to the NCAA and the media that I'd never accepted bribes. None was ever offered to a guy like me. My family had money and plenty of opportunity for me and my brothers to work and earn more of it, and invest it wisely. I was no Greer Scott, who labored sweatshop-hard creating cool designs, to earn every blessed cent for her and her family. But I wasn't going to pretend to be someone else. I was a Camillo. And I wasn't ashamed of the nice things I had, like my car or where I lived.

But a lot of schools were apprehensive about adding a former Michigan player to their rosters. They didn't want, or need, to risk bad press. Coach Phillips fought for me, and I appreciated him for it. He also understood exactly how I fit within this team. Tripp Saunders was a decent quarterback, but he was not exceptionally fast, and he wasn't smart. Guys like him were a dime a dozen in my opinion. But with players like Dylan Ryder and Nico Camillo on the line, he could shine.

He must have figured out my value to him because he was

being nice to me this morning. I still knew he was a total douche at heart.

After a hard drill set run by Coach Phillips, where I worked both the left and right sides of the line, I stretched and then got in the ice bath. My torso was fine, but I was now used to how awesome I felt about an hour after spending ten minutes chest-deep in fifty-degree water. Tripp was in the tub next to mine. Not too unusual for a Monday morning. He was sacked four times after all because his boy Ryan Edwards was a shit tight end.

"Hey Nico." This had to be the first time he didn't refer to me as "Nicole" when the coaches weren't around.

"Tripp," I replied coolly.

"Rumor around here is that you're going to ask Caroline Scott to the Delta Gamma formal," he said. "True?"

I glanced over at him. "Nope."

"I wonder who started that," he said.

Caroline Scott, I refrained from saying. The less I said about Greer's sister, the better off I was.

"Then are you cool if I hook up with her?" he asked.

I hesitated before answering his question. Obviously, I didn't care if he hooked up with Caroline. It would get her off my back and, as far as I was concerned, they were equally superficial people. It would never last because Caroline wanted the next Tom Brady, and Tripp Saunders didn't have it in him. But I also didn't want Greer anywhere near him. What if Caroline invited Tripp over and Greer was forced to sit beside him on that cozy front porch?

Once the straight males on this campus realized how much Greer Scott outshined the other girls, she'd be hunted down. No one was worthy of her as far as I was concerned. I had to do everything in my power to protect her from boneheads like Tripp Saunders.

"Why do you need my blessing?" I asked him.

"I heard she's a friend of yours from Virginia," he said. "That you guys had a thing going on."

"Is that why you're interested in Caroline Scott?" I asked. "Because you think I'm interested in her? You're trying to take something that you think is mine?" Now I had the upper hand with Tripp. Ever since I rescued him from losing the season opener on Saturday, I could talk to him however I saw fit. And he deserved to be put in his place by me.

"That's not it at all." He was contrite, just as I expected him to be. "Ryan said she wants to go to the dance and hasn't been invited yet. I broke up with my girlfriend, so I'm available."

"Take my advice Tripp." My time was up, and I needed to shower before heading to Smythe Hall for Dr. Simmons' class. "If you like a girl, ask her out. Let her decide whether she wants to go out with you. Asking a guy like me for permission just because we're from the same hometown makes you look weak."

I hoisted myself out of the tub and walked away. Not many guys could achieve that. Most had to limp, crawl, or stand still until feeling returned before walking.

GREER MADE it to class just in time. I'd yet to ask her why she was usually the last one to arrive. I was here early, again, because I wanted to see Greer. Her eyes found mine and she smiled. *Thank God.* After dropping her off yesterday afternoon and leaving her angry, I wasn't sure how she'd react to me today. But Professor Hawk got right into her lesson, so we didn't have the chance to talk.

The lights were soon dimmed for a slide presentation. We were still in the Middle Ages, and Dr. Simmons flashed pictures of feudal societies until the Industrial Revolution. To me, it was like she was narrating the highlights of a European vacation.

Dukedoms with never-ending wheat fields worked by peasants. Small medieval towns with powerful guilds. Famous sea ports where trade began. Her voice was soothing. Greer's scent surrounded me. The only thing that could make this morning more comfortable was if my partner's desk was touching mine.

The professor turned the lights back on with about fifteen minutes left of class. "Use this time wisely and try to finish your term papers due on Wednesday."

I pulled out our paper now ensconced in a spiffy report cover, university red of course, and raised my hand.

"Yes, Mr. Camillo."

"What if our term paper is finished?" I held up our project, which reminded me of my fifth-grade science project that my mom helped me type.

"Is that yours and Miss Scott's?" she asked. "How professional!"

"We thought you'd appreciate that," I said firmly. Greer grunted, trying not to giggle.

"Oh, I do." She took it from me. "Has any other pair finished their term paper?"

No one raised their hands, including Blake and Liam in the corner.

"Well, I guess there's nothing for you to do here," she said to me and Greer. "You two can cut out early, but it would be nice if you talked about your next project. The topic is social class and capitalism. I'll give out the details on Wednesday, but the two of you can get a head start today."

Greer had on another cute outfit today with her combat boots. An ink-colored skirt and a Scotty top, like the one I wanted to peel off her yesterday. This one was black. With her dark hair and boots, she looked a little goth. At least next to me as we walked out of Smythe Hall. My wardrobe consisted of khaki shorts and whatever clean T-shirt lay on top of the pile.

"You headed to work after this?" I asked.

"Yep. Class for you?"

"I have about thirty minutes. You have time for a sweet tea?"

She nodded. "Sure."

"I want to hear *all* about what happened last night."

She laughed, so it must not have been that bad. The air was warm, but most classes were still in session so there were few people walking around. We stopped at the café in the Adams Center, which was on Greer's way to her van. She didn't argue with me when I paid for our teas. We found a shaded bench on the path near the lot. A patch of mature red-and-white impatiens just starting to brown lined the brick walkway. She chose her spot first, and I sat right next to her and extended my arm along the backrest, her silky hair brushing my forearm.

"Spill it, Greer. Tell me what happened."

She was hesitant at first, especially about her mom's reaction. She said her mom understood who I was, that I was Nico Camillo, but then her mind tricked her into believing that I was my father back in high school here to rescue her and bring her back to Virginia. I wasn't the spitting image of my dad, but out of my brothers and me, I looked the most like him.

Greer's mom needed serious help, and it was clear to me Greer either couldn't or wouldn't get it for her. I refrained from saying anything because it really wasn't my business. Even though campus security intervened last weekend, Caroline and Sophia Scott were no real threat to me. And my parents were never coming to Butler.

"And my sister assumes that I asked you not to invite her to the formal, Nico." Greer's eyes widened. "I didn't admit to it, but she has a sixth sense when it comes to stuff like this. After I finally convinced her that I wasn't trying to *steal* you away from her."

I laughed. "So what did you tell her about us?"

"The truth," she said. "That we're partners for history of capitalism. She was surprised you were admitted into Professor Simmons' class."

"She's right about that. I had to get special permission from the coach to even register. It's one of those classes they discourage athletes from taking because of the workload."

"Well, your secret is safe with me."

"And what's that?"

"How smart you are," Greer said. "Caroline's not stupid, but she uses her brain for all the wrong reasons. She manipulates people. And once she finds out that you're better than her at something, she attacks you for that ability rather than being supportive. She doesn't even recognize she's doing it." Greer was still making eye contact with me as she spoke, but I sensed she was also thinking out loud. As if she finally realized what made her sister tick. "So even if you were to ask her out, Nico, it would never last. She'd figure out she couldn't control you, especially the way you think, and you'd mean nothing to her anymore."

"Hey Greer," I said when she stopped talking.

"Yes."

"We need to set the record straight." My hand on the backrest squeezed her bare shoulder, and I looked into her violet-grey eyes. "I was never going to ask out your sister. She's not my type at all."

Greer didn't respond right away. Her mind was trying to process what I just said, and maybe my hand touching her shoulder was affecting her the same way it was affecting me. *You're my type*, I wanted to tell her but couldn't. Since yesterday, Greer Scott was constantly in my thoughts. I knew it would never work out between us, because of my parents, but I still wanted her. This was a dangerous game I was playing.

I told myself this morning that she and I could just be

friends, good friends even. But when we were together, I couldn't stop myself from closing the distance between us and squeezing her shoulder. What would happen if she finally agreed to have dinner with me at my place? This girl had all my senses fired up, and I didn't think I'd be able to *not* make a move on her.

"Were your parents in town last weekend?" she suddenly asked. It was almost as though she read my thoughts and drove the wedge back between us. I released her shoulder but kept my arm behind her.

"Nope."

Greer's expression turned serious. "Why?"

I hesitated. "I wasn't supposed to play."

"It was the season opener. I don't know your parents well. But I do remember how involved they were with football." She shrugged. "I'm surprised they wouldn't have come to your first game."

Now which Scott daughter had the sixth sense again? I took a deep breath. Lying to Greer was risky. I considered doing it now to protect her, but Greer was smart and tougher than even me. Maybe coming clean about this would allow her to come to terms with the gravity of Sophia Scott's diseased mind.

"Greer," I began, "my parents are never coming to Butler. They don't support my decision to be here."

She closed her eyes. "Is my family – is my mother – the reason your parents don't support your decision to be here?"

I waited until her eyes locked with mine again. "Yes," I answered.

She jumped off the bench and put her backpack on. She was about to run away, so I grabbed both of her hands. "Greer," I said softly. "This has nothing to do with you. I hope you know that."

She didn't answer but looked up at me when I tightened my grip. "I'm sorry," she said.

"You have nothing to apologize for."

"Will they be at your away games at least?" she asked. "I mean, my mom and my sister can't go to those?"

"We haven't talked about it," I answered truthfully.

She pulled her hands away gently. "I should get to work," she said. "Thanks for the iced tea."

"Friends don't have to be polite with each other all the time." I changed the subject.

Her dark eyebrows furrowed in confusion. "What are you talking about?"

"It bothers me when you thank me for stuff." My tone was teasing. "I don't want you thanking me. Taking care of you makes me happy. You're my partner."

"You won't let me pay my fair share when I'm with you," she said. "And now I can't thank you either? You are *legit* bossy. I wonder if Blake and Liam want to swap partners."

"Don't even joke about that," I glared at her. Her teasing tone was just matching mine, but the thought of her working with a guy who wasn't me sobered me up fast. The campus' pathways started to fill with students, which meant I had to get to my next class. First, I wanted to walk Greer to her car. We didn't talk about our new project for Dr. Simmons' class, but what we did talk about was more important.

I hated when I parted from her though. I couldn't kiss her. Or hug her. Or squeeze her hand. Just words. This left me feeling unfulfilled, my body reverberating but not in a good way.

AFTERNOON PRACTICE WAS another tough drill set, followed by weights with the trainers, and then film study. Dylan, Tripp, and

I couldn't rely on what worked for us against Florida to succeed with Carolina. Their defensive coordinator would have a response. And since this weekend was Carolina's first home game, the crowd energy would be with them. Our team was favored, but a win was never guaranteed. Ryan and Beau had to get their heads into the game, and their asses out of parties, for us to dominate.

Dylan and I left the stadium together. Every player in the locker room gave him shit for his T-shirt, but he just laughed it off. It looked familiar, but one of the other guys had to tell me that it was Ed Sheeran's official tour shirt. Dylan was taking Lila to a concert in Atlanta tonight, and he was wearing it to surprise her.

That girl had him wrapped around her finger, but Dylan didn't mind one bit.

"Did you invite your *mystery* girl to the dance yet?" He laughed.

"I haven't gotten around to it."

"Sorry about the other night. Caroline Scott had been telling everyone you were taking her to the dance. I had no idea you weren't into her."

"It's complicated."

"Well, you don't have to say anything," he held out his hand, "but between you and me, I'm glad. There is something off about that girl. I keep telling Lila to be careful of her. I mean, why is she still hanging around campus? Lila told me she had two really good job offers, and she turned down both of them."

"No shit." My voice was quiet, but my blood was instantly raging. As far as I could tell, Greer was still supporting Caroline. Why would she choose not to move on with her life and help her family?

"Because I consider you a friend," Dylan said, "you should

know Tripp's been trying to find out who you are taking to the formal since it's not Caroline Scott."

"He's so predictable. Listen, Dylan, it's doubtful I'm going to be taking anyone with me. My *mystery* girl is also complicated. But let's let Tripp keep guessing."

"I like the way you think."

BACK AT MY APARTMENT, I packed up rolls, the barbecue I made the night before, and a bowl of salad for dinner at Greer's studio. If she wouldn't have dinner with me here, then I'd take dinner to her. She'd said that she'd be working late from now until the homecoming formal in October. Her kitchenette may not have the equipment to cook the food, but it was well equipped to heat up meals, store leftovers, and wash all the dishes. I couldn't wait to see her reaction when I showed up.

My dad called just before I walked out the door. "Hey Dad."

"Nico," he said. "How are you?"

We talked about today's practices and watching film, and some of Coach Phillips' thoughts on the Carolina game. He listened and responded but the call seemed unusual. My dad was in his car, not at home next to my mother.

"Is Mom in the car with you?"

"No. I'm coming back from a meeting, but she is why I'm calling. She's more anxious than ever, reading all the press coverage of last weekend's game. There's no way Sophia Scott doesn't realize who you are by now. And your mother is worried about you living alone, in the same town as that woman."

"I told you I'm handling it, Dad."

"What do you mean you're handling it? Has Sophia reached out to you?"

My parents despised lying above all else, and I told myself I wasn't a liar. But I also couldn't tell my father the truth right now. He and my mother would freak if they knew security had to pull Sophia off me after the game last Saturday.

"I told you I have class with Greer, Dad. Caroline's graduated but she still hangs around campus. She's exactly the way she was in high school. Greer is the opposite. She goes to class and works. Please believe me, Dad. They're not a threat to me, and I can handle myself."

"Do they know what their mother did in Charleston?"

"Caroline has no idea, and Greer doesn't know everything," I answered as honestly as possible. If she did, she would have gotten her mother to a doctor by now.

Greer was the reason my being here at Butler could backfire. My parents warned me dozens of times to stay away from the Scotts. Greer asked me to keep my distance too. Yet, the first chance I got I defied all of them and dropped Greer off at her front door, essentially poking the bear.

"This entire situation is so messed up, Nico." He sighed. "Jack Scott would be devastated if he knew we are considering hiring *armed* security to protect you from his wife and daughters."

"I don't *need* armed security down here. Butler is a safe town." I laughed. "And Greer is nothing like Sophia or Caroline."

"You say that like you know her, Nico," he said. "Are you friends?"

"Sort of. She's my study partner."

My dad didn't answer right away. I heard him exhale. Then he said, "Listen, Nico. I have to go. But, for now, let's not tell your mother this."

I parked my car next to Greer's van and carried the food inside. A couple of suits were conducting business in the atrium. If I had to guess, a real estate transaction was taking place. Looking through the glass door, I knew Greer wasn't alone inside the studio. The machines were hopping, but no one in the atrium could hear the noise.

Her face broke into a smile when I walked inside. It was genuine too because she blushed at the same time. I'd surprised her. She was pulling pink fabric out of one of the machines. At the station next to hers was a petite grey-haired Asian woman, one hundred pounds soaking wet, sewing a different shade of pink. I winked at Greer before I turned on the charm.

"You must be Isabel Flores." I placed the bag on the table and held out my hand to her.

"I am." She shook my hand. "And you're the handsome football player from the television the other day. Congratulations on your win, and call me Aunt Isabel."

"Do you like barbecue?" I asked her.

"I've never had it." Her brown eyes lit up with curiosity. "But I'll give it a try."

"We were just about to order food," Greer said. "I can't believe you did this."

"You said you'd be busy," I carried the bag to the kitchen area, "so I figured I'd bring dinner to you. But don't let me get in the way. Pretend I'm not here."

Today there were Scotty bags, phone cases, and clothes wrapped in clear packaging stacked up by the mail station. The farm table was also full of what must have been orders waiting to be packaged. Now, it was clear to see they were working on the Delta Gamma dresses. Greer's hair was tied in a bun, and a strip of yellow measuring tape hung around her graceful neck. The dummies were on full display, but Greer didn't attempt to cover them up this time. If she did, I would have tackled her.

I was here to help, not to stop them from working.

There was enough food to feed the three of us and the group in the atrium. When I started carrying everything into the free spot on the table, Aunt Isabel said, "Good gracious that's a lot of food, Nico."

"I knew you'd be here, Aunt Isabel," I deadpanned.

She started to laugh, and then we all sat down to eat. Like Greer, Aunt Isabel wore Doc Martens. I asked them why, and Greer explained that they had to wear comfortable shoes with protective, steel toes when operating the machines. Canvas sneakers weren't strong enough, and sandals were out of the question. This explained Greer's goth look on campus.

Once we finished, I cleared and washed the dishes while they continued working. But I didn't leave. Each of the packages had a label affixed to it, so I asked Greer if I could package everything.

"Are you sure?" she asked. "I usually do this before I leave for the night and drop at the post office in the building."

I insisted. Each task was easy. Stuff each product in the brown envelope and attach the Scotty label. Weigh each package and print out the postage stamp. Drop in the mail containers – one for U.S. orders and another for international – lined against the wall. As I worked, I chatted with the two of them. They were constructing dresses piece by piece. Isabel did not stop talking. Though she'd just started at Scotty, her niece Melanie who was on vacation had been with Greer for more than a year. Isabel was having so much fun here in Georgia with her brother and sister-in-law and their children, and Greer, she didn't know if she wanted to return to the Philippines.

Greer and I never got around to talking about our new project for history of capitalism. But I left there feeling less worried about her. Caroline and Sophia Scott were toxic, but Greer had a family in the Floreses.

13

GREER

*E*ach morning over the following week, Caroline and my mother were up and dressed in athletic clothes when I left for class. They either power-walked or went to yoga. Both of them seemed content and normal, almost happy. Rather than question the reasons why, I went to class and then straight to the studio each day.

Aunt Isabel's work was incredible. She was efficient and creative, too. She started adding the finishes to Scotty accessories – the violet buttons, custom hardware, embroidery – something I'd never permitted Melanie to do. With Isabel sewing throughout the day, and Nico arriving each afternoon after practice, with his shopping bag full of homemade food, to package and stamp, Scotty Designs had nearly all fifty-two Delta Gamma dresses finished. Granted, we still had to schedule fittings and make alterations. But the scale of the job was still impressive, considering this work was on top of all website orders *and* I was taking six classes.

My dad swore that people accomplished more when their lives were busier. For now, that sentiment was true.

My silent partner had always handled the numbers side of the business, but Nico's mind kept busy. Each evening as he was packaging up the orders, he kept a tally of Scotty's daily sales. In the first week alone, not including the Delta Gamma dresses since these were separate, Scotty sales were between ten and fifteen thousand dollars per day.

This surprised me, but I'd never really thought about the business in terms of money. To me, it was always the number of orders that I had to complete.

Since Nico was leaving with the team on Friday, Aunt Isabel gave her gift to Nico on Thursday at dinner. He'd made grilled chicken kabobs with saffron rice and roasted summer tomatoes. As we sat down, she placed the box in front of him. Inside was a large canvas tote bag, insulated, with a reinforced bottom and sturdy zipper closure. She created it from our dark denim canvas, and because it was a Scotty, she placed one violet button on a leather logo patch.

There was nothing like this on our website. In addition to the design being a great transport tote for hot or cold food, with pockets for serving spoons, salad dressings, or a bottle of wine, it was our first masculine-looking design, ever.

"Aunt Isabel," he said, "this is amazing." He stood up and walked over to her chair, bent down and hugged her tightly, like he'd probably done countless times to his own mother and grandmother. Then Isabel grabbed his face and gave him a kiss on his cheek.

"Your cooking is amazing, Nico," her small hands still held his cheeks, "and now you can transport your cuisine in style and with ease and share it with all of your friends like Greer."

Nico blushed. He probably wasn't used to receiving compliments on his cooking. I was blushing too. For a different reason entirely. I wanted to feel his arms hug me tightly. And kiss him. But not just a peck on the cheek.

. . .

How was it that I went from despising Nico Camillo on the first day of college to thinking about him all the time and craving his touch by the end of the second week? Being with him, whether it was during class, on the walkway to my van, or at the studio in the evening felt thrilling. He was intelligent and funny. He treated Aunt Isabel with the same teasing charm as Professor Simmons, and the two women were smitten with him. Our paper on mercantilism during Renaissance Italy received an A, of course, and a dose of hefty praise from Dr. Simmons on the Wednesday before the Carolina game.

I wanted to be a fly on the football field and observe Nico with his teammates. He couldn't be a charming tease with them. Was he quiet or did he taunt? It was obvious to most experts that Nico was agile and strong but also read the defense well. Based on how perceptive he was, I was sure his mind was never idle on the field. Football was part of his life I'd probably never experience, unless the camera was on him during or after the game.

Yet when I lay down at night to rest, I did feel overwhelming guilt about liking Nico. Nico's father created my mother. It wasn't totally his fault; my mother and her confused mind were also to blame. But the result for our family was that life was a constant struggle and held very little joy since moving to Georgia. We weren't in dire straits, and we were safe and in good health. But the happiness and security we took for granted when my father was alive were gone.

Once Caroline got a job, she'd get married and have children, and leave my mother and me behind. There was no doubt in my mind about this. She spent time with my mother now because all of her sorority friends were busy.

Though I was only a college freshman, I worried sometimes

that I'd never find someone. Who would choose to spend their life with me? Scotty Designs was demanding, and my mother and me were a package deal. Caroline would never assume the responsibility. And I was not shortsighted. I knew my mom's needs, both financial and emotional, would only increase with time.

Nico, on the other hand, would marry someone like his mother. Beautiful and capable. They'd have adorable children who were strong, charming, and with confidence to succeed in life. Their happily ever after was guaranteed.

In fact, I was probably making his future wife's homecoming dress right now.

So at night, in the dark, when my imagination wanted to picture Nico Camillo hugging Greer Scott, I stopped myself and went through Scotty inventory lists in my mind until I fell asleep.

"DID you wear that dress for me?" Nico asked, smiling, when I walked into history of capitalism on Friday morning. His khakis and white dress shirt were pressed, and a university tie was fixed to his neck, just like the rest of his teammates. His damp hair was neatly combed but not in a fussy way. Even though the game was in another state, the whole campus was decked out in red-and-white clothing.

"Do you like it?" I asked. It was the same Scotty signature dress I'd worn a handful of times already, but in a new print. Aunt Isabel also suggested altering the pattern, making the dress more fitted. "I ordered fabrics last week in the school's colors and they just came in. I made this last night after you left. What do you think of this as a new product? Game day sundresses for college girls? We could customize them for any team." Until last Sunday, I never imagined myself bouncing designs off any guys, ever. Especially a guy like Nico. But he enjoyed sharing ideas, and he was always making observations. Last night, after Isabel gifted him his tote bag, he told her she was on to something and had suggestions for a dozen more.

"Where are your boots?" He was eyeing my wedge sandals.

"I was trying to blend in with sorority girls," I joked quietly, "not scare them away. They're the target market."

Nico nodded. He was considering what to say to me, but Professor Simmons started a new unit that consumed the entire period. Partner breakout sessions would resume the following week, she said at the end of class. Students rushed out. It was Friday after all. As we were leaving, she stopped Nico and wished him good luck during the Carolina game.

Then she said, "Miss Scott, your dress is simply delightful. I've never seen anything like it, and I'm always looking for quality spirit wear."

I glanced at Nico, whose green eyes were smiling. I knew he wouldn't pass up this opportunity to tease.

"Greer made that dress, Dr. Simmons." Then Nico lowered his voice, "If you're on your best behavior this semester, I might be able to convince my *partner* to make one for you."

I gasped. Nico went too far this time.

But Dr. Simmons laughed. "Mr. Camillo, you are wicked!"

Nico couldn't walk me to my car or he'd miss his next class. He said he was just turning in an assignment because he had to catch the team bus at the stadium. But once we were outside Smythe Hall, Nico flagged down a girl neither one of us knew.

"Would you mind taking our picture?" He unlocked his phone and held it out to her.

The girl, who wasn't rushing to class, was happy to do it and found a shady spot on the brick path, next to an aged southern live oak. Before she aimed the camera, Nico whispered that the dress I made for Professor Hawk better be more *delightful* than the one I was wearing, or else. I laughed and couldn't stop. Nico, of course, pressed his rock-solid body against mine and wrapped his arm around my waist, squeezing me close. He smelled clean, like wind on a summer day.

"I got a good one," the girl called out.

I'd forgotten we were even having our picture taken.

"It's perfect," he said to the girl. "Thank you."

"Can I see?" I asked.

"I've gotta run, Greer." He ignored my question. "Have a good weekend and stay out of trouble."

"You too, Nico." I giggled. "Good luck."

BEFORE I WENT to the studio, I stopped by my house to change my outfit and pack dinner. I was looking forward to going to the studio today. Since the Delta Gamma dresses were mostly finished, fittings scheduled to start next week, Aunt Isabel and I were going to experiment with the violet zippers and closures that arrived yesterday along with the new fabrics. Now that Nico was out of town, we had to feed ourselves however.

Caroline was packing the small trunk of the Mini when I arrived, my mother beside her handing her items. I double-parked the van and put on my hazard lights.

"You better not block me in," she said when I stepped out of the car. "I can't be late today."

"Where are you going?" I asked.

Caroline stared at me from head to toe, glaring. She hated Scotty dresses as a rule, and I'm sure she wanted to ridicule this new red-white-and-black pattern.

"Caroline is headed to the game!" my mother squealed. "Isn't that exciting?"

"Since when?" I asked.

"Since Tripp Saunders messaged me," she gushed.

"How did you get a ticket?" Admission to away games was pricey and hard to come by. "And where are you staying?"

Caroline loaded a brand-new Yeti cooler backpack, glass bottles clinking inside, into the rear. "Not that it's any of your business, Lila had an extra ticket. We've got a room in the same hotel as the team. But I need to leave, Greer, so hurry and get out of here. We're following the players' bus up there!"

"Caroline," I said delicately. "How are you paying for all of this?" Even if she got the ticket for free, which I seriously doubted, hotel rooms, gas, food and alcohol still cost a few hundred dollars. The cooler bag alone cost three hundred bucks, based on the research Aunt Isabel and I did after she gifted Nico the tote. We didn't have that kind of money, and Caroline wasn't working.

"How can you say that to your sister, Greer?" my mother said, annoyed. "After all she's done for your business with the homecoming dresses. Your father was never a tyrant! Let her have fun this weekend without having to stress out about money."

My mother never mentioned my father, but when she did, it was usually to make me feel terrible about myself. Her words were a direct hit, as she knew they would be. I left the two of them still scowling at me. I changed into my boots and an older Scotty dress since working with hardware always left a residue and I didn't want to ruin my new one. Then I tossed snacks and a half loaf of bread into my bag.

The studio was empty when I arrived. Isabel did say she'd be performing her alteration work at the Flores' store this morning. Something had been bothering me on my drive to the studio. After I printed out the new website orders and answered online queries, I opened my email. Nico was on the bus headed north and probably wouldn't read this until after he returned. I considered texting him, but we'd yet to communicate that way.

And I didn't want to sound the alarm over something that was not a big deal.

> *Dear Nico,*
>
> *We never talked about our new project for Dr. Simmons' class. What about focusing on laborers during the Industrial Revolution? (Is it true capitalism when the majority of the population is working in factories?)*
>
> *Aunt Isabel hasn't arrived yet. Fingers crossed she won't also bug out early when she sees peanut butter and jelly on the menu tonight ;)*
>
> *Greer*
>
> *P.S. My sister has made last-minute plans to attend the game this weekend and stay in the team hotel. Consider this your official warning. If it makes you feel better, I believe she will be tattooing herself with the QB's jersey number. But I can't be sure because I didn't help her pack.*

His response came within just a few minutes of me hitting send.

> *Hey Greer.*
>
> *Since you're the expert on sweatshops, I'm cool if you take the lead on this one. (FWIW, I love the idea.)*
>
> *Just make sure you don't serve grape jelly tonight. Aunt Isabel is a red raspberry preserves kind of woman.*
>
> *Nico*
>
> *P.S. I see the Mini.*

I stared at his reply, unsure what to think. Had Caroline already embarrassed herself? College wasn't what my sister was addicted to. If that were the case, she'd have enrolled in a master's program. College life, on the other hand, was a different story. But didn't part of her feel like a loser? I mean, she'd turned down good job offers for this? Chasing a bus full of football players in a car that she couldn't even afford to buy gas for? Before I could even move away from the screen, my phone pinged alerting me to a new text. I dug it out of my green backpack on the floor. It was from Nico:

> Text me with anything even if ur not sure it's
> important. I'm here for you G.

Nico read between the lines *and* read my mind. My response was lame, a boring "ok," but what else could I say? My cracked family was my problem, not his.

BECAUSE CAROLINE and Nancy were both out of town, my mother came to the studio with me on Saturday. She didn't want to, but I promised her Aunt Isabel and I would make her a new outfit. Just like Caroline, my mother found Scotty clothes too plain and generally not to her liking. While Caroline went further – she found Scotty clothes beneath her – my mother did allow me to alter some of our basic patterns for her body.

She had to really. Clothes made at the studio were a lot cheaper for my family than having to pay for brand names at Nordstrom. She would scroll through websites or catalogs and show me what she was looking for, then I'd try my best to piece something together using leftover fabrics. Given her breast enhancement and tiny waist, she needed most store-bought clothes altered anyway.

This city was like a ghost town on away game days. There were house parties, of course, but closer to campus. The studio's business park was quiet. But that didn't stop my mother from creating a party atmosphere. She dressed in her game day denim shorts, heels, and tight T-shirt. She refrained from the face tattoos. What Aunt Isabel and I were grateful for were the tailgate snacks. Dip and chips, sliders, and iced football cookies, all spread out on the farm table.

Aunt Isabel didn't know what to make of Sophia Scott. She must have asked her a dozen times if she was really my mother or my older sister. Isabel didn't mean for her questions to be flattering but that's how my mother took them. When Isabel gazed from my mother to me and back to my mother, her face wrinkled in deep thought, she asked, "Where does Greer get her looks?"

"Her father," my mother stated. "He died on Greer's fourteenth birthday. Tomorrow will be five years. I still can't believe it."

It was the most lucid, caring statement I'd heard from her in a long time.

"I'm so sorry," Aunt Isabel exclaimed. "But it's your birthday tomorrow, Greer! What are you going to do to celebrate?"

"Not much," I said as I stitched website orders. Though we hadn't been slammed overnight, I knew I'd be watching for Nico at the game, so I was trying to work fast. "I have my study group in the morning, and then just hang out I guess."

The truth was I avoided celebrating my birthday. Sudden death will do that. My mother had tried to make my fifteenth birthday special by inviting girls from school over as a surprise, but it failed. I held it together while we ate and had cake around the new kidney-shaped pool in our Virginia home, my mother parading around in a string bikini. Once the last girl left, I had my mother swear she'd never attempt that again and disappeared to my room for two days. The certified mail started showing up shortly after that, and the rest was history.

The pregame coverage started around noon. When the cheerleaders came out in their away uniforms, my mother started to dance around. They were just like their home uniforms but white instead of red. "Oh Gree!" She pointed to the screen. "Look at those cute uniforms."

"Do you really like them, Mom?" I asked. "The sequins are overdone, the fake boots are awful, and that fabric looks totally uncomfortable."

"Listen to Greer on this, Sophia," said Aunt Isabel. "She understands fabric and comfort. You should see her pink dresses."

"But they *stand out* against the green football field," my mother argued. "Look at Carolina's. Those are way too busy."

She was right about that. Carolina's cheerleaders wore blue on top and white on the bottom. The girls blended with the crowd of people on the sidelines.

The afternoon passed without drama, which was unusual for my mother. Butler gained another win but it was ugly. Nico played the entire game and did have one score. Whenever the announcers called out his name, Aunt Isabel said, "Oh, we love Nico here!" My mother was too busy scanning the crowd for Caroline and Nicholas Camillo to grasp what Isabel was saying.

After the game, Tripp Saunders was interviewed by the pretty reporter who interviewed Nico the week before. When she asked him about his performance, which was terrible, he didn't mention any other player except for himself. It was as if he blocked, threw the ball *and* caught the ball for the entire sixty minutes of play. Yet his passes were sloppy. The running backs and defense were the players who gave him another win.

This was another ill-suited match for my sister Caroline. While my mother suggested to Aunt Isabel the quarterback could be her son-in-law one day soon, I envisioned how disastrous a relationship between them would be. Both were takers. For most of her life, Caroline manipulated every situation to benefit herself. My first impression of Tripp was that he took credit for the entire game despite having dozens of players standing shoulder-to-shoulder with him on the sidelines.

Before we locked up, Isabel and I outfitted my mom in black palazzo pants in a viscose and spandex blend. They were thin and stretchy, perfect for all seasons. We cut and sewed a few of our Supima cotton crop tops in multiple colors to accommodate her large chest and still show off her belly button, and we added a backless halter top in the same viscose and spandex blend as the pants. It was made from blush pink fabric leftover from the Delta Gamma dresses. Though my mother insisted on exhibiting cleavage, we convinced her that the backless top was just as sexy.

She must have agreed since she wore it home.

14

NICO

The hotel lobby was so loud and crowded that I almost missed my parents standing by the front desk. I was shocked to see them. Even though it was less than a month since I'd left home, so much was different now. I was different. For the first time in my life, I wasn't depending on them. Emotionally at least. They still helped pay my bills.

I told Greer the truth too. My parents and I never talked about away games. They were so opposed to my decision to come to Butler that I assumed they just canceled football altogether.

They also weren't the type of people to hover on the periphery, like now. They looked lost in the Butler sea of red, white, and black surrounding them in the lobby. In high school and Michigan, they were the ones hosting team dinners and organizing tailgates. Here they knew no one other than me.

My mother hugged me first. I held her tight the way she liked. Then it was my father's turn. He hugged me the way that I hugged my mom. Sometimes guys would ask why my dad was so affectionate, and I'd say it came from being raised with four sisters who doted on him. But that was just a joke. It was more than that. He lived his life to the fullest and never took anything for granted, after he watched Jack Scott die.

"You look so handsome, Nico." My mom straightened my tie. "Your hair is longer."

"When did you get here?" I asked.

"We only arrived about thirty minutes ago." My dad glanced around us. "This is intense."

"Where's Enzo?" I knew my little brother didn't have a game this weekend.

"Matteo is spending the night with him," my mom said.

"He seems to really like Penn," my dad added. "He's met a girl from South Philly, just like your mom. I told him not to make a move until he samples her meatballs and gravy."

My mom started giggling. This was how their marriage worked. He teased, and she giggled. Even though our relationship was strained, it felt good to see them. I'd missed them. But I also didn't have much time. After the team checked in, we were heading to the stadium for a quick practice followed by our team dinner.

I studied both of them, then took a deep breath. "I have to ask. Why are you here? I mean, you guys were pretty clear about Butler."

My parents looked at one another, and then my mother was the first to speak. "We missed you. Watching you on TV last week just felt," she paused, "wrong."

"We figured your away games would be on neutral ground," my father added. Then he lowered his voice, "And the Scotts wouldn't be such a threat."

As if his words were a cue, a high-pitched squeal echoed through the crowded lobby. "Oh. My. God. Mr. and Mrs. Camillo!" Caroline Scott was suddenly beside us, having stepped out of line with Lila and other Delta Gammas. My parents didn't have time to brace themselves for Caroline's hug.

"It's so good to see y'all," she gushed in a perfect southern drawl. "We are so excited that Nico is playing for Butler now." Caroline clasped my forearm and squeezed it. "You two look amazing."

My parents were socialites, skilled at navigating large gatherings, yet were both rendered speechless at the moment. They gazed at Caroline, who was a younger version of Sophia Scott, as though they were seeing a ghost.

"You staying at this hotel?" she asked.

Since I wasn't sure, I had to wait for one of my parents to speak. My mother eventually said, "Yes."

"Perfect!" She clapped her hands. "We're going to hang out by the pool while the guys are practicing, and then we're meeting up at the hotel bar tonight. You should come! Tripp – the QB – he's my boyfriend by the way." She placed her hand on her chest. "He says Nico's coming along. The SEC is just a little more competitive than his other conference." She laughed.

When my mom glanced over at me, her expression stunned, I shook my head. Caroline was so full of crap, so desperate to be the better half of the it-football couple, that I didn't want them taking anything she said seriously.

Caroline squeezed my arm again, and it was starting to piss me off. "I better get back to the girls. But find me tonight." She smiled at my parents. "Nico, I told Tripp to save you a seat at the team dinner to discuss his strategy for beating Carolina tomorrow. Good luck!"

When she was gone, my mom said wearily, "Nico—"

"I can't talk about this now." My teammates were filling up the lobby, and we only had a short time before we were due back on the bus.

My dad blanched. "Caroline is dating your QB? Why didn't you tell us, Nico?"

Unable to reveal to my parents the truth behind Tripp and Caroline and risk getting them even more upset, I shrugged and walked them to the elevators. I made plans to meet up with them in the lobby around eight.

ON THE BUS back to the hotel from the team dinner, Dylan, Malik and I were sitting together. The three of us were sharing a room. Even though road trips for NCAA football teams were monumental efforts, Butler was a well-oiled machine. The coaches, staff, and players were pumped for tomorrow's game. Carolina, Dylan said, was one of the biggest away games because so many students and families made the trip. While the cost of tickets was inflated for this particular game, our cheering section would be huge. His parents were arriving later tonight, and they told him they couldn't wait to see how the new offensive line played.

"It's you." Dylan elbowed me. "My parents can't wait to shake your hand."

"Hey man," Malik lowered his voice, "sorry for that hit I gave you when you first arrived. I didn't know you were the real deal."

I listened to him with a steely expression, nodded, and then told him he'd be sleeping on the rollaway bed.

"Come on, man," he complained. "I got like twenty pounds on you."

Dylan was laughing. "I'm with Nico on this one, Beech. You should never have opened your mouth." Dylan was right. As the new guy on the team, the rollaway bed was mine. But now I had a queen-sized bed to myself. It was *almost* worth a week of bruising.

Dylan asked, "Are you hanging out for a little in the lobby tonight?"

"Yep," I said. "My parents are here."

"Cool. Lila and I need a little privacy if you don't mind. I'll text when the coast is clear?"

"Sure."

"She said her sorority sisters are bombed. I've got to find Tripp and warn him."

When he got up from his seat, I pulled out my phone. Greer hadn't texted me again, and I was disappointed. She still didn't trust me. I knew Caroline's presence here right now troubled her. Why else would she mention it to me? I was curious how Caroline afforded her carefree lifestyle. Scotty Designs made a ton of money based on this week's sales alone, but Greer lived frugally. The old car, clothes she made herself, low-maintenance hair and skin.

I opened my pictures and found the one of Greer and me from earlier today. I felt real affection for her sweatshop boots, but seeing her in those sandals with her polished toes peeking through unleashed raw desire for her. Holding her briefly underneath that magnificent, gnarled tree left me wanting more. Professor Simmons was right. Though *delightful* described more than just the game day dress that looked beautiful on her. Delightful was Greer herself.

A sliver of sunlight touched Greer's dark hair. And she was laughing, which happened more and more when we were together. Her nose crinkled, which was adorable. I didn't look too bad either. This picture would be perfect for her website or social media. We matched, and my name could boost new product sales given the way I was playing football right now. But I didn't want to share this picture with anyone yet, even Greer. It was too precious. Besides, what went down in Michigan was still very recent. Even though I wanted to help

Greer, endorsing a small business that sold women's clothes and accessories could come back to burn me and her. And what we had was special.

I was in this protective state of mind when I stepped into the lobby and spotted Caroline Scott leaning against a bar stool yards away from my parents. Out of all people in the crowd, I hated that my eyes found her. I literally wanted to rip her clothes off her. And not in a carnal way. She was wearing Greer's new red-and-white dress, *our* dress, and flaunting her body like she was on a runway. On Caroline, who was taller than Greer, without the stiletto heels she now wore, the dress barely covered her ass. And it was so tight on her, clinging to her breasts and hips.

This was the exact same dress Greer made the night before. On Greer, it gave off a flirty vibe. On Caroline, it screamed, "Fuck me."

Lila, who was beside Caroline, beelined her way to Dylan, and the two of them disappeared. Caroline, on the other hand, waited for Tripp Saunders to walk over to her. Her eyes were seductive and wielded power over him. She was as predictable as he was. I went to my parents' table and sat down, trying not to let my anger and intense dislike of Greer's sister show.

I failed.

"I know what you're thinking, Nico," my mother started. "I'm fine. Don't worry about me. She was already over here, chatting up your father and me as though we were old friends."

"Are you okay, Mom? I can get her to leave."

"It's a public place, Nico," my dad said. "And for whatever reason, she doesn't harbor any bad blood between us. All she really wanted was a free drink."

"What were the girls like before Jack died?" my mother asked, eyeing her outfit.

My dad shrugged. "Jack was laid-back but he had a strong

sense of right and wrong. He was the type of guy who brought out the best in you and, at the same time, you didn't want to disappoint him. He was the nurturer in the family. It's so hard to believe that Sunday is the five-year anniversary of Jack's death. I still remember that day like it was yesterday. His daughter standing next to us in shock."

My mother reached over the table and squeezed my dad's hand.

Five years, I said to myself. Which meant that Sunday was also Greer's birthday. When word got out in our hometown that Jack Scott had died, it was followed by the news that it had happened on Greer's birthday as they were picking up her gift, a sewing machine. My parents and I felt bad that we didn't know that at the time. But I honestly don't think it would have made a difference. Knowing Greer as I did now, she would have fled no matter how we tried to help her.

I had my work cut out for me on Sunday. Making her birthday special was my new mission.

Before my dad had the chance to tear up about Jack, Caroline was at the table again, this time with Tripp.

"Babe, let me introduce you to the Camillos." Both of her arms were wrapped around one of Tripp's. She either dragged him over to our table or needed him to support her drunken ass. He smirked at me, but naturally my father stood up to shake the notorious QB's hand.

"Pleased to meet you." Then he introduced himself and my mother, and heaped a bunch of praise on Tripp. My dad had a pretty good asshole detector, but it obviously wasn't working at the moment.

"Mr. Camillo was my father's best friend. My mom still refers to him as 'My Nicky.'" Caroline then winked at my mother. "Of course, when she met Nico after the game last week, she was so excited she leapt into his arms. Isn't that right,

Nico? The security agents just didn't understand our history with the Camillo family."

I watched the color drain from both of my parents' faces as they turned to me.

"That was *your mom?*" Tripp laughed. "I had to be escorted to my car from the locker room last week because of some *crazed* fan. I had no idea your mom jumping Nico was the reason."

"We are very passionate about our football team." Caroline giggled.

"Maybe Nico isn't used to passionate fans," Tripp said. "I mean, have you seen those girls in Michigan?"

Caroline playfully smacked Tripp's chest as though his offensive comment was offensive, but she was laughing alongside him as though his joke was actually funny. They both had to leave, now. I stood up.

"We have less than an hour before lights out," I announced.

"Oh, just one more drink!" Caroline squeezed Tripp's arm. "Come on! Let's hang out for a little longer. Goodnight, Camillos!" She pulled Tripp back to the bar, and I sat down to face my parents.

"Jesus, Nico," my dad hissed. "Sophia Scott? Security? What the fuck is going on?"

"Nicholas—" my mother's whisper was a warning.

The only time I'd heard my dad swear is when he thought he was alone or when he was extremely angry.

"She broke through the barricade and came at me. Security pulled her off. That was it. I didn't tell you because it was handled. And because you guys were never coming to a Butler game."

"Nico," my mother said quietly. "Do you have feelings for Caroline Scott?"

I laughed and shook my head. "You can't be serious, Mom."

But her expression was serious. So was my dad's when she glanced at him.

"Your mother's question is a good one and deserves an answer. I'm wondering the same thing." My dad's tone was loaded with controlled anger. "You're deliberately hiding the truth from us. You know what your mom went through four years ago. And you're choosing to protect *Sophia* over her."

"That is not true." My face was as flushed as Greer's when she was angry with me. I was pissed at my father's accusation.

"Ana," my dad stood, "let's leave Nico alone. We all need our rest."

My dad nodded at me while my mother hugged me, kissed the top of my head. I was too angry to acknowledge either one of them.

CHAOS WAS the only word to describe breakfast on Saturday morning. A few of the players, including Tripp Saunders, were missing, and the coaches huddled in the corner, scowling and speaking heatedly at one another. Dylan, Malik and I piled our plates with bacon, eggs, and grits. Dylan made a second plate full of fresh berries for the three of us.

Last night, Malik and I went up to the room after Dylan texted the all-clear. Apparently, Lila was having trouble with her girlfriends and needed her boyfriend's advice.

"If all she needed was advice, why didn't you invite us up here, man," said Malik, laughing at Dylan. "Nico's a smart dude. He'd have told her exactly what to do."

"She doesn't need anyone's advice but mine." His tone was serious.

When it came to Lila, Dylan couldn't take a joke. At least I was smart enough to keep my mouth shut. Fortunately, the three of us crashed. By the end of the week, practices and the heat – and my parents showing up – took their toll. Getting a full eight to ten hours before game day was just what we all needed.

"What's going on over there?" Malik asked, pointing at the coaches' table.

"Take my advice," said Dylan. "Stay out of it. Do your job today, and we'll be fine. Tripp and some others got in a little trouble last night from what Lila texted me." He looked into Malik's eyes. "Be glad you weren't with them, Beech."

A bunch of the players broke curfew and went to the party floor. Lila, who went to bed just like we did, described the hallway as busy all night long with security popping in and out. Someone must have noticed one of the players because it was the coaches who put a stop to it. But whoever was involved was keeping it quiet because even Lila couldn't get any details.

The second surprise came after breakfast. My mom texted, saying that they'd left before dawn and were heading home to Virginia. "It wasn't a good idea to surprise you. Good luck today. We love you."

I felt my anger rising again, but it was also mixed with relief. I was on my own again, which was how it was always going to be when I chose Butler.

So I sat with Dylan's parents and listened to them discuss their restaurant on Amelia Island, catching Dylan up on local events. The conversation was pleasant and helped to ease some of the tension around us. My parents would have enjoyed getting to know Dylan's family, and I couldn't help feeling guilt in addition to anger that they'd left without saying goodbye.

Usually, I was calm on game day. But now that Tripp may not be playing, I had no idea what to expect. I'd yet to work out with our backup QB.

And Greer still hadn't texted or emailed. At the very least, I was hoping to hear about Aunt Isabel's peanut butter and jelly sandwich. Her radio silence left me feeling uneasy, and even more alone now that my parents ditched me.

By mid-morning, all players had to pack up and check out before heading to the stadium. Dylan learned that Tripp was at the hospital with Coach Phillips getting an IV. The moron QB got wasted during the night. But rather than punish him, the Butler football machine was patching him up to start. Granted, it was better to have him than the backup QB who none of the starters had worked with. But could this guy be any more of a douche?

We were loaded onto the bus watching some of the Butler fans stream out of the hotel. Again, my hawk eyes found the one person I didn't want to see: Caroline Scott. She was primped for the game. Wavy hair, full makeup, short shorts, football tee, and high sandals. This week, she had Tripp's number glitter-tattooed on her cheeks. In her hand was the game day dress of Greer's. She laughed as she held it up for all her friends to see. Red wine or some other ruby-colored beverage had stained the length of it. Then I watched, helplessly, as she scrunched the thin fabric into a ball and tossed it in the trash.

She continued on to her Mini as if she hadn't just shit all over her sister.

15

———

GREER

I woke up on Sunday morning, my nineteenth birthday, to steady rain. Emma and I were still meeting at ten. Caroline arrived home late last night and went straight to bed, but not before telling me that Tripp Saunders had asked her to go to the Delta Gamma formal. And she'd need a pink dress.

"I want the one you made for Lila. But I want mine to be a mini dress. And in hot pink."

"Those dresses are only for current sorority sisters. I can't make one for you."

"But I'm going with the QB."

"We had to sign a non-compete, Caroline. The custom-designed, pink gowns are only for current Delta Gammas."

"Jesus, Greer. Why do you always have to say things like that?" She was pissed. "Just forget it. I'm going to get something on my own. It will be much prettier than one of your stupid dresses anyway."

My mother was up when I came into the kitchen and wished me a happy birthday.

"Thanks, Mom."

"What would you like for dinner?" she asked.

"Whatever you feel like."

"Nancy asked to come over, too." She kissed the top of my head. "I told her six."

I grabbed my mother's hand. "You didn't invite anyone else, did you Mom?"

"Greer Scott!" She was defensive. "I learned my lesson. I promise that no one else is invited. And the only reason Nancy is coming is because she's making your birthday cake."

My mother was acting differently. More like herself before Nico Camillo arrived to town. When I asked her why she was in such a good mood, she revealed that Caroline ran into the Camillos at the team hotel.

I froze, then chose my next words carefully. "Did anything happen?"

"She said they were very nice to her." My mother smiled. "Why would you think something happened?"

The Camillos went to the away game after all. I was happy for Nico. But I changed the subject. I didn't want to share with my mother that Nico's parents were never coming to Butler because she lived here.

When I went back upstairs to shower and dress for the library, I saw a new text on my phone. From Nico:

> Wear old tennis shoes and comfortable clothes.
> Don't forget a raincoat.

This meant that Nico would join our study group this morning. Based on last week's reaction to Blake and Liam sitting at our window table, I had a feeling I'd see him there today. Knowing Nico, this text had something to do with our report on "sweatshops." But I couldn't read between the lines on this one. Instead, I replied:

Bossy much?

I followed Nico's orders and put on athletic tights and a Scotty tank, an old pair of running shoes, and a rain jacket. In my school bag, I added a flannel in case the library was cool. My hair was wet from the shower, but what was the point of blowing it dry when the rain would soak it anyway? Then I grabbed my keys, waved goodbye to my mom under a blanket on the couch, and ran for the van parked a couple of blocks away.

Nico's black SUV was double-parked, blocking in my van. He must have spotted me running because he stepped out of the car and held the passenger's side door open for me.

"I figured you'd be mad at me if I waited outside your house," he said. "So I came here, taking the chance you'd drive to the library."

I stood near the opened door, too stunned to move. What a nice thing to do, and he didn't even know it was my birthday today. "Am I allowed to say thank you for this?"

"No." He smiled. "Just get in the car before my leather seats get ruined."

I climbed inside and he shut the door then walked around the car and got back in. The rain was heavy, and like me, he wore a rain jacket with the hood raised. Even surrounded by the odors of new leather, rainwater and water-repellant polyester, Nico's fresh sunshine scent found me.

"What time do you meet your study group?" he asked. His deep voice in such close quarters sent a shiver through me. I didn't know whether it was just because he was thoughtful enough to pick me up not even knowing it was my birthday or that I'd missed hearing him speak these past two days, but my entire body felt tingly.

I knew I was blushing. "Ten," I croaked out, then cleared my throat.

"Let's get to it."

I asked him about the game, and he said it was okay. Butler should have done better but at least they got the win. I decided against asking him about Tripp Saunders and Caroline. It was my birthday after all, even if he didn't know that, and I didn't want to spoil it by even talking about them.

"How are your parents?" I asked. Even though the Camillos were a source of stress in my household, they were important to Nico. I didn't want to be someone who got in the way of that.

"They came to Carolina," he said softly. "They didn't stay for the game, but we had the chance to hang out."

"And how are Matteo and Enzo?" I asked. Like his parents, we never talked about his brothers. He knew all about Caroline, so as friends, it was only fair of me to learn about the people who meant the most to him.

Nico wouldn't allow the conversation to be awkward. He loved his family, and spoke the rest of the way to campus about what each of his brothers was doing. Matteo, who was Caroline's age, was at business school in Philadelphia. And Enzo was a junior in the same Virginia high school where we both went. And he played football.

"My brothers are hoping to come down for a home game soon," he said. "I'd love for you to meet them, Greer."

As he said these words, he was pulling into the parking lot closest to the library. I smiled at him but didn't respond. Meeting any member of his family was *not* a good idea, but since it was my birthday and my mother and now Nico were being so nice to me, I chose not to get into it with him and spoil everything.

Nico was also wearing running shoes, so we both tightened

our hoods and ran for the library. Since the ground had been so dry, there were mini rivers of water and giant puddles everywhere. Nico made it a competition, and we took turns attempting to clear the puddles. I was laughing so hard that I landed in water most of the time. By the time we arrived, my old shoes were soggy and my tights were soaked. My hair, which had been wet from the shower, was dripping. Nico was only slightly less wet. We took off our jackets and shook out the excess water before entering the library. Even my flannel, which I pulled out after removing my jacket, was damp. But it was better than just a tank top.

Most students chose to stay in their dorm rooms this rainy morning. We had no trouble finding a table by the window, and we didn't have to wait long before Emma, Blake, and Liam showed up.

At first, the three of them were quiet, not knowing what to make of Nico being at the library on Sunday morning after a huge away game. Blake and Liam just stared at him. Emma was the one who broke the ice.

"What happened to Tripp Saunders yesterday?" she asked Nico. "He played like crap."

"It happens sometimes," he answered her. "But the defense stepped up."

And then Blake and Liam entered the conversation, with specifics about yesterday's highlights, and Nico tried to explain what was happening on the sideline. He was diplomatic always, never once criticizing another teammate or bragging about his own performance. He missed catches, but that was mostly due to Tripp's bad passes. The receptions he did make were pretty impressive because the balls were either too high or too low.

The table had room for four people, but Nico had pulled over an extra chair so that he was sitting next to me, sharing my table space. While Blake and Liam talked about their own project for history of capitalism, one they had to ace because their term paper grade was a C, Emma and I went over our prerequisite classes. English lit and philosophy were easy. We'd both caught up on the readings and exchanged notes. Emma had already started on her phys ed culminating project with a local elementary school, and I still didn't have a topic.

"Did you find out what your sister's project was?" Emma asked.

"Don't laugh," I said. "But she did a Pilates class for football players. And her sorority sisters filmed it on the stadium turf for her."

Emma and Nico started to laugh.

"Your sister is obsessed with football," Emma said.

"My sister is obsessed with football players," I corrected.

Nico put his head down, suddenly uncomfortable with this conversation. After all, he was the object of her obsession for at least a week.

"The only idea I had isn't technically a curriculum," I said.

"That professor is so flexible, though," she reasoned. "I mean, come on, it's phys ed. What's your idea?"

"What about designing a new cheerleader uniform?" I asked. "Those ones the girls wear look so uncomfortable."

"I guess I hadn't really noticed," Emma said. "What about you, Nico? Do you like the cheerleader uniforms?"

"I hadn't really noticed either." He actually blushed, and Emma and I giggled at him. Of course, he noticed the attractive and athletic cheerleaders standing alongside the team each week.

"It's not that I personally think they're unflattering on the girls," I said, "but they're also not athletic wear. There are so many better fabrics to choose from."

"Talk to the professor," said Emma. "Maybe she can help."

"Coach Phillips is friends with the cheer coaches," Nico

offered. "You want me to ask him? Maybe you can speak with the coaches about it?"

"Only if it doesn't put you in an awkward position."

"Not at all." He lowered his voice. "I'd do anything for you. You're my partner."

I studied him but didn't respond. *Did he really just say what I think he said?* His focus returned to his econometrics textbook. When I glanced at Emma, her eyebrows raised at me and she smiled, then she looked away. She must have heard him too.

When Emma, Blake, and Liam broke for lunch, Nico and I went over our rough outline for Dr. Simmons' new project. We'd have to do more research, increase the number of sources, but the writing wouldn't be as heavy. According to the assignment, each group had to present the final report, using visual media, as though we were in a board room.

"Is that why we're dressed like this?" I asked. "Are you planning to recreate a sweatshop from the early nineteenth century wearing old sneakers?"

"Actually, no. That wasn't my intention. But I like the way you think, Gree."

My nickname came out of him so naturally, he couldn't have known how much it meant to me. My family sometimes used it, but it was my father who started calling me Gree when I was little. I changed the subject.

"I'm nervous about this presentation," I said. "Most of my high school classes were online, so I've never really had to speak in public." Nico, on the other hand, was able to deliver poised and thoughtful answers during interviews conducted by beautiful sidelines reporters on national TV.

"We're partners, remember?" he said. "We'll practice, and you'll be great." His green eyes smiled as he spoke. "You ready to get out of here?"

The rain had stopped but the sky was still overcast, threatening more rain. "What did you have in mind?"

"Do you have anything else planned for today?"

"No, but I have to be home by six."

"Sunday dinner?" he asked.

"Something like that," I answered.

"Okay," he said. "I'll have you home by six."

We walked back to his car, and he announced he had a surprise for me. I wasn't allowed to ask any questions. But once he turned onto Route 153, I had a feeling we were heading towards one of the state parks along the Oconee River. So I wasn't surprised when he turned into the parking lot, but I was surprised when he opened the trunk. There was Aunt Isabel's Scotty tote bag.

"You ready?" he asked.

"Did you make us lunch?"

"Of course, I did," he said. "It's your *birthday*, Greer. Aunt Isabel would expect no less of me."

I gasped. "How did you know?"

"I have my sources." He winked. "Now let's go before it starts raining again."

The trails, normally crowded on Sundays in September, carried few other hikers. Like the library, most people stayed home. But most of the rainwater had already receded. So even though there were muddy spots, walking in old sneakers was not too difficult. The air was humid though, and both of us soon had our jackets tied around our waists.

Nico wanted to know what was happening at six o'clock. "Just dinner with my family, and Nancy is coming over. My mother asked her to make a cake." Since he'd gone to so much effort today for me, I decided to open up to him. "I hate my birthday, Nico. It's the anniversary of my dad's death, so we usually don't do anything. My mom knows not to invite anyone over. She did that for my fifteenth birthday, and it was a disaster."

"I get it. Let's just pretend it's a regular Sunday."

We hiked to the riverbank and found a large flat rock to picnic. Nico had even brought a blanket, which we spread out. Then he unloaded enough food for ten people. When I asked him how he had time to make so much food, he confessed that most of it was store bought. There were tomato and mozzarella sandwiches, fruit salad, vegetable chips, cookies, and large bottles of water. As he was unloading everything, he spoke in an infomercial voice, demonstrating how each practical pocket of Aunt Isabel's tote worked.

I laughed so hard my face and stomach hurt.

The sun peeked through after lunch, and we stretched out on the rock in companionable silence. Nico admitted he was tired from the week and traveling to a tough away game. Then he asked me how I did it.

"Do what?" I was confused.

"You never stop, Greer," he said. "You work all the time and you have six classes."

"I'm not getting tackled though. My work isn't strenuous."

"That's not true. You are always on the move, in and out of your chair, kneeling and squatting next to your dummies. I've watched you, Greer, and I don't think many people have your kind of energy."

I didn't respond. No part of me wanted this moment to end, staring into Nico's green eyes, his hair still damp from the rain and messy. My hair was just as tangled but I didn't care. The sun soon went behind the clouds, and Nico suggested packing up.

While Nico repacked the tote, I folded the blanket. The river below had swelled from the rain, and the rapids were higher than usual. When I handed him the blanket, he had pulled out a small gift box.

"Is that for me?" I asked, stunned.

"It's for you."

"Why did you do that, Nico?" I asked. "You didn't have to get me a gift. Lunch was so nice."

"Greer." He smiled. "Remember what I said before? You're my partner, and partners take care of each other. Especially on their birthdays."

I'd already confessed to Nico that I dreaded my birthday. But I was also wary of gifts. On my fourteenth birthday, my father and I picked out the Singer Quantum Stylist 9960, a gift that still meant everything to me but reminded me of his death. I'd been asking for a real sewing machine for a few years at that point. Nothing would ever compare to what that gift meant to me.

Inside the gift box was one of the most beautiful things I'd ever seen. A pink diamond necklace on a pale rose gold chain. I covered my mouth. But before I could even protest him giving me this gift, my eyes started to overflow with tears. Ever since my father's death, I could do that. Cry without making a sound. With my free hand I started wiping away the wetness.

"Don't cry, Greer. It's just a necklace."

"It's so beautiful. I can't accept this from you."

"You can and you will," he insisted. "When I saw that, I knew it belonged to you. It matches your eyes. Let's try it on."

Because I was still wiping my face, Nico took the necklace and clasped it around my neck. His voice was upbeat and friendly, and I'm sure he felt embarrassed because the tears kept coming. I was helpless to stop them.

"There." He held onto my shoulders until I could look into his eyes. "You don't even have to look at it anymore. Just know that it suits you perfectly."

I didn't speak, but then did something so unexpected and out of character. I hugged him, awkwardly, both of my arms wrapped around his waist. And I leaned my head against his chest, something I'd wanted to do five years ago today. I'd caught him off guard because his arms were limp for a moment. But I didn't let go, and I soon felt him holding me too.

I couldn't let go until I knew I'd stopped crying. Deep breaths helped, and inhaling Nico's summer beach day scent calmed me even more. His T-shirt was damp again, my wet face plastered to it. But I was no longer crying. Despite this, pulling away from him seemed impossible. Eventually my breathing evened. His hand moved to my chin, and I glanced up. His eyes were green fire against the darkening clouds, and I found myself staring into their depths, wanting to know what his intuitive mind was thinking. And I was hoping he could see how grateful I was to him for being a friend at that moment.

Nico's eyes lowered to my lips, and then his head bent forward. He was going to kiss me. *Finally*, I thought, surprising myself. Suddenly I didn't care how wrong this was. I should never have hugged him the way I did. Nico Camillo and Greer Scott should not be kissing. We should not even be friends. But it was my birthday, and it was just one kiss.

But it wasn't meant to be.

The skies opened and rain pelted down, separating us. Nico grabbed the tote bag and jumped off the rock, and assisted me down. We put our raincoats on and hurried back to the car, Nico's hand holding mine because the trail was slippery. I didn't pull my hand away, or tell him to stop this time.

The drive back to my house went quickly despite the darkening skies and the heavy rain. Nico pulled up to my house again, but no one was out on the porch to witness it so I didn't mind.

"Happy birthday, Greer."

"Thank you, Nico. For everything." I jumped out before he could reprimand me for thanking him.

On the porch, I waved to Nico and watched him pull away. Then I took off my jacket and hung it on a chair to dry outside. I'd been soaking wet for most of the day and in desperate need of a shower. When I walked inside, my mother was wearing the palazzo pants with one of the new Scotty tops we altered to fit her bust. Her tan belly and navel were on full display, and her hair and makeup were done. She looked like she was going to a club rather than Sunday dinner. Nancy was at the table with her, sipping a cup of tea.

"There's the birthday girl," she said cheerily.

"Happy birthday Greer!" said Nancy. "Looks like you were caught in the rain."

Before I could answer her, heavy footsteps were descending the stairs. My sister Caroline, who looked as primped as my mother, followed by Tripp Saunders.

"This is my sister Greer, Tripp," Caroline said. Her eyes found my necklace immediately, and I held onto the diamond, hiding it from her. I vowed then to never remove Nico's necklace for fear she'd take it from me.

He smiled. "You look familiar. Have we met before?"

"I doubt it," Caroline answered for me. "Greer is hardly ever on campus. Did you meet your study group in a kennel today, Greer?" My sister held her nose. "You smell like a wet dog."

I ran upstairs for a shower, suddenly wishing Nico never brought me back here.

16

NICO

efore I fell asleep on Sunday night, I texted Greer.

> How was bday dinner?

She replied right away.

> Not as nice as bday lunch. Gnite.

Her goodnight meant she didn't want to keep texting. But I already heard what I wanted to. My lunch was better than her family's dinner. Not that I was trying to outdo them. I wasn't. But I was happy that she had a nice afternoon.

Her crying made me sad for her, but even that was worth it. Greer hugged me. And I knew that was not something that came to her easily. She didn't grow up in an affectionate Italian family. Her mom was crazy, and her sister was cruel. Her father seemed like the one person in her life who loved her unconditionally and supported her genius, yet he left her for good when he died on Main Street.

The small jewelry shop was across the street from the Carolina hotel, and I ran in there five minutes before we were scheduled to head back to Butler on Saturday. I had no idea what to get Greer, and the pink necklace was the first item that caught my eye. The jeweler had designed it herself. When she told me that, I knew Greer would love it. My only hesitation was her sister Caroline. Based on the way she treated Greer's dress, I had no doubt she'd try to get her hands on her necklace too. But how do you tell someone their sister is depraved?

The rain saved me today. I stood as still as a statue with my hands wrapped around her upper body. But my insides were in overdrive, the blood pumping fast and racing to one place only. Her hair was soaked, and I detected the sweet honeysuckle scent through the rainwater. Then Greer kept burying her face deeper into my chest, her full breasts pressed against me, which felt incredible but made me scared to move. Greer was inexperienced. That was as plain as day. She had no idea what effect she was having on me, or half the guys on campus.

I'd just decided to kiss her when the rain started again. It was for the best. If she'd realized how turned on I was, she might have fled. But I learned something important today. I couldn't get physical with Greer unless I was all in. She was strong and perceptive, but she also felt emotion deeply. She just didn't wear it on her sleeve. But if a guy like me took advantage of her, I knew it would crush her. Maybe for good.

The rain didn't let up all night, so Monday morning's practice was wet and messy. The coaches also blamed all of us, not just Tripp and his asshole friends, for the poor performance on Saturday. I still didn't know the whole story – my only concern about Tripp's bad judgement was that he didn't make it again – but I suspected Caroline Scott was involved.

Coach Phillips stopped me after drills to tell me Ryan and Beau would be working out with me this week. "I want them on the field, in the weight room, and watching film with you, Nico," he said. "We can't keep relying on you and Dylan. Everyone on the offensive line needs to make plays."

Because Tripp Saunders sucks, I finished for him.

"No problem, Coach." I nodded. "My friend wants to talk to the cheerleading coaches about her culminating project for the semester. Could you introduce her?"

"I'd be happy to," said Phillips. "Have your friend email me and mention you, and I'll remember this conversation."

"Thanks." I ran off the field.

Just like every Monday morning, the locker room was noisy. Guys rehashing the game, talking about what they did afterwards and on Sunday, which was a rest day. I grabbed a quick shower and was changing when I overheard Tripp Saunders bragging about his weekend.

"I'm telling you," he said, "Caroline Scott is fucking wild, man. And then I was at her house last night, and I swear to God I could have had both the Scotts. They both wanted to fuck me."

I walked up to him, grabbed him by the neck, and shoved him into the locker. He started to scream but I held him tight, practically choking him. Chaos erupted around us. Dylan soon wrestled me off him. And Tripp started shouting at me. "What the fuck is your problem, Camillo? You told me you didn't want her, you fucking asshole."

"What the hell are *you* talking about?" I said. "Who wanted to fuck you last night?"

"Caroline Scott and her mom," he shouted, "not that it's any of your goddamn business."

When Tripp Saunders said "both," it felt like Malik Beech hit me again, knocking the wind out of me. All I could think about was Greer with this piece of shit. I took a deep breath and slowly released it, trying to calm down.

"Show some respect," I spit out to Tripp.

I walked away listening to the guys whispering about me. As long as no one realized my fear was about Greer, I didn't care what they thought of me. If a guy like Tripp knew how much she meant to me, he'd exploit that.

And now I had to go through the day knowing that Tripp Saunders was at Greer's birthday dinner? It wasn't her fault. She didn't invite him. And since I'd dropped her off a few minutes beforehand, she probably didn't even know he was inside. But she should have told me. Or, I should have never taken her home in the first place. Or, I should have been there with her.

The whole situation was screwy. I couldn't be a part of Greer's life because her mom stalked my parents? But Tripp Saunders, one of the biggest jerks in the league, was welcome with open arms?

After my behavior this morning, I realized I had to distance myself from Greer and the Scott family. My decision yesterday *not* to kiss Greer in the rain was the right one. Being her friend and her partner had to be the extent of our relationship.

BUT THEN I walked into history of capitalism with one minute to spare and saw Greer standing by her desk chatting with Blake and all of my senses were back in overdrive. She was not dressed provocatively, but it didn't matter. She had on a pair of jeans with her Converses and another one of her tank tops that hit right at her waist. She was proudly wearing her diamond necklace and smiled at me as soon as I walked through the door. For the first time, I noticed Greer's dimple on the right side of her blushing face. Her sleek hair fell down her back and around her face.

This look was dangerous for her. Most guys I knew wouldn't try to look beyond a goth look, assuming the girl was fringe. But this mainstream look on Greer would get every guy admiring her. There was not a doubt in my mind that she was the most beautiful girl on campus.

"Mr. Camillo has finally joined us," said Dr. Simmons in a cheery tone. "We can begin."

The lesson went quickly. There was so much to the Industrial Revolution that the professor said we'd be on this topic for a couple of weeks. Greer and I, like the rest of the class, had our work cut out for us with our presentation. So we spent the last thirty minutes of class meeting with our partners.

Greer must not have hung out too long with her family and Tripp the night before because our rough outline from the library yesterday was fully mapped out. She'd spent a lot of time on it since I'd dropped her off and now. When Dr. Simmons left us and moved on to check the progress of another group, I asked Greer in a low voice how dinner *really* was.

"I know Tripp was there, Greer."

She blanched. "Is he a friend of yours, Nico?"

"Why do you ask?"

"He just doesn't *seem* like you."

I had to tread carefully here. Football players weren't allowed to badmouth teammates. It broke the honor code. And Greer had only been my friend for a short time. I wanted to trust her but I also had to be careful, especially after my attack on Tripp this morning. Whatever I said next could get back to Caroline and then be broadcast everywhere. Rather than answer her question, I changed the subject.

"Coach Phillips said that you should just email him, and he'll introduce you to the cheer coaches."

"Thank you," she said. "But do you think making new cheerleader uniforms is a dumb idea for a culminating project for phys ed? It's not a curriculum."

"You'll never know unless you ask, Greer. But I have the sense that the faculty and staff here are required to hear you out. So just follow up. What's the worst that can happen?"

"They say it's a dumb idea." She laughed.

"You can handle that," I said. "Although if I were you, I'd bring Aunt Isabel along. She'll straighten them out."

"By the way," she said. "I don't know if you are planning to come to the studio again this week, but tonight's the only night we're staying open. I have fittings the rest of the week at the Delta Gamma house."

"Then count on me bringing dinner tonight."

WHEN I ARRIVED at the studio with my awesome tote bag full of food, Greer and Aunt Isabel were not at their machines but searching through cabinets. A camera on a tripod was pointed at a white screen.

"What's going on?" I asked.

"Nico!" Aunt Isabel said. "I'm so glad you're here. We need your tote bag. We're photographing new products."

"Before we post anything new," Greer explained, "my partner likes to review everything. But I couldn't find the new game day dress at home. Aunt Isabel modified the pattern, and I can't seem to find that either."

Now was my chance. "Could Caroline have taken it?"

"Definitely not," said Greer. "My sister hates Scotty clothes. I asked her about it this morning, and she told me that she wouldn't be caught dead in anything I made. Then, of course, she told me how much fun she's been having searching for a *real* designer pink dress for the formal." She rolled her eyes. "I think my mom threw it away without realizing it."

"Let's just make a few new ones," Aunt Isabel suggested. "We have plenty of new fabrics for other teams as well."

While they got to work, I unloaded all of the food. Since this was my last dinner for a while, I'd made my mother's lasagna. It wasn't her meatballs and gravy, unfortunately, but those required at least two days to make them right. While I was in the kitchen grabbing plates and utensils, two little dark-haired kids came running through the studio. They both hugged Aunt Isabel and Greer. They spoke Filipino with Isabel and English to Greer. Then their mother came in and was talking fast in both languages about all the progress Isabel and Greer made the week she was away. This was Melanie and her twins, Sam and Beatrice, who I'd heard so much about. Sam, I noticed, was wearing a Butler football jersey with seventeen on the back. Cool.

No one had noticed me standing there, but Isabel had asked the kids to help by picking up the pieces of fabric she'd cut for the game day dresses and carrying them over. I could tell this was something the kids were used to doing since they both ran to the table and started to argue about who was carrying what. On their way back, Sam in the lead, the little boy stopped suddenly and dropped his fabric, pretending that he hadn't just trounced his sister on the game they'd been playing. She didn't miss a beat, picked up his pieces and delivered everything to Isabel.

Sam stared at me. And I knew exactly what was going through his mind.

"I'd have dropped that fabric too," I said with a straight face. "Tennessee is the worst. Let's go find the Butler colors." I walked over to the cutting station and sorted through them, finding Greer's red-and-white fabrics and handing them to the little boy, still shocked I was here.

"Nico Camillo?" Melanie shouted. "I thought Aunt Isabel was

joking. You *are* Greer's friend! We were at the Carolina game on Saturday. My husband surprised us with tickets on our way home from the beach. This is number seventeen, Sam!" She turned to me. "He's a big fan of yours."

"We are all big fans of Nico here!" said Aunt Isabel.

After all of us had dinner, Sam, Beatrice, and I stuffed all the daily orders into their packages, weighed and stamped them, and then they took turns being pushed by me in the plastic bins down the hallway and into the mail room. By then the building was quiet, and the kids squealed the entire time. It was a blast, but bending over and running was almost as hard as Coach Phillips' football drills. I'd definitely feel it in the morning. Keeping them occupied and out of the studio helped the others since they were able to make what they needed to and photograph everything. For a small studio, Greer had her system down well.

At the end of the night, Greer turned her keys over to Melanie and Isabel since she had to spend the next few days at the sorority house with the pink dresses, and they'd be in charge of running the studio.

"Finally, you are letting go of some control over this place, Greer," said Melanie. "We will take care of orders and call you with any problems, okay?"

Greer nodded. She and I were wheeling out her portable wardrobe, which was much heavier now with all fifty-two dresses, the lights, screens and mirrors. We loaded everything into her van and said goodbye to the Floreses. Sam and Beatrice gave me high-fives and chest bumps, just like they'd seen in the end zone.

"Poor Melanie," said Greer when they pulled away. "The twins will never want to come back unless you're here."

"We did have fun tonight."

"You're amazing. Sam and Beatrice warmed up to you within

seconds. Do you know they didn't speak to me for months after Melanie started? I think they were scared of me."

"You do run a sweatshop, Greer," I said. "To them, I'm just a kid who plays football."

She laughed. "Dr. Simmons is right. You are wicked!"

My thoughts about Greer Scott right now were definitely wicked. She switched her white Converses for her boots, which did funny things to me. They weren't feminine in the least, but they were Greer. As she stood before me in the dusky light, the white from her smile visible as well as her cropped white tank and pink diamond necklace, I felt just as I did on the rock when I was holding her. I wanted to kiss her. She was waiting for it also.

An image of me holding Tripp Saunders by the neck sobered me up fast. Even if I didn't have issues with the Scott family, he'd go after Greer next if he knew she meant something to me. As it was, I could be facing disciplinary action by the team for my behavior today if Tripp ratted me out. And I suspected he already had since Coach Hampton texted me to see him tomorrow morning in his office.

This Butler football machine might be willing to overlook Michigan on my behalf, but they would protect Tripp at all costs. And if it was between him and me, they'd choose him.

I broke our staring contest and closed the back door of her van and handed her the keys. Then I opened up the driver's side door, said goodbye, and closed it for her. There was no point in me asking her what time she was due at the sorority house tomorrow. She wouldn't tell me, insisting that she could transport the wardrobe by herself.

But I had my sources, and I'd be there to help her.

17

GREER

Nico was acting differently.

He was still friendly and kind, always trying to make me laugh. He showed up each night at the Delta Gamma house with Dylan to carry in the dresses and then wheel them back to my van when we finished. The girls begged me to leave the portable wardrobe there, but I refused. I couldn't risk the whole sorority taking the dresses out and trying them on without me, ripping out pins and ruining all of our hard work.

It was when we were alone that I sensed the shift. Before my birthday, Nico was always invading my personal space. The way he yanked my desk to his during history of capitalism, or walked me to my van, his arms and torso always brushing up against me. And when he spoke to me, his face always dipped close to mine so I could spot the brown flecks in his green eyes.

That all changed after I hugged him on the rock.

I believed Nico when he said Caroline wasn't his type. But I now realized I wasn't his type either. And while my mind knew this was for the best and, if I was honest with myself, exactly what I'd wanted from him in the beginning, my heart still stung.

A lot. I was almost unsure whether to wear the pink diamond necklace. Part of me was convinced he regretted giving me such a beautiful and expensive gift. But then I couldn't take it off because I knew Caroline would steal it from me. She demanded to know who gave it to me, and that she needed to borrow it the night of the formal.

"As the QB's date, everyone is going to be looking to *me* to support breast cancer," she argued. "*I* should be the one who wears the necklace."

Liar.

She wanted it because it was stunning. Everyone complimented me on it, and all I could say was that a friend gave it to me. Caroline was convinced it was the Flores family, and I didn't say anything to make her believe otherwise.

I also loved how Nico's necklace made me feel. Pretty because he said it matched my eyes. And strong. Whether I was at school or home, or helping the Delta Gammas with their dresses, all I had to do was touch the stone to feel Nico near me. I knew now that he didn't intend for this gift to signify more than friendship. To him, it probably wasn't even that precious an object. Nico did feel sorry for me sometimes, though I always turned away from him when that look entered his eyes. I didn't want his pity. Maybe he just wanted to give me something for my birthday, and this necklace was the first thing he saw?

The good news was that the dresses Aunt Isabel and I made for the girls were a success. The fittings went smoothly, and even though some of the alterations would be substantial – girls wanting major changes, like flowy pants instead of skirts – most were minimal. There were even some who didn't require any more work, and the girls carried them upstairs to store in their closets until the dance. Lila asked me a million questions about how Scotty had accomplished so much in so little time.

"I hired a part-time seamstress whose work is incredible," I said. "Between the two of us, we got everything done. Even I was surprised." I left out the part about Nico helping with the daily packages, which freed up our time to focus exclusively on the sewing work.

"And what does Caroline do then?" she asked.

Before I could respond with the truth, that Caroline didn't work for Scotty, my sister walked through the cloakroom door, as if she'd apparated here upon hearing her name.

"I keep Greer on track," Caroline announced, winking at me. She was fully primped and in bar attire: heels, tight denim jeans, and a tube top. I'd never seen these clothes before, which made me think she'd raided one of the Delta Gamma's closets. She couldn't afford them otherwise. The heels looked like Louboutins. "Lila, Dylan is looking for you."

The two of them left, and I completed the rest of the fittings. It was Thursday night. My plan was to return to the studio tomorrow with all of the dresses, and between Isabel, Melanie, and myself, we'd have the alterations finished by Saturday night. I was about to text Nico not to return since Caroline was here and could help me. Also, I wanted to spare him a run-in with my sister. But Lila returned without her.

"Where's Caroline?" I asked as I was packing the last of the dresses into the wardrobe.

"She already left," she answered. "She was meeting Tripp and his roommates at his house. Dylan's afraid they're having a party tonight."

"My friend Emma invited me to an off-campus party tonight," I told Lila. "Could that be the same one?" I'd considered going too, thinking about Melanie's advice to experience college life. Branching out beyond Nico, given his recent distancing, was also tempting. But then I realized the timing was all wrong. Scotty was stretched to capacity. Going to parties with Emma could wait until after homecoming.

"There are dozens of off-campus parties on Thursday night," Lila said. "But the football players aren't allowed to party. They have to stay dry throughout the season."

Caroline won't like that, I said to myself.

Just then, Nico and Dylan arrived to both take the wardrobe back to my van. Lila and I followed them as they wheeled it up Midvale in the dark. While the Georgia air was still warm in September, the days were getting shorter. Our walk was slow, lingering, because Lila had a lot to say. She was telling both of them about Tripp's probable party. If the information surprised or bothered Nico, he didn't let it show. His expression was fixed, but knowing Nico's mind, he was processing everything she said and making conclusions.

He just wasn't sharing them. In fact, he wasn't sharing any of himself.

Once the two guys loaded my van, Nico held the drivers' side door for me as he always did and gave me a quick goodbye. Lila and Dylan were waiting for him. I suspected that they were all headed back to the sorority house tonight.

Just then, I realized that Nico never told me who he was taking to the formal. Was that why he was being so reserved around me? Because he now had a girlfriend and was afraid I'd be upset?

I wasn't my mother, and I wasn't my sister. I thought he realized this. Steeling my heart was something I'd mastered after my father died. *I'd survive Nico,* I told myself as I pulled my car out of the commuter lot and headed home.

Perhaps he needed to hear this from me?

. . .

FRIDAY'S HISTORY of capitalism class went by quickly. Most of the period was given to partners to work on Industrial Revolution projects. Nico insisted that we include information about workers in New England cotton mills before the start of the nineteenth century.

"We don't always have to focus on textiles," I said, thinking about the mercantilism essay we'd written. "We could talk about the railroads, steel, or an industry that interests you."

"True," he said. "But because of you, sewing interests me too. And I know you want to get Elias Howe in this report somehow."

I laughed. Elias Howe invented the sewing machine. "I've already read all about him, Nico," I said. "I'm happy to study another industry."

"Does it really matter, Greer?" he asked. "The workers, the millions of immigrants who allowed capitalism to succeed here, are our focus. Let's study something that might help Scotty Designs while we're at it."

His head dipped towards me then as he said this. Old Nico was back for a moment. I held my breath as he stared into my eyes while I studied his. Then I exhaled slowly and gave him a slight smile. But then, after class ended, New Nico walked me to my van, never once brushing up against me. Something was bothering him though.

"What's wrong Nico?" I asked. "I can tell you want to say something but won't."

His smile, like mine earlier, was tight. "I presume Caroline will be at the game tomorrow. Is your mom also going?"

I stopped walking. He did too, and we stood feet away from each other, just staring at each other.

"My mom works for a dermatologist, and he gives her a ticket. But she's been different. She hasn't mentioned your father in a while."

He nodded.

"Caroline will be there. But she's forgotten all about you. All she talks about is Tripp Saunders."

"If I got you tickets, would you go, Greer?" he asked. "Maybe your mom could go with you instead?"

Was he asking me to go to the game, or did he just want me to babysit my mother? "Nico, you know I don't miss the games on TV, right?" I asked.

"I know that," he said. "I thought it might be fun for you. You do deserve to be a college student sometimes."

"Maybe after homecoming." I smiled at him. He was just being kind to me, like always. "My mom watched the game with Isabel and me last weekend at the studio and had fun. I'll try to convince her to come again tomorrow."

And then I wished Nico good luck and hurried to the van.

MY MOM REFUSED to miss the game. As much as I hated to do it, I texted Nico on Saturday morning.

> Mission failed. My mother and sister are both going to the game. I told them to be on their best behavior.

My face flamed as I typed out the message because I felt ashamed of my family. And then I thought of my father, and my shame was compounded by guilt. He was always proud of us and respectful of my mother. It was with this mood that I went to the studio. Melanie and Isabel had been amazing the week before, keeping on top of all the Scotty orders and making tote bags and game day dresses when they had extra time so that when we launched the new products, we'd have inventory. The pink dresses for the formal were also back in the studio. With luck and hard work, we'd have them finished by the end of the day.

My silent partner liked the new products but set the prices for the game day dresses higher than our existing sleeveless minis. The decision was very unemotional:

This product has a new cut with bolder colors. From all indications, it should perform well in sales. We should raise the price on this style and see what happens. No downside for Scotty. Send me one of the food tote bags through our third party.

Call me crazy, but I didn't think my silent partner had any interest in ever getting to know each other.

Nico had another strong performance. Aunt Isabel cheered every time the announcers said his name or number. I glanced up from my work during the game, but I refused to be less productive for him. At the same time, I didn't want Melanie or Isabel thinking anything had changed between us. They were fond of Nico, particularly Aunt Isabel. Who was I to get in the way of that? But I also felt jittery, afraid my mother would misbehave today, and Nico would be right about her and our entire family.

Something must have happened though. Nico outshone the other players, yet the reporter interviewed Tripp and Dylan. Dylan thanked Jesus, while Tripp thanked no one. Granted, the game wasn't a tough one, Butler won easily against Notre Dame, but why wasn't Nico, who was always diplomatic behind the camera, chosen to speak?

We locked up the studio shortly afterwards. Melanie and Isabel wanted to drop off their alteration work for the Flores' dry-cleaning business, and I wanted to get home and make sure my mother hadn't gotten herself in trouble.

. . .

D̲r̲. W̲ilson walked her to the door that afternoon. I was sitting on the porch with a glass of sweet tea. Nancy, who'd gone to the game, sat on her side with her hot tea. The town was always happier when the home team won, but I felt my whole body relax when I saw my mother return home in one piece, without her psycho mask.

"Hi Dr. Wilson," I said when he stepped onto the porch.

"Hi Greer," he said. "Please call me Mark."

I smiled as they both sat down. "Can I get you both some tea?"

"Thanks, Gree," my mother said. "Was it me, Nancy, or was the stadium intense today? I don't think we sat down once."

I disappeared inside to bring out drinks. My mother didn't appear crazed and laser-focused on Nicholas Camillo today. Instead, she seemed like any other middle-aged mother. What she did miss though was Mark's obvious attraction to her. He looked at her *almost* the way my father did, as though she was the most beautiful woman on earth and he was a lucky man.

Mark was also good looking. He had dark hair and eyes, and a body that showed his devotion to working out. Caroline had called him a hottie the first time he brought my mother home from work, and I'd cringed then. But she was right.

We grilled burgers and ate on the porch, watching all the Butler fans pass through the neighborhood either on their way home from the stadium or off to a party. Caroline probably wouldn't be home all night. After Mark left and my mother went into her room to watch TV, I locked up and went to my room to work on our history of capitalism project. The format was a slide presentation limited to ten minutes of material with three minutes for questions. Each slide, whether delivering information, a graphic or picture, or a short video, had to be concise.

Our PowerPoint already had our outline mapped out. I spent about two hours working on cotton mill workers. It was impossible not to touch on the shipping industry and slavery, so by the end of the night, I felt like I'd doubled our number of slides, weakening the presentation. Nico would have to weigh in on this tomorrow.

Just as I was about to power down for the night, a new email from Nico appeared.

> *Hi Greer.*
>
> *Thanks for your text today. It helped.*
>
> *Even though I'm an unofficial member of your study group, I won't be at the library tomorrow or next Sunday. In case you are looking for me.*
>
> *I also won't be free in the evening to bring dinner to Scotty. I hope Aunt Isabel isn't upset. But practices are ramping up and coaches are cracking down. Curfew starts right after mandatory team dinners.*
>
> *The good news is I'll have plenty of time to work on our project, and think about you of course.*
>
> *Nico*

This email proved my suspicions to be true. Nico was distancing himself from me. This was what I'd wanted from the beginning, but he'd insisted on *meeting in person* and *dinner at his place*. He got me to like him, just to shut me out of his life for good. I didn't want to know how my text "helped" him. And I didn't want him thinking about me.

But now I had to pretend none of this bothered me until I'd convinced myself. I also couldn't act like some spurned lover. Other than brushing up against me and invading my space, he never led me on. And I was the one who hugged him on the rock. Maybe he thought I was just like Caroline, and this was his way of turning me down gently.

I had to be impersonal but cordial. And never could I show him how much this hurt. Because, right now, my chest felt crushing pain and my eyes were leaking tears. I was pathetic.

Nico,

Here is the draft of our slide presentation. There is more material than we talked about on Friday, but I trust that you'll edit out what's nonessential.

Isabel will be cranky in the sweatshop this week.

See you later,

Greer

Nico wasn't in class on Monday, which worked out fine for me since we didn't break into our partnerships. Based on Professor Simmons' demeanor, she must have known that Nico wouldn't be there as she'd started class early without him. That was the day I was meeting the cheer staff at the stadium. Coach Phillips replied to my email about my phys ed culminating project with instructions to meet him at the stadium this afternoon, and he'd walk me to the cheerleading office.

I carried my brown Scotty tote with my fabric samples and laptop. I wore what I thought was my most flattering dress with my wedge sandals. I smoothed my hair and added makeup. I also wore Nico's necklace. Before my birthday, this meeting was something I'd have discussed with Nico and he might have helped to calm me down. Whereas Caroline could preen around campus like she owned the place, I knew how much power the offensive coordinator wielded at this university. All the coaches did. Most times, they were more worshiped than the players. So I was nervous.

Coach Phillips was talking with a player who I didn't know when I arrived at his office, his door wide open. He appeared larger than on television. Nico once told Isabel over dinner how grateful he was to this man for believing in him when few other NCAA coaches did. I stood outside until he made eye contact with me and waved me in.

"Time's up, Edwards," he said. "My two-thirty is here, and she's cuter than you."

Edwards didn't appreciate being kicked out. He looked me up and down, a glint in his eye, and walked out angry. I would be too if this were my coach and I was dismissed so abruptly.

"Have a seat," he said when Edwards left.

"My name is Greer." I remained standing. "I'm just here to meet with cheerleading."

"I know who you are. Please sit down. I want to ask you a few things."

I took a seat at the edge of the chair.

"You're Nico Camillo's friend, right?" he asked.

I told him I was.

"And why do you want to meet the cheerleading coaches?"

"There's an idea I'd like to explore for my culminating project for phys ed," I explained.

"That is what your email said." The entire time he spoke, his eyes were boring into mine or staring at my chest. To say I felt uncomfortable was an understatement. This guy gave me the creeps. "Tell me what your idea is."

My face must have betrayed my surprise.

"It's okay." He smiled. "Cheerleading is separate from football, but we work closely together. I'm curious. Phys ed students are always requesting to do curriculums for football players. But I've never heard of anyone wanting to collaborate with cheer. I mean, Coach Evans is pretty tough. She won't work with just anyone."

Even his smile was creepy. But I told him my idea. He wasn't going to introduce me to the head coach, who was notorious for being difficult, unless I came clean. And Nico may be distancing himself from me, but he wouldn't intentionally set me up with this guy to waste his time and mine.

"Is sewing like a hobby for you?" he asked after I'd finished.

"Well, yes and no. I mean, I have an online business." I pulled out a card and gave it to him.

He took the card and placed it on his desk. "Are you related to Caroline Scott?"

Oh shit, I thought. My sister was the reason he was acting so strange.

"She's my sister," I said. "She graduated last year."

He nodded. "And who is Sophia Scott?"

I gasped. Where the hell was this conversation going? "My mother," I answered, annoyed. "I'm not sure what they have to do with this."

"I'm just trying to figure something out. That's all." He shrugged. "Don't look so stressed. Nico's my friend too. I want to understand what he has to do with the Scotts. Tripp Saunders is the one dating your sister, right?"

"Nico has nothing to do with my family." I stood up. I'd find a new idea before I endured this guy's scrutiny. "We're just from the same hometown in Virginia."

He stood from his chair before I had the chance to tell him I was leaving. "Okay," he said. "Let's introduce you to Coach Evans. Don't hold it against me if this doesn't work out for you, okay?"

I exhaled and nodded. We exited his office, which was surrounded by others just like it. Large glass panels and doors with sleek workspaces and desk chairs. From there we walked down a well-lit hallway and through another door. That's when things got even more unnerving. The corridors were empty.

The numbered doors had no windows to see into the offices beyond. Coach Phillips placed his hand on my lower back to guide me through several hallways. Goosebumps surfaced from my neck to my feet. With my free hand I held my pink diamond and planned my escape. My bag was heavy with my computer. I'd hate for it to break, but I wouldn't hesitate to smash the guy with it if he got any more physical.

Finally, we stopped in front of an ordinary door with Coach Evans' name on the plate. Coach Phillips knocked then escorted me into her much smaller and more cluttered office. More evidence that football was king on this campus and every other program was subservient. The offensive coordinator introduced me to the coach as a friend of his who wanted to talk to her about a culminating project. He exited but not before his hand gripped my elbow.

"Bye Greer." His tone was familiar, as though we'd been friends for years. "Keep me posted on the project."

The door closed and my exhale was audible.

Never once had I seen Coach Evans on campus or on the sidelines at games. I would have remembered her. Other than the brassy red hair, she looked similar to my mother. Her lips and cheeks were full of fillers, and her skin was taut and smooth. My guess was she was a patient of Dr. Mark Wilson. Coach Evans' reputation was that she was unpredictable, moody, and a total bitch to anyone who wasn't a cheerleader or Coach Phillips apparently. All I saw was an insecure hot mess.

This I could handle.

Coach Evans was a former cheerleader for the Dallas Cowboys, hence her affinity and attachment to the boots. She also loved sequins. Considering these were the two items I most hated on the uniforms, I had to tread lightly.

When I explained to her that I didn't want to create a curriculum for phys ed, but design uniforms for comfort and performance, she didn't immediately shut me down. "I would donate most of the materials and do all the work myself," I said. "And it wouldn't have to be a game day uniform. I could design practice wear if you weren't interested in making any major changes. I'd want the team's input too, of course."

She'd yet to speak, just nodded. With her frozen facial expressions, I was having trouble gauging her reaction to me. At this point, all I wanted to do was get out of here. After the perv offensive coordinator, I didn't know if I was willing to follow through on this, even if Coach Evans begged me to.

"Your athletes have amazing physiques," I added. "That's why all the guys and the girls can't take their eyes off of them. With uniforms that are more comfortable, and figure-hugging, I think they'd get even more attention."

"Let's go ask the girls." Coach Evans stood up. "They're always bitching about something. 'My skirt's too itchy. I'm sweating in this top.'" She stepped into the hallway and fast walked down the corridor. I had to run in my wedges to catch up with her. We exited through a door into one of the tunnels that led to the field.

Since moving to Butler, I'd walked or run by the stadium countless times. But until this moment, I realized I'd never been inside. Unlike Caroline and my mother, who were hooked on attending games. And now I was about to walk onto the lush green field.

Because my head was lifted, my eyes following the curve of the topmost seats, trying to process the enormity of this place, I missed the football players standing outside the tunnel. They were fully suited in pads and helmets, and appeared taller and twice as broad as usual. Coach Phillips was about twenty feet away, talking with another coach. I noticed Dylan and Tripp by their numbers. Before my eyes could find Nico, I heard Tripp's voice.

"Look who it is," he said. "Caroline's little sister. Grace, right? What are you doing here, and why do you look so hot all the sudden?"

"Come on, Tripp," said Dylan. "Leave her alone, man."

"What's the big deal?" he asked in a voice loud enough for the players around him to hear, but not the coaches. "The Scotts *love* me."

Where is Coach Evans? I asked myself. My eyes searched for her while I touched Nico's necklace. But then they spotted number seventeen standing behind Dylan and Tripp, his eyes locked on mine. It was as though we were the only two people on the field, and we were facing off. He broke our gaze and glanced at Tripp, still laughing, and then to Coach Phillips. As though he was finally realizing why he was seeing me on his turf.

I was just about to walk over to him when he turned his back to me, grabbed a football, and ran onto the field.

18

NICO

I loved my parents, but after this week, I was glad they were never coming to Butler. They were the ones obsessed with the Scotts, not the other way around. Whatever Greer had said to her mother and sister on game day worked. Sophia Scott kept her distance and never posed a threat to me at the stadium. But their family *was* the cause of my standing with the team.

When my parents learned I'd been placed on probation for getting physical with Tripp in the locker room, they insisted upon meeting with Coach Phillips after the Notre Dame game. I had no choice but to join them on a Zoom call. Up to this point, Coach Phillips stated he didn't want to know why I went after Tripp, just that I was never to do that again or I'd be off the team. But with my parents online, I had to explain what happened. I had to admit to him, in front of my mom and dad, that Tripp disrespected Caroline and Sophia Scott, and that's why I did what I did.

It was because of me that the team was forced to have mandatory dinners and curfew before the Louisiana game. Not

Tripp Saunders and his out-of-control parties that university security covered up from the coaching staff and administration.

When the meeting ended, my parents Facetimed me back. My mother started to cry. She didn't understand why I'd risk *everything* for the Scotts.

"Nico," she said. "You know what happened in Charleston. You know that she broke into our room and asked your father *to get rid of me* so that they could be together."

I didn't say anything because she was right. I was risking my future, here and with the NFL, to defend two women not worthy of my support. Caroline Scott was, in my opinion, worse than her mother. Sophia was clearly mentally ill and in desperate need of meds and therapy, but she had threatened my mother's life. Her daughter was as calculating and sinister as a witch. Just the sight of her made my blood run cold.

Greer Scott was my dilemma.

She was just so likeable. Nothing had been the same between us since her birthday, and I missed her. I'd been in her presence almost as much, but none of our time together was the same. Everything changed after she hugged me. I knew now that in order to save myself and my future, I had to distance myself even further. And the irony of this situation was that distance was what she had wanted from the beginning. A partnership via email only. That wasn't good enough for me. I was the one who fueled this attraction between us, and now I had to squelch it for good.

It was almost as though my mother read my mind. Her eagle eyes zeroed in on the Scotty tote bag hanging on its hook in the entryway behind me.

"Where did you get that bag?" she asked.

I glanced at my father who shrugged. He didn't know what she was asking. He was about to find out. Even though he didn't want my mom knowing about my partnership with Greer, I now had to tell her.

"It's from Greer Scott's studio, Mom," I admitted.

She was quiet, and my father shook his head.

"It was a gift," I said.

"Are you going to tell me what's going on, Nico?" Her voice was raised, desperate. "I feel like I'm in the Twilight Zone. We want to hire a security service to buffer us from the Scott family, but it seems to me like you are wrapped up in their lives. Please help me to understand."

I sighed. "Mom, I told you that Greer and I have a class together. It's one of the electives for the entrepreneurship program. It's a small class and hard to get into. And somehow, we ended up as partners. It's not a big deal. She's not like her sister or her mother. At all." My eyes met hers, to assure her of this. "But we do have to work on projects. And since she spends all of her time outside of class at her studio, that's where we've been meeting. I bring food, and one of her employees made me that bag to transport everything. Her name is Isabel, and she was just thanking me, Mom."

My mom looked pained, and my dad hugged her shoulders. "Ana, you've always supported Greer," he said. "I think what Nico is trying to say is that he's trying to make the best of a bad situation."

But my mom's face, which always relaxed when my father hugged her, was still pale. If my parents got to know Greer the way I did, they'd love her more than me. But my mission was now clear. I couldn't allow my mother to suffer like this. I'd have to get through this semester by not getting too close to Greer. Hopefully she was still amenable to an email-only partnership.

.   .   .

I MISSED history of capitalism on Monday because Coaches Phillips and Hampton wanted to make sure I understood I was indeed walking a fine line around here. When Phillips told me I was expected in his office, I told him I needed to email my professor. Dr. Simmons would not appreciate a no-show.

"I already took care of that for you." He placed his hand on my shoulder, then walked me upstairs.

"We like you, Nico," said Coach Hampton. "You've been the missing puzzle piece the offense needed this year. And you've really stepped up with Ryan and Beau. They've learned a lot, and they enjoy working out with you. Not something I'd have expected after the first week."

I nodded.

"But the reason we called you up here is pretty clear," Hampton said. "You've got a shady past. We know you didn't take bribes." He smiled. "But you can't disrupt the hierarchy of this team. Tripp Saunders is a senior. He's the face of our organization. He's the guy who's going to lead this team to a conference championship."

I didn't respond or nod again. Tripp wasn't worthy.

"So whatever your issue with him and his girlfriend *and her mother* is, stay out of it," he said. "That's not a suggestion. It's a demand. Butler will glorify him no matter what he does. This organization and its national network will not support the guy who tries to take him down."

This was where the coaches were wrong. Tripp Saunders would expose himself as the grotesque person that he was. So would Caroline Scott for that matter. Neither one of them needed my help. For Tripp, it could be today or a few years from now. Given his masochistic tendencies, he'd end up hurting someone who would save themselves over this team and university or even the NFL.

Tripp might be drafted, but he'd never live up to his hype. He didn't have the talent or the self-control.

"Understood," I replied.

Little did I know then that I'd be tested later that day. Greer walked through the tunnel with her brown Scotty tote. She looked more beautiful than the picture on my phone before the Carolina game. She was sophisticated with her sleek hair and classy dress and sandals. On her face was an expression of awe as she glanced up into the empty seats. A feeling I knew well since it hit me every time I stepped onto the field.

Then Tripp recognized her and went *there*. He disrespected her and her family out of earshot of the coaches. Not that it mattered. They'd overlook his asshole behavior no matter what. The only saving grace from the entire encounter was that he'd called her by the wrong name. The less he knew about her, the better, as far as I was concerned.

But he made her uncomfortable. She rubbed her diamond necklace between her fingers, and I was unable to help her. I glanced from her to the coaches down the field, and realized I had to distance myself. I had to walk away, fast, before I tackled Tripp and smashed his head into the concrete floor of the tunnel near where he was standing.

Once I left, Dylan and the others followed me onto the field. In one way, I *had* helped Greer. Not that she'd see it that way. I kept an eye on her too as she talked to the cheerleaders and coaches and showed them her fabric binder. At one point, she pulled out a sketchpad and shared that with the group too. There was no way for me to know if the meeting was a success or not for Greer. Coach Evans waved Coach Phillips over at the entrance of the tunnel. Again, I had no idea what they discussed. All I knew was that Coach Evans then walked Greer out of the stadium.

My fantasy of her being in the stands, cheering for me, at

games was over. But I could still explain myself to her so she didn't think of me as a total jerk.

She wasn't in class on Wednesday though. It bothered me so much that I had to email her.

Greer,

We missed you in class today. And then I had to work on condensing our project with the help of Professor Hawk, who pulled her chair next to mine during partner time. Her advice was to cut out the material on slavery and capitalism because another group is already covering the subject in depth. I attached the revised presentation with my contributions included. We are scheduled to deliver this next week. Would you like to arrange time to meet and practice? Given my football restrictions, somewhere on campus at lunchtime would work for me.

I missed on Monday to speak with the coaches. Where were you today?

Nico

Then I made myself baked chicken and steamed broccoli. The mandatory team dinners were at the cafeteria, and I didn't want to fill my body up with crap before one of the biggest away games of the season. Louisiana was a tough team, but we definitely had a shot at beating them. After I ate, checked in with the coaches so they'd know I was home, and showered, I opened my email. Greer replied.

Nico,

I will clean up my slides and send back to you. As usual, yours are perfect without any misuse of the word "to." I'm sure your delivery will also be flawless. Pretend you are speaking with the beautiful sideline reporter next week if you get nervous.

Blake and Liam are rehearsing theirs at study group this Sunday, with a stopwatch. They agreed to listen to mine too. Meeting on campus at lunchtime won't be necessary.

I was in Atlanta today for Scotty. Professor Hawk knew all about it and even excused me from class since I was getting "real-world experience."

Greer

Her reply messed with my head. Greer and I were partners. And even though we'd yet to talk about the reasons why, we both seemed to be on the same page now about distancing from each other. Yet practicing her presentation with Blake and Liam over me insulted me as a student and as a man. Greer was *my* partner, not theirs. She clearly didn't want to meet with me. Because of my position with the team and my family, I should have wanted the same thing. But I didn't.

Instead, I missed everything about her.

And then she baited me about going to Atlanta for Scotty Designs. I had no idea what "real-world experience" she was talking about. My only thought was that she was being taken advantage of. She was always praising her silent partner, but something didn't add up. Literally. That small studio made a fortune, yet Greer seemed to be receiving none of it. The irony of our upcoming report was lost on her though. As a small-business owner, Greer Scott was a capitalist. Yet, she lived the life of a sweatshop worker. The bottom line was that *I* should have been by her side in Atlanta.

I stood up and walked around my place to process all of this. It was such a cool unit, one of only four refurbished apartments in an old red brick building. I couldn't believe my luck when I found the place since it was within walking distance of all the trendy bars and restaurants downtown offered.

Ever since the first day of school when I chased Greer in her grey dress and Doc Martens to her car, I'd pictured her here with me. This was even before I got to know her too. The place seemed as cool and hip as she was. I knew she'd love the barn doors that sealed off the living room when watching a movie. And the exposed brick in the kitchen. Now, of course, I pictured her in my bed too.

After I calmed down, I shut off my laptop and packed it in my school bag. Tomorrow was the team's last day on campus. We were leaving by bus right after practice on Friday morning, so I'd miss history of capitalism again. Since Saturday's game was late and nationally televised, we weren't planning to be back to Butler until Sunday night. I had to get Greer out of my system. Ignoring her email seemed like the best way to start.

AFTER PRACTICE ON THURSDAY, we were all told the mandatory team dinner in the cafeteria was canceled. Instead, we had to go to the Delta Gamma sorority house for tuxedo fittings for the homecoming formal. After the week I'd had, this was the last place I wanted to go. Dylan, of course, was excited for it. He hadn't seen Lila all week due to the curfew. A lot of the players were also happy for the change of scenery. Many guys asked Delta Gammas, but a lot of players dated girls outside the sorority. Either way, they were all looking forward to the formal.

I think I was the only guy who wasn't. There was only one girl I wanted on my arm, and no matter how much I buried my desire for her, my brain couldn't picture myself with anyone else. But I still had a few weeks before the event. At least Greer wouldn't be here tonight. Last week, we were on friendlier terms, and I knew her work with the sorority was basically done.

Given the number of players on the team, I was surprised how quickly the line moved. Since the offense was kept late in the film room tonight, we were the last in line. Dylan disappeared to find Lila, and I was left with Tripp, Beau, Ryan, and a few others.

"Who are you taking to the formal, Camillo?" asked Tripp.

"Wouldn't you like to know?" I replied. The coaches weren't around, and being obnoxious wasn't the same as being threatening.

"I might be able to talk Caroline's mom into going with you," he said. "Her tits are amazing."

I glared at him. *This is the best you can do?* I said to myself.

"Ryan and I asked these two Delta Gammas outside the stadium last week," said Beau. "They're new pledges and both really cute. But we don't remember who's going with who." He started laughing.

"It's so embarrassing," added Ryan.

"Not really," said Tripp. "Go as a foursome, and then maybe you'll both get lucky at the end of the night. I've had two at the same time. One of the best experiences of my life."

There was such a thing as locker-room talk, but Tripp always crossed the line. He was a total pig. I was grateful when Dylan returned, and we were the last to walk into the dimly lit cloakroom. All three measurers looked familiar to me. I thought I was having déjà vu until I glanced at the placard on the table. Flores Tuxedo Rentals. This was Aunt Isabel's brother and extended family.

Each of us had to try on jackets and then get measured for shirts and pants. The Floreses were efficient, which didn't surprise me in the least. I stood in the older man's line because I knew this was Isabel's brother who I'd heard so much about. He had a tape measure like Greer's hanging from his neck. Did he have his sister's wit? That was what I wanted to know.

Just as it was my turn, Mr. Flores glanced outside the room and shouted, "Greer!"

There was only one Greer I knew on campus. And then she walked into the shadowy room, in her Doc Martens, carrying a handful of garment bags, and smiling so wide my heart stopped.

"Mr. Flores!" She hugged him, her eyes closed to me. "It's so good to see you!"

"What are you doing here?" he asked. "I thought Isabel was working with you tonight."

"I took her home early," she said. "A few of the girls wanted their dresses, so I'm just dropping them off."

"I've been meaning to thank you for taking my sister off my hands," he said. Greer started to giggle. He was teasing her and Isabel. And I loved it. "Then she comes home and beats our ears about your pink dresses, and all your little bags with the cute little buttons, and the amazing food your friend makes for you guys. My wife and I rejoice when we drop her back off the next day!"

I laughed then too, and Greer turned my way, noticing me. Her smile disappeared, and she turned back to Mr. Flores. "I didn't realize you'd be here tonight," she said. "I'll let you get back to work."

"Greer, would you do me a huge favor?" he asked.

"Sure."

"Can you finish measuring these two gentlemen?" He pointed to me and the guy behind me. Tripp Saunders. "I need to call the warehouse before closing."

She glanced at me and Tripp. The two people she least wanted to see, if I read her nonverbal body language. Her shoulders sagged and she exhaled. "Of course," she said to him. Mr. Flores was someone she respected, someone she couldn't refuse.

She hung her dresses on an available rack and took the tape measure and pen he handed her.

"Mark down the jacket size, and then measure the neck, arm, waist, and outside seam. That's it. Thank you so much. I'll be back as soon as I can."

Greer wore a mini skirt and tank top with her boots. I was happy to see she still wore the pink diamond necklace. *Did she think of me when she put it on each morning?* This was one of her fringe looks, so my hope was Tripp would overlook her entirely or get into a different line.

I handed her my form. She asked me what size my jacket was, and I reported the number in a clear voice. I was a size bigger than douchebag Tripp, and I hope he heard it. Then Greer's hands touched me, and I lost my ability to think clearly or speak. She gently wrapped the tape measure around my neck, her fingers pressed softly into my sternum. Her purple eyes met mine before looking down. She released her hold a moment later. She wrote down the measurement on my form, my face above her honeysuckle-scented hair. I took a deep breath. Then she asked me to turn around.

This was almost worse. Her fingers dragged the yellow strip from the middle of my neck, along my shoulder and down my arm until she held my wrist. My blood flow surged, and I felt my entire body tense to counteract my response to her. She attempted to take my waist measurement with my back to her, but I turned around, needing to see her face again. Her cheeks were flushed. Whether with embarrassment or desire matching my own, I couldn't tell. Probably a mixture of both.

But I craved her touch, and I wanted to see her reaction. Her arms circled my waist and she brought the measuring tape around to my abdomen. The back of her hand touched the muscles through my thin T-shirt, and I swear her face darkened even more. She released it, jotted down the number, then traced the measuring tape down the side of my leg, touching my exposed calf muscles, before reaching my shoes.

She got to her feet and wrote everything down, handing me back my form. I just stood there. No experience had ever turned me on quite like the last two minutes, and I didn't want it to end. I wanted her fingers and hands to measure every single inch of me, including my erection filling my boxers which I could not stop.

"You're good to go," she whispered.

I still couldn't speak. So I nodded and stepped aside. Tripp was behind me. I walked over to one of the racks to return my tuxedo jacket. Dylan joined me. He was just finishing up, asking me if I wanted to stay for dinner with him and Lila. I knew I wouldn't be staying, so I shook my head, still not sure words would form. Then I turned to Greer as she was measuring Tripp's pant leg. She was squatting, touching his tennis shoe, when he spoke up, clearly wanting everyone in the room to hear him.

"From this view," he said, "I can tell you're a Scott."

Dylan must have watched me charge because both his arms were on me pulling me back. Ryan and Beau, whose reaction times were for shit and caused most of their issues, didn't flinch and were both in front of me, pushing me deeper into the cloakroom. Greer's face, which had just been bright with healthy desire for me, blanched. But she didn't waiver. She wrote down his measurements, handed him his form, collected her dresses, and then left the room. She never glanced back at me.

Tripp was laughing at his own joke. No one in the room joined in, but Tripp didn't notice or care. Then Caroline Scott ran into the cloakroom and hugged Tripp, her legs soon wrapped around his waist.

"I'm good," I told the guys in a low voice. "I promise I'm cool."

Dylan still walked me out of the room, blocking me from Tripp. It was for the best, too, because I didn't trust myself at that moment. I'd wanted to kill him.

Then Dylan walked me up Midvale to my car in the lot.

"Does Greer know you like her?" he asked.

I shook my head. "I told you it's complicated."

"I'm a good listener," he said, "when you're ready."

"Thanks for back there." I tipped my head in the direction of the sorority house. "That would have cost me everything."

"I know," he said. "And all of us really. Tripp's nothing without me and you. He knows that too even if he's too stupid to admit it. But there's only one thing that's going to stop this thing between you guys."

"What's that?"

"Make Greer yours, man," he said. "You claim her as your girl, he'll back off. He won't even glance in Lila's direction because he knows she's mine. You see what I'm saying, man?"

We were passing Greer's van in the parking lot. I hated leaving her in the house with Tripp still inside. But I knew that I needed distance now more than ever. On one level, I knew Dylan was right. But he also didn't know what he was asking me to do. Choosing Greer meant losing my parents.

"I hear you man," I said. "Can you do me a favor and walk Greer to her car?"

He nodded then waited for me to drive away.

19

GREER

y mother was crying when I returned home from the sorority house on Thursday night. Nancy was comforting her on the couch and explained that my mother had yet to tell her why she was upset. Upon seeing me though, my mother looked relieved I was here. I thanked Nancy and told her I would take over and she could go home.

"What is it, Mom?" I asked when we were alone.

"Mark fired me," she cried. "He said he won't perform any more work on me until I see a psychiatrist."

I exhaled slowly, thinking about my words. "Why does he think you should see a psychiatrist?"

"He thinks I'm one of those patients who's never happy," she explained, "constantly believing that the next procedure will *fix* me. Or something like that."

"And why do you think he's wrong?"

"Greer, why are you never on my side?" She started to cry again. "Caroline would be angry at Mark with me! She wouldn't ask me such a question."

Don't react to her. A little voice inside my head said. *Stay calm and don't ruin this opportunity.*

"I *am* on your side, Mom." I touched her face. "You are already so beautiful. Maybe Mark doesn't see any way to make you prettier?"

"Obviously, there's something imperfect about me, Greer!" she said. "Nicky Camillo chose Ana Romano. His son has been here for weeks, and Nicky is never coming *here* to see me. Instead, his lawyer had the sheriff deliver a restraining order. I'm not allowed at the stadium anymore!"

My body felt a tremendous blow at her words, but I had to stay strong for her in this moment. I still hadn't recovered from Nico's rejection earlier. "May I see the order?"

She pulled out an envelope and handed it to me. Inside was a restraining order that was signed by a judge and filed at the courthouse. It referenced my mother's history of "breaking into" a hotel room and threatening Ana Camillo and compromising a Butler police barrier to stalk her son Nico Camillo. Nico never spelled it out in black and white, but now I knew what went down in Charleston.

"Did Mark see this?" I asked.

"He was here when it was delivered," she said. "And he was there when a security guard at the stadium a few weeks ago warned me it might be coming. But I was so good last week, Greer. I stayed beside Mark the entire time."

"Mom?" My voice was soft. "Can you tell me why you love Nicholas Camillo?"

Her eyes glazed over. "Nicky is just so much fun, Greer. All the girls were after him when we were kids. And he picked me. I loved how strong he was, how beautiful his eyes were when they looked at me. And then Ana came to town and took him away from me."

"What about Dad?" I asked. "Did you love him?"

"We were all friends, Greer, for years before Ana came to town. Your dad was so funny. I mean, everyone loved him." She sighed. "But when Ana took Nicky away, I thought I was going to die. Your dad did save me. And I do love him for that."

I supposed that she was telling me the truth. It was an ugly truth, but I was grateful for her honesty.

"Do you want to know what I think, Mom?"

"I don't know. Caroline makes me feel better. You usually make me feel sad."

"I love you and I want what's best for you. So, keep that in mind when I say this."

My mom covered her face with her hands. She was about to cry again. I pulled her hands away, and made her look at me.

"I think you should talk to a psychiatrist," I said. "Not just about plastic surgery. But about this letter from the Camillos. You have nothing to lose from this. And if you really think you want work done after you talk to someone, maybe Mark will be open to helping you again. You are his favorite patient."

That didn't make her smile, but she said, "You sound just like your father when you try to reason with me. But I don't want to have to go on all those pills again."

And that explains the nosedive after Dad died. It amazed me how little I understood at age fourteen compared to now. Of course, my father made sure her mental illness was under control while he was alive.

"According to my friend Emma, meds are getting better every day."

She wiped the mascara from her eyes. "I'm glad you're making friends again."

"About that, Mom," I said cautiously. "I have a class with Nico Camillo. And he's nothing special. Maybe he can play football and make the people like our professor laugh. But the Scotts are beneath him." I pointed to the restraining order. "He's learned it from his family. Whatever affection you have for Nicholas and Nico, I'm begging you to let it go. It's not too late for you to move on." I held her hand. "Mark looks at you the way Dad used to."

Her smile was tight, but at least it was a smile. We watched an episode of *House Hunters*, which took her mind away from all the drama in her life. Then, I waited for her to get into bed, and shut off all the lights. Caroline would likely be out all night with Tripp Saunders, who was a total pig. Between him, Nico, and Coach Phillips, I wasn't sure I'd ever root for the home football team again.

CAMPUS WAS SURPRISINGLY SUBDUED before the Louisiana game on Friday. There was still the sea of red-and-white clothing throughout the campus, but students and faculty like Professor Simmons were on edge. Last year, Louisiana beat Butler in the conference championship. It was a close game, and people were still devastated by the loss. No one wanted a repeat performance, and I had to hear about how this year, with Nico Camillo, the offense had a chance to win.

Blocking out all the chatter about him was impossible. Professor Simmons sat in Nico's seat on Friday. Our slide presentation was finished, but she didn't let me leave early. Instead, she asked me questions about my visit to manufacturers near Atlanta earlier this week.

"I met with two companies, and I liked one of them better," I said. "It's been hard to let go of my original products. Out of everything, I'm attached to my bags the most." I pointed to my backpack. "My partner feels that in order for Scotty to continue, we have to keep designing new products and we need to outsource some items. The accessories are the most time-consuming."

"Growth is essential to capitalism," she acknowledged. "What about hiring more?"

"This town isn't flush with seamstresses." I laughed. "I think I've exhausted the Flores' family resources."

"With sound advice, which I think you have, you will find a way," she said. "There's a certain chutzpah about you. I'm really looking forward to that dress Nico promised me."

"Right," I said. I'd forgotten about the dress. And at this moment, I wished that Nico and I were on good terms. I could already hear him laughing at the email replaying this conversation with Professor Hawk. Whatever I designed for Dr. Simmons, I'd be telling her *exactly* which pair of her designer shoes she had to wear with it. Right now, she had on the sweetest pair of Gucci loafers, black with gold accents, with red-and-white capri pants. She'd have been better off matching her cotton pants with white sneakers than the sophisticated shoes she chose, even though they were gorgeous.

When I arrived home that afternoon to check in on my mom, her spirits were better. We called her doctor and found the name of a psychiatrist who could see her on Monday. We had some money saved, but I'd be willing to incur credit card debt if it helped her.

Caroline had already left for Louisiana. In the Mini. What could I say? Even Lila was staying behind this weekend. The ride was nearly ten hours without stopping. My mother knew no more details. I didn't want to upset my mother, after my breakthrough with her the night before, but I had to ask the question.

"How is she paying for all of this, Mom?"

"She must have money saved from babysitting during college," she replied. "She even bought a dress for the formal because you can't make her one."

Before I left for the studio, I peeked in my sister's room. Sure enough, there was a dress hanging on her door sealed in a Nordstrom garment bag with a price tag of close to six hundred dollars. Twice what we were charging each of the Delta Gammas. Even if Tripp came from wealth like Nico, he wasn't a giver. He wasn't considerate of anyone other than himself. Tripp didn't buy this for her.

So how the hell did she afford this?

We were swamped in the studio the day of the Louisiana game. Since most of the Delta Gammas were in town, Lila suggested that they come to me to pick up their dresses rather than me having to wheel the wardrobe to the sorority house. Girls filtered in and out of the studio all day. They'd try on their dresses, and we'd make adjustments right there. Melanie and Beatrice, who were on vacation the week Isabel and I made them, fussed over each one.

What we hadn't anticipated was the volume of on-the-spot sales apart from the formal wear. The game day dresses were a huge hit, and some of the girls even purchased bags and cases for phones or laptops. One girl, who was from Birmingham, purchased Alabama game day dresses for her younger sisters.

"I'm the black sheep of the family for coming here," she said. "But they will *love* these."

The day flew by. Sam missed Nico, but he was excited for the game later. My mom called to ask if I'd be home soon. I told her I wouldn't. We were working through the game again. Then she asked if she could come to the studio, with Mark, and just hang out.

"Does he know about your appointment on Monday?" I asked her.

"Yes," she said. "He's glad, Greer."

The Floreses and the Scotts sans Caroline watched the

Louisiana game together. My worlds were colliding. But my mother supplied tailgate food. Isabel and Sam were getting *very* into the game. For someone who didn't grow up with American football, Isabel understood the sport better than I did. She also understood Nico's role, which blew my mind since the tight end was not often seen on camera.

At one point, Nico caught a short pass for a first down and then dodged a tackle and ran twenty yards into the end zone for a score. Everyone jumped up and cheered. Nico chest bumped Dylan and then pointed into the camera. It was unlike him to do that, but Sam and Beatrice started to go crazy.

"Mom! He did that for us!" they screamed. "He told us he was going to point to us if he scored a touchdown!"

My mom wasn't paying attention because the camera then went into the stands, and there were Ana and Nicholas Camillo, in Butler colors, cheering for their son. Her face blanched, but I walked over to her, squeezed her shoulder, and whispered that it was going to be okay. She reached up and squeezed my hand back, and said, "Thank you, Gree."

Mark, who went to Butler for undergrad, didn't realize the significance of that moment. Maybe he would one day. He seemed like a nice man. He and Isabel were too busy analyzing Nico's performance anyway.

The entire game was close, but in the end, Butler won with a field goal. The reporter did get Nico on camera this time after the game. He was standing with Tripp. Like always, Tripp made the victory about himself. There really was nothing redeeming about him. He said that *he* had a lot to prove tonight and *he* got the job done.

When she held the microphone to Nico, he bent down again to hear her question. His hair was soaking wet with sweat, his face flush under the stadium lights, and his eyes were bright. This reporter was lucky, but not as lucky as me. When I got to measure him, I had to run my fingers down his powerful arm and leg, and touch his chest and abdomen. It lasted only seconds, was a bit awkward, but gave my body a rush. Tripp, of course, turned that moment into something dirty.

"Your team is now 4 and 0. What does that mean personally for you?"

Nico hesitated to answer. He wasn't the type to ever talk about himself, and it was almost as though the reporter was baiting him to move out of his comfort zone.

"Well, there's a hundred guys here who are very much looking forward to going home," he said, "and celebrating this victory with our fans. So I'm personally very proud to be a part of this team that got it done for Butler tonight." He dropped his smile and added, "And I'm excited to continue to build upon this momentum with Tripp and the rest of my teammates."

Diplomatic Nico. Always. The Nico Camillo I'd gotten to know over the last few weeks would hate Tripp Saunders. Nico was a jerk to Blake and Liam, and they'd done nothing to hurt me personally. He seemed so protective of me because we were partners, except when it really mattered. Twice Tripp insulted me and my family in Nico's presence and he did nothing to stop him. Given my mom and sister's behavior, I wouldn't expect him to defend their honor. But to ignore what he said, or walk away, made me question his judgement. Nico was perceptive. And smart.

Why couldn't he see the monster in Tripp Saunders that I saw?

STUDY GROUP WAS a little dull without Nico. Blake and Liam's presentation was weak in detail, but they delivered it well and came in right at ten minutes. Theirs dealt with the railroads, so when it was time for questions, I did something obnoxious and asked them whether the steamship line helped or hindered railroad construction during the Industrial Revolution. It was intentionally difficult for them to answer adequately. I held a straight face as long as possible, and then cracked up.

"You got us, man," said Blake. "I thought we were so screwed."

"Actually," Liam started. "Let's find the answer to that question. Greer, you should ask it next week. And when we answer it *intelligently*, Dr. Simmons might be impressed. We need an A on this one."

"I don't even know if railroads and steamships influenced each other!" I laughed. "But let's find something that will work and stage it. You can do it for me too."

"Nico won't put up with that," said Blake. "That dude is smooth. He doesn't need our help."

"Well, I might," I argued.

"But you guys have that thing going on," Liam said. "He'll kick the shit out of us if we ask you a question."

"That's ridiculous." I shook my head.

"I think they're right, Greer," said Emma. "He is totally into you."

My cheeks turned red. "I think he feels sorry for me," I told them. "Pitying someone is not the same as liking someone."

"Why would he pity you?" Liam asked.

I shrugged. "It's just a feeling I have. That's all. Are you going to time me?"

My presentation was heavy in detail. My delivery was stilted because I read it, and too long. I'd have to consolidate or omit some of the information. While the rest of them finished up whatever they had to, I weeded out details. And because I was a fair partner, I emailed Nico.

Hi Nico.

My portion of the presentation ran over. I'm eliminating the information about the cotton mills in South Carolina and will only focus on Massachusetts to illustrate the main points. Hopefully that will be sufficient. The final is attached.

I had the pleasure of watching the game with the Floreses while making Professor Simmons a new dress. Sam and Beatrice went crazy when you delivered your secret sign.

Greer

P.S. You are paying for half of Professor Simmons' dress.

As usual, his reply was immediate.

Greer,

I'll skip my class after Hawk's. Let's go over it then.

Thank you for telling me about the twins. That made my day.

Nico

P.S. Only if it's delightful.

I didn't reply because meeting with him was impossible. Even if I wanted to, my mom had her first psych appointment tomorrow. As we were packing up, the three of them were headed to the cafeteria and asked me to join them. I'd promised my mother I'd be home this afternoon since Caroline was still away. So I told them that I wouldn't be able to join them for lunch.

"That's cool," said Blake. "My roommates and I are having a party tonight. Pretty low key. We have a keg we need to kick. You should come, Greer."

"Yes," cheered Emma. "You should come! It's in your neighborhood. How about I pick you up, and the two of us can walk over together?"

This was the opportunity that Melanie warned me not to

miss out on. I wasn't planning on going to the studio today, and I'd finished all my homework. Caroline should also be home by this afternoon and could stay with my mother.

"That sounds really fun." I gave Emma my address, and she said she'd be there around six.

When Emma arrived, my mother and I were sitting on the front porch chatting with Nancy. Caroline had already returned home. She was taking a power nap because Tripp was having a huge party tonight when the bus got back to campus. Earlier today, when my mom announced that I was also going to a party tonight, my sister laughed, looked me up and down, and told me I was underdressed.

"If you want to get noticed by a superstar, Greer, you need to step up your game," she said before disappearing upstairs.

Fortunately for me, I had no interest in attracting the attention of guys like Tripp Saunders. And knowing Emma, Blake, and Liam the way I did, they would laugh at me if I showed up in heels and a tube top.

I liked Emma because she was nice and laid-back. Some kids on campus ignored you when you told them you were local and still lived at home. But Emma wasn't like that. This was her first time meeting my family though.

Mark was taking my mother out to dinner. The restaurant, she said, was too casual for her new palazzo pants. So she had on heels, tight white jeans, and a navy cowl neck top. On anyone else, this would be a conservative outfit. On my mother, she looked like a Victoria's Secret model.

Emma didn't gawk like Tripp Saunders had. Instead, she sat down and chatted with my mom and Nancy about how she was from Maryland and was studying psychology. Like me, she had on jeans and tennis shoes. Even her brown hair was pulled into a ponytail and covered with an Orioles baseball hat. She was the picture of low maintenance but comfortable in her own skin.

In her bathrobe, my sister stepped onto the porch to ask my mother where her curling iron was. I introduced her to Emma.

"Wait," she said, "what party are you going to again?"

"It's my boyfriend Blake's house," Emma said. "They only live a few blocks from here. They're juniors. They're all in a band together."

"That sounds…really *boring* actually. Have fun!" And then she rushed back inside, letting the porch door slap the frame.

I rolled my eyes. "Ignore her," I told Emma.

But Emma was laughing, and Nancy joined her. "At least she's honest!" said Emma.

When Emma and I left to walk to the party, Emma said, "Your mom is gorgeous, Greer. Your sister looks just like her. And you're so different."

After I explained to her that my father had dark hair, I shared with her a little bit of my mother's fragile mental state. I figured she was safe to confide in because her interest was psychology.

"Wow. You really have a lot going on, Greer. I'm glad your mom is getting help. Keep me posted."

"I will."

"What's up with your sister then," she asked.

"She's just a bitch," I said. "It's been getting worse, too. Once the formal is over, she's promised to get a job. That's half her problem."

"We all have crazy families," she said. "The reason psychology appeals to me so much is because my siblings and I have always struggled with my parents' divorce. We never had therapy, and we should have. So don't think you're the only one, Greer."

"There are some people where everything in life seems easy." I thought of Nico. "You know what I mean?"

"I do," she said. "But most of them have issues too."

When we arrived, the scene was pretty mellow. It was outside since the evening was so mild. The band was set up by the detached garage playing covers from artists like The Killers, Zach Bryan and Taylor Swift, and some kids were tossing corn hole. Like most off-campus parties, the crowd continued to grow and everyone moved inside eventually to keep the noise down.

Not that this surprised me because these were friends of Blake's, but everyone here was really down to earth. Even though I'd gotten to know many of the Delta Gammas and liked them, they were still a lot like my sister, always focused on their appearances and achieving a certain social status on campus. Their world also seemed to revolve around Butler football. This group was different.

I'd felt *so* comfortable, I'd almost tried beer from the keg. But my mother asked me to be careful about drinking tonight because alcohol, she said, made her crazy. Caroline was also super-obnoxious when she drank. And then I was terrified of being cited for being underage by the local police, after my mother's recent restraining order. So I avoided it altogether and stuck with water.

I'd spent most of the night talking with Liam and some of his friends. We stood in the basement. There was a TV and bar area on one side and a pool table on the other. The keg was sitting in ice by the sliding back door. More and more people arrived, and Emma and Blake kept being pulled in all directions by their different groups of friends. For two people who'd just met each other, they seemed to be the host and hostess of the party, and reminded me of Lila and Dylan. I could see them staying together long term.

One of Liam's friends stopped to say that we were in the same social media class. That class was huge, and I didn't know him. He was skinny with long dark hair. I thought maybe he was one of the guys from the band. He knew me because he really liked what I was doing with Scotty Designs' Instagram account.

"It's really cool you have your own business," he said. "And it seems like you're targeting new markets effectively. I'm not sure why the professor doesn't highlight your work more."

I think I blushed, because the feedback from the professor and TAs was pretty weak. And I was surprised how much fun posting cool pictures of new Scotty products was. "What other classes are you taking?" I asked.

We were standing in a far corner of the basement. The pool table was in front of us with a light hanging above it. The noise level in the room increased, and I had to lean in to hear what the guy was saying. Suddenly there was a shadow over us. I glanced up thinking one of the pool players needed us to move in order to make a shot.

But it was Nico. Standing next to him was Emma. She had a silly, drunk grin on her face. She grabbed me around the shoulder and whispered in my ear, in a voice loud enough for the entire room to hear, "Now do you believe me? He definitely has a thing for you!"

2 0

—

NICO

Greer's email reached me somewhere in Alabama on Sunday and finally allowed me to relax. On Friday morning, when we were loading the bus at the stadium, getting out of town and away from her had seemed like it was exactly what I needed to clear my head. But by Friday afternoon, thoughts of her were constant. Was she at the studio? Did she blame me for Tripp's insults? What did she think about her sister coming to Louisiana and staying in the team hotel again? All I wanted was to call her, but I was too chicken to follow through.

Just like the Carolina game, my parents were at the hotel when the bus pulled in. Apparently, Coach Phillips reached out to them and said it would be good for me to have support in the stands, given how much the coaches, Butler Nation, and the network were expecting of me.

I greeted them as though nothing had changed between us, even though it had. I was not cool and collected, but my parents' presence did not ground me. If anything, it made me feel even more conflicted about Greer. I was like a snapped live wire thrashing around in a storm.

Caroline Scott wasn't helping matters. She spent the afternoon hanging out at the bar again, pretending she and my mom and dad went way back. It was bizarre behavior. As far as I'd witnessed, Caroline was manipulative and selfish, but she wasn't deranged like my parents always described Sophia. Greer would never pretend to be close to my parents. To her, they were the cause of her family's suffering. My only thought was that Caroline was doing it to get ahead in some way. She had no loyalty to her family, and she didn't care about anyone other than herself. Even Tripp. The coaches may have covered up his drunken ass before the Carolina game but they didn't forget. Greer's sister kept trying to get him to sip her margarita in the hotel lobby and pouted when he pushed her away. She had no clue how dangerous the game she was playing was.

After the team dinner, we returned to the lobby. Caroline was buzzed, but the two Delta Gammas who drove down with her were wasted. They were underage too. Before the head coach noticed, Coach Phillips stepped in and got the girls back to their rooms safely. Caroline stayed behind in the lobby. Fortunately, my parents missed all of this since they went straight to their room after dinner. Dylan, Malik and I did the same.

Because party-girl Caroline was getting so much attention from the team, word was getting around about me and Greer. Beau and Ryan had told players what happened with Tripp the other night, how I had to be restrained in the Delta Gamma cloakroom when he disrespected Caroline's sister. And it wasn't long before Tripp figured out that Greer was my Achilles' heel and that her name wasn't Grace.

Somehow, I managed to ignore him on Saturday. His insults were more of the same, completely unoriginal. *I've never had three women at one time. Greer may be fun on days I'm not into blondes. Caroline says her sister is a virgin; that could be interesting.* My control amazed even me. Dylan did deserve some credit for keeping me in check because he didn't let me out of his sight.

That night on the field, all my anger and frustration with Tripp was transferred onto Louisiana. The game was tough and gritty, but football kept me focused that night. Thoughts of Greer still slipped in like when the cheerleaders would perform in their boots, when I pointed at Sam and Beatrice in the end zone, and when the sideline reporter interviewed me. Greer was right; the reporter was beautiful. She was also about a decade older than me and married to an NFL player. Standing on the sidelines with her, I wondered if Greer was jealous of her. The thought gave me hope.

Greer didn't answer me about getting together on Monday. So I closed my eyes hoping to catch up on sleep. Most Butler fans, my parents included, left town first thing in the morning. But we had a late breakfast followed by a light workout and training session. The coaches and trainers wanted us to loosen up before taking the ten-hour bus ride back to campus.

As we crossed into Georgia, Coach Hampton walked to the middle of the bus and announced that he was lifting curfew this week. But if he found out that any of us were partying excessively on campus due to the Louisiana win, the entire team would be on lockdown for the season. He looked directly at me when he spoke, most likely because I'd made a comment to the reporter last night about celebrating the win, but the rest of the team looked at Tripp.

Once the coach returned to his seat, Dylan turned to Tripp. "You better tell your girl to cancel the rager she's got planned," he said. "I will let you get sacked next week by Tennessee – whose defense sucks – if I'm put on curfew again."

"Security doesn't give a shit," Tripp said. "They're not going to say a word."

"Don't take the chance, man." Dylan turned his body and leaned across the aisle, to talk in a low voice. "Phillips was hanging out with those Delta Gamma girls last night, including Caroline. He knows what's going on. And he's told Hampton. You and your crew are being tested, Saunders. Don't be a moron. Find some other party to go to. You're the QB. Anyone will let you in."

Dylan's speech worked. Within thirty minutes, Tripp got the message out that his party was canceled. Then, as we pulled into the stadium where a huge crowd of fans was waiting for us, Tripp said Caroline just texted him about another party near campus.

"How about just going home, Saunders?" Dylan, frustrated, gathered his bag and walked to the front of the bus. Lila was somewhere in the crowd.

"That dude is way too serious." Tripp smiled and shrugged. "This party could be fun. Greer Scott is there with her geeky band friends. Wait until they see us show up with a carful of alcohol."

On the outside, I stayed calm but adrenaline spiked inside me. As far as I knew, Greer never went to parties. She was almost too adult for them, having been forced to run a business for long hours every day and provide for her mother and sister. But she was also nineteen. What if she was drunk or roofied and being taken advantage by someone? She was gorgeous and didn't know it. And then add Tripp Saunders and Caroline to the mix, and anything terrible could happen to her.

Greer had to be with Blake and Emma. Blake was in a band and lived somewhere off campus. I'd have to find out where she was before Tripp and Caroline arrived. That bothered me too.

Why would Caroline even go to a party that was so beneath her? Blake and Emma were the type of people Caroline would sneer at on campus. She and Tripp were also old enough to just go to a bar if they were so desperate to party. Nothing made sense, which is why getting Greer out of there was so urgent.

I grabbed my stuff and went right to my car, never stopping to talk to anyone. Before I drove away, I checked my email and managed to find Blake's and Liam's phone numbers on history of capitalism threads. I texted both of them and asked where they were, then just started driving. Blake was the first to reply with his address and an invitation.

come over!

The address was near Greer's house. Townhomes and city streets. I had to park a few blocks away and then run back to the house. This is what Greer had to do every night in her van, and that pissed me off too. My building had a garage, and if anyone deserved to live comfortably without having to park a mile away with a van full of merchandise in the dark, it was Greer.

The house was relatively quiet from the outside. If Tripp showed up with alcohol and fifty guys, the cops would be here in minutes. I let myself in, and Blake and Emma, both wasted and happy, screamed. Emma hugged me. "Greer's here too! She's downstairs." Before she pulled me away, I warned Blake that the Butler football team was headed this way with booze.

"Really?" he asked.

"Their own rager got canceled, and someone told them about this one. But you're going to have the cops here if you don't do something."

"Let me go talk to my neighbor." He put his beer down and heading to the door. "He's a cop. Maybe he can help."

Emma dragged me through the house and down the narrow basement stairwell. People were chill. Not everyone knew who I was, but some shouted either "Nico!" or "Seventeen!" If trouble wasn't on its way, this would be a party I might enjoy. Greer wasn't in the TV room with the bar. "There she is," Emma said, and pulled me to the pool table. Greer's face was blushing, and she was leaning into some skinny dude with long dark hair. He was smiling and telling her something. She had on jeans, a tank top, and tennis shoes, and a flannel shirt was tied around her waist. Her fingers were touching the pink diamond necklace. The only sign that she could be drinking was her red cheeks, but she could also be reacting to what this guy was saying to her.

I had to duck my head around the exposed pipes in the basement ceiling, but we made our way to Greer, and then Emma wrapped her arms around her and called out: "Now do you believe me? He definitely has a thing for you!"

Greer's face turned white. I couldn't read her eyes because my own body was blocking the light from reaching them. Then Emma released her and said, "I don't think he pities you." She turned to me, "I'm going to get a drink. What would you like, Nico?"

"Nothing for me, thanks," I said, never taking my eyes off Greer. It seemed like forever since we'd been together, and my mind and body felt instant calm in her presence.

"Let's see," the guy next to me was still talking. "I think that's five." He counted off the fingers of his left hand. "Social media, real estate law, investment banking, and then I have intro to psychology and U.S. history." Then he leaned into my girl and said, "Do you want to get together sometime and study social media?"

I held my breath. This guy deserved credit. He had balls. Here he was standing next to me, the guy who Emma just announced *definitely had a thing* for the woman before us, and still delivered his pickup line. And I had him easily by six inches and fifty pounds.

Greer didn't respond. She was still staring at me, in shock that I was in front of her. Finally, she cleared her throat and turned to the thin guy, "What?"

Time was of the essence because Tripp and Caroline were on their way. I wanted to get Greer out of here. Before the guy could answer, I said, "Would you excuse us a moment? I have something important to say to her."

"Oh, um, I guess."

Once he was gone, I had so much to tell Greer. Not just about the firestorm headed this way but how much I'd missed her. Dylan was right. If I wanted Tripp away from Greer, the only thing I could do was make her mine. And even though it had only been a few weeks, there was an attraction between us I could no longer deny. It was there the afternoon her father died, when I'd wanted to hold her and take away her pain. Ever since she showed up, late, to history of capitalism, that attraction kept getting stronger and stronger until I felt like I couldn't live without her. If she was willing to give us a try, and her hug on the rock told me her heart beat for me, then I'd take the chance. My parents would just have to get over it.

With the skinny dude and Emma gone, the light reached Greer's eyes and left me mute. There was a fire in there. She was wary, possibly still mad at me. But she was also excited and happy I was here. I could just tell.

I leaned down and kissed her. My lips were gentle because I didn't want to scare her but firm at the same time. So she knew this kiss was for real. For someone who was inexperienced when it came to guys, she didn't back down. And then her sweet lips parted for me. And I wrapped my arms around her and deepened the kiss, inhaling her perfumed hair and firing up all of my senses. She tasted better than her honeyed scent. Pure Greer. Her tongue tangled with mine as I pulled her soft curves against my strong body.

There wasn't a trace of alcohol in her system, and I wondered where on earth this woman found the strength to be herself and not act like every other college kid in this place blowing off steam.

Emma's loud voice reached me. "Get a room!" And I realized that I was in a dark corner of an off-campus house where my teammates and the cops were on their way. I released the kiss and smiled at her until I saw her dimples appear. Then, I grabbed her hand and walked through the room. The keg was by a slider door, and I asked someone where that led to.

"There's an alley through the yard," a familiar voice said. I turned my head and saw Liam standing by the bar. "Have fun, kiddies." He sounded disappointed. Like the thin guy, Liam probably had a thing for Greer. What straight guy wouldn't want her?

Once we were outside, through the yard, and onto the alley, I turned us to the right, in the direction where my car was parked. The alley was narrow, large enough for one car. A few streetlamps illuminated the concrete path, the only sound the rubber of our sneakers hitting the pavement. The party noise didn't follow us.

"Where are we going?" Greer asked.

"My car's this way. Blake was going to talk to the cops. Tripp and Caroline are crashing Blake's party with a bunch of guys from the team."

"Wait." She stopped. "What?"

"Your sister and Tripp Saunders are on their way to crash this party."

"Caroline said Tripp was having a party."

"He was," I said, "until he got called out by the head coach. They are coming here instead."

"That doesn't make any sense." She tried pulling her hand out of mine, but I held on. "Caroline would never do that. When Emma came to pick me up, she said we were lame."

I took a deep breath. "But her initial plans fell through."

"Nico," she said. "I really don't think you understand my sister. This isn't her scene."

What Greer didn't realize was that I understood her sister better than she did. "Maybe for tonight it is," I pleaded. "Tripp specifically said you were here with your band friends." I was still holding her hand, even though she'd tried to make me let go when she'd stopped walking. "We can talk more in my car, but we need to keep moving. I can't afford for the cops or anyone from the team to see me here."

We resumed our way through the alley and then reached a side street and turned left. My car was parked another two blocks down. "Is that party about to get raided? I mean, are Emma, Blake, and Liam going to get in trouble?"

"Blake's neighbor is a cop," I said. "They'll be okay."

"Why are you here, Nico?"

This time I stopped. "I care about you Greer. You weren't safe there."

"I was fine." She pulled her hand out of mine. "I wasn't drinking. Blake and his roommates are all twenty-one. I was having fun. If the cops came, I would have just walked home." Her words were confident, but I detected some uncertainty in her tone.

"That's not how it would have gone down." There was some soft yellow light from the tightly spaced houses that reached us, but I couldn't see Greer's eyes. I sensed a shift in her. Not just pulling her hand out of mine, but her brain was also firing and not fitting all the pieces together. As if on cue, a police car without its sirens sped by us, the blue-and-red flashing lights showing fear on Greer's face.

Silently I took her hand, and we picked up our pace in order to get to my car. She and I weren't breaking any laws walking down a neighborhood street, but I did breathe a sigh of relief once I closed the passenger's side door with her safely inside. If any of these cops wrote my name down, the entire team would be on curfew through January.

"It's early," I said. "Do you want to go to my place?"

My question didn't scare her as much as annoy her. "I better go home."

"I think we need to talk."

She shook her head. "I disagree. Email has been working fine for us. We didn't even have class together once this week, and our project was still turned in on time. There was no need for you to come and get me tonight. I'm sorry for what just happened—"

"A lot just happened," I said. "What specifically are you referring to?"

Her deep blush told me exactly what she was sorry about.

"You're sorry for kissing me?"

She turned her body towards mine. "Yes," she said. "I was right in the beginning, Nico. We don't have to be friends. I know you feel somewhat responsible for what's happened with my mom now, but I'm taking care of it. And, believe it or not, I'm grateful your parents did what they did."

I didn't know what she was referring to, particularly regarding my parents, but I wanted her to keep talking. I thought about Emma's comment too. "Do you think I pity you?"

"Why else would you kiss me?"

"I kissed you because I like you. A lot. And I think you like me too. You kissed me back. In front of that skinny dude trying to hit on you."

"You kissed me because that guy was talking to me?"

"No." I leaned over so that I was looking into her eyes. "I've wanted to kiss you since the first day of class. And I want to kiss you again now."

She turned away from me. "That's not a good idea."

"Why?" My voice was quiet.

"We don't get along."

I clasped her hand. "I'd rather be with you over anyone, Greer."

She glanced over for a moment, looked at our hands, and then turned back to the windshield. "I can't do this." Her eyes were blinking, trying to hold back tears. "With work, and school, and home, I just can't do this too. I'm sorry."

"Let me help you. Unless Tripp does something stupid and gets us all in trouble, my evenings will be free again. I miss coming to the studio."

"It won't last, Nico," she said. "You and me together." She squeezed my hand and then removed hers. "Can you just take me home?"

I started the engine and pulled away. I still had time to convince her since I had to take the long way back to her house in order to avoid whatever was now going on at Blake's. "Are you worried about my family? Because I really think they'd like you."

She laughed. "Are you trying to make fun of me?"

"Of course not," I said. "I would *never* make fun of you."

"Then why would you say something so ridiculous?" she asked.

"I'm telling you the truth, Greer. I really think my mom and dad would like you."

"I don't even know your parents," she said, "but I know something you don't. Your mom and dad do *not* like me."

"If they met you, they'd like you."

We were on her street. There was a spot outside her house, but I pulled to the curb a few houses away. We were out of sight of her front porch, but I would make sure to walk her home.

"Nico, I'm not going to meet your parents," she said. "Please don't ask me that again."

"Why not?"

"Because I don't want to be with you."

"I don't believe you," I said. "You like being with me, Greer."

"Fine." She took a deep breath. "I give up. I have enjoyed being with you. You're charming and funny, and you make me laugh. You're a good partner in history of capitalism because you are smart and efficient. I'll also admit that you are really good looking, but you already know that so it's not like I'm revealing some big secret. But there is a huge barrier between us."

I smiled when she told me I was good looking. "What is that?"

"I will never be your equal," she said. "It's like Tripp Saunders and my sister. He has no respect for her."

For the first time tonight, I feared what she would say next. Because right now, her words hurt. "Greer—"

"Actually, it's worse," she continued. "You couldn't even defend me or my family in front of him and your teammates."

Her words stung. They also weren't true, but how could I explain what happened when I defended her family in front of the team? I didn't want to hurt her by telling her that I was one wrong move away from losing my spot on the team because of her mother and sister. I didn't get the chance to respond though.

"The only reason I'm saying this to you is because what you're proposing is impossible," she said. "I'm not trying to hurt you personally. I never asked for your loyalty. Hearing this might be helpful for you." Her eyes found mine. "You and I will never be together. I'm a Scott. You're a Camillo. You will always view us as beneath you, just like Tripp Saunders."

I took a deep breath because she was starting to get me mad.

"I can't control my sister." She started to wipe tears from her eyes, just as she'd done on her birthday. Crying without making a sound. "But my mother has finally agreed to get help because of the restraining order. I will never abandon her, Nico. I'd never be able to live with myself."

"What are you talking about?" I asked. "Is this about Charleston?"

"No." She laughed while still wiping tears from her eyes. "Your parents filed one here."

"I didn't know, Greer." I grabbed her hands. "I'll talk to them."

"Please don't." She pulled away immediately, like my touch burned her. "I'm glad they did. I mean, I never want to speak to them. Ever. But maybe something good will come from it."

How did tonight, which started off with the most intense kiss I'd ever experienced and the promise of more, deteriorate into this?

She reached her arms to her neck and removed her necklace. *My* necklace.

"I don't want that back."

"I feel guilty wearing it. Especially now," she said. "And if I take it off at home, Caroline will steal it."

"Don't do this, Greer." I was angry. "Deep down, you know we're meant to be together. Relationships. Families. Life. These things aren't always easy. But I know my parents and my brothers. And you. And I know we can work all of this out."

She didn't say anything, but her violet eyes met mine, studying me. She held the pink diamond necklace in her hand. Her mind seemed impenetrable right now.

"What are you thinking?"

"Life *is* hard," she said. "But I don't want this to be. Good-night Nico."

The chain of the pink necklace pooled in the plastic cup holder with a rattle. Greer unlocked the door and jumped out. By the time I got out of the car to stop her, she'd already turned up her walkway to her porch.

Her pain was real. Greer's cry wasn't silent after all.

21

GREER

The house was empty when I left Nico. My mother was still out with Mark, and I had no idea where Caroline was. I wasted no time running upstairs and getting into the shower. I didn't want to wash Nico's clean scent off me, or the feeling of being surrounded by his powerful arms and chest. And definitely not his kiss. Which felt like liquid fire coursing through me, from the ends of my hair to the tips of my fingers and toes. But this was an ugly cry, and I needed the sharp prick of heated water and white noise to get it out.

Of the twenty thousand males on this campus, why did Nico Camillo have to be the one? *I'd rather be with you over anyone, Greer.* I felt the exact same way about him, as much as I tried to convince myself otherwise. A relationship between us, a Scott and a Camillo, would never work. We'd both turn more bitter than we already were. Meeting his parents? Was he crazy? *Hi Mr. and Mrs. Camillo. Don't worry, my mother is locked back at the house.* What would he say when he met my mother? *Hi Mrs. Scott. I'm so glad you didn't convince my father to ditch my mother and be with you instead.* Some barriers were insurmountable, and a relationship between us was one of them.

The only option for me was to let him go. And cry. I'd learned to hold so much inside me and not cry over the years. But I knew the pain of losing Nico would fester unless I released it now. He was there on the worst day of my life, the day my father died. And knowing him now, he was trying to comfort me then. Deep down, Nico was kind and good. He would always have a special place in my heart.

When the water turned cold, I wrapped myself up in a towel and went into my room. My face was puffy and red, yet the pain lingered. The house was still quiet. So I sent a quick text to my mother, ignoring the new texts from Emma, Nico, and Caroline, and told her I was home and in bed. The last thing I needed was for her to return and see me in this state. Her note back to me just said goodnight and that she'd be home soon. I dressed and climbed into bed, and cried until sleep took over.

Monday morning came too soon. It would be so easy, and healthier, for me to skip classes. No one would even notice if I missed the first two, except maybe that guy from social media who I met last night at Blake's house. I never did catch his name. Once Nico appeared before me, I pretty much stopped processing anything other than him.

He was the reason I had to go to school this morning. I'd look like a coward if I didn't show. All I had to do was get through the next few hours. And be strong. Since I'd never brushed my hair the night before, it was a tangled mess. I showered again, combed my hair and dressed in one of my studio outfits with my boots. The studio was my refuge, and I needed that more than ever. But it would have to wait until after my mother's first psychiatrist appointment today. Caroline was curled in her bed, still dressed in her party clothes. My mom was also asleep in her room when I left for campus.

Josh was the guy's name, and he sat down next to me in social media. I didn't even need to talk, which was nice. But he informed me that the party broke up shortly after I'd left. There was some kind of confrontation in front of the house, but no one stayed to watch. Instead, Blake had everyone leave quietly out the back, the same place where Nico and I had exited.

"I was back at the dorm early, but that was cool. My roommate and I watched Netflix," he said. "I know you're with that football dude, but my offer still stands. I'm happy to get together sometime and study social media platforms. I think you've got a really good eye, Greer."

Josh seemed like a very nice, normal guy. And he was a musician, a fellow artist, which was appealing. There were hundreds of guys like him on campus. Not everyone was as gross as Tripp Saunders. Why couldn't Josh be the one? As I listened to him, I tried to imagine him kissing me the way Nico did, and I felt…absolutely nothing. In fact, I had to tell him right away that meeting with him was not possible.

"Thanks, Josh," I said. "But other than class and one study group, I'm hardly ever on campus. My work is full time."

"That's cool," he said.

I smiled and then tried to process the lecture. My anxiety level increased as the class neared the end. Nico didn't make me nervous. At all. I felt calm when I was near him. Even last night, when I said those things to him, I was sad but didn't feel awkward. But I feared for myself. Would I burst into tears the moment I saw him?

I CLIMBED the steps to the second floor of Smythe Hall with only moments to spare before class started. Nico was waiting for me outside Professor Simmons' room. It wasn't fair how good he looked. His hair was still damp, and his gorgeous face was still reddish from practice. He was the picture of physical and emotional health. I sucked in a huge gulp of air, trying to calm my heart.

"Hey," he said, stepping up to me. "I just want to make sure you're okay."

"I'm okay," I said, too quickly.

He leaned into me, his green eyes piercing into mine and then checking out the rest of my face and my hair. "You don't look okay to me."

"Gee, thanks." I shook my head but smiled. "We're late for class."

"We don't have to go," he said. "I'll ditch it for you. We can hang out and finish our conversation."

"Nico—"

"I'm serious, Greer. There is nothing you and I can't work out." He lowered his voice. "And if talking doesn't work, a make-out session will cure almost anything."

I felt my face flame.

"That's better." He smiled. "I can still make you blush." Then he held out his hand, an "after you" gesture, and he followed me into history of capitalism.

"Miss Scott and Mr. Camillo," said Dr. Simmons. "Glad you could *finally* join us! Since you're the last ones here, you'll be the first to give your presentation."

"Ours was scheduled for Wednesday," I said.

"Schedules are always subject to change, Miss Scott. As a businesswoman, you should get used to this." The wooden chairs now formed a horseshoe. She pointed to two empty chairs in the center of the room, where the equipment was set up and aimed for the whiteboard. Then, she took a seat next to Blake at one end of the semicircle. Nico was already pulling out his laptop and hooking it up to the projector. Now my anxiety spiked. Nico gave me a reassuring smile, but even I knew his calm would not help me now.

The presentation went worse than even I expected. Nico, of course, spoke smoothly and authoritatively, delivering his slides on the manufacturing giants in New England with natural grace. I, on the other hand, sped through my slides so fast that I knew no one would have processed anything I'd stated, much less find my material interesting. It was a shame, really, because the cotton-mill workers in New England, the "mill girls," were fascinating. And though they'd suffered through harsh working conditions – many died – their labor allowed for capitalism to thrive in the United States.

Nico's contribution might have given us a passing grade, but my part was a bomb. Even Blake tried to salvage my portion at the end by asking me a softball question about the weaving process. I just stared at him, empty – grasping for the necklace I'd returned to Nico – as his facial expressions encouraged me to get out a few words about spindles and steam power.

Thirteen minutes couldn't come to an end soon enough.

Nico insisted on walking me to the lot despite my protestations. When he started to invade my personal space by brushing up against me, I deliberately increased my distance by walking faster.

"We weren't *that* terrible," he repeated to me.

I glared at him. "*I* was terrible. Not you. *Me*. And I'm sorry about that. But I really need to be somewhere. You don't have to walk me to my car."

"When are we going to talk, Greer?" he said. "Why are you running away from me?"

"This is so silly." I stopped walking. "I'm taking my mom to see a psychiatrist. Right now. Then I'm going to work. The presentation was a disaster because of me, Nico. The only good thing is that it's over. Last night probably hurt my performance today, but honestly, I'll never match your skill when it comes to speaking in public." My voice was raised, and other students walked by us, a few staring. But I didn't care anymore. He needed to hear this. "If you really care about me, Nico, please leave me alone. I promise that I'll do my fair share of work in that class, and I'll try to do better if we have to present again, but I can't do this."

"What can't you do, Greer?"

"I can't be your friend. I can't be anything to you." I lowered my voice. "It's too painful."

My words must have finally penetrated. His face was grim. And pale. I'd never seen him look so sad. Maybe now he understood how I was feeling and accepted my choice. Because when I turned around and hurried to the parking lot, he didn't follow me.

THAT NIGHT, I crashed. I felt so drained physically and emotionally that I went upstairs without eating. Isabel and I closed the studio around eight, just after the orders were complete. Had it not been for her, no Scotty orders would have made it to the mail room. Usually sewing allowed my mind to wander and reset. Between my mother and Nico, I didn't know where to start to untangle my thoughts. Isabel sensed how troubled I was and kept me on task.

My mother's psychiatrist appointment ran long but went better than expected. The psychiatrist was a woman, attractive like my mother, and understood Sophia Scott better than even me. Like my sister, my mother was skilled at using her looks to get her way. Men were easier for her to manipulate than women. All you needed to do was to take my mother to a grocery store, and she'd have guys of all ages, in every aisle, falling down to help her.

Dr. Jane Forrester would not be treating her with kid gloves. My mother wanted me to stay for the first thirty minutes, to help her share her history. She did most of the talking but I was there to hold her hand and encourage her to get to the root of the problem. My father and his death, Nicholas Camillo, and what meds she was taking five years ago and why. These were topics that must be worked out, we both reported to Dr. Forrester. I also brought the restraining order for the psychiatrist to see. When I left to sit in the waiting room, Dr. Forrester smiled and asked one question: "Caroline is your older sister. Where is she now?"

"She's home," I said. "She graduated in May and is still looking for a job." The homecoming formal was less than two weeks away, and Caroline promised that she'd resume her search in earnest afterwards.

The doctor nodded and smiled at my mother.

About an hour later, my mom exited with a face as red and puffy as my own was the day before. She hugged me, and I started bawling. For someone who'd become skilled at crying without making noise, I was making up for lost time after walking away from Nico the night before. Then my mother held my face in her hands and kissed my forehead, and we each started laughing. A release we both needed apparently.

"Thank you, honey," she said when we got into the Mini. She let me drive her, but before we went home, we stopped at the pharmacy for her prescription. A low dose to start. Dr. Forrester also suggested spending more time outside the house. Regular work that was not tied to the dermatologist she was in a new relationship with would be beneficial too. But the doctor suggested waiting a month or two, until she had several weeks of meds and therapy under her belt, before entering the workforce.

"You're welcome to come to the studio," I said, "but we're not always having football parties."

"She warned me *not* to rely on my teenage daughter." My mom shook her head and smiled.

I thought of Coach Evans, who reminded me so much of my mother. Maybe the two of them could be friends. "Tomorrow the cheerleading coach and the captains are coming to the studio," I said. When the coach asked me to return to the stadium with samples, I lied and said it was easier at the studio. But I didn't want to run into Nico and his teammates, and I was legit scared of Coach Phillips. "We're going to try some new patterns. You could be really helpful with this project, Mom."

"Oh, that sounds fun, Greer!" She rubbed my hair, something she used to do when I was little. "But only if you don't mind."

"Just not too many sequins," I said. "That's all I ask."

"There's no such thing as too many sequins, Greer."

She sounded *exactly* like Coach Evans.

The following morning, I finally scrolled through Nico's texts. Most were just him checking in to see if I was okay. A few were attempts to make me laugh about Isabel, or Sam and Beatrice, or coming to his place for dinner. He asked me to go to the homecoming formal with him, which wasn't intended to be funny but I laughed anyway. I'd be tucked away in a hotel suite during the formal, helping the girls with their dresses and makeup. I'd even planned to bring the Singer Quantum Stylist 9960, my five-year-old machine that was equipped to fix any sewing-related issue, to the hotel. There was no way I'd be attending as a guest. His last text from this morning told me to check my email. Apparently, Dr. Simmons requested we stop by to see her during office hours. *Ugh.*

Rather than text Nico, I replied to the email with the only time I was available today, right after phys ed with Emma. Coach Evans was due in the studio in early afternoon, and I'd have to allow time to pick up my mother. Before Dr. Simmons could even confirm the time, Nico replied that he was available then too.

We rock climbed in phys ed. Emma struggled while my arms were able to handle the heavy pulling. Not as well as the guys in the class, but I was excited about how high I was able to climb. My mom and Caroline were gym rats, not me. Perhaps the studio work was more physical than I realized.

I had to skip the shower and run to Adams Center in my yoga tights and one of Caroline's Lulu tissue tank tops that I borrowed from her room this morning. She'd pull my braided hair if she saw me wearing this now.

Nico, of course, was already seated when I rushed in, my face flushed from rock climbing and then running to get here. He was a starter for the number one college team in the country, yet somehow managed to always get where he needed to be ahead of time. Dr. Simmons was laughing at something he'd just said, but his expression turned serious the moment I arrived. His hair was combed and he wore a slub knit polo and shorts, neat without being overly preppy. Our professor's striped sweater clashed with her printed Oxford and her tortoise shell glasses. I took a seat and tried not to focus on her fashion faux pas.

"Thank you for coming," she started. "I wanted to tell you together in person that I had to grade your presentation as a C. This is probably very disappointing to you both. The content was excellent, which did help raise the grade. But your presentation was flat. It had no spark whatsoever."

I opened my mouth to interject, but she held up her hand to me to stop me from speaking. "Let me finish, Miss Scott. I know that yours was the first one. My hope was that you'd start the class off on a high note, and the rest of the teams would have to elevate theirs. Instead, you set a low bar. Now the others know what *not* to do. I'm very disappointed. And I must ask whether you even bothered to practice?"

"Greer had to practice on her own because I was out of town," Nico stated.

"Dr. Simmons," I cut in. "Nico was very good yesterday. I deserve the poor grade, not him."

"That's admirable, Miss Scott," she acknowledged, "but you are a team. You win as a team, and you lose as a team. Mr. Camillo understands that better than either of us. As far as being out of town, your computers are equipped with distance learning capabilities and cameras. You two are smart. You *should* have figured this out."

Neither one of us responded. This time, music did not play in the background, and the silence was awkward.

"Another thing," she said. "You removed all of the data on the cotton mills in South Carolina and the rest of the Piedmont region. That would have been of tremendous interest to your audience. It provides regional context."

"That was my decision, not Nico's," I admitted.

She ignored my comment. "Moving forward, I urge you to take these projects more seriously. Understanding our history is critical in all areas of study, including capitalism. But the value of this class is learning how to work as partners. It is essential to any position you will have one day. No CEO worth his or her salt made it to the top without learning how to collaborate." Then she dismissed us, adding, "Thank you both for coming."

Nico's shirt was sage green, which made his eyes greener if that was even possible. He was studying me outside Adams Center. Neither one of us had spoken since walking out together.

"I'm sorry," I said.

"For what?"

"For *that*." I pointed to the building. "I'm the reason we tanked."

"I don't care about that grade." He reached out to touch me but pulled away suddenly. "Are you headed to the parking lot?"

"Yes."

"Can I walk you there?" When I didn't answer right away, he said, "I promise I won't try to touch you again."

We descended the Adams Center steps and took the brick path that would eventually lead us to the parking lot. Nico was not relaxed. I was about to ask him what the matter was when he blurted out, "Do you have a flannel shirt in your bag?"

"What?" I asked.

"It's just that you may want to cover up," he said. "You don't want to get sunburnt."

"It's cloudy."

He was blushing. "It's just that I can see everything." He pointed to me. "I mean, any guy can see everything."

I looked down at my clothes. My sister's tank was thin and white. I wore a lilac sports bra underneath. My tights were similar in color to Nico's sage green shirt. My Nike sneakers were black with a white swoosh and soles. I looked like every other girl on campus and told him so.

"I've never seen you dress like this, Greer."

"I always wear this to phys ed," I said. "What else would I wear?"

He fingered his hair, messing it.

"Nico, I think you're being irrational."

"Sorry. It's just—" He didn't finish.

I stopped. "What is it, Nico?"

He exhaled. "Guys are going to look at you and like what they see. And I don't want that."

I burst out laughing.

"This isn't funny," he said. "I can see your cleavage *and* your belly button."

At that moment, a female student walked between us. She wore a tank dress that barely covered her nipples and heels, and smiled flirtatiously at Nico. My outfit was double the coverage of hers. And I tilted my head and gave him a look to prove my point. But he wasn't looking at her. His eyes were on me, and they were smoldering. I felt my skin heat under his gaze. This was the same look he gave me at Blake's house, before he kissed me and I hungrily kissed him back. Suddenly I wasn't laughing anymore. Releasing a slow breath, I turned and continued walking.

"You're ignoring my texts," he said. "I know you want me to leave you alone, and I'm trying to respect that. But I can't pretend that I don't care about you." His deep voice felt like sunlight warming my skin, causing goosebumps to form all over. "I can't force you to be with me. But could you please just answer me so that I know you're alive?"

The meeting with Professor Simmons was evidence that we'd have to communicate better. Even though it was beneficial for me and my family, shutting Nico out of my life wouldn't be possible until the end of the semester.

"Yes," I answered.

He didn't smile but nodded. And then, just after I'd given him an inch, Nico took a yard. "Will you go to the formal with me?"

"Nico!" I said in a stern voice. "I can't be a guest at the formal. I'll be there all day for Scotty. The Floreses and I are getting the girls ready, and I told Lila I'd stay in case anyone has a wardrobe malfunction. But even if I could go with you, it's not a good idea." Then I said words that made my heart feel like it was ripped in two. "Have you thought about inviting someone else? It may be good for you."

He glanced over at me and just shook his head. Caroline believed Tripp Saunders to be the biggest catch of all on the football team, but she was mistaken. Nico Camillo outshined Tripp, and every other player I'd seen up close, in every category.

"Any girl would be crazy not to say yes to you."

"Don't say that," he said quietly. We'd arrived at the parking lot. Nico was upset, but he asked me for my keys. Because I didn't want to distress him anymore than I already had, I handed them over. He unlocked the driver's side door and held it open for me. He gave me a tight smile when he closed the door. I backed out of my spot, and watched his eyes follow my car out of the lot. Then he turned and walked back onto campus.

THE DAYS LEADING up to the formal were calmer. The psychiatrist said my mother needed weeks of meds before she'd start feeling better, but to me, she was more like herself when my father was alive. Back then, she functioned as our mother. She was up early with my father, she packed our lunches and schoolbags, she enjoyed putting our outfits together. Though she never sewed, my mother loved to iron and made sure each of us looked primped before we left. Yes, she pined for Nicholas Camillo, but she never acted on those feelings. She was content with my father and with us.

Besides the psychotic behavior and the obsession with her appearance, the most significant change in her after his death was her sleep habits. Because of this, Dr. Forrester was treating her first for depression. Looking back, the signs were all there. But Caroline and I were too young and self-absorbed to truly understand that she was suffering.

Caroline didn't like our mother on meds.

Though I was either at school or the studio, my sister texted me frequently.

> Why is Mom so annoying all the sudden?

> She keeps yelling at me to get out of bed

My favorite:

> Mom won't stop bitching about me getting a job. Tell her to leave me alone. I told you both I'd get one after homecoming!

Caroline still wouldn't say what happened at Blake's party. It was like she was under a gag order. Her text to me that night was evil.

> Hahaha…little miss perfect was arrested!

She blew me off when I called her out on it, saying she knew when she wrote that that everyone escaped out the back door. Still, it was cruel.

My mother and I were right to give her a hard time. A job was what she needed.

She was seeing less of Tripp Saunders, and that also put her in a bad mood. The team had three home games in a row, and the homecoming game and dance were sandwiched in the middle. She thought she'd be seeing more of him since the team wasn't traveling, but his time for her was limited.

"It's only understandable," she'd say. "He is the MVP and every single NFL team wants him."

Nico and I had also reached a truce of sorts. He still walked me to my car after class each day but never let the conversation drift to studio talk or the two of us. I'd considered asking him who was going to the formal with him, but then decided against it. The logical choice would be a Delta Gamma, and I wasn't sure my heart could endure helping her get beautiful for Nico. I cared about him and, like any good friend, wanted him to be happy. But he was still my one.

Instead, we spoke only of history of capitalism. Teams were still delivering their Industrial Revolution presentations, but we were working on term papers due in a couple of weeks. Both were focused on twentieth century capitalism before 1950, one before the Great Depression and one after. This time, I wouldn't let us study anything that dealt with the clothing industry. We picked automobiles and telecommunications. There would be an oral component to these, but Dr. Simmons hadn't decided on what that would be. Nico wanted to work ahead because the team was in town for a while.

Homecoming marked the halfway point of the semester. Once the term papers were out of the way, all teams would be working on their culminating projects. We'd each be tasked with an in-depth analysis of one Georgia company, examining its capitalistic principles, successes and shortcomings. Interviews with company leaders were required. Dr. Simmons had yet to assign each team its company, and Nico was chomping at the bit to get that started as well.

"Football takes over in November," he said one day during class. "I don't want to let you down, Greer."

"Research doesn't bother me, but presenting does." I lowered my voice. "Professor Hawk would never let me go without you anyway."

"True. We're partners. But there's a lot more involved than just presenting." Then he lowered his voice. "All-nighters at my place can't be ruled out."

I rolled my eyes.

He smiled.

22

NICO

hat went down in Michigan messed with my head. Until the scandal, my life was charmed. My parents doted on me. My brothers respected me. My community, with the exception of Greer Scott on the day she turned fourteen, cheered for me. Then my teammates and coaches, guys who I believed were among the best I'd ever known, admitted to taking thousands of dollars to perform poorly at football. Cheat for money.

As a result, I trusted people less. Guys like Tripp Saunders and girls like Caroline Scott were dangerous as far as I was concerned. At the same time, I stopped taking the people I loved for granted. Like my parents and brothers. I was learning to trust again. Dylan and Coach Phillips were good people.

And then there was Greer.

What I told her was the truth. I wanted to be with her over anyone. Yet her life was intrinsically linked to Caroline and Sophia Scott, and by extension Tripp – three people who were toxic, to be avoided at all costs. She wasn't just trying to protect herself when she said we can't be more than partners for history of capitalism. She wanted to protect me. Manipulation and deceit were not tools in her arsenal. Her honesty, intelligence, and overall goodness shined through her violet-grey eyes.

She needed me in her life.

No one here had her best interests at heart *and* the means to be there for her. The Floreses came the closest, but they had no idea what was going on with Sophia and Caroline. Out of everyone in her life, Greer trusted her silent partner more than anyone, yet that person was likely ripping her off every single day.

My physical attraction to her was now all-consuming. All I had to do was think about her, and my blood rushed, my skin hot to the touch. Our one and only kiss was just a tease, a distant memory. I fell into bed each night with a raging hard-on and woke up with one too, images of her crowding my mind. Greer in her short dresses. Greer in her boots. And the latest. Greer in a sports bra and tight pants showing off her smooth curves. How did I let her drive away that day when all I wanted was to wrap her in my arms and kiss her senseless in the back of her van?

Greer wanted me too. I knew that once I held her again, she'd see things my way. She'd give us a chance. She was the only reason I was still going to homecoming.

COACH PHILLIPS STOPPED me the Monday morning after the Tennessee game, which was the first of three home games. We dominated as expected. Tennessee's defense was a little better than its offense, but they could not penetrate our line. Together, we made Tripp Saunders look like Peyton Manning.

"Hey Nico. Owen Ross will be getting into this week's game.

You and Ryan are going to start working with him. We'll let Dylan move between you guys and Tripp during drills this week." Owen was a sophomore and the backup QB. The homecoming game this week was against Garrison State, another team we were expected to beat pretty easily. The coaches intended to give the starting line less playing time, which was fine with me.

"Sounds good," I answered him.

"How's that friend of yours by the way?"

My look to him matched my confusion.

"That Scott girl who I hooked up with Coach Evans?" he asked. "The one who has her own business?"

"Right," I said. "She's good."

"I thought I'd see her around here," he said. "Coach Evans is secretive about what they're working on together. But she's happy, and I've never seen her like this."

Everyone on the team thought that Phillips and the cheerleading coach were dating. But I wasn't convinced. Because if they were, why didn't everyone know about it? Neither one of them was married. I assumed Phillips was too chicken to ask the woman out.

"That girl's website is impressive." Phillips' admiration was something we all had to work for. Leave it to Greer to earn his respect after one meeting. "I'm anxious to see what the new uniforms look like."

"I wouldn't know." I laughed and bid him a good day.

My chest felt puffed with pride for Greer. Her work ethic was unparalleled. And I knew that whatever she designed for the cheer squad would be a thousand times better than what they had now. But breaking through a tough nut like Coach Evans? That just showed how irresistible my girl really was.

After class that day I asked her how her cheerleading project was going.

"It's going better than I expected," she answered.

"What about Coach Evans?" I asked. "I heard she can be really difficult."

She nodded. "I'd heard that too but she's really sweet."

"Sweet?" I asked. "I'm not sure I believe you. I've witnessed her…coaching."

Greer laughed. "If you came to study group," she said, "you'd have known that she had dinner with us last night. She and my mother are becoming…friends. Sort of."

"That sounds like a good thing, right?" I asked.

"Yes." She smiled.

My own relationship with my parents was deteriorating, but I was happy Greer was making progress with her mother. I gave my mom and dad hell for hiding that they'd filed a restraining order against Sophia Scott. I didn't fault them for taking action, but they should have told me.

"Coach Phillips was asking me about you today," I said. "He wanted to know how it was going."

"Why would he care?" she asked, annoyed. "He has nothing to do with the cheerleading team, right?"

"I suppose not," I answered. "But he and Coach Evans are friends. A lot of people say they're dating."

She shrugged. "That's not the vibe I get."

It felt wrong not to touch her when we parted. But I had to respect the boundaries she set.

SOMETHING FINALLY GOT through to Tripp Saunders. After the night of Blake's party, he calmed down a bit. Rumor had it that the cops laid into him when he showed up with Caroline and a Mini full of booze and threatened to arrest them for serving minors. Unlike campus security, the local cops weren't as permissive. But the two of them still got off with a warning, not even a slap on the wrist. Hampton didn't punish the whole team so we weren't even sure he knew about the incident. My senses told me he wasn't totally in the dark. Hampton was keeping Tripp on a very tight leash.

When a group of players asked Tripp if he was having the pre-party before the homecoming dance, he shrugged. "Nah. It's up to someone else. I'm dry for the rest of the season."

"It's about time," said Dylan.

"We can have it," announced Beau. "The girls are getting ready at the hotel. Just don't trash the place, guys."

My apartment was within walking distance of the hotel, but there was no way in hell I'd be inviting the entire team over for drinks beforehand. Dylan was planning to come over after the game, get dressed in our tuxes, and then walk over together. Since it was Lila's night, he'd rented a suite for afterwards.

Greer turning me down, twice, was a bummer. Since Scotty Designs was one of the sponsors, she was expected to be there for part of the event according to Lila. I knew two hundred people, many of them drunk, wouldn't be Greer's scene. It wasn't my scene either. But in case she was overwhelmed, or made uncomfortable by douchebag Tripp, I'd be there. She was the only reason I was going.

The homecoming game was supposed to be cakewalk, and Butler handled Garrison State easily, with Owen Ross playing the second half. I was in and out of the entire game, but only on the field about half of the total offensive minutes. Next week's game against Tech was supposed to be just as tough as the Louisiana game, so I tried to soak in the atmosphere. The hot weather finally broke into a perfectly sunny and beautiful seventy-degree day. Rather than a sea of red and white, the fans and players were wearing red, white, and pink for breast cancer awareness.

Alumni players and their families filled up two sections. The NFL had a presence too. Retired NFL players who were also alumni generally came, but since the Atlanta Falcons were also at home the following day, some of those players who also played here came to watch. They were honored before the game and stood on the sidelines with us during the first quarter. They shook our hands, told us stories, and generally wished us well.

One guy who had to be in his seventies said, "I heard you boys are having a formal tonight with some sorority girls." Then he pointed to his seats. "My wife's up there, and she's a Delta Gamma. Prettiest girls at this school."

"Amen, brother," said Dylan, slapping the guy on the back.

The cheerleaders were still wearing their original uniforms, which meant Greer's project was still under production. I was never quite sure what she had against these outfits because whenever the squad came onto the field, the crowd went crazy.

She should observe this phenomenon for herself before she completed her project. But then I didn't trust myself. Was I wanting her to come and study the cheerleaders, or did I just really want her here for me?

I sounded needy when my mind had thoughts like that, but Greer enjoyed football. There were nearly one hundred thousand people here, yet she wasn't one of them. Emma, Blake, and Liam never missed a game, and I was annoyed on her behalf that she always felt she had to work instead of just being a college girl.

DYLAN and I went from the stadium after the game to the business school commuter lot. I'd left my car there overnight because I knew I'd never get a spot on campus today. Both tuxes were already in the car. Fans were still tailgating even though the game ended about an hour before, and all the players were pretty hyped for the formal tonight. Typically, sorority formals were kind of generic for guys. But this one was different. It was homecoming. The perfect fall night at one of the oldest hotels in Georgia. And Lila, with the help of her committee and Butler football, had raised a ton of money.

Dylan still lived in the dorms, so he was pretty stunned when he walked into my apartment. The kitchen, particularly the range with six burners, impressed him the most.

"Your car is pretty sweet," he said, "but this place is unreal. Maybe when I sign with the NFL, I can afford to be your roommate."

"It's just an apartment."

"How many bedrooms you have here, man?" he asked.

"Two and an office." I showed him around the place. The master was a little bigger than the guest bedroom, but both were equally lavish with large bathrooms. The office was empty. I typically worked at the kitchen counter. What I didn't tell Dylan was that I now pictured that as Greer's home studio, which was insane. She didn't want a relationship with me, yet we were already cohabiting in my mind?

We had more than an hour before Lila wanted Dylan there, so we did something we'd promised our coaches and teammates we wouldn't do until after the bowl game in January. We each had a beer. It wouldn't impact our training, but it sure felt good after the game today.

"Nico, man." He was seated at the long dining table and looking around the place. "You need to have a dinner party. I'll cook unless you want to share in those responsibilities. I'm not talking the whole team. Just a few friends, and girlfriends."

"You sound like my mom." I laughed. "She loves to *entertain*."

"I'm serious though," he said. "That would be fun. I mean, I love cooking for a crowd, but I never really sit down and enjoy myself. It would be awesome to use that Wolfgang Puck kitchen, fill this table, and just hang out. What do you say?"

"Sure," I said. "You tell me when." If I was honest with myself, a dinner party didn't really appeal to me unless Greer would agree to come. The beer went down too easy. It was light. I offered him another, and he accepted.

"What's going on with you and Greer?" he asked. "You don't have to tell me. I know you value your privacy when it comes to her. But did you think about what I said?"

"Yes," I told him. "Your advice was good. I've been asking her out ever since. But it's com—"

"What the fuck is so complicated, man?"

I took a deep breath. *Her mother's psychotic and tried to have my mother killed to be with my father.* That was the easiest explanation, but I knew Greer wouldn't want that getting out, despite it being the truth.

"Nothing that's between us." I shrugged. "It's just shit from my parents and hers, and she's still dealing with it. She won't let me help her." I gazed into the empty office. "But deep down, I think she trusts me. She knows I won't hurt her."

"Does she realize Tripp's about to dump her sister?"

"I doubt it. What do you know?"

"I have my sources." He smiled. "Hampton wants Caroline out of the picture. I think Tripp was just waiting until after tonight."

"Why? So he doesn't hurt her feelings? Tripp doesn't give a shit about timing," I argued. "If what you say is true, he'd have dumped her already."

"You're probably right," he said. "But Tripp seems worried about something. He's not his typical cocky self."

I tried not to think about Tripp and said this to Dylan.

"The Scott sisters don't seem at all alike," he said. "What's up with that?"

"They're four years apart," I said. "And Greer's the only one working in that family. I wish I understood them better, but Greer doesn't let me in."

We finished our beers. Dylan brought his stuff into the guest bedroom while I showered and changed in my bedroom. The tux was nice, and even though Greer didn't make this, she measured me for it. And for that reason, I felt like part of her was with me.

Dylan took longer getting ready than me. And then he had to pack up all of his stuff for his big night with Lila. The town was hopping as we walked over to the hotel. Women gave us wolf whistles. Both guys and girls screamed our numbers. I smiled and laughed along with Dylan, but I didn't fully embrace the adoration. After Michigan, I'd always be wary of die-hard fans.

Even though we were among the first guys to arrive at the hotel, girls in pink dresses I'd recognized from Scotty Designs roamed the lobby. They did nothing for me because they weren't Greer Scott, but each one looked beautiful. Lila ran over to Dylan. Her dark hair fell in long waves. Her pink dress was soft and flowy. Dylan, the guy who didn't shut up all afternoon, stopped speaking.

"Jesus," he finally said. "Forgive me for taking the Lord's name in vain, but you look like a supermodel."

Lila giggled and then pulled him away. I was left on my own. My eyes found Caroline Scott standing at the bar. Her dress was different than the others. I could tell Greer didn't make it. It was shorter, for one thing, and wasn't quite as formal. The girls Greer dressed looked like they were at a black-tie event in a historic hotel. Caroline seemed like she was attending a casual outdoor wedding. But it was pink.

Just as I stopped a girl in a Scotty dress, I noticed Owen Ross walk in with his girlfriend, who wasn't a Delta Gamma but happened to be wearing the same dress as Caroline. The girl-friends of the starter and backup QBs were wearing identical outfits.

"Where is Greer Scott?" I asked the girl I'd stopped.

"Greer?" she said excitedly. "She's in suite 205. You can take the stairs."

"Thank you. You look very pretty by the way." Ana Camillo taught me to compliment all women in situations like these.

"I love this dress," she gushed. "I can't wait for Ryan to see it."

"What's your name?" I asked.

She told me, and I made sure to text it to Ryan and Beau since they'd yet to arrive. They still weren't sure which Delta Gamma they asked, and hopefully this information would prevent them from embarrassing themselves.

I thought about hanging around to help out Owen if and when Caroline verbally attacked his girlfriend, but there were at least a hundred people here. Surely Caroline Scott would behave herself?

Greer was here, and I wanted to see her.

I KNOCKED ON SUITE 205. The door opened wide, and Aunt Isabel was on the other side.

"Nico!" she called. "Nico is here! Come in! Come in!"

"Are you sure, Aunt Isabel?" I asked. "I am a guy, and according to my sources, this is the ladies' dressing room."

"Greer's the only one left." She waved me inside. "You can help us dress her."

The door closed behind me, and I felt me entire body freeze. My face had to be red. Isabel said, "I've missed you Nico. Greer said the coaches are very strict. When the season is over, you must come back to the studio and visit. Or teach Greer to cook like you do."

"I miss you too, Aunt Isabel." And then I leaned down and hugged her, still afraid to walk deeper inside and encounter Greer in some state of undress.

"Come on," she said. "Greer will be happy to see you."

Since this was a suite, I walked down a very short hall into a sitting area with a small kitchen. The bedroom door was closed. Greer had to be on the other side of the door. Her portable wardrobe on wheels was in the center of the room, and she had her mirrors balanced against one wall. On the other side of the room was her camera on a tripod aimed at the white screen. A sewing machine sat on the desk.

Isabel, dressed in her Doc Martens, handed me a water bottle and told me to take a seat on the couch.

"How was it here today?" I asked.

"Busy," she answered. "The sorority girls looked beautiful. They really did. The hairdresser was a very nice young man. He was gay, Nico. He was very comfortable with all the girls running around in their bra tape and itsy-bitsy panties."

"Are you sure he wasn't just *pretending* to be gay?" I asked.

She laughed immediately. I forgot how easy it was to make this woman laugh. "I hadn't thought about that," she said. "Anyway," she lowered her voice, "Greer should be proud of herself. She only had four designs, yet every single one of those fifty-two dresses is a work of art. Not one of them looks like the other."

"You made them too."

"I can sew Nico," she said. "But I don't have Greer's eye." Isabel pointed to the bedroom door. "Her task was pink dresses for fifty-two sorority sisters. Most designers would have made all the girls look like bridesmaids. Instead, each one looks like a bride. I tell my brother all the time. I say, 'One day, the whole world will recognize the name Greer Scott.'"

I smiled at her. "How is Greer?"

"Melanie's helping her now," she said. "Lila told her she has to come downstairs and be recognized with all the other sponsors, and Greer said she wants to go home. She said she has nothing to wear." Aunt Isabel shook her head. "We fitted one of the samples. She looks gorgeous."

Just then, the bedroom door opened and Melanie followed by Greer walked into the room. Melanie saw me first and said hello. Then Greer realized I was here and stopped in her sexy strappy heels. I stood up the moment the door opened, just as I'd been raised to do. But I almost sat right back down because I felt like someone knocked the wind out of me.

Greer looked nothing like what I'd expected. Her dark hair was smoothed into a long glossy curtain. Her eyes were smoky and her plump lips were painted pink. Her dress was black, but the fabric was light and shimmery with the setting sun still filtering through the windows. I tried not to stare, but the neckline dipped between her full breasts, stopping somewhere above her navel. Greer didn't have a spray tan like the sorority girls. Instead, her skin was smooth and creamy, and I wanted to taste every single inch of it.

There was nothing teenager about her. She was all woman.

"What are you doing here?" she asked.

I cleared my throat and concentrated on looking into her eyes and not at her chest. "I heard you were here."

"Aren't you going to the formal?"

"Eventually," I said.

"Where's your date?"

"I'm looking at her." I smiled. "I hope."

"I told you I'm not going," she said. "I mean I have to go for a little while, but then I'm coming back here and cleaning up."

"That's cool," I said. "I'll help you."

Aunt Isabel started clapping. "Perfect! Melanie and I can *finally* go home."

"That sounds good, Aunt Izzy," said Melanie. "Sam and Beatrice are dying to see you again, Nico. Let's get a picture of the two of you before you go downstairs."

Greer, still stunned, walked with Melanie to the white screen. I followed and then took my place beside her. When she aimed the camera, I wrapped my arm around Greer's waist and smiled. Melanie took several trying to get Greer to smile. It was Aunt Isabel who broke Greer by telling her she looked constipated. Melanie then took a few with her cell phone. Before they left the suite, I made her text me the pictures.

When we were alone, Greer looked nervous. I walked over, held her hands and gazed into her eyes. "What's wrong?" I asked her. "I figured that if you have to go, and I have to go, we should go together. I won't try to kiss you again. Unless you want me to. I have a feeling your lipstick won't survive the experience."

Greer blushed. "It's not you exactly. I mean, it's you a little. We're...complicated. But every girl downstairs is dressed in pink. I don't have a pink dress. I feel like I'm disrespecting Lila by showing up in this. She's worked really hard on this, and I don't want her to think I'm insulting her."

"She'd never think that of you," I said. "But I think I can help."

"Did you bring a pink dress?" she deadpanned.

When it came to Greer, I did orchestrate scenarios in my mind on how I might bump into her on campus. They never worked, which is why I always walked her to her car after history of capitalism. But this moment wasn't planned. I just happened to see the pink diamond necklace on my dresser when I was tying my bowtie tonight. And I placed it in my pocket.

"Close your eyes and turn around," I said. "No peeking." I steered her over to one of the full-length mirrors she had propped against the suite wall, under a high-hat light. I gently moved her hair to the side. Her scent filled me, and I was tempted to bury my face into her neck and kiss her sensitive skin. Instead, I pulled out the necklace and fastened the clasp around her neck. Then I put her hair back in place and told her to open her eyes.

23

GREER

"Open your eyes," Nico said. His voice was almost hoarse, like he'd spent the day screaming on the sidelines at the homecoming game. My skin flushed at the sound.

I knew exactly what he clasped around my neck, and I was smiling before I even opened my eyes. The pink diamond necklace. Before I came to the hotel today, I'd assumed that I'd talk my way out of attending the formal in any capacity this evening. Then I felt guilty. Lila had worked so hard to make the event special, and she planned to acknowledge Scotty Designs along with the other major sponsors. The obligation was there to show my face tonight. But the only dresses we had were here accidentally. The original sample dresses Beatrice and Sam helped us make weeks ago, tucked in the portable wardrobe along with the heavy mirrors.

Of course, it didn't take long for Isabel to make one of them fit me. The fabric, while beautiful, was as far away from pink on the color spectrum as possible. It was as black as my hair. The ideal backdrop to Nico's gorgeous necklace. "It's perfect," I said. We smiled at each other in the mirror until I felt so self-conscious, my gaze fell to the floor, my skin flaming.

Nico stepped away so he was facing me. "Hey." He lifted my chin and his green eyes shined into mine. "You're perfect. And right now, I feel like the luckiest guy in the world."

"Thank you."

If he leaned down and kissed me, I wouldn't have pulled away. He was staring at me like he wanted to. Melanie had just put makeup on me, and maybe that was what made him hesitate. He said he was lucky, but I wasn't stupid. It was me who was the lucky one. Without him next to me, I would be a complete mess right now. Nico Camillo never bragged about his skills as a player because he didn't have to. He was the best. Even Aunt Isabel, a Filipino native here for a couple of weeks, figured that out immediately. He was more intelligent than anyone I'd met on campus, including the professors. And I imagined all twenty thousand women on campus, not just me, pictured him in their fantasies at night. Kindness was stamped on his beautiful face, and his body carried graceful power.

He was confidence personified.

And when he held my hand in his and we left the suite and took the elevator to the lobby, I didn't pull away. I'd let him be my rock tonight. I felt invincible at his side, like I could conquer the world. That all my dreams would come true. If this was the euphoria my mother felt dating Nicholas Camillo, no wonder everyone after him came in a distant second. Even my father.

I pushed those thoughts from my mind as we entered the lobby.

It was like God was testing me right away. Caroline glared at me from her spot at the bar and rushed over.

"*Why* are you here?" she asked.

My sister didn't come upstairs to the suite, so this was the first time I was seeing her. As usual, her hair and makeup were on point. The pink of her dress was bold rather than soft, and while it wasn't a hue I'd have chosen, it suited her perfectly. Caroline was a force to be reckoned with in all aspects of her life. Of course, she didn't want me, her little sister who she thought was a weirdo, around her tonight.

I opened my mouth to tell her about Lila's acknowledgement, but Nico spoke up. "Greer's *my* date."

"Ugh," she said. "You could have at least read the memo about breast cancer awareness. What is it with you and the color black?" She lowered her voice and leaned into my ear, "You are such a freak, Greer."

Before I could answer her, she turned and rushed away. I exhaled. Nico didn't say anything – our families were off-limit topics between us – but he squeezed my hand, a sign of support. I wasn't sure why I deserved him right now, but I squeezed his hand back to say thank you.

"Let's go find Lila and Dylan," Nico said. "If I know you as well as I think I do, you're going to worry about your black dress all night long."

I smiled. "Okay." And we cut through the crowd, Nico's head above mine searching for the couple. As we passed through, guys were calling out his name and some of the girls said hello to me or stopped to thank me again for their dresses. Not every woman in this room was wearing pink either. Some had pink shoes, or pink wraps, even pink sashes. I wasn't the only woman in black.

Out of the corner of my eye, I spotted Caroline's six hundred-dollar dress on a different girl. No wonder my sister was in such a bad mood. She did not like being upstaged, even if the other woman did not match her beauty.

"Over here, Nico!" Dylan boomed.

Nico pulled me towards the banquet room where all of the guests would soon be seated.

"You're sitting at our table," Dylan announced when we reached him. "Hello Greer. You look beautiful tonight. Lila could not be happier with the way this event has turned out, and you're a big reason why."

"We're a small part of this," I said, taking in the lobby and banquet room. "Lila's done an incredible job. She's amazing." The ceiling of the hall was covered in twinkling white lights, but with the pink floral arrangements and soft-pink linens, the entire room looked bathed in blush-colored warmth. It was quintessential Southern elegance and charm.

My face was still looking up when Lila arrived. "Hey girl." She bumped my hip with hers. "You ready to have a good time?"

"Lila! I hope you pinned everything. If someone hasn't already told you this, you could be a professional event planner. This room is enchanting."

"I had plenty of help," she said. "Come here!" She pulled me away from Nico. "I want to show you something." Lila took me to the long wall opposite the band. She'd converted it into a gallery of Delta Gamma photographs throughout the years. Lila's mother had also been in this sorority, like many of the other girls here tonight. With the exception of her bobbed hair, she looked like Lila and I told her that, which made Lila happy. In addition to photographs of formals throughout the years, she had photographs of the sorority's breast cancer victims and survivors. It was an inspiring tribute. What motivated her to do this was the memory of her own mother, yet she also honored as many mothers, daughters, and sisters as she could.

"I wasn't really planning to come here tonight," I admitted, "which is why I don't have a pink dress. But I'm really happy to be here for you, Lila. And I'm glad Scotty Designs could be a part of this event too. Thank you. Truly."

She hugged me. "I'm glad you're here. And I *know* Nico

Camillo is glad you're here with him. That boy is *in love* with you, Greer Scott."

I laughed. "Nico is not in love with me."

"Oh, he is." Her smiling face turned serious. "Trust me. You know you're the reason the whole team was put on curfew a few weeks ago?"

I looked at her, shocked. "What are you talking about?"

"Don't look so upset. Everyone was on Nico's side. He fought with Tripp in the locker room for talking about you." Lila put her arm around me. "Tripp is a pig. I'm glad someone had the courage to put him in his place. I feel bad for Nico though. Another incident and he's off the team."

"Nico didn't tell me any of this." I was horrified. Caroline was the one dating Tripp, which made me realize almost immediately that he was defending her as well.

"They're not allowed to badmouth teammates," she whispered. "Dylan told me in confidence."

"Does Caroline know about this?" I asked. "I mean, what exactly did Tripp say?"

"I'm sure Tripp didn't tell Caroline that he could score *all* of the Scott women," she said. "Deep down, Caroline knows Tripp's not a good guy, but she wants the fame and glory, Greer." She clasped my shoulder. "She always has. Let's get back to the guys. And don't worry about this anymore. I only told you so that you'd see what we see. When it comes to you, Nico wears his heart on his sleeve."

Right now, he did as his eyes found mine walking towards him. He was listening to Dylan but smiling at me. Rather than try to analyze why he liked me, or what motivated him to go after Tripp Saunders in the locker room, I decided to relax for the next hour or so. The suite upstairs needed to be packed up, and I'd eventually have to go home and make sure my mother was okay. Caroline would never pull herself away from this. For now, though, I could afford to enjoy being with Nico.

"Hey Lila," Dylan said when she reached him. "I asked the band to make the change. Was there anything else you needed before everyone sits down?"

"They're good with opening with Ed Sheeran?" she asked.

"They're happy to. And the photographer knows to get pictures of the dance floor."

Lila said to Nico and me, "I really want an aerial view of the dance floor while we still have some daylight coming through the windows. But I want a slow song, so we picked Ed Sheeran." She turned to me. "What girl doesn't love Ed Sheeran, right?"

My whole body tensed all of the sudden. After five years, I still could not listen to Ed Sheeran without remembering the day my father died and breaking down. I guess that made me a freak. I tried to take deep breaths, but they did nothing to slow down my beating heart. I knew that once the band struck the first few chords, I'd embarrass myself, and by extension Nico, if I didn't get the hell out of here.

The entrance to the banquet room was now inaccessible because happy hour was over and couples were pouring in. Nico must have felt my distress when he reached for my hand to walk to the table.

"You okay?" His head dipped down to stare into my eyes.

Do I tell him I'm about to lose control of my emotions? What would he think of me then? According to Lila, I was the reason the whole team was punished weeks ago. How would it appear if I ran away from him now?

Caroline and Tripp Saunders stopped.

"You're at *our* table," my sister announced, as though we were the lucky ones.

Tripp looked me up and down then stared at my chest, smiling at what he saw. He was such a creep. His hair was slicked back with some kind of product, and his brown eyes were dull, emitting no brightness or warmth. She pulled the two of them past us, and my eyes found Nico's again. I still hadn't answered his question.

I tightened my grip. "I'm okay," I said. And as we walked over to Lila's table in the center of the room, I wasn't sure I was okay. But there was something about the man holding my hand. He made me feel calm. And whole.

One thing the Delta Gammas said to me this afternoon, over and over, was how they felt like princesses on their way to a ball. I thought they were being dramatic. But now, I wanted what they did. Nico Camillo was a prince, and right now, I was his princess. For the next hour, I wanted a fairytale.

JUST AS WE all found our seats, the first notes of "Perfect" started on a guitar. Lila squealed and pulled Dylan onto the dance floor. Nico, of course, stood up and asked me to dance, and I placed my hand in his. My father died before this song became popular, and the singer's voice was nothing like Ed Sheeran's, though it was still smooth. The music from the band was even more dramatic than anything recorded, so I concentrated on exhaling through my nose as the song opened.

You can do this, I told myself.

The wooden floor was filling up when we stepped onto it and Nico walked us to a far corner, eager to get away from Tripp and Caroline who stopped front and center. Surely my sister knew where Lila's photographer would aim and wanted history to record her beside an NFL-bound quarterback. An unkind thought, but I was grateful for the distraction even if it lasted only a second. Because now I stood before Nico and he gazed into my eyes with such affection, emotion came to the surface.

He didn't notice right away because he smiled down at me. Then his powerful arm wrapped around my waist, his hand gently gripping my hip, and pulled my body flush with his. My right hand was entwined with his, and my left arm and hand were draped on his shoulder. We started to move to the slow and tender melody. My body was braced against his chest and abs, and his handsome face bend down to mine, our foreheads grazing.

I'd never danced like this before. But Nico knew how to hold me so that we were the only two people on the dance floor. His green eyes studied mine as we moved, and I saw sixteen-year-old Nico dressed in his royal-blue jersey, his face streaked with dirt and grease looking at me with concern. I felt tears wetting my cheeks, likely smearing Melanie's makeup, but I didn't look away from him. Instead, I tightened our grip, and with my hand on his shoulder, pulled him closer and fingered his hair.

The intensity of our eyes locked upon one another was like a cord about to snap. The violin joined the music, and Nico's lips touched mine, breaking the tension. Our kiss was brief but sweet. When he released me, I leaned my head onto Nico's shoulder and silently cried.

I cried for my father, and for me, my sister, and my mother as we were still so lost without him. But we were also getting better. My mother and myself, at least. And it was due in part to Nico Camillo being here at this school. Even though his parents hated the Scotts, Nico cared enough about me as a friend and partner.

When the song ended, neither one of us let go right away. I was afraid for him to see my face. But because he was a gentleman, and the tuxedo was from Flores', Nico pulled out a handkerchief from his pocket. I pulled my head away, shaking my head. "I'm sorry," I said. "Did I ruin your shirt?"

"If you did, you can return it to Aunt Isabel's brother."

I laughed, and then he gently wiped whatever smudged under my eyes and cheeks. "I think I got it all," he said quietly. "You sure you're okay?"

I was about to tell him what made me cry, that it wasn't him. But Caroline walked over to us. "Does Ed Sheeran still make you think of Daddy? You have to get a grip, Greer." She grabbed my hand and started to pull me away. "Excuse us, Nico."

When we were off the dance floor and headed for the exit, I stopped. "What is it, Caroline?"

"You need to leave."

"Why?" Suddenly I had no interest in leaving or even being acknowledged by Lila. I only wanted to dance with Nico for the next four hours.

"Because I need your dress. And your necklace."

She would notice the necklace because I was already back to rubbing it between my fingers. I missed touching this stone of Nico's. "I don't understand."

She lowered her voice but was shaking with anger. "That bitch here with fucking Owen Ross is wearing the same exact dress," she yelled at me. "If you weren't so wrapped up in your own little world all the time, you'd have made me a pink dress like every other Delta Gamma here!"

"Caroline," I said slowly. "You know I couldn't do that. Besides, you hate Scotty dresses."

"Well, I changed my mind."

"You're being ridiculous," I said. "Everyone has already seen you and me. No one really cares that you're in the same dress as someone else. Most people are already bombed."

"You don't even belong here," my sister hissed. "You're not a Delta Gamma. As soon as Lila acknowledges sponsors, you need to leave. And, remember this, Greer." My sister's face met mine. "I will never help you again. Scotty Designs can crash and burn for all I care."

And then my sister walked away, back to the table where I was expected to sit.

Nico was standing at the edge of the dance floor, having given my sister and me distance to argue. I walked towards him.

"Everything good?" he asked.

"Yeah."

Nico was so perceptive that he had to know I was lying. Caroline was screaming at me in front of the entire room. Yet I was still too proud to admit to him that she'd affected me. We walked back to our table, where Caroline was now seated, glaring at me. The only good news was that she and Tripp were about as far from Nico and me as possible. Nico was on one side of me and Lila was on the other. The wait staff was serving salads when Lila walked back onto the dance floor.

For the first time, I noticed two tables full of sponsors and donors, older adults and their spouses, directly in front of the dance floor. That was where my silent partner and I would have sat if we interacted. We'd agreed to donate twenty percent of our proceeds to Lila's cause. In exchange, we were posting pictures of the sorority sisters in their dresses on our website and social media accounts. It was a great deal for us.

My partner thought of it. She or he was convinced that high-end couture was the future of Scotty Designs, not cotton-polyester game day dresses or Isabel's food transport totes. The gorgeous women of Butler's Delta Gamma were ideal spokespersons of such fashion, according to my partner. I wasn't convinced, but these were arguments we made through a third party that went unresolved.

Lila performed beautifully. She spoke from her heart, acknowledging how personal this fundraiser was to her and all the girls who'd lost loved ones to breast cancer. When each of the sponsors was called, we were asked to stand. I was the only outlier sitting with the sorority girls, but I received applause not only for our donation, but for all the Delta Gammas dressed so happily in pink.

Nico and Dylan whistled at me, which should have made me feel special. Instead, my eyes fell to Caroline who was still giving me the evil eye. Tripp looked about as miserable as she did.

When Lila returned to the table, Dylan was the first to praise her speech. I thanked her after he did since her praise of Scotty was especially kind and generous.

"Thank you, Greer." She lowered her voice. "When I saw that Scotty was donating over five thousand dollars, I was shocked."

"But that's not right," I said just as quietly. "We're donating twenty percent of proceeds."

"Exactly."

I knew this wasn't the time or place for this discussion, but since I'd just received the email from my partner this morning about the check for thirty-one hundred dollars cut for Delta Gamma, I had to clear the air. "My math must not be what it used to be," I joked. "The dresses were three hundred each."

"That's what you quoted us. But then Caroline collected the two hundred-dollar cash deposit for each dress, remember?" She flashed me a smile that said she was finished discussing this here. "Don't worry, Greer. We all *love* our dresses. Scotty gave us a deal, and according to Caroline, these will sell for double online."

The room spun. My face blanched. I felt like I'd just been tackled, repeatedly, by every football player in this enchanted room. I stood up. Nothing could make me glance over at Caroline right now. "The check's not right then, Lila," I whispered. "I'm going to go take care of it now."

She started protesting, and then Nico asked what was going on, but I ignored both of them. I had to keep moving forward.

My fairytale lasted for one song. One song! Far shorter than the hour I'd been hoping for.

This was like the September day five years ago. When my father's aneurysm caused him to fall, shattering my first sewing machine. This time, my sister's lies and twisted maneuvers were as deadly as lighter fluid and a match. Her wish came true tonight. Scotty Designs had effectively crashed and burned, exactly as she'd wanted.

I'd lied to Lila. My math was pretty fucking good. Caroline pocketed over ten grand in cash from her sorority sisters. The expensive clothes and shoes. The weekend trips away. The designer dress from Nordstrom. All the nonsensical pieces fell into place to explain how my jobless sister was living in luxury.

Not only did we owe Lila the funds she was expecting, I'd have to return all the money Caroline stole. And the worst part, the most damning part for me: This was a total breach of my silent partnership. I didn't need a business degree in the entrepreneurship program to realize this.

There was no recovering from this.

And Nico Camillo was here to witness our family's collapse once again.

24

NICO

Caroline jumped from her seat when I stood up to follow Greer. She stopped me before the dance floor. "Don't chase her, Nico." She held the sleeve of my tuxedo. "My sister's crazy. She's like my mother."

I glanced at where her hand was holding onto my jacket and then into her eyes. She'd been drinking, but she didn't seem drunk or even buzzed. Instead, she looked terrified. Tripp was watching us quietly. Something was up with the two of them. I didn't trust either one of them, and I sure as hell knew Greer wasn't crazy.

"You can let me go now, Caroline," I said quietly. "I want to make sure your *sister* is okay."

"She's *fine*." Caroline lowered her voice. "She's just immature. Greer can't handle college life. Knowing her, she'll run home and sew all night long. She was sobbing when she was dancing with you."

I'd overheard the words "Caroline" and "cash" in the same sentence uttered by Lila right before Greer's face went from rosy pink to ghostly pale. Then she rushed out in complete shock. There was a reason Caroline didn't want me to find Greer. I glanced over to Tripp, who was studying Caroline and me, a smirk on his face. I had to extricate myself from this situation without calling any more attention to myself, the Scotts, and Tripp.

"I'll be back, Caroline," I said in as kind a voice as I could muster. "You're probably right. Greer didn't want to stay very long. But she is my date, so I need to at least make sure she gets off okay."

She didn't respond and she was still clutching my arm.

"Would you like to come with me?" I asked her. "Or do you want to return to Tripp?"

She flinched. Neither option appealed to her. For the first time, I asked myself if even Caroline Scott, one of the most toxic individuals in this town, realized that Tripp Saunders was a real-life bogeyman. But she let go and I walked away. My heart was pounding with worry, but I kept my stride natural and smiled to my teammates as though nothing was amiss.

When I emerged from the banquet room, I saw Greer leave the registration desk and hurry to the elevator. She carried a key card in her hand. Her original key to suite 205 was tucked in my front pocket. The doors closed before I reached her, so I took the stairs. As fate would have it, we met outside the suite door.

Greer's eyes were dull. They emitted total and complete defeat. "Nico," she said. "You don't want to be here with me right now, okay? Trust me when I say that you should go back to the dance and be with your friends. I *have* to be alone right now."

I let her finish and took a deep breath. My words to her were careful. "You know I can't do that," I said. "Let me help you pack up and load your van."

"Do you remember the day my dad died?" she asked.

"Of course, I do. I remember everything, Greer. Including your dad's T-shirt. I know why you were crying tonight." It clicked when Caroline made fun of Greer on the dance floor. Jack Scott was wearing a shirt with math symbols. It was similar to the one Dylan was wearing on the day he took Lila to the Ed Sheeran concert, and we gave him a hard time.

"This is worse," she said. "Please just go."

"No."

She exhaled. "I'm not going to cry. I'm too angry right now. But I don't want to fight with you, Nico. If you care about me, at all, please leave me alone."

I waved the key card in my hand and unlocked the suite, opening the door for her. She walked inside reluctantly, and then rushed into the bedroom, closing the door behind her and locking it. If she wasn't out within a few minutes, I would call security.

There was nothing for me to do but pack up. It helped settle my nerves. The mirrors were packed into her wardrobe, along with the white screen and camera. I walked over to the sewing machine on the desk. The white outer shell had yellowed. I ran my fingers along the lettering "Singer Quantum Stylist 9960." I shook my head, realizing that this was the machine my parents bought that day Jack Scott died.

When we'd learned it was Greer's birthday and they'd been picking up her gift, my parents said they had to do something. I went back with them to the fabric store. They purchased the same machine and insisted that the owner deliver it right away. The owner agreed and promised to keep the Camillo family out of it. My takeaway from that day was how cool it was to be generous like them. How I wanted to be magnanimous one day, a Robin Hood, someone who had the power to give.

I never really thought about what that gift meant to Greer. Until now. This machine most likely saved her that day. It sure as hell saved her family. I packed it carefully in the hard-shell case on the desk and placed it next to the wardrobe. Next, I collected the plastic cups and plates scattered around the place and threw them in the trash. There was nothing else to do but wait for Greer.

I stood in front of the bedroom door and knocked. "Answer me or I'm calling security."

She opened the door. Her black dress was tossed on the bed, crumpled. She walked back into the bathroom and I followed her. She wore ripped jeans, a Scotty tank, and her boots. She hadn't taken off her necklace. Yet. Her hair was in a ponytail and she was scrubbing her face with a wet washcloth.

"Melanie did my makeup tonight," she said. "It's not coming off easily. I'm not going to hurt myself if that's what you're afraid of."

I released the breath I hadn't realized I was holding. "Are you going to tell me what happened?"

"I don't want to, but I can't keep this a secret either."

"You can trust me, Greer. I'm on your side."

She shrugged. "Why did you leave Michigan?"

"My teammates and coaches were taking money," I said. "Then they made sure we lost certain games. They broke the NCAA rules, Greer. But I didn't do that. In fact, I proved that no one even offered me a bribe."

"But you were guilty by association, right?"

"Yes." I sighed. "It was terrible. It still is sometimes. There will always be a dark cloud over my name because of it."

"How do you handle it?" she asked.

I wasn't sure why she was bringing this up now, but I'd share anything with her if it kept her talking. "I knew I wasn't guilty," I said. "People are going to believe what they want to, Greer. Early on, I decided I wasn't going to hide anything from anyone. I proved how I paid my bills, including my car, and I never apologized. I still refuse to do that." I stepped towards her. "The people who mattered most to me believed me," I said, "and that helped keep me sane. They still do."

Rinsing her face and patting it dry with a clean towel, she glanced at me in the mirror and gave me a tight smile. "Thanks."

"Are you going to tell me what's going on?"

"Scotty Designs charged the Delta Gammas three hundred dollars each for the dresses. My partner and I agree to give back twenty percent of the proceeds, so roughly three thousand dollars." Her voice was even, the words matter-of-fact, emotionless. "Unbeknownst to me, Caroline had each of the girls give her two hundred dollars apiece extra, in cash, as some sort of deposit we never agreed to." She shook her head. "She's collected over ten thousand dollars from them, and I'm sure she's spent most of it."

"Jesus, Greer." No wonder Caroline looked terrified when Greer walked out. She realized what Lila had just revealed.

"Lila's expecting five thousand dollars for our donation, which shouldn't be a problem. But I have no way of returning ten thousand dollars to all the girls right now."

"We need to find your sister," I said. "Now. It's not too late to fix this."

"Believe it or not, she's not my biggest problem."

My face must have showed my confusion.

"It's Scotty Designs." Her eyes met mine. "This is a clear breach of our agreement. My silent partner owns the majority of the business. I'm finished, Nico."

My mind was spinning. Caroline was one issue, but her partnership wasn't equal? I was already convinced the guy was ripping her off. "You need an attorney." I pulled out my phone. "And the police."

Her hand covered my phone. "You don't understand Nico," she said. "I won't fight my partner for anything. Whoever that person is deserves the business. They have saved me and my family so many times, I've lost track."

"You can't let Caroline get away with this."

"What if she spent all the money?" she said. "Then what do I do?"

Have her arrested, I wanted to shout at Greer.

"What would you do if this were your brother?" she asked.

My brother would never have stolen from me, but telling this to Greer wouldn't help. She proved her point when I didn't have an answer for her.

"I'm not afraid of Caroline," she said. "She has to get a job someplace far away from here. I'm not sure what this will do to my mother."

"Your mother has to have your back on this." I thought about Caroline and Sophia at the season opener, looking like twins. Surely her mom wouldn't take Caroline's side?

Greer's eyes were not just dull, they were tired. She'd had a long day and now faced a sleepless night. "My mom will not understand how depraved my sister is." She shrugged. "Does that make sense?"

"No. Your sister stole ten thousand dollars," I said. "Cash. What's so hard to understand about that?"

"My mom's not rational." Greer started to pack up her Scotty backpack on the vanity. "She's been showing signs of progress. She likes her psychiatrist. She's dating again for the first time since my father died. And she's made a friend in Coach Evans." Greer buttoned her backpack and walked into the bedroom. She grabbed her dress and shoes off the bed. I followed her into the other room and watched her stuff them into one of the garment bags on the wardrobe. "But Caroline is her partner in crime. If she leaves town, my mom and I will be fine. If she stays, my sister's behavior will probably get worse." She exhaled.

"Maybe the best thing is for my mother and me to move. Start over someplace else."

I stalked over to her side. "That won't solve anything."

"It worked for you," she said. "You left Michigan."

I wrapped my arms around her waist and pulled her to me, like I'd done on the dance floor earlier. "Greer," I started. "I can't be the only one who's feeling this connection between us." My forehead leaned on hers, and we started turning slowly in a circle as though we were dancing. "I want to be with you. All the time. Let me help you. Move in with me if Caroline won't leave."

She gave me a half smile. "You know I can't do that," she said. "But I do feel something for you, Nico, which is why we have to end this."

I stared at her, confused. "Huh?"

"Your mind works much faster than mine." She smiled. "But you don't want to be associated with me when the whole town finds out Scotty Designs committed fraud against the Delta Gammas."

"Greer—"

"Lila told me about what happened with Tripp in the locker room," she said firmly. "You don't get another chance."

"That has nothing to do with helping you."

"You are better off staying away from me," she said. "Depending on how this blows up, I'm now linked to Tripp, to Coach Evans, and to you. You must see how dangerous it is for you to be associated with me."

Greer was making sense, and right now, I didn't want to listen to reason. So I pulled her closer to me so that I could feel her. Her breasts were full and soft against my chest. Her hair smelled divine, and I leaned her head against my shoulder so that I could inhale her sweet scent. Her toned waist and hips fit nicely into my large hands.

I could start kissing her. Greer would respond. I'd carry her into the bedroom, taste her lips and mouth again, and trace her creamy skin with my tongue. My palms wanted desperately to test the weight of her breasts. Getting lost in her was what my body needed so desperately. Though she wasn't ready for sex with me yet, I could give her release. Something to take her mind and body to a new level, where she could forget about all of her troubles for one night.

Once I really showed her how much I cared for her, cherished her, she'd crave the intimacy. There was not a doubt in my mind how great we'd be together. Her body started to shake. I released her to make sure she wasn't crying. But she was laughing.

"What is it?" I asked her.

"I just remembered the restraining order your parents filed against my mother." She looked up at me. "It's kind of funny. There are so many reasons why we can't be together. It's like the universe is against us."

Since my mind had been more favorably engaged, the different ways I was going to make this woman scream my name in bed, I didn't laugh with her.

She let go of me and glanced around the room. She thanked me for packing up all of her stuff, but wanted to load everything in her van in the garage and go home.

On the elevator, I asked her how she brought everything to the suite without help. She made multiple trips. "I'm used to doing this on my own, Nico," she said. "It's no big deal."

I loved this girl's independence, but I needed to break it too. She didn't trust me. Sure, she liked me and enjoyed our dance tonight. But she wasn't ready to give herself to me yet. And with all she had going on now with Caroline and her mother, and her partner, I wasn't sure when she'd get there. Normally, I'd turn to my parents. They were experienced businesspeople. They'd know what to do in this circumstance. But since it was Greer

Scott, Sophia's daughter, would they be willing to help me help her? Or was it up to me to be magnanimous on my own?

Greer let me hug her goodbye this time when I opened the driver's side door for her. In her mind, this was the last time I'd be holding the door open for her. In my mind, I was never again letting her leave me without at least a hug. When I asked her if she'd be okay, she shrugged. Her brain was already trying to work out how she was going to fix the mess Caroline got her in. The one thing she did let me do for her that night was return the keys to the registration desk and check out.

I watched her pull away, then went back upstairs to the lobby and did as Greer asked. It was hard to believe that I'd been gone less than an hour. Dinner had apparently ended, so there were some Delta Gammas and guys from the team hanging out in the bar area. Caroline Scott was one of them. She came running over to me when she noticed me.

"Where's my sister?"

"She went home," I responded. "I told you she didn't want to stay long."

Caroline nodded. My eyes bored into hers, communicating to her that I knew every shitty thing she'd done to Greer and the girls wearing her sister's dresses in this hotel.

"Did she leave anything for me?"

I shook my head.

Tripp walked out of the banquet room and stood next to Caroline. He nodded to me, then turned to Caroline, "What's up?"

"Nothing," she said. "Greer didn't give me her dress *or* her necklace. I can't go back in there looking exactly like the *backup* QB's date. Greer is such a bitch!"

"You don't mean that Caroline," I spoke up. Greer wouldn't want me engaging with her sister like this, but there was only so much venom spewing from this wicked woman's mouth that I could take.

"Yes, I do!" she shouted.

"I'm going to head back in there," Tripp said to Caroline. "I'll catch you afterwards. Unless you're going to leave now?"

Before Caroline responded to her date, I left the two of them and exited the hotel. If I was betting, I'd put money on the two of them ending their relationship tonight. Caroline's manipulations were no longer working on him. That was as clear as day in the dimly lit lobby.

Greer and I had Caroline's number, and Lila was pretty close to figuring out her deceit. Soon everyone would know what a terrible person she really was. Right now, she was like a wild animal boxed in. There was no telling when she'd attack.

The clear night was as pleasant as the day had been. The air was cool but a welcome relief from a hot September. So much had happened since I walked here with Dylan that I'd almost forgotten how beautiful Greer looked in her black dress. Caroline didn't just want the dress because she wasn't unique tonight, she wanted to steal her sister's beauty away from her.

As I passed by outdoor cafes and restaurants, wishing that my girl was still by my side, I thought of one person who might be able to help us. Knowing Greer, the neurons in her brain were firing like mad trying to get herself and her business out of the situation Caroline dragged them into. She didn't want my help. She wanted me out of her business. But I think I figured out a way in.

GREER

Sleep would be elusive the night of the formal, I thought to myself on the short drive home. Inside, my body hummed with emotions. Anger and sadness at Caroline, but also delicious electricity when I remembered Nico's touch. On the dance floor and again in the suite, Nico's body told me exactly how much he wanted me. My body wanted him too. If he'd made a move tonight, I wouldn't have stopped him. Nor would I have regretted it. That was how safe he made me feel.

But it was for the best we never crossed that line.

When I arrived home, Nancy was on the porch with a cup of tea. I sat with her, chitchatting about the weather and the highlights of the homecoming game, until my mother and Mark arrived. When my mother asked me how the formal was, and how Caroline looked in her expensive dress, I lied and said everything turned out well.

Mark was a man in love. Even though my mother wasn't going to the homecoming formal, she wore her pink backless halter top and black palazzo pants that Isabel and I made for her to be there in spirit. And for breast cancer awareness. Her long hair was draped across one shoulder. She giggled and smiled at everything he said to her, and it became obvious they didn't need an audience.

When Nancy said goodnight, I also left them. They both looked like they wanted privacy. Would Mark still be here in the morning?

It was an event I'd been preparing myself for. Caroline wouldn't be home tonight. Before I went upstairs, I told my mom that I had to leave first thing in the morning. "I'll be gone most of the day," I added.

"Don't work too hard, Greer," she said.

"Goodnight," added Mark.

I showered and put on cozy pajamas. Then I pulled out my computer. The only way I'd sleep tonight was if I told my partner what was going on. So I sent an email to our third party, with the subject line, "Emergency – Please Respond."

Please deliver this to my partner:

We have a situation. At the formal tonight, when we were being acknowledged for our donation and the dresses, the head of the sorority informed me that my sister collected $200 cash from each of the Delta Gammas, on top of what we charged, as a bogus deposit. This means we owe $10,400, cash, back to the sorority. Since they don't know the deposits are bogus yet, they are expecting a $5,200 donation, not the check for $3,120 you cut today.

My sister must have convinced her sorority sisters that she was representing Scotty. I didn't know she was doing this. She hates our products.

I know this is fraud and therefore a breach of our agreement, and I take full responsibility. But I think it would be helpful to meet in person and sort this out.

I don't know what my future here is now.

> *I'm devastated, and so sorry that you are involved in this mess because of our partnership.*
>
> *Greer*
>
> *P.S. The girls looked beautiful and were happy with their dresses.*

Because it was late on Saturday night, and I was impatient, I texted the emergency cell phone number of our third party and said there was an important email that had to be delivered. The news was devastating, but it felt better to share it than conceal it. Even telling Nico, the one person who needed to be kept out of it, lessened the weight piled on my chest when Lila revealed what Caroline had done.

I'd told Nico that this was worse than my father's death. On the surface, I knew that wasn't true. Caroline and my mother were very much alive thankfully. But our family was destroyed. I never wanted to speak with my sister again. My father would not support this decision, but for the first time, I didn't feel guilty about it. She had to leave, or my mother and I would go. But I would no longer be Caroline's enabler.

Before I came upstairs, I took ibuprofen p.m. that my mother sometimes used to sleep. My mind and body soon felt blissfully sleepy. As I was about to sign out of my email, a new one appeared. From Nico.

> *Dear Dr. Simmons,*
>
> *I know you are planning to assign partners a Georgia company to study for the final project of the semester. Greer and I request to start this immediately. Football comes first now that we've passed midseason, and I want to do my fair share. The team's on campus for the next ten days.*
>
> *We also have a second request. Can Greer and I study Scotty Designs, the small business that she runs but is also a*

minority owner of? The majority owner has been silent since it formed three years ago. It is my belief that this will provide the class with intrigue and suspense found in the best history lessons as well as insight on how a young company succeeds. Greer Scott is modest but she's a hell of a businesswoman.

I've copied Greer and my athletic advisor on this email.

Thank you for considering this,

Nico Camillo

Was he crazy? Yes, he definitely was. He knew how volatile Scotty's situation was now, and he went there? And, yuck, his athletic advisor was Coach Phillips, one of the creepiest people on campus. The good news was that I'd read the list of Georgia companies spotlighted in the past for history of capitalism. Home Depot, UPS, Coca-Cola, and Delta were on the short list. There was no way Professor Hawk would let us focus on Scotty. We were too new and small, and there was nothing *historic* about us. My reply was just to him:

Are you high?

Then I signed out for good and climbed into bed. Caroline didn't scare me, but I'd locked my bedroom door in case she happened to come home before I left in the morning. My plan for her was not formulated. How would I kick her out of the house? Change the locks? My mother wouldn't be able to handle that. Somehow, I had to entice her to leave. For good.

My alarm went off at five-thirty. Almost seven hours of sleep, which was incredible considering I didn't think I'd ever sleep again after the formal. I stepped into the shower, to wake up and clear my foggy brain. The ibuprofen was almost too effective. Caroline was sound asleep in her bold pink dress when I passed by on my way back from the bathroom. This could mean only one thing. She and Tripp had broken up. There was no other explanation for her being in her own bed after a night she'd been anticipating for months.

I dressed and packed my bag. My room faced the front of the house, and I spotted Mark's car still parked outside. So I braced myself as I tiptoed down the stairs, grabbed the van keys, and left the house without even stepping into the kitchen to eat or drink. Though my stomach was empty, I wouldn't risk passing by my mother's first floor bedroom and seeing Mark in bed with her. *Let Caroline deal with that*, I told myself. *Maybe that would get her to leave.*

The roads were empty on my way to the studio. I'd texted Emma, Blake, and Liam last night to tell them I'd be missing study group this morning. Spending the day in the studio was what my brain needed. Since all of us were at the hotel yesterday for the formal, no website orders were processed. I'd spend today, by myself, catching up on orders, sewing products for inventory, and waiting to hear back from my partner on what my future held.

But the studio parking lot was not empty. Nico's shiny black SUV was already parked, with him inside, smiling at me when I pulled next to him. Like me, his hair was damp.

"What are you doing here?" I asked when we both stepped out of our cars.

"Didn't you read your email this morning?" he said. "Professor Hawk loved my idea. She gave us the green light."

"What happens when Caroline's theft is revealed?" I asked.

"Think about Michigan," he said. "It would have been worse for me if I didn't come clean right away. By spotlighting Scotty Designs, laying everything bare, the truth will emerge. And the truth is that you had nothing to do with your sister's bad choices."

We lifted the wardrobe from the van. When Nico reached for the Singer case, I stopped him. "That machine can stay in the car," I said. "I brought it to the hotel yesterday because it can do anything. But it stays at home."

"If it can do *anything*, why not keep it here?" he asked.

"It's not a commercial sewing machine," I explained. "It's a great home sewing machine, and I still use it all the time. But it's mostly to work on new ideas." I looked into his green eyes. "I keep it in my bedroom at home."

We closed up the van, and then he stopped at the passenger's side of his car. He pulled out coffee and bagels, and my mouth watered. "Oh my gosh, I'm starving!" I said. "How did you know?"

"I didn't," he said. "These are for me and Aunt Isabel."

I started laughing. "Since she and Melanie don't work on Sundays, I guess it's my lucky day."

"You mean we have the studio to ourselves?" His voice was low and sultry as he stepped into my personal space. He leaned down and kissed me on the lips as if it was the most natural act in the world. "Lucky day indeed."

My insides felt like a busy butterfly bush all of the sudden. Nico's eyes found mine, and neither one of us moved. Finally, he asked, "Do I make you nervous, Greer?"

"No." My answer was immediate.

"Good." He smiled at me.

We wheeled everything into the studio. While I put yesterday's items back where they belonged, Nico spread out breakfast on the table. He had brought enough food for the Floreses, but he promised not to let anything go to waste. "The Tech game is this weekend," he said. "I'll need all the calories I can get."

"Do you think it will be like the Louisiana game?" I asked once I joined him at the table.

"I think it will be tougher," he admitted. "Their defense is better than ours. The offense has to be perfect, and that includes Tripp. So let's hope he keeps his promises and stays dry for the rest of the season."

"My sister came home last night," I shared.

Nico's face immediately hardened.

"I didn't hear her come in, and she was asleep when I left. But I thought that was odd. Do you think they broke up?"

"Maybe." His face relaxed. "It's the best thing really – for both of them."

"I agree."

While we ate bagels and cream cheese, I opened my email and read through Professor Simmons' reply, giggling. She must not have a social life since she answered Nico's email within an hour. She said that his idea was excellent and that we should get started right away. Then she attached the project's requirements and samples of her favorite culminating projects over the years. Coach Phillips also emailed last night, after Professor Simmons, congratulating both Nico and me on being such exemplary students and leaders on campus.

To me, Phillips' email seemed disingenuous. Nico, on the other hand, was pleased with his support. Nico was smart and read people well. Was I wrong about Coach Phillips?

We were reviewing the project's guidelines when a new email sounded on my computer. I must have gasped because Nico asked me what was wrong.

"My partner replied," I said.

"Do you want some privacy?" he asked.

"No," I said. "I'm glad you're here." When he walked over and leaned over my shoulder, I clicked it open:

Greer,

 Sell the Mini. It's in your name and should cover what's

owed back to the sorority. The Ruxton dealership on Davidson Boulevard specializes in used imports and is expecting you. Ask for Mike.

Jill Suter, an attorney in town, can see you at three this afternoon. She will represent you when you meet with the sorority leadership, explain what happened, and return the money. Taking care of this immediately, today or tomorrow at the latest, is advisable.

I can't help you with your sister. All I can do is wish you luck. But is this a picture of her? It seems to me that she does like Scotty products.

We don't know what the fallout from this will be. It goes without saying that I'll be with you until the end. If your sister's actions ruin us, then you rebuild. Don't lose hope yet.

P.S. Of course the dresses were a success. You made them. They photographed well on social media too.

I clicked on the attachment and found a screen shot of Caroline wearing the first game day dress Isabel and I made before the Carolina game. I didn't recognize the account, but it had to belong to one of the Delta Gammas standing by her side, in the lobby of a hotel. She stole the dress from my room and lied about it.

My exhale was audible, and I felt tears threatening. But I swallowed them because Nico was above me. He touched my shoulder and whispered in my ear, "If it makes you feel better, it doesn't look *delightful* on her."

I shook my head.

"You have to move on, Gree. Ruxton is where I took my car for an oil change. They're great. I'll go with you."

"Now do you understand why I *love* my partner?" I asked.

"He's got your back," he admitted. "And I like this plan. It's good advice, and you should follow it."

I nodded. "I think he's a she."

"Maybe. But this email doesn't change what we're doing for history of capitalism," he said. "Studying Scotty Designs will benefit you the most. Maybe your partner will consent to an interview?"

I laughed. "My partner values privacy. I doubt they'll agree to an interview."

"There's no harm in asking," he said.

Because we still had a couple of hours before the dealership opened, Nico and I spent the morning reviewing Professor Simmons' list of requirements. The project was a short documentary on a company. Origins, mission, how it started, and how it grew. We needed primary sources so much of my homework now involved going through old photographs and bins at home to find original Scotty products. These, I'm sure, would provide hours of entertainment for our documentary. Fourteen-year-old Greer's phone cases were vastly different from the products now offered online.

Nico wanted all the financial information I had. He was suspicious of my silent partner, and I was getting slightly frustrated with him. So I gave him access to everything our third party ever sent to me. I also provided him with the spreadsheets generated directly from the website orders.

Basically, the orders came in. Scotty Designs completed them and shipped them. My partner handled all the money. The supplies, like fabrics, threads, and notions, were ordered by me and paid for by my partner. I'd never had, nor had I ever wanted, access to company funds. As an owner, my name was on the accounts. But because of my mother and sister, I could never risk them gaining access. A wise decision in light of my sister's recent theft.

The financial piece was never easy, especially when I was

still a minor. But my partner set up an account at a local bank in my name, and my mother's, and that was where my salary went.

"But you've grown so much since this was all set up," Nico said. "And your salary has stayed the same. All I'm saying is that you could be living better. You could have a new car."

I shook my head. "I love my van."

"Fine," he said. "But you should have an idea of where the money goes. Fair enough?"

"My partner has never hidden anything from me," I said. "I'm glad you're looking at this. Maybe you'll see how fortunate my family and I have been since my fairy partner appeared."

Nico's phone rang and he answered. I couldn't hear what was said on the other line, but his face turned even more serious than when he was talking about Scotty finances. When he hung up, he said he had a mandatory team meeting at the stadium in one hour.

"Is that unusual?" I asked.

"Very," he said. "I wonder if anything happened last night." He called Dylan who had received the same call Nico had, but didn't have a clue about why. In fact, he was still at the hotel with Lila. According to them, the formal went well. No incidents whatsoever.

"That's even more unusual," said Nico. "Dylan *always* has the scoop." He looked around the studio. "Well, I'm going to assume the worst. And that's mandatory curfew for the rest of the season. So how about you print out everything you can think of for me to take a look at from that computer," he pointed to the desktop where Melanie, Isabel or I printed out the orders each day, "and I'll forward everything from your laptop to my email. Does that sound okay?"

"I told you it was," I said. "But what will happen if you have mandatory curfew."

"It means I'm on house arrest and you will *have* to come to my apartment now." He winked.

I blushed.

He left me shortly afterwards, bothered that he couldn't go with me to the dealership. And depending on what happened, he wasn't sure he'd make it to the meeting with the attorney later.

"I'm fine on my own," I assured him. "It's for the best that you're not involved, Nico."

"Don't say that." And then he pulled me towards him and hugged me tightly. When he released me, he leaned in and kissed me.

It wasn't just a peck either, but a firm lingering kiss. When we separated, his face was as enflamed as mine felt.

His behavior was so strange. Was he just being friendly or testing the waters? I didn't know what to make of him as I watched him walk out the studio door.

NICO

*G*reer had a plan for returning the sorority's money. But I still felt uneasy leaving her to execute it on her own. I also didn't like the phone call I'd just received. Something huge happened for us to all be brought in. When the Michigan College scandal broke, there was no mandatory team meeting because so many of the coaches and players were complicit. I'd learned about our disgrace from the media. So perhaps this wasn't as bad as that considering the team and coaching staff were intact.

Maybe the fact that I was already on probation had me worried.

I was one of the first players to arrive for the meeting. Coaches Phillips and Hampton were already here too. Their faces were grim. When I saw them, my guess was that someone had died last night. But that news would have reached us by now. Maybe something happened with one of the alumni from yesterday's game?

We were told to sit in front of our lockers. That was it. So little by little the team trickled in. Some guys were still in their tuxes from the formal the night before. Dylan arrived right before the meeting started. As far as I could tell, the only person we were waiting for was Tripp Saunders. But the doors closed before he arrived. Everyone was instructed to turn over their phones. No one was to record what was said within these walls.

Coach Hampton spoke first. "Gentlemen. Thank you for being here. I know many of you value your one day off each week, so I appreciate you coming here so quickly." As he spoke, he looked into each one of our faces. "The news is about to break that Tripp Saunders has been suspended indefinitely from the school as well as the football team."

The entire room gasped or cursed. My mind reeled. What the hell could have happened? Greer said Caroline went home last night. Their breakup was imminent, but Tripp seemed calm and sober. Resigned almost. Very unlike his typical brash, cocky self.

"What happened?" someone shouted from back of the room.

"You're going to find out, so I don't mind you hearing this from me," the head coach continued. "There was a credible threat of sexual assault by Tripp last night. The police were called. Fortunately, no one was hurt. That's all I'm going to say right now. As a team, we need to move on. Immediately."

"Goddamn!" said Dylan. He slammed his locker door. I wasn't sure what exactly he was reacting to. That Tripp was a misogynist. Or that the season was in effect over. Tripp wasn't a great player without the offensive line firing on all cylinders. But he was more experienced than Owen Ross, and had a better arm. Owen was faster but lacked confidence. We'd be slaughtered this Saturday, and the SEC Championship was no longer "our" game.

At least Greer wasn't his victim. Tripp thought I didn't see him staring at her chest last night, but I sure as hell did. Tripp probably leered at every guy's date last night, come to think of it. That he was finished with Caroline Scott was obvious.

"What's important right now," Coach Phillips raised his voice to quiet the rumbling, "is that we remember there's a victim in all of this. We're worried about the season, and we'll address that later. But there is a victim who's facing a mental battle much tougher than ours. Dylan, I know you're already praying for her, and for your old teammate who made a bad choice last night. I want all of you to do the same. Coach Hampton started off this meeting by addressing you as 'gentlemen.' Don't any of you lose sight of what's important. We are gentlemen first before all else."

For the rest of the meeting, the focus was not on football but our emotional health. Did we need to talk to someone? Help was outside the door. Naturally, the biggest issue for the team was how each one of us was going to handle the press. All the coaches had to do was lift the Ziploc bags that held our cellphones. They looked like Christmas lights blinking and sounding off. The news broke about Tripp, and those closest to us were trying to reach out for the inside scoop.

My parents would be devastated. I dragged them through one scandal, to now face this? No wonder they wanted me to get my degree and work for them. When Hampton said we'd soon be hearing from the team's public relations department, flashbacks of Michigan returned. The media were a nightmare. Phillips and Hampton did not need to worry about me talking to the press. As far as I was concerned, they were as evil as Caroline Scott. I hated Tripp Saunders' guts, but the press would never get me to say one word to them.

The only time I ever agreed to speak was on camera after the game. Live and unfiltered. And no room for manipulation.

Coach Hampton and Coach Phillips called me into the hallway when the PR people arrived.

"I guess we owe you an apology," Hampton said. "Looking back, you were on to Tripp before us."

I didn't reply. He and Phillips knew exactly what Tripp said that day. That Tripp was a total pig was not a surprise to anyone, the coaches included. But Tripp's aggressive words went too far. My guess was that this victim wasn't his first. More would come forward. At what point would the public start to question who knew what about Tripp Saunders?

"You and Dylan are due thirty minutes early tomorrow. With Owen Ross." Phillips put his hand on my shoulder. "I know you're an intense guy who likes to get his schoolwork done on time, but the offensive line will have very little freedom this week. You understand that, Nico?"

"I do," I replied. "Are we on mandatory curfew?"

"Not yet," Hampton said. "Practices will run long, and there will be a strict gag order. If anyone says anything to a reporter, or anyone for that matter since half the time reporters are incognito, curfew will be back."

"Understood," I answered.

"Nico," said Hampton. "We are counting on you and Dylan to help Owen through this. This season is not over. Owen's stats were better than Tripp's in high school. But we have our work cut out for us this week. Right now, that kid is terrified. Anything you can do to help him is appreciated."

"Sure," I said.

WHEN I SPOKE to my parents late that afternoon, I didn't know much more than they did. Naturally they were freaking out, renewing their objections of sticking with football and then joining this team. My mother wanted me to quit, come home, and start again. "Any school would be lucky to have you, Nico," she repeated. "You can go to an Ivy if you want to. You're *that* smart!"

After my parents, I called Greer. She was back in the studio working on website orders. She'd already sold the Mini and met with the attorney. Even though the scandal was all anyone wanted to talk about, Jill Suter insisted they visit with Lila and the rest of the sorority that night. The attorney said they were basically using the scandal to their advantage. As long as everyone was paid back what they were owed, and Delta Gamma had their money for the charity, no one would remember that Caroline misrepresented Scotty Designs. And she was bringing fifty-two non-disclosure agreements along with her.

"Lila's extremely intelligent," Greer said. "She will not forget what Caroline did."

"You're right," I said. "But what's most important is that she knows you weren't involved. Does Caroline realize she doesn't have a car anymore?"

"I don't know," she answered. "She wasn't home when I collected both sets of keys."

"What about your mom?" I asked.

"She spent the day with Mark," she answered. "It affects her just as much, but my mom hardly drives. There's about three thousand dollars left over. Maybe they can buy something older?"

"Greer," I said. "I know you don't want me in your business, but don't buy Caroline another car."

She exhaled, then changed the subject. "How are you?"

"I'm hosting a dinner party on Thursday night," I said. "Dylan and Lila. Owen Ross and his girlfriend. And Emma and Blake. They're only allowed in if they have you with them though." I laughed.

She didn't respond. Then she said, "Are you serious, Nico?"

"Yes," I answered. "Dylan and I have taken Owen under our wing. And Dylan's been bugging me about a dinner party. So I'm cooking, Dylan's making dessert, and you have to come. Don't worry, Greer. This isn't a trap. This won't be just the two of us, although I'm still hoping you'll consent to that sometime soon."

"I don't know what to say."

"Say you'll be here."

"Do you want me to bring anything?"

"No. Just yourself, please."

She didn't answer.

"Greer, you're not nervous about this, are you?"

"Maybe," she answered. "But not because of you. I've never been to a dinner party. It sounds like something my parents used to do."

"I can't wait to tell Dylan you said that." I laughed.

THE WEEK FLEW BY. No one spoke about Tripp Saunders in the locker room or on the field. Private security protected the stadium and the locker room at all times. Reporters were still everywhere, though. The Butler machine protected Tripp until he pissed off a donor. Apparently, Tripp's victim was the wife of one of Butler's biggest boosters and a former player. And Tripp was just being Tripp. Flirtatious and then he boldly groped her. When she called him out, her husband wanted to beat the shit out of him, which is why the police had to intervene. No one was naming names, however. That made me feel good for the victim and her husband, that they had friends who wouldn't sell them out to the first reporter who offered cash.

Caroline Scott was not so discreet. Since she had been Tripp's girlfriend until the very night he was arrested, she was gaining attention. When major news outlets offered to drive her in a limousine to Atlanta to talk about her relationship with Tripp, she readily agreed. Greer tried to stop her, said she was risking exposing her own crimes with Delta Gamma, but Caroline blamed Greer. "If you hadn't *stolen* my car, maybe I wouldn't have to go on TV." Her argument had no logic.

What worried Greer, and her attorney, was Caroline's volatility. "Your sister can still kill you with one bad word," Jill Suter told Greer. "That girl is playing with fire." Though all fifty-two sorority sisters signed the NDA, the court of public opinion was mightier than the court of law. Scotty would suffer if Caroline's actions were revealed.

I wanted Greer and her silent partner to get ahead of the story by telling their side first. When I wasn't at football practice or having team meetings, or planning my dinner party menu, I was working on our history of capitalism project. I'd written to her silent partner twice, the first time requesting an interview for our project. And, the second time, to help expose Greer's sister. I'd yet to hear a response, which bothered me. Whoever this person was spent a fraction of time on Scotty Designs. They had deep pockets to help her in the first place, but Greer averaged at least sixty hours per week. Revenue steadily increased over the years too. Greer didn't want access because she was afraid her mother would overspend, but was this partner actually putting her profits aside? There were so many unanswered questions.

THE DINNER PARTY fell on a good night. According to Greer, Caroline was being interviewed the following day. No decision was made on when the interview would air. Before the game on Saturday? Or would they air it afterwards, using the three hours of national television to advertise Tripp Saunders' girlfriend's exclusive? Since the interview had yet to take place, the team and Greer had nothing to worry about. Yet.

"Let's forget about Tripp and Caroline for one night," I said to Greer Thursday morning after practice. "Emma and Blake are picking you up at five-thirty, but I'll drive you home."

"Blake lives right by my house."

"I was hoping you would help me do the dishes," I lied.

"What are you making?"

"Something vegetarian. Owen's girlfriend doesn't eat meat."

"Do you want me to come early and help you?"

I told her that I didn't. That wasn't true, of course, but I didn't trust myself either. If Greer came early, I might not let anyone else inside.

After practice on Thursday, Dylan came home with me. I'd decided on a risotto with butternut squash, walnuts, and kale. I paired it with my mother's insalata, which was simple arugula, grape tomatoes, hearts of palm, and a lemon vinaigrette. Much of the main dish I made beforehand, so I just had to add the kale and reheat. The salad required minimal work. Prepping in advance had helped since Dylan needed the oven for his family's apple crisp. Though we weren't allowed to drink, I'd picked up some wine and prosecco for dinner. It was hard to serve Italian dishes without it.

Lila was the first to arrive around five. Dylan told her to arrive early, which was no big deal. She made a fuss over the apartment then asked if I needed help setting the table. This I'd never even considered. She took charge and made herself at home, going through my cabinets and setting the table with plates, glasses, and silverware. When she asked me where I kept my napkins, I realized that I didn't have any. So she stuck the roll of paper towels at the center of the table, giggling. She poured herself a glass of prosecco and chatted with us while we finished dinner.

"Before Greer gets here, I wanted to know what the reaction was at the sorority about the phony deposits," I said. "I know you signed NDAs. Was anyone upset with Greer?"

"Not at all," she said. "With Caroline, yes. I don't think she's going to be able to show her face around the Delta Gamma house until everyone who went to the formal graduates."

I nodded.

"We all feel pretty stupid though," she admitted. "Scotty Designs provided each one of us with a receipt, which itemized everything we ordered and had customized. We all should have questioned why we were being asked for two hundred dollars, in cash."

"It's not your fault, babe," said Dylan. "Caroline is Greer's sister. Would your sister do that to you, if you had one?"

"I hope not," she said. "But then I feel horrible again for Greer. I mean, I practically yelled at her the night of the formal to stop talking about her donation. I had no idea that she'd just realized her own sister stole ten thousand dollars from all of us."

There was a knock on the door, and five people stood outside when I opened it. Owen, his girlfriend Tess, Greer, Emma, and Blake. I wasn't sure who was most shy at the moment. Greer, Tess, or Owen. Emma and Blake were immediately cool, calling out "Nico" and "Seventeen" and patting my back as they walked inside. Owen shook my hand and introduced me again to Tess, who had a pretty smile and thanked me for inviting her. Like a lot of people on this campus, Tess and Owen were high school sweethearts. From a small town in northern Florida. How he and she would handle the media attention this weekend was anyone's guess.

The PR team met with Owen every day. Once he left them, I gave him my advice afterwards. Talk about the specifics of the game, praise your teammates, and always be positive.

Greer was the last one inside. Lila and Emma looked like

they were headed to the bar later, in heels, jeans and dressy shirts, while Tess wore a dress. All the guys were in khakis and shirts. Greer had on jeans and Converses. Her hair was in a loose braid and her white sweater was V-neck, showing off the delicate expanse of her shoulders and neck. She wore my pink diamond necklace. Her face was bright with light makeup and pink gloss.

My heart beat faster at her sweet beauty.

I didn't let her pass me without first giving me a hug. When I released her, she handed me a gift bag. "This is for you," she said. "Thanks for inviting me."

"You brought me a gift?" I asked her.

She blushed.

"Should I open it now?"

She laughed as we walked inside to join the others. "You can open it whenever you want."

When I glanced inside, I couldn't believe what I saw. "Did Lila call you about fifteen minutes ago?"

She shook her head, confused. When I pulled out her gift, a stack of white napkins, embroidered by Greer, Dylan and Lila started to scream.

"How did you know Nico needed napkins?" Lila shouted. "But, oh my god, these are gorgeous!"

Greer had made me football-themed linens. Some had the logo or mascot of our Virginia high school, some had Butler's logo and the red wolf mascot, others had the number seventeen in either red or royal blue and yellow. None were of Michigan. These were things my mother would covet for her own dining table, but I appreciated them because Greer made them for me. I didn't really have the opportunity to study her workmanship because Lila grabbed them and finished setting the table.

"Thank you," I said to her. "They're really nice."

Her violet eyes shined under my kitchen lights. She smiled.

What I loved about this apartment was how open it was. Dylan had been right. Soon everyone relaxed and chatted around the kitchen island while Dylan and I finished making dinner.

No one talked about the upcoming game, or Tripp Saunders, or Caroline Scott. For most of us here, it was exactly what we needed.

When we were all seated, Dylan insisted upon saying grace. We all joined hands. Dylan's prayer was from the heart. "Tonight, we come together as a family to share a meal. We'll see if you've blessed Nico with the gifts you've bestowed upon me. But we thank you, Lord, for granting us this wonderful rich food and this time together. Each one of us has our own demons to face, but we rely on your strength and guidance, and the friends you put on our paths and at our tables, to conquer them. Amen."

"Amen," we all chimed in. Everyone let go, except for my right hand grasping Greer's left. Since she was right-handed, and I was left-handed, we never had to let go except to pass the food around the table or serve.

Everyone had a good time. Since half the table knew each other, most of the conversation focused on Owen and Tess and Emma and Blake. Emma and Blake were not obligated to be dry and finished off the wine. They were also the first to leave since they were headed for a bar downtown.

"You sure you don't mind driving Greer home?" Emma asked.

"I'll get her home," I assured her. "And you guys better Uber if you've had too much to drink. Leave your car here overnight."

When they left, we talked about the game this weekend. Both of us assured Owen he'd do well. Tess, at one point, expressed frustration with Tripp for putting Owen in this position. "Don't get me wrong. I'm happy that he's getting a chance to play. But who wants to be the one who follows Tripp's footsteps?" she asked. "He was so rude to us at the formal. And his girlfriend was worse!" Tess said. "She accused me of stalking her at Nordstrom because we were wearing the same dress. It wasn't even my dress; it was my roommate's. She is horrible."

No one spoke. Dylan and Lila were looking at Greer. When I turned to her, she looked into my eyes and started laughing. Then Lila joined her. Soon, the two of them were wiping their eyes of tears.

"What's so funny?" Owen asked.

"She's my sister," Greer admitted. "And she *is* horrible."

"Oh, I'm really sorry." Tess was upset. "I would never suspect you two were sisters."

"Don't apologize," said Greer. "It's okay."

Before Tess and Owen left, Greer pulled the two of them aside and talked to them in a quiet voice. Whatever she said to them, they felt better since they were embarrassed about trash-talking Caroline at the table. Lila and Dylan followed them out. It was only eight-thirty, which meant that Greer and I finally had a couple of hours to ourselves.

When she started to do the dishes, I joined her and we talked about how well the night went. Greer searched my cabinets for Tupperware because she wanted to pack leftovers for Aunt Isabel. Dylan's apple crisp was also a hit. The foods were rich — it was autumn after all — but nothing was too heavy.

"We'll have to do this again sometime," she said.

"Yeah," I said.

Because Greer said "we," alluding to her and me, together, my whole body flooded with emotion. I wanted her, badly, but I also saw the two of us together, for good. Until I'd met Greer on the first day of classes, I hadn't thought about committing to one person. Commitment was something I'd be doing in a decade rather than now. But Greer wasn't someone I ever wanted out of my life. I wanted her in it.

Greer wasn't ready for that. She'd never done more with a guy than kiss. And that was with me. She didn't have to even tell me that. She'd worked all the time the past few years, having skipped going to high school for online classes while running a studio. Her only social outlet had been Melanie and her family, and her neighbor Nancy.

When we finished cleaning up, I led Greer around the apartment. As we wandered, I told her how I thought I needed the extra square footage for my parents and brothers to visit. But my parents were resolute; they were never visiting Butler.

She was staring at me and not speaking. Since she was probably thinking about my family, I changed the subject. "Do you want to watch a movie?"

"Do we have time?" she asked. "You have practice in the morning."

Her hands were in her back pockets. The light was behind her, and her braid was draped over her shoulder. I stepped towards her and pulled one of her hands into mine. She held my gaze. When I wrapped my arm around her waist, she smiled. She wasn't afraid of me, and she wanted this as much as me.

"Have you ever been with a guy, Greer?"

"No." She shook her head. "Does that bother you?"

My eyes bored into hers. "If you told me that you *had* been with another guy, that would bother me. I'm not the caveman type, but the thought of you with someone other than me makes me want to smash something."

Her face turned animated. "Smash something?"

"Yes," I answered. "Something large and heavy. Or someone." I pulled her closer. "I only want you. And I only want you to want me."

She swallowed. Her neck was delicate, and I wanted to suck

it, mark her as mine. I was possessive and possibly scaring her. I needed to lighten the mood. "So we could watch a movie, or—"

She stared at me. "Or?"

"Or we could talk more."

"What do you want to talk about?"

"You haven't been with a guy," I said. "But have you been curious about sex?"

"Isn't everyone?" She blushed.

"True," I said. "I'm not sure where to start. I've literally dreamed about kissing every single inch of your body."

"Nico!" she laughed.

"I'm serious."

"I have an idea," she said.

"What?"

"How about we stop talking. And you kiss me."

When my lips covered hers, they were not exactly gentle. But Greer, I realized right away, didn't want gentle. She was starving for me and greedily kissed me back. My tongue went deep into her mouth and she responded by tangling hers with mine. When she moaned I lifted her, and her legs wrapped around my waist. I was used to being semi-aroused around her, so my erection was immediate and touching her center as she grinded on me. She'd never had sex, yet her body knew instinctively what to do.

My cock grew thicker.

I started to carry her into the family room, thinking I would lay her onto the couch. But something made me press her against one of the sliding barn doors. Bracing her against the hard wood, I ran my hands along her thighs, squeezing her gently when I reached her ass, pulling her towards me. Her fingers were touching my face, running down my scalp, and holding my neck and shoulders, sending electricity down my spine. I groaned when her nails grazed my skin. She tasted like apples, and her honeysuckle scent teased me until I pulled her braid out and fingered her hair, inhaling her thick shiny locks.

I broke from her lips and trailed kisses down her neck, nipping and licking the sensitive flesh. Her breasts were heavy against my chest. I slid my hands under her white sweater. Her waist was smooth, and when I palmed her breasts, I almost came. They were as full and firm as I imagined. Greer pulled my face back to hers, and we sucked on each other's mouths as I played with her breasts and rubbed my thumbs over her nipples until they pebbled.

Her own hands dove under my shirt and traced the skin of my abdomen and chest slowly. She broke from our kiss and said, "I've always wanted to touch you here."

"You're killing me, Greer." I claimed her mouth again.

Just as I was about to unclasp her bra, I heard a loud knocking on the door. Followed by my name. Part of my mind realized someone had been knocking for a while. Greer gazed down at me, looking ravished but curious. Her usual sleek hair was messy, half pulled out of her elegant braid. Her lips were dark pink, her cheeks bright red.

I might have succeeded in marking her because there was a pink patch near her collarbone. One of my palms was still squeezing a breast.

"Is that Blake and Emma?" she asked.

"Maybe," I answered. "But it sounds like a crowd. Wait right here." Once Greer was on her feet, I smoothed my shirt and ran my hands through my hair. Before I left her, I smiled and kissed her softly on her plump beautiful lips.

"Hang on!" I shouted walking to the door. I couldn't answer with a raging hard-on. I took a few deep breaths to tamp down my desire. Then I pulled my shirt up and wiped my mouth since it was still wet from Greer.

I pulled open the door, and five people screamed, "Surprise!"

My mother and father, my little brother Enzo who rushed at me, Matteo, and a petite blonde-haired woman with a huge smile. Matteo's girlfriend Isabella.

My family were huggers. And kissers. Before I could get back to Greer and prepare her for this "surprise," I greeted each one of them. My father and mother started talking all about the drive down, the nonstop construction zones on I-95 and I-85. Enzo interrupted to ask about what kind of food I had in the refrigerator, followed by how much Owen Ross was going to suck on Saturday. Matteo was trying to say how happy he was to see me while introducing me to his girlfriend Isabella. This was someone he was obviously very proud of.

My father saw her first. I heard the "oh," followed by my mother's gasp. Enzo was in middle school when the Scotts left Virginia, so he didn't recognize her. He stopped and introduced himself, shaking her hand, on his way into the kitchen. Matteo and Isabella were still talking to me, so they weren't really aware of what was taking place a few feet away.

Greer had smoothed her hair out. Her sweater was back in place, her face wiped off like mine. Her cheeks and lips were still heated, whether from me or surprise that the Camillos, archenemies of the Scotts, had just walked in on us attempting to rip each other's clothes off I couldn't tell. She did not cower, but I knew she needed to get out of here.

Since my parents, usually very sociable, were speechless, I interrupted Matteo and Isabella talking by saying, "Come on in!"

Then I quickly walked to Greer's side. "Mom and Dad. Matteo. You remember Greer Scott?"

Matteo was as speechless as my parents.

"Isabella, this is my friend Greer," I said. "Greer, this is Matteo's girlfriend Isabella."

"Hi," Greer said.

"It's nice to meet you," gushed Isabella. "You've got such pretty hair. And what a gorgeous necklace. Are you coming with us to the game on Saturday?"

"Oh," she said. "No. I work on Saturdays."

Before I let this conversation last much longer, extending the pain Greer and my parents were obviously feeling, I interrupted Isabella. "I was about to take her home. Make yourselves comfortable. I'll be right back."

Greer stopped and said, "Bye. Have fun this weekend." Then she headed towards the door. Without realizing the consequences, or maybe subconsciously I knew exactly what I was doing, I clasped her hand as we exited my apartment.

GREER

*R*esisting Nico's touch was becoming impossible for me, so I didn't pull away when he took my hand in his apartment, in front of his entire family. As we walked down-stairs and he led me to his garage and then his car, he had his arm wrapped around my shoulders and then my waist. He kissed me when he opened the door for me.

When he pulled the car out of the garage, I finally spoke. "You know my biggest fear about my mother finding out about us is because she is still fixated on your dad," I said. "But what do you think is going through your parents' and brothers' minds right now? Please be honest."

"I don't know," he said. "They've always just said, 'Stay away from the Scotts.' This was after Charleston, Greer, not when your dad was alive."

If his mother broke into my parents' hotel room, we would think the same way.

He sighed. "My parents aren't huge fans of Caroline's," he said quietly. "At the last two away games, she tried to hang out with them in the hotel lobby. They bought her and her friends drinks, but still thought her behavior was odd."

I stayed silent. My sister always put herself before others. She'd bargain with the devil if she could.

"We've never talked about this," he said, "but my dad did love your father. He still cries when he talks about him. So—"

"So?"

"I don't know. Maybe there's a chance they'd embrace you." He clasped my hand again. "You're not like Caroline at all. Even Tess and Owen, who just met you tonight, saw this right away."

"You know what I think?"

"Tell me."

"That it's a good thing we didn't go too far tonight."

"Greer—"

"Hear me out, please," I pleaded. "It's still going to hurt not being with you, Nico. But you and I can both walk away, right now, relatively unscathed."

"Did you hear me tonight?" he asked, his anger rising. "I don't want to be with anyone but you. And I can't watch you with someone else. The thought of it makes my skin crawl."

"But you love your family," I said quietly. "And I'm a reminder of a time and place they want to forget. They're bitter. I would be too."

"You have nothing to do with that." His car pulled onto my street and stopped at my house. The porch light was on, but the house looked dark. It was later than I realized.

"Think about where I'm coming from," I said. "Your brother and Isabella are down for the weekend, and everyone looks happy. It wouldn't be that way with me, Nico. And you have to see that. It would always be awkward."

"I wouldn't let that happen to you."

"You could find someone new," I said. "And I wouldn't blame you for it."

He grabbed me before I could open the door and escape. "I'll forgive you for all this crazy talk," he said, "but don't leave without saying goodbye to me."

His face was so close to mine, I could see the green in his eyes. His clean summer scent was a fresh contrast to the odor of wet leaves that hung in the cool October air. Nico was intense, never showing vulnerability. I saw his affection for me when his eyes softened, but the angles of his handsome face were rigid. It had to be his mind constantly working, trying to figure out a way out of this maze he and I didn't create. His full lips parted, like he was about to say something, but I pressed my mouth to his.

The street was dark, and I let his tongue light my entire body on fire. My free hand slipped under his shirt so I could explore the hard muscles of his abs and chest once again. Next time we were alone, if there was a next time, I would make him take his shirt off so I could see everything I was feeling.

At first, back at the apartment, I worried my inexperience showed. But Nico responded to me and seemed to feel as excited and heated as I was. Sometime between the formal and tonight, I stopped feeling self-conscious around him. My outfit was all wrong tonight, jeans and tennis shoes while even Emma knew to dress up for a dinner party. An epic fail for a fashion designer. Thankfully, my hair looked like I put some effort into my appearance tonight. But Nico still looked at me like I was the most beautiful girl in the world. His hand constantly touching mine under the table made my blood race so that when we were finally alone, all I wanted was him.

I pulled away first this time. "Goodnight," I said. "Will I see you in class tomorrow?"

"Of course. Don't be late, Miss Scott."

I giggled as I stepped out of the door. Before I knew it, he was at my side walking me to my porch. "What are you doing?"

"Seeing you home," he said. "I apologize for not doing this before. I wasn't raised to leave a girl on the curb."

He kissed me goodnight again before I ran up the porch steps and stepped in the door. I went to the kitchen for a glass of water. My mother was asleep in her bed. Upstairs, I went directly to my room but heard my sister moving around in hers. When I went to the bathroom, she was packing. Her hair was piled on top of her hair, and she was dressed in sweats. Her brow was wet, like she'd been sweating. I asked her what she was doing.

"Moving," she said. "I'm staying in Atlanta after tomorrow."

"Do you have somewhere to live?"

"Yes." She turned to me and put her hand on the door. "Not that it's any of your concern, Greer. Unlike you, I have an entire network of friends. You haven't succeeded in poisoning all of them against me."

I held back my retort, which wouldn't have been pleasant. Caroline wasn't delusional. Somewhere in her mind, she knew she did this to herself. She slammed the door in my face anyway. After the bathroom, I locked my bedroom door and climbed into bed. Caroline was still making noise, not caring that my mother was asleep right below her. I covered my ears with a pillow, and tried to imagine Nico's lips and hands all over me.

At least tomorrow night I could once again sleep with my bedroom door unlocked.

CAROLINE MUST HAVE CRASHED because she was lying face down in her bed when I passed by that morning. I showered and dressed in a new game day dress, my boots, and a denim jacket. I switched out my backpack for a black one. Caroline would hopefully be gone by the time I returned home. Was it terrible of me that I couldn't wait for her to leave?

My mom was awake when I walked downstairs. She was upset Caroline was leaving us. I hugged her but said nothing. The three of us had argued about Caroline's theft. My mom tried to justify it, saying that when I didn't give her a finder's fee for getting the Delta Gamma business, she took matters into her own hands. Caroline accused me of hoarding money. I pulled out the bank statements and credit card receipts to prove to her that we were all barely getting by, that most of the recent charges were hers.

My sister hated to be challenged and immediately attacked me for my pink diamond necklace that I likely bought for myself and pretended was a gift. I shouted at both of them then, saying that Caroline should be thanking me the police hadn't come for her. That finally got both of them to stop talking.

"What are you doing today?" I asked my mother.

"I'm working in Mark's office. He has a few cosmetic consultations, and he thought I may convince the patients to go with him," she said. "He's going to the game at the stadium tomorrow. Do you mind if I hang out with you at the studio?"

"Not at all." And then I left.

AFTER CLASS TODAY, I wouldn't see Nico until Monday. The Tech game had suddenly become the biggest of the season, and the tension surrounding Tripp Saunders' removal was thick on campus. The student body still dressed in red and white, but everyone was nervous. News crews were situated in front of certain entrances, stopping nearly everyone who walked by for an interview. Given how hungry the reporters were, I texted my mother to tell her to go out the backdoor to walk to Mark's office.

My sister wouldn't be a problem since she was waiting for her exclusive interview sometime today or tomorrow. She wouldn't talk to anyone outside the Atlanta studio.

Enzo sat beside Nico in history of capitalism. Since he was a high school sophomore, and he was technically on a college visit, he was shadowing his older brother for the day. Professor Simmons couldn't be more excited. To her, this was a guest of honor because he was Nico's brother. Her game day outfit was awful again – paisley pants clashing with a floral-printed Oxford – reminding me that Nico never did see the dress I'd made for her. Had it not been for the drama after the formal, we could have delivered it sometime this past week. Even if it wasn't as delightful as Nico was hoping, it would have looked better than her outfit today. She had to wear the dress with her Gucci loafers or a pair of white sneakers though. I wasn't sure how to tell her this.

Today's lesson was a short one even though a lot was happening in the twentieth century. The rise of socialism in Europe was an ideal foil for understanding capitalism in the United States. Since Nico and I had already finished our pre- and post-Great Depression term papers, I easily grasped her lecture on the rise of Marxism in Germany. When we broke for partnerships, most of the teams were still working on their term papers. So Professor Simmons allowed the three of us to work on our Scotty Designs documentary in an empty classroom.

If Enzo knew the Scott-Camillo family drama, he didn't let it show. He was as tall as Nico but fifty pounds lighter. His hair was dark and curly. One could tell they were brothers, even though Enzo's eyes were blue. Both had a similar quick wit about them, and this showed as they were setting up the camera and testing the room's lighting. But Enzo's intelligence was playful compared to Nico's intensity. From my black Scotty backpack, I pulled out some of my original phone cases that I'd made back in Virginia. I was lucky to also find old iPhones in the house. To Enzo, these dinosaur devices, which were only about five years old, were way more fascinating than my button cases.

"See?" I laughed at Nico and held up a pink case with a purple button. "It's not too late to switch to a different company. Who is going to find *these* interesting?"

"Everyone who watches this," he said. He looked extra handsome today. He was dressed as he usually was on Fridays before home games — khakis, a white dress shirt and red tie — but he'd combed his hair off his forehead so his eyes were insanely bright under the lights and against the classroom's white board. I had the urge to kiss him and mess up his hair the moment I saw him.

Enzo was going to film Nico interviewing me about the start of Scotty Designs. He didn't share his questions with me beforehand, and I was nervous. I didn't want to cry on camera, yet my father and his sudden death *were* the reasons why Scotty started and still continued. Before we began, Enzo filmed me showing Nico the first cases I'd made. Because it was Nico, I found myself forgetting all about the camera. Instead, I explained to him that once I figured out how to get my original Singer machine to handle the hard polyester material, the details like the liners and button closures were easy.

"That was what my friends loved about these cases," I explained. "They could pick the outer shell, the liner, and their closures. Some liked the buttons, but others wanted zippers or snaps. And I wanted to learn how to sew it all. So all of these early cases were experiments."

When we sat down, Nico's body was close to mine. As we spoke, I allowed his calm and power to wash over me. We never touched, but I imagined my hand in his, my body pressed deliciously against his unyielding one. I never let my gaze stray from his either.

"When did you start to sew?" he asked.

I wasn't expecting this question and told him so. But I did remember what made me learn. It was buttons. "I was little," I answered him. "My sister and I still played with dolls and had bins of doll clothes. My grandmother on my dad's side, whose name was also Greer, took me to the pharmacy one day. I saw one of those little travel sewing kits at the counter, and I told her I liked the buttons. She bought it for me, taught me how to tie the thread. And then I added buttons to the doll clothes." I laughed at the memory. "And then it became a slight obsession. I stopped playing with dolls altogether and just altered the clothes."

Then he hit me with a boom. "Company names are meaningful. What made you settle on Scotty Designs?" Nico asked.

Nico didn't know the answer. I'd never told anyone. I took a deep breath and exhaled slowly. For this, I had to pretend Nico was someone else and that there was no camera in the room. "My father died suddenly, on Main Street in our hometown in Virginia. He collapsed on the sidewalk, and his best friend from childhood happened upon us and tried to revive him. It was the worst moment of my life, but this man, Nicholas Camillo, kept referring to my dad as 'Scotty.' I never knew that was his nickname."

Nico stared back at me. I'd never acknowledged his father in any favorable light, and here I was revealing a very deep secret.

"At the time, my father and I were buying a sewing machine. It was my birthday, and it was the first machine I'd ever owned. It happened to break when he collapsed, but the owner of the store delivered a new one to my house that night." Nico swallowed. I still hadn't answered his question. "Anyway, 'Scotty' is in honor of my father. He always believed in my sister and me.

But, the name 'Scotty' reminds me of the best part of him. To me, the name is fun, and young, and very much alive."

"Cut," Enzo said. "I'm sorry but I have to stop right here. *You're* Scotty's daughter? Did you know this, Nico? Holy shit, your dad is like famous in our family. My dad has a Scotty wall in his office. It's crazy. Nico, you have to bring her there sometime. She has to see it."

Professor Simmons happened to walk in then to tell us class was ending and we needed to wrap up. The timing was perfect because I don't think I'd have held it together much longer. I noticed that Nico's eyes darkened, like he was getting emotional, when I started to talk about both of our fathers.

We packed up, and Nico asked Enzo to wait for him outside. Once we were alone, Nico asked me if I was okay.

"Believe it or not, I am okay," I said. "I've never told that story to anyone."

"Thank you for sharing it with me. And with Enzo," he said. "You have no idea how much that means to us."

I smiled at him. He wrapped me in his arms and we kissed. It was brief but still made my body tremble with desire for him.

Since he and Enzo were headed to his next class and not walking towards the lot, I wished Nico good luck at the game the next day. Enzo said, "You should come with us, Greer. We have an extra ticket."

Because Nico knew how awkward that would be, he said, "She'll make it to a game one of these days." He winked at me. "But I know she and Aunt Isabel will be watching."

"Who's Aunt Isabel?" asked Enzo.

"I'll tell you in a minute," he said. "Bye Greer."

We went our separate ways. And for the first time, ever, I was disappointed I wasn't going to the football game. Standing next to Enzo, cheering for Nico, sounded like a lot of fun. Then I pictured his parents alongside us, and my mother at home, prohibited from entering the stadium, and I realized such a moment would never take place. I exhaled. Nico deserved to be with someone who could love and support him openly. He was wasting his time with me, and I was selfishly holding him back because being with him felt so good.

The right thing to do was to let him go.

BEFORE HEADING TO WORK, I stopped home. Coach Evans texted me to say she and the captains would meet me at the studio this afternoon with an emergency request. I knew this meant my afternoon and evening would now be hectic, so I wanted to grab food and a change of clothes.

Judging by the black limo double-parked in front of our house, Caroline hadn't left. *Just keep driving*, my mind told me. Instead, I parked and hurried up the walkway. As if on cue, Caroline stepped onto the porch as if she'd been inside waiting for this moment.

Her golden hair fell in soft waves. She wore a black skirt and blazer, and nude heels. This was my sister's interview outfit. She looked amazing, and when she dressed like this, it was easy to see how she'd landed two offers right out of college. Had she taken one of those, none of this nightmare would be happening to her, or us, right now.

"Bye Greer," she said, dabbing her eyes with a tissue.

"Are you really crying?" I blurted.

"Shut up and hug me, okay."

I should have known she was using me. As soon as she hugged me, I heard cameras clicking. I released her and noticed photographers on the street, next to the limo. How did I miss them earlier?

"You are unbelievable," I said. "I know you're planning to

play the victim card. You better hope that this interview doesn't blow up in your face."

"You don't know anything about me."

"I know what you used to be like, Caroline," I said. "You *used* to be fun. And if Daddy were alive, you'd have never stolen money from people."

"If Daddy were alive, everything would be different, Greer." Her voice was low and angry. "But he's dead, and you're not him. So stop trying to tell me what to do with my life." She moved for the steps then turned around. "Do you know how easy it was to take money for those dresses? We could have been living so much better these past few years, but you are too stupid or weak to run a successful business. I will never be like you."

I stood there, stunned and in silence, and watched her climb into the limo. When it pulled away from the curb, Nancy called my name.

"I didn't see you there," I said to her. She was seated at her table, working on her puzzles. She wore a sweater and a blanket over her legs.

"Caroline didn't either," she said. "Don't listen to her, Greer. Your sister is a troubled young woman. Deep down, she and your mom know that if it hadn't been for you working so much, they'd starve."

I gave Nancy a half smile, went inside and gathered what I needed then hurried back to my van, hoping there were no photographers still lurking nearby. I'd never seek the spotlight like Caroline. Ironic, considering that Enzo Camillo had filmed me this morning on camera. But that documentary was only for the twenty students of history of capitalism. And Professor Simmons of course.

.   .   .

The afternoon flew by. Even though the Butler vs. Tech game was a local rivalry, it was now being televised nationally due to the Tripp Saunders' scandal. The rumor was that Tripp had propositioned the wife of an alumni player who was staying in the hotel last Saturday night. It explained why no one on campus knew the victim, and every woman from the formal had been accounted for.

Because the game was now going to be carried across the country, Coach Evans wanted new uniforms. Scotty was working on several outfits for the cheerleading team. Home, away and practice. We'd also started on a special uniform, heavy with sequins, to be revealed at the championship game. But since that game was no longer guaranteed, we decided to hold off on it.

These uniforms looked nothing like what Scotty had ever done before. I wasn't sure what my partner would think of them. They were risky and not what other college cheer teams were wearing. Because Coach Evans was so attached to boots, I started the design with a white bootie I found from an online supplier. Not a fake boot. These booties were designed for athletes, comfortable as sneakers. The girls could run and jump in them without risking any injuries. We could add fringe or sequins, depending on the uniform.

From there, I designed boy shorts in a high-performance, recycled nylon and spandex blend. The base was garnet red with black and white striping at the waist, which gave the illusion of a belt. The top was a well-constructed, supportive bralette. With thick straps and a band of fabric below the bust-line. The main color was again garnet red, but the straps and accent colors were white and black. A cropped white jacket with red sleeves and black piping, my mother's idea, tied the outfit together. The school's classic BU logo was on the back of the jacket; it sparkled with sequins.

With the jacket off, the girls would be showing off their toned abs and trimmed waists. Their muscular legs would also be on full display. And, overall, the girls could move around, dance and cheer, as though they were in gym clothes.

They loved them.

Coach Evans, normally a badass, cried when she saw them. The booties moved her the most. But she agreed with the girls that black sneakers also went perfectly with the uniforms and would be a nice change on occasion.

Our problem was that we hadn't constructed all of them. When the rest of the team arrived, I called Melanie in to see if she could help me and Aunt Isabel. Since this was also my phys ed project, I had to write another emergency note to our third party and explain how I'd offered my services for free. The cheerleading team readily agreed to pay for the boots, the fabric, and the Floreses' time. Given the Delta Gamma debacle, I wanted everyone, including my partner and customer, on the same page.

The green light came quickly, and soon the three of us had a packed studio and all the machines working. When my mother texted to say she'd be going out to dinner with Mark, I told her not to expect me home until late. Coach Evans stayed through evening. There were twenty cheerleaders, but each uniform had three pieces. Until this afternoon, we'd only assembled half of them. Which left us about thirty separate products to construct before morning. And the jackets were time consuming. I pushed everyone, Caroline and Nico, from my mind and just sewed.

The studio was loud. The machines were grinding. Coach Evans had the girls on a rotation so that they could try on their uniforms, making sure they fit perfectly, before taking them home. It was like the day Delta Gamma came to pick up their dresses. I was grateful that I changed into yoga pants and a tank top because the work was high intensity, and the studio was hot. Even Isabel, always cool as a cucumber, was sweating.

She spotted the Camillos before me. "Nico! And Little Nico! And Big Nico!" called out Isabel over the noise of the machines. The cheerleaders chimed in. "Nico!" and "Seventeen!" I was operating one of our sergers, constructing the piping on the jackets, when I glanced up, ruining my work.

Nico had walked in with his father beside him. Enzo was filming the entire scene with his camera. His eyes were wide when the cheerleaders started to make a fuss over Nico's little brother. I stood up from my station, yanking my mistake out of the machine.

Nico smiled at me from across the table. I was so confused. Why was he here and not at his team dinner? Then I noticed how late it actually was. He said something about how I really did operate a sweatshop, but my mind was having trouble processing all that was going on at once.

When I glanced at Nicholas Camillo, I knew why Isabel had referred to him as Big Nico. Nico favored him. Same height and build. Their hair was similar, though Mr. Camillo's was streaked with grey. But Nico's eyes were nothing like his father's. His were dark, a blue from where I was standing, and pained. He stared at me as if he was seeing a ghost. Before Nico or Enzo had a chance to help him, Big Nico started crying. His eyes were leaking tears faster than he could wipe them away. Like me, he knew how to cry without making a sound.

As far as I could tell, no one had noticed his emotion. Nico was chatting with the cheerleaders, teasing Isabel about how he needed to fatten her up, and asking Melanie about Sam and Beatrice. Enzo was still filming, and Coach Evans walked him over to the straight-stitch machine where Melanie was finishing up a pair of boy shorts. When I glanced back at Mr. Camillo, he was still crying, his eyes not leaving mine. Something propelled me to him. The story I told his sons earlier today was the truth. I knew Nicholas Camillo loved my father. Loved Scotty. And that Scotty was who I chose to celebrate when I formed this company.

I hugged Nicholas Camillo, the man who'd come between my father and mother without wanting to. My intention was to comfort him, but then I started to lose my tight control and cry with him. We were complete strangers, bound together by our love for Jack Scott. What we didn't have to say with words was that we both knew we loved him best. My mother's love for Jack Scott was clouded by her illness, and Caroline, for whatever reason, had buried his memory so deep she'd lost him

But Nicholas Camillo and I kept Jack Scott close to our hearts. After five years, we were finally sharing our grief.

2 8

NICO

Melanie was telling me about how much Sam and Beatrice were loving preschool when Enzo nudged me, telling me to look where his camera was pointed. When I noticed my dad and Greer hugging and crying, I froze. My first instinct was irrational. I wanted to lunge at my father for touching her. I didn't, of course, but that's how possessive about Greer I'd become. It scared me, a little. My second reaction was sane. I turned to Enzo and told him to stop filming. This was a private moment, years in the making, and not meant for an audience.

I hadn't planned to come here tonight. It just so happened that my dad and Enzo picked me up from the team dinner — Enzo who had his permit at the wheel — and so we decided to drive around town. My brother had already shared his footage of my interview with Greer from this morning with my father at lunch, and I guess it was still weighing on him. When he asked to go and see Greer's studio, I had no idea she'd still be working, with the crowd she had, on Friday night.

While my dad and Greer cried on one side of the studio, I

329

decided to interview Coach Evans and the cheerleaders. They refused to show the camera their new uniforms, which was kind of a neat twist for our documentary. Enzo could film the big reveal tomorrow at the game. But what the coach and squad could discuss was how fun it had been working with Scotty Designs on planning and executing a whole new look.

"Greer came to me to work on her phys ed project," the coach said on camera. "But we've had the opportunity to give feedback every step of the way. So it's been more of a collaboration rather than a designer telling us what we have to wear. All Greer cared about was comfortable fabric for my athletes. And we got so much more. I can't wait until our fans see the girls tomorrow."

Melanie and Isabel were focused on the project at hand. According to them, they only had two more uniforms left to finish. Greer was working on the more complicated pieces. "Don't worry, Nico, we will all leave together," Isabel said. "Melanie and I will make sure she doesn't close the studio on her own tonight. You should get home and get some rest before tomorrow. Go take care of your father. We'll take care of Greer."

The Floreses were kicking us out. But it was late, and they couldn't really finish up with three guys hanging around. I nodded and walked over to my father and Greer. He'd stopped crying but was talking in a low voice, calmly unloading decades' worth of thoughts he'd wanted to say to Jack Scott's daughter. Greer was still wiping fresh tears from her eyes. How was I going to leave her?

I touched my dad's shoulder. His eyes were red, but he grinned at me. This had been cathartic for him. "Dad," I said, "we need to leave. The girls are trying to finish up."

"Okay, Nico." He turned to Greer. "Your dad would be so proud of all you've accomplished here, Greer. And I want to thank you for letting me come here tonight and finally tell you what he meant to me and how much I miss him."

She nodded. "Thank you."

Enzo was right behind me, and we pulled my father away from Greer because I didn't know if he would leave her. It was funny. I saw my dad with Caroline Scott, and he never unleashed onto her the emotion he just showed Greer. It wasn't just that she resembled her father, she had a different energy. She was good. You felt it right away. Even the day she told me that she hated me five years ago, I never fully believed her. She didn't seem to have hate in her.

When Enzo and my dad walked out the studio door, I turned to Greer.

"You okay?" I asked.

"I think so."

"I'm going to call you tomorrow. And you can tell me what the hell just happened."

She laughed. "Fair enough. Good luck tomorrow."

"Thanks." I squeezed her hand and turned to leave.

"Nico—"

I turned back to her.

"I wish I could be there for you."

"I know you do," I said. "But someone has to keep Aunt Isabel from breaking the TV. She seems a little hyped up for tomorrow."

I made her laugh again. "Bye Nico."

When we pulled into the garage at my apartment and we all got out of the car, my dad let Enzo run up the stairs ahead of us. He stopped me on the landing, his voice serious.

"Son," he said. "I know you like Greer Scott. It's obvious. And I think you care about her too. But your mom's not ready for welcoming Sophia Scott's daughter into our lives, even if she's nothing like her mother."

"What are you saying, Dad?" I asked. "Because I do really like her. And she likes me too."

"I'm looking out for you because you're my son and I love you. I'm also looking out for Jack Scott's daughter because Jack would want me to." He rubbed his face. This was hard for him. "Your mother will eventually love whoever you love, Nico. I know that she will. But don't go for Greer Scott unless you love her. There's so much ugly history there. If she's not the one, then let her go now before all of us, the Camillos and the Scotts, are ripped apart at the seams."

I stared back at him. He was asking a lot of me, and of Greer, right now.

"I blame myself for everything that happened to your mother," he said. "And I won't have her hurt again. Do you understand?"

"I think so."

He nodded. "Now let's get some sleep so you are ready for tomorrow."

We lost the game.

The good news was that the offense played amazingly well. Owen Ross stepped up and executed. He had nearly four hundred passing yards and more than two hundred rushing. Had the defense got it done in the last two minutes of the game, it would have been the game of his life. But Tech got us in the end. A Hail Mary pass that put them over us by two with no time left.

Owen still got an interview at the end with the pretty sideline reporter. Coach Phillips asked me to stand with him. The running backs and wide receivers deserved the honor tonight because they were amazing, but Phillips thought I could keep the focus off Tripp Saunders and on Owen and the team.

"Remember what I said," I told Owen when we jogged over to her. "Talk about game strategies rather than anyone personal."

"Owen Ross, what a performance. You didn't get the win, but how did it feel having to fill Tripp Saunders' shoes tonight?" was the first question.

I put my hand on Owen's shoulder. He didn't answer right away and I thought I was going to have to take over. But then he said, "Once Ryan Edwards completed the screen pass in the opening drive of the first quarter, I only thought about football. Jackson and Tyler were solid on the run, and the grabs by Harris and Gordon were just inspiring. Those guys made my job look easy tonight, and I'm really happy our team can move on."

"Nico, we've crossed the midway point in the season and you've been a leader on the offensive line. What are your take-aways from this game?" she asked me.

"The Butler coaching staff has been incredible this season. Each one of us is trained and prepared for any scenario," I said. "And we didn't get the win tonight, but we really feel that our team made a statement. We're still contenders for the championship game in a few weeks, and based on how well the entire team performed tonight, we feel no one can count Butler out."

"The crowd was pretty mellow in the beginning of the game, and by the end, energy was high. Do you think the fans were thinking about Tripp Saunders?" The reporter was persistent.

When Owen didn't answer, I did. "The cheerleading team really got the crowd moving like they always do. The new uniforms were a huge hit with the fans, and I really think their positive energy rubbed off on everyone."

My final comment stunned the reporter. She thanked us and sent us on our way. En route to our teammates on the sidelines, Owen asked, "The cheerleaders got new uniforms?"

I laughed out loud. The tension on the sidelines was so heavy throughout the game. If the coaches caught us studying the cheerleaders' new uniforms, we'd have been called out for not focusing on the game. It was a random enough to divert attention from Tripp. I hoped that Greer and Aunt Isabel heard the shoutout from the studio.

Owen ran over to Tess in the stands, who leaned down and kissed him. My family were all standing by the railing, waving and cheering. Enzo still had the camera rolling. I hoped that he did get a shot of the new cheerleading uniforms for our documentary. Isabella and Matteo were holding hands. I was happy for my brother. She was cute, and smart like my mother, which is why they got along so well. But she'd asked me, or Enzo, or Matteo, or my parents a dozen times why my "girlfriend" wasn't coming to the game today. She knew something was off about us, and I also sensed she wanted a female closer to her own age to hang with.

I wished Greer could have been there, that I could kiss her in the stands after each game. My family also had reservations at one of the nicest restaurants in town tonight, a short walk from my apartment. I'd have loved it if she'd have joined us. But that was not possible. Like Greer said, and my dad confirmed, her presence would be too awkward, too uncomfortable, for my mother.

My dad was right. And Greer was right.

So why did not seeing her feel so wrong?

GREER CAME into history of capitalism late on Monday morning. Her skin looked dull, her eyes dark, as though she hadn't slept in two days. Professor Simmons didn't say anything, likely because Caroline Scott threw everyone under the bus on Saturday night after the game. According to her, the university itself as well as the football hierarchy promoted a culture of sexual assault against women. While Tripp had never "raped" her, she'd never felt comfortable around him yet was always pressured by her friends and family to keep dating him.

The interview made no sense. Caroline admitted that her physical relationship with Tripp was consensual. She'd be a terrible witness for either side when Tripp eventually faced trial. And everything afterwards was total speculation. She had no firsthand knowledge of any sexual assaults perpetrated by anyone on campus, including other football players. Yet she argued that her sorority made her be the host of the most exclusive parties because they all wanted what she had, a relationship with a sexual predator.

"My family has struggled financially since my father's death," she told the interviewer. "So I always felt pressured to look beautiful and find boyfriends with NFL potential. Joining Delta Gamma at Butler was a demand, not a choice." Then she added, "After Tripp's violence was exposed, I decided to leave my family for good. I need a fresh start away from them and that campus."

It was an absolute train wreck for the Scotts. Lila and Delta Gamma were furious too. Caroline lied throughout the entire interview, manipulating the truth, and cried on cue. But no one could challenge her without appearing to be attacking the victim.

Where did this leave me and Greer?

We hadn't even spoken yet. My dad had already messed with my head about letting Greer go for the sake of my family, and then Caroline's interview sealed our fate. The worst thing I could do would be to associate myself with Greer after her sister painted her and her mother as pimps for NFL hopefuls.

Caroline had also effectively destroyed all that the team had worked to overcome since Tripp's arrest. The entire country forgot about Owen's unbelievable game and were now rooting against us. We were back on mandatory curfew, honor-bound not to watch ESPN or any sports news, for our own mental health.

It was now up to the coaches to handle the fallout, too. They'd granted interviews and tried their best to control the damage caused by Caroline. When Coach Phillips stopped me this morning after practice, he'd asked me if it was true Greer and her mother pressured Caroline to only date football players.

I laughed in his face. "You can't be serious, Coach?" I said. "I can't speak for Sophia Scott, but I can for Greer. She'd never pressured her to date anyone," I told him. "I can also let you in on a secret. Greer's company makes a ton of money. None of what her sister said was true."

Professor Simmons dismissed the class early, then asked Greer and me to stay behind. Since we hadn't broken into teams, I'd yet to speak to her at all.

When the class emptied, Dr. Simmons said, "I've received your recent term papers on the Great Depression, which are excellent. You will still have to present on these, and I encourage you to figure out how to prepare for these remotely." She glanced at both of us. "Can you give me an update on your final project. How far along are you?"

Each of us talked. Greer was writing the company's business plan retroactively. She'd also been able to compare the company's website offerings year to year, with a detailed description of the changing trends in products and fabrics since the company's inception. It was up to Greer to discuss her part-time employees and their contributions. Greer also planned to answer questions about her silent partner and how that person impacted Scotty Designs.

Since I was handling all of the financials, I told Professor

Simmons that I had everything I needed to write and create visuals on the company's growth. Due to my family's background in real estate, it was up to me to discuss the company's physical location and equipment and weigh in on how Scotty Designs could best expand. Would it make sense to outsource production to Atlanta factories, proposals Greer had already collected? Or rent larger space elsewhere, closer to campus, which would include a storefront? Or buy property, which was something Greer hadn't considered? Or stay put where space was cheap and Scotty could focus only on expanding the website storefront?

What I didn't tell either of them was that I was still trying to convince Greer's silent partner to finally reveal themselves.

"If you both had to guess, would you say you're fifty percent finished?" she asked.

Greer and I turned to one another. She guessed closer to seventy-five percent, while I gave a conservative estimate of fifty. I didn't want to finish the project without her silent partner's input.

"Good," she said. "Here's the bad news. Nico's academic advisor wants this project done by this week, before the team leaves on Friday. And—" She held up her hand before either one of us could object. "You are not permitted to see each other, or be seen together, outside this classroom."

"Could you repeat that?" I asked.

"Your advisor wanted one of you out of this class," she said. "I refused because it's not fair. We barely have four weeks left in the semester. But I had to make concessions. Neither one of you can work on history of capitalism outside this classroom. You can work remotely. But you can't be seen together," she said, "until this drama blows over."

Greer took a deep breath.

"Perhaps if I had let Miss Scott have her way two months

ago," she said with a grin, "this never would have happened. I'm sorry I couldn't fight better for the two of you, and your partnership. I still maintain that keeping you together was the right decision. Who could have predicted this plot twist?"

"Just so I understand," Greer spoke up. "Nico and I now have an email-only partnership? Unless we *want* to chat or speak to one another online?"

"That's correct," the professor said.

Greer thanked her then asked to be dismissed. I attempted to follow her when Dr. Simmons reminded me that we couldn't leave together. Greer didn't even wave or say goodbye.

I called her when I left the building on my way to my next class, but she didn't answer. When she ignored my call after my last class of the day, I sent her an email.

> *Greer,*
>
> *Obviously you're ignoring my calls. I thought we were beyond these silly games. We have a lot to discuss so can you please pick up your phone?*
> *Nico*

I met a few of the players from the team for lunch in one of the smaller cafeterias on campus. Everyone was given orders similar to what Professor Simmons just gave me. Limit our time with people outside the team. Guys with girlfriends, like Dylan and Owen, were even told to distance themselves for at least the next week or two. The team wanted zero distractions or complications from this point forward. Advisors and tutors were available around the clock. The team didn't just want my history of capitalism report finished by Friday. They wanted every player to work ahead and finish what they could now. This, more than anything, would keep players too busy to dwell on the bad press.

I checked my email after lunch, and Greer had responded.

Nico,

I thought Professor Simmons made it clear. Our partnership is email only from this point forward. We don't have to communicate remotely (i.e. phone or video) unless we want to. And I don't want to talk to you again. I've blocked your number.

As I've explained repeatedly, verbally and in writing, this relationship was doomed from the start. It was a ticking time bomb that finally went off. One can argue that none of this trouble with the team and Caroline would have happened if I got my way and dropped out of history of capitalism.

From this point forward, I will trust only one person. Myself.

Greer

Each time I read her email, I cursed. It didn't surprise me though. Greer was consistent. Since classes started in August, she fought the partnership and the relationship. Was she right about the team and Caroline? I didn't think so. Caroline and Tripp had been trouble from the start. She wanted a good time and a QB who could party and perform well. No player at our level could abuse alcohol or drugs and get very far.

Why did Caroline throw Greer under the bus? Had it not been for Greer, Caroline would not have the life she had. An education, a place to live, food to eat, and until last week, a car to drive. What Greer always failed to see was that Caroline was holding something against her. I believe it to be her success in Scotty Designs. Caroline was not a tough nut to crack. She was simply blinded by jealousy.

But Greer's email bothered me for another reason. My dad told me not to go for Greer unless I loved her. Unless she was the one. What if what Greer had known what I could never see? What if she knew that when it came to us, it had to be all or nothing?

I reread her last line: *From this point forward, I will trust only one person. Myself.*

Had she been trying to tell me all this time that she didn't want me? That she didn't want us?

29

GREER

When Nico didn't call me after the game on Saturday like he said he would, I was hurt. His father and I had poured our hearts out to one another Friday night at the studio. For the first time since my father died, I'd felt free. Like I could finally move on from grieving and find happiness of my own. And in my trusting heart, I believed that happiness started and ended with Nico Camillo. That our intense glances, and constant smiles, and sweet kisses and touches were love. True love.

But then he didn't call me.

And Caroline's devastating interview was not an excuse in my mind. He more than anyone would know how much I needed a friend after my sister accused my mother and me of essentially whoring her out.

My sister announced to the world that she needed a fresh start. It was the only part of her lie-filled interview that resonated. I hoped she did get her fresh start. My mother and I, and Scotty Designs, needed the same thing. Caroline wasn't as good as me at execution though. This had been an ideal town to start over five years ago. The Floreses had been wonderful to me, too. Our lease was up in January. My goal was to finish this semester and start over someplace else in the new year.

We wouldn't be following Caroline this time around, and we'd distance ourselves from Nico and his family for good. When Nico's email arrived, I was sitting in the waiting room of my mother's psychiatrist's office, after our meeting with Professor Simmons. I was here so that I could talk to the psychiatrist afterwards. I had lied to Nico when I replied. There was one person in my life whom I still trusted. That was my silent partner. Once I'd formulated a better plan, with my mother's psychiatrist's input, I would write to them.

My mom had been getting better with the medication, but she was still a needy person. I wasn't sure she would ever be capable of standing on her own two feet. Which is why I'd always envisioned my future with her in it. In my mind, we had to leave this town for good. Townies and the campus community loved the university's football team above all, and Caroline opening fire on them meant that we would never be accepted here again. I'd already suspected this, and Dr. Simmons confirmed it less than an hour ago when she said Nico could not be seen with me. My worry was Mark.

When Caroline was being interviewed on Saturday night, all my mother noticed was how good she looked on camera. My sister was beautiful, which is probably why she was still trending on social media. But all of my sister's lies and direct cuts to her own family flew right over my mother's head.

When Dr. Jane Forrester and my mother stepped out of the office and invited me inside, I asked my mother if she wanted to stay. "Oh, you go ahead, Greer," she said. "I'll finish my magazine in the waiting room."

"Come on in, Greer," Dr. Forrester said. "I've been looking forward to talking to you again."

When we were both seated, I told the doctor that I wouldn't take too much of her time.

"I'm not sure if my mother told you about my sister's interview over the weekend," I started.

"I watched it," she said. "I'm glad you brought it up. Sophia doesn't seem to understand *exactly* what your sister revealed to the world."

"She doesn't," I agreed. "Considering what my sister accused us of, maybe it's for the best."

Dr. Forrester did not respond in any way. I exhaled. This was wasting precious time, and I needed her advice about my mom's new boyfriend.

"As you know, my business is here. But the lease is up in two months. Given what's happening, I've decided the best thing to do is move," I said. "I don't know if that will harm the progress you've made. My mom has also been seeing Mark, which has been good for her. I don't want her to suffer, but I don't see how we will survive here any longer."

"Greer—"

"And Mark likes her," I added. "But in the long term, I'm really the only person my mother can rely on."

"You're enrolled in college," she spoke calmly. "Have you thought about that?"

"At the end of this semester, I should have thirty credits total," I said. "I'll need six months to restart the business, so I plan to reenroll next fall."

She nodded.

"But if I don't go back, it's not the end of the world. My business does fine. If I have to change the name, I will. It might be rocky in the beginning, but I think my chances of surviving a move and transition are better than staying here. Does that make sense?"

She shrugged.

"It's my mother's mental health that I'm worried about."

"Can we talk about your sister for a minute?"

I looked at her, confused.

"How did her interview make you feel?" Jane Forrester wore bootcut suit pants and a crisp linen Oxford. Her pumps were at least three inches, with a spiked heel. Her hair was styled in a long sleek bob. Professional. Attractive. But intimidating at the same time.

I shook my head. "Are you interested because of Tripp Saunders?"

She laughed. "I'm not a reporter Greer."

"Right," I said. "Her interview made me angry and very sad. There's not much more to say. She's not the reason I wanted to talk with you."

"Tell me about the money she stole."

"My mother told you about that?" I asked. "I'm surprised because she took Caroline's side." I told her about the bogus deposits, and how Scotty handled the situation. "Maybe we should have pressed charges, but my sister is very skilled at manipulating the truth. She could have convinced the police she'd done nothing wrong. It was easier to return the money."

"And what about your boyfriend?" she asked. "Nico?"

"He's not my boyfriend," I corrected. "I'm not sure why his name would have ever come up in my mother's conversations with you."

"According to your mother, he's your study partner. And he took you to a dance. And you went to his house for a dinner party."

"He is my partner for one of my classes," I stated. "We went as friends to the dance. And he did invite me to his house with a group of others. We aren't dating. I actually have him blocked," I added, proudly.

"Your mother thinks he's the boy who's come between you

and your sister," she said. "Apparently Caroline is not happy Nico chose you over her."

I shook my head. "Dr. Forrester, what does any of this have to do with my mother and Mark? I'm here about that. Can my mother handle a big move, or should I consider staying somewhat close like Atlanta or Greenville?"

"I can't answer that for you," she said. "You, your mother, and Mark should talk openly. Your mother understands more about you than you realize, Greer. And I'm sorry about what's happened with Caroline." She stood up, ending our conversation. "But running away from problems never solves them. I didn't learn that from medical school. My mother told me that when I was about your age."

I stood up too. "Thanks for your time."

"I know money is tight, and Sophia is now coming twice a week, which is good for her," Dr. Forrester said. "But if you ever want to talk to someone, I'm always here for you."

Yeah right, I thought. I gave her a tight smile and left.

When I arrived at the studio, I printed out the Scotty orders. So far, our sales were not impacted by Caroline's bombshell interview. But it wouldn't take long for the world to make the connection. The best thing we could do was deliver quality goods on time. Because my sister's interview was so damning on Saturday night, I'd spent Sunday in the studio working by myself, missing study group once again. And waiting for Nico's call that never came. Work was the only thing that was keeping me from falling apart.

Before I started filling orders, I wrote to my partner through our third party.

Our lease is up at the end of December, and I no longer see a future for Scotty Designs in this town. Caroline helped seal our fate, but there are other reasons too. I think my mother and I need to start over, someplace far from here.

We were likely going to have to invest in a move anyway. I'm asking that the moving van take the studio a little farther now.

If it were up to me, I'd pick a university town similar to this one but away from the East Coast. My mother may have a different idea. We're discussing it later.

I also plan to withdraw college after this semester and restart next fall.

Greer

It felt good to hit send on that one. Now that I'd informed Dr. Forrester and my partner of my plans, they felt more real. For me, execution meant completing difficult tasks right away. It was why working with Nico on history of capitalism had been so productive. Neither one of us procrastinated. Speaking of Nico, he responded to my email.

Greer,

Blocking me is extreme. What has happened?

I may be on curfew, but you can still come to my apartment. I have a private garage. Dr. Simmons and Coach Phillips would never know you were there. We can accomplish a lot over dinner.

Nico

This email pissed me off. My reply was immediate:

Now who's playing silly games, Nico?

You will have my entire contribution for this culminating

project by Friday morning, as we've been asked to do. (Focusing on Scotty Designs was a mistake btw. I should have refused, but I wanted to prove to you that my silent partner was clever, a true entrepreneur, and a good person, and not the grifter you make them out to be.)

Friends don't promise friends they are going to call and then don't. You are not my friend, Nico. So please don't pretend to be anymore, even through email. It makes me feel like you are insulting my intelligence, after hurting me.

Regarding the presentations for the term papers we've already turned in, I can't promise you I won't tank those like I did the one on the Industrial Revolution. So maybe you should prepare yourself for Cs.

After Friday, we shouldn't have any reason to communicate.

Greer

P.S. Emma is good with splicing videos. When the time comes, she's doing Blake and Liam's. She offered to do ours too.

I hit send before I thought too much about it and forced myself to shut down and work on orders. I didn't think my email would make Nico rush over here and apologize, but I locked the studio door and pretended to be closed.

30

NICO

 ngry Greer was better than Shy Greer. Her email upset me because she was right – I didn't call her on Saturday night like I said I would – and now I was trying to pretend that she was the one ignoring me. But it also told me she still cared.

I screwed up and sent mixed messages, because I was conflicted. On one hand, Greer was who I wanted beside me always. But she, and my dad, were right. My mother would be miserable, and that wasn't fair to anyone. And then there was Greer herself. Was I *her* one? She was inexperienced and had never had a boyfriend. Was it even fair of me to expect her to know the answer to that question?

And I wasn't stupid. The coaches wanted all the players away from their significant others for one reason only: They wanted me away from the sister of Caroline Scott. Coach Phillips asked me about her this morning, and then Professor Simmons basically confirmed that he wanted one of us out of the class. Knowing the power of the football team at this school, it was Greer he wanted to withdraw.

348

"You ready to walk to the stadium, Nico?" one of the guys shouted. When we weren't at practice or class, we were encouraged to work at the library.

"Yep." But when I went to shut down my computer, there was a new email from Scotty Designs third party.

I told the guys I'd catch up with them and opened the email.

Dear Mr. Camillo,

I consent to an interview. On camera. Email me back with the time and place.

My recommendation is to keep Caroline Scott out of this video. Greer handled it promptly, and her execution was, as always, flawless.

P.S. Greer likes my anonymity. I presume the interview will just be with you, and that you can pixel me out and alter my voice?

For the first time, I realized that Greer may not like what I was about to do. Someone had to challenge this silent partner on her behalf. Unlike her, I believed this guy to be a man and ruthless. Based on the revenues over the last three years, this guy had to have pocketed at least a couple million dollars. Greer's family lived on a fraction of this. Where was her money? And why didn't she have access to it?

My size alone would intimidate this person. I couldn't wait.

But since we had the Penn State game this weekend, this team's first road trip across the Mason-Dixon line in decades, the interview would have to wait until next week. I sent a quick reply asking if he could meet next Tuesday at the library on campus. I'd prefer a coffee shop in town, but a quiet room on the second floor would be best for audio and visual recording.

Then I wrote to Professor Simmons and Coach Phillips,

copying Greer, letting them both know that we needed until the end of next week to complete our project.

My email back to Greer would have to wait until after practice.

31

GREER

By the time I got home from work, Mark and my mother were having a cup of tea on the porch. With Nancy, who sat on her side of the wrought iron railing. I grabbed a plate of food from the kitchen and took a seat across from them. They were chatting about Caroline. My sister had received an offer with a major television network to be a sidelines reporter for the NFL.

I laughed so hard I nearly choked on my food.

"Why are you laughing?" my mother said, angrily. "You're not happy for Caroline?"

I shook my head and waited to calm down. "It's just such a *perfect* job for her. I'm sorry I didn't think of it myself. Where will she be living?"

"She will be with NFC East teams almost exclusively, so she's looking for a place in New York."

"Good." I felt relieved. "I was hoping to move Scotty Designs to the West Coast."

"You're moving Scotty Designs?" Mark asked nervously.

"What do you mean you're moving?" my mother chimed in.

"It was something I wanted to talk to you about first obviously," I said. "But I don't see how we can stay here now that Caroline is public enemy number one. I think she's more hated than Tripp."

"She didn't hurt anyone," my mother defended.

"What does she have to do with you, Greer?" Nancy asked.

I thought about Professor Simmons' comments earlier. "Her interview's already affecting me at school," I said. "And I think what she's done will hurt the company. Since the lease is up in January, I thought the best thing to do would be to move."

"What about your schooling?" Mark asked. "Do you really need to work so much?"

I glanced at my mother. Had she explained to him that without Scotty, we had nothing? "It is our livelihood, Mark," I said. "If we start to get bad press or bad reviews, or start to be targeted by trolls, and sales drop, my mother and I can't sustain ourselves. And for the record," I waved my hand at my mother, "I'm not moving in with Caroline, even though she'd never ask us to anyway."

"What about your boyfriend?" Mark asked.

"Yeah," my mom said. "What about Nico Camillo?"

"Mom, he's *not* my boyfriend. Why did you tell Dr. Forrester that he was?"

"Caroline said he was," she answered. "And his car is always here. You went to the dance with him. He invited you to his apartment, and you spent an hour on your hair."

I exhaled. "That doesn't mean he's my boyfriend, Mom," I said quietly. *He's not even my friend.* But I got up. Not having slept in two days had taken its toll. Tomorrow was my easy day. I'd see Emma in class and then Isabel would be back in the afternoon. I needed her help now that the documentary was due on Friday. When I glanced around, all three of them were quiet.

I'd apparently dampened everyone's spirits. I said goodnight and headed upstairs.

I didn't open my computer until I was showered and tucked into bed. Nico had answered my reply to him from earlier.

Trust me, Greer. You coming to my place for dinner will not involve any silly games. It will be all business with no interruptions this time.

Looking back, I can see how you think I hurt you. I'm sorry. Let me make it up to you immediately so that we can get back to being friends.

Nico

P.S. I've already edited the video we shot so far, but I'll be sure to thank Emma for her offer next time I see her.

Nico was back to being flirtatious, which was worse than pretending to be friends. Despite his stating otherwise, I felt like a pawn in his game. He was using me. He knew that I had been right. A relationship between us was impossible. His family's weekend in town showed him that. It was time to tell him the plan I'd been executing all day so that he could move on.

Nico,

Since this impacts our project, you should know that I'm moving Scotty Designs out of Georgia, hopefully to the West Coast, at the end of the year. The lease is up anyway, and given all that's happened, my mother and I could use a fresh start.

This should be good news to your family.

Caroline got a job as a sidelines reporter for the NFC East. She's moving to New York. I know you can't control where you're drafted. But at least you are now prepared for the day she interviews you.

No more invitations to dinner. Okay?
Greer

My mind was in that nearly asleep zone when I was pulled away by a knock on my bedroom door. Since Caroline had moved out, I'd stopped locking myself in at night. The shadowy figure was too tall and bulky to be my mother and I shot from the bed, terrified.

"It's me, Greer," said a voice. Nico.

I exhaled and cursed. "You scared me."

"I'm sorry," he said. Then, "May I come in?"

I shook my head in the dark. "What are you doing here?"

"I got your email and just got in my car. Your mom told me where to find you."

"My mother? Oh my god, Nico. Did she think you were your father? Is she psychotic again?"

"No," he said calmly. "She and her boyfriend are staying at his place tonight. She seemed glad I was here." He laughed. "I was nervous when I first stepped onto your front porch, but then she introduced me to your neighbor Nancy as your boyfriend."

I released the breath I'd been holding. I turned on my desk lamp. Nico still stood in the doorway, his eyes finding mine. I had on little shorts and a tank top but felt naked under his observant gaze. He glanced away and studied my room. It was tiny compared to his apartment's bedrooms, but neat. The furniture was all secondhand, but I'd painted everything the same color, a distressed white, so that it didn't appear so mismatched and worn out. In Virginia, my bedroom was my studio and was typically covered in works in progress. The only evidence that I sewed was the Singer Quantum Stylist 9960 on my desk, a prototype for the cheerleading uniform beside it.

Nico's mind was always so perceptive, and I had no idea

what he was thinking about right now. He had on sweatpants and a long-sleeved football tee. I'd never seen him dressed so casually. His appearance was relaxed, but I could tell from the hard lines of his face that he was anything but relaxed.

"Nico, I—"

He crossed over the threshold and stalked over to me. He held my arms and stared into my eyes. His cheeks were red, like he'd ran here from wherever he'd parked his car. I could also tell that he'd recently showered since his hair, like mine, was damp. I felt my entire body blush at his touch, betraying my logical mind that had pushed him aside and was looking forward to a new life in a sunnier, less humid university town.

"I can tell you haven't slept in a few days," he said in a low voice. "I'm not going to try to talk you out of moving tonight. And I'm not going to kiss you. No matter how much I want to." He sighed. "I just want to hold you. And smell you if you don't mind because I think I'm addicted to your shampoo."

"You're complicating everything by being here," I protested.

"No talking, okay?" he asked. "You need sleep. I'm not leaving you by yourself tonight. I have one question though."

"What?"

"Does your bedroom door lock?" he asked. "In case your mom comes home and goes psycho on me?" Nico said this in a light voice, but I could tell he wasn't joking.

"You're serious, aren't you?"

"Kind of."

I walked over to the bedroom door. The house was quiet. My mother must have gone to Mark's, which was almost as surreal as Nico being here right now. I closed the door and locked it. When I turned around, he was staring at my bed. It was full size, but still looked too small for both of us.

"I know what you're thinking," I said. "The bed is too small for you. It's okay if you don't want to stay."

"I was thinking the exact opposite," he said. "It's cozy. Everything about this room is warm and homey. Just like you. Go ahead and get your spot back. I'll find my way." While I got back into bed, Nico turned off the light. Then he took his shirt and sweatpants off.

"What are you doing?" But I couldn't help but laugh.

"I can't sleep with all these clothes on," he said. "Trust me. You'll wake up with a fever." He got in and pulled my back against his bare chest, snaking his arm around my waist. Like the night in his apartment, I felt his erection through his boxers. His other arm went under my pillow so he was cradling my head. My arm rested on his. He was not joking about my shampoo because the buried his face in my hair and inhaled. I felt his entire body relax into mine.

"Greer," he whispered.

"Yeah."

"I swear I'm not going to try anything with you tonight. But my hand might graze your breasts. And I can't promise you I won't have a wet dream about you. Do you know what that is?"

"Nico!" I laughed. "I may not have had sex before but I'm not a prude!"

32

NICO

I woke up before my alarm, just as hard as when I went to bed. Greer was still asleep. But I moved to check the time on my phone, and she shifted with me. I was on my back, and her head rested on my chest, her hand beside her exquisite face. Her black silky hair was tangled, covering her nose and mouth, so I gently pulled it from where it was stuck on her cheek. It didn't matter that I'd taken off most of my clothes. Greer fired up my blood all night long. The tight white tank top that revealed her full breasts and rosy nipples along with the little shorts that I wanted to rip off her with my teeth. We were both damp with sweat because of me.

She stirred and sucked in a deep breath. It was still dark outside.

"What time is practice?" she asked.

"I still have a few minutes before I need to leave," I whispered.

We sat in silence for a while. The sheet covered me up to my waist, and before I knew it, Greer started to run her palm along my chest and stomach, her fingers tracing my pecs and abs. This was payback because I cupped both of her breasts, underneath her flimsy tank, for hours last night.

I didn't bring condoms with me. When I read her email after the shower, I got my keys and left. Greer leave me? Not a chance in hell. I had to see her. Never in my wildest dreams did I expect Sophia Scott to invite me into her daughter's room to spend the night.

If either one of us initiated anything last night, and I had protection, we'd have probably gone all the way. And it would have been amazing. But I'm glad we couldn't. Greer's beauty never failed to take my breath away, but she was exhausted. The circles that were there from history of capitalism had only darkened. When we finally had sex, we should both be fully alert and willing.

My alarm sounded. I wrapped my arms around her head and shoulders and kissed the top of her head. Then I sat up and put my clothes on. When I stood up, I turned and said, "Could you please unblock me?"

"I did that yesterday," she paused, "when you didn't answer my email right away."

I smiled in the dark and told her I'd call her later.

OTHER THAN PROFESSOR Simmons class on Wednesday, I didn't have the chance to see her before we left for Pennsylvania on Friday morning. I had mandatory study hours now after practice too, and she had work. She was also determined to submit her pieces of the documentary by our original deadline of Friday.

But she was talking to me, and texting, so I felt content. We hadn't spoken about her decision to move Scotty out of town. I wanted to interview her silent partner first. She'd obviously told him already. If he was pushing for an out-of-state move too, then I'd be prepared to fight both of them.

It sucked to be the sister of Caroline Scott, but people would forget. Other than Phillips wanting her out of Dr. Simmons' class, which Professor Hawk prevented, no one who knew they were sisters blamed Greer. As far as the rest of the campus, no one connected the cute dark-haired girl in Doc Martens who was hardly ever on campus with the opportunist headed to the NFL. People had no sympathy for Caroline. They did for Tripp Saunders' victim, whose identity was still protected but who did announce that she wasn't blaming the entire team, or university. The blame, she'd announced, rested entirely on the shoulders of Tripp Saunders.

We needed the community's focus back on the team, and not on Caroline or Tripp. That's what we talked about at practice, at meals, and at mandatory study sessions.

Owen Ross was pumped. And so was the rest of the offense. The defense was nursing their wounds from Tech, but Hampton and the defensive coordinator spent most of the week with them trying to get them focused for the remainder of the season. After Penn State, we had two more away games and three home games. All should be winnable. Tech already had two losses, one to Louisiana, a team we beat. Provided we kept winning, it looked like the conference game would be Louisiana vs. Butler. In Atlanta, so we'd be the home team.

This was the scenario we were hoping for.

Not many fans made the trip to State College. Even my parents skipped so that they could see one of Enzo's final games. I was lucky because Matteo and Isabella made the trip out from Philadelphia. They didn't spend the night, but they did hang out with me for a little while in the hotel lobby after our win.

"Matteo tried to explain your family's trouble with the

Scotts," Isabella said. "But I don't understand why you and Greer can't see each other. You guys are so cute together."

"Her mom tried to kill our mom," Matteo deadpanned. "They've got the crazy gene."

"But your dad was her dad's best friend," she argued. "Greer didn't seem crazy to me. I only met her once, but I have a sense for these things."

"Greer's not crazy," I said. "And her mom's getting help now. She was off her meds when she broke into our parents' room. And we don't know that she wanted to *kill* our mother. She just wanted to marry our dad."

"Nico must really like the girl if he's defending Sophia Scott." Matteo laughed. "Next he'll be praising Caroline Scott for her courage in trashing your team, your school, and possibly your NFL chances."

"That's not happening," I told them. "And don't worry. Greer wants to move to the West Coast to get away from her sister."

"That's so hard," Isabella said. "Well, I like her. And I hope you two figure it out."

"I don't know." Matteo shook his head. "Our mom will never accept Greer Scott. Nico's got to get over whatever he has going on with her. If I were you, man, I'd end it and wish her all the best in California."

I PRACTICALLY RAN to the library after my classes on Tuesday morning. University tutors held study hall for the team on the first level. But I'd reserved a small room on the second floor. It wasn't the one where I'd first cornered Greer. For this interview, I wanted privacy so I picked one of the closed rooms. I also didn't want to take a chance and have Greer walk by and see me conducting this interview without her.

Getting there early was essential. I had to set up the tripod and camera and find the perfect angle. Before I conducted the interview, I wanted to show Greer's partner what I'd pieced together so far. So I pulled up the unfinished documentary on my laptop. I considered Greer's testimony about how she named the company the most powerful segment by far. Enzo did a nice job in capturing her emotion, as well as mine, when she talked about my father. But Greer also sent me video of herself talking about her silent partner, and I needed this person to see her pure, unadulterated trust and admiration for the guy I was about to meet. The guy who'd lined his pockets pretty well.

Even without this interview, Scotty Designs was a great example of capitalism at work. The company employed most of the tenets of capitalism – capital accumulation, wage labor, voluntary exchange, a price system, and competitive markets. The only piece missing was private property, which is why I was arguing for the company to purchase a storefront closer to campus here in Georgia. Greer could have the studio in the back, sell products in the front, and keep the online business. She'd need more employees, but the growth would offset those costs.

Provided this guy wasn't shady, the partnership worked for Greer. She controlled the quality and design, but always had the capital she needed. Because he took the initial risk in her, he was allowed to profit. I just hated that Greer did all the work.

There was a knock on the glass. I'd closed the heavy plastic blinds to keep the light in the room even for the camera. Today I'd worn khaki pants, a shirt and tie. It was as close to a power suit as I had with me. I squared my shoulders and pulled the door open.

"Hi, honey," she said.

And then my mother walked through the door.

33

NICO

"Don't look so surprised, Nico." She hugged me tightly, like she always did, then kissed my cheek. "I've always loved Greer's work."

"This can't be happening, Mom." My hand still gripped the doorknob. "*You're* Sophia Scott's daughter's silent partner? Is this some kind of joke?"

"Close the door, honey," she insisted. "Where do you want me to sit? I have a plane to catch in Atlanta, and the traffic is awful. Your father doesn't know I'm here, so we can't waste any time."

"Dad doesn't know?" I shouted. "You've kept this a secret from him too?"

"Right now," she said, "you're the only person who knows I'm Greer's partner."

When I envisioned how this interview was going to go, this wasn't it. I planned to intimidate whoever walked through the door. I even told Dylan to be on standby in case things got physical between us. Because Greer's partner was shrewd, ruthless, and rich off of her labor. I swore that if I didn't like what I heard, her partner would need to know, in no uncertain terms, that I had her back.

"Why don't you take a seat and a few deep breaths," she said. "Once you *really* think about it, me being her partner makes sense. I'm shocked no one has figured it out before now."

"Was it before or after Sophia Scott threatened your life that you decided to help Greer?" I asked sarcastically.

"After." She sighed. "Of course, it was after."

I stared at her. Like me, my mom took this interview seriously. Her hair and makeup were just the way she liked. She had on her favorite color. A light blue dress. She'd always said light blue made her eyes stand out, and right now, they shined under the lights. I sensed that my mom was happy to finally get this information off her chest.

"You seem angry, Nico." She reached for my hand and gripped it. "Now that you know Greer, I have the sense that you *really* like her. And you're here because you want to help her and Scotty Designs. Is it so hard for you to see why I wanted to help her too?"

I exhaled. "No," I admitted. "It's not." My mother was also there on the day Jack Scott died. She wasn't some sixteen-year-old kid. She'd had the power to help her back then, not me.

My mom glanced around the room. "Here's my advice. Since time is of the essence, just let the camera roll. This could get emotional for me, and for you. You're now as close to this as me, so I'll leave it up to you to take out whatever you don't think Greer can handle." My mother had always been efficient. In addition to shrewd and ruthless apparently.

"Do you want your identity protected or not?" I asked her.

"Greer has never wanted to know who I am," she said. "She thinks I was someone who invested in successful Etsy sites. But it's time. Especially now that you're involved. I don't want to keep this a secret any longer."

"What if she really doesn't want to know, Mom?" I asked. "What if she's furious that we reveal this? This may not be good for any of us."

"Then we set her free," she answered. "Greer has made our family a fortune. But if this upsets her too much, we dissolve our partnership, and she goes on her own. I would never force her to stay, and I won't hold her back."

I stared at my mom, unsure of what to think.

"Get the camera rolling, Nico," she said. "I don't have all day."

WHEN MY MOM saw the early footage, she cried. I hadn't brought tissues for the shrewd and ruthless partner I thought I was meeting, so I had to run to the rest room and get her a roll of toilet paper. When I returned and then told her that Enzo shot that, she started to cry some more. Then we saw Greer describe their partnership in such glowing terms, and I realized it was my mother she was unknowingly describing, I started to fill up. *Football players don't cry, you pussy*, I said to myself. According to Greer, her partner, my mother, saved her family from being homeless and destitute.

"My partner took a chance on me," Greer said on camera. "But we were never charity. My partner believed that I could make Scotty Designs successful. There's a tremendous difference in handing out money and saying, 'Here, spend this carefully' to someone saying, 'Let's create a website so you can sew more bags and sell them.'" She was sitting at the farmhouse table in her studio when she filmed this. "My partner forced me to believe in myself and my skills. It was very empowering. And once someone tells you that you're good at something, and then the product sells out, it's very easy to build upon that success."

"Why did you help Greer?" I asked when my mother and I collected ourselves.

"Everyone always associates Jack Scott with your dad," she started. "Nicholas Camillo *was* his best friend. But I knew Jack too. He taught me everything I needed to know about how to run a business and how to invest wisely. Sophia never knew this but your father and I were clients of Jack's. If it wasn't for him in the early days, we would not be where we are today." She looked up at me. "Jack Scott was one of the smartest and most generous people I've ever had the pleasure of knowing."

I didn't respond because I had to let that sink in.

"His death was tragic on many levels." My mother took a deep breath. "Sophia spiraled, and we all watched it happen. Those who knew Jack well understood that she had to be either off her medication or in desperate need of medical help, yet none of us intervened. We assumed someone else would, but her teenage daughters were not equipped to give her the help she needed. After the dust settled from our Charleston trip and the Scotts left, I realized I was more to blame than Sophia was."

"Mom—" I protested.

"Hear me out, Nico," she said. "And all of what I've revealed so far really shouldn't be on your documentary. It's private, honey, and you don't want to hurt the Scott family anymore. But those of us who knew Jack and had benefitted from all of his advice over the years and who loved him should have been there for his family. We should have gotten Sophia help. When they left, and I realized they had absolutely nothing left, I knew buying a bag or two on Etsy was not going to sustain them. I had to do something."

So my mother went on to explain how, at first, she funded Greer's website though a third party. Then she bought a couple of commercial machines, then the space for the studio, and the rest was history. Greer took online classes and worked all the time. My mother had toured the space without Greer and made sure security knew to watch out for her. Greer was the one who found the Floreses, but my mom went in there as a customer to meet them and had them thoroughly checked out.

"Greer is an old soul, Nico," my mom said, "but she was still a child when we started. I've always treated her as a colleague. Except when it came to her attending college. I've had to force her to go. You have no idea how much it's bothered me that her high school years were spent in her bedroom sewing, but it was the only way she'd get Scotty off the ground." She laughed. "Little did I know Scotty Designs would have its busiest quarter during her first few months of college."

"How does the partnership actually work, Mom?" I asked. "I mean, I really believed that Greer was being taken advantage of."

"Very creative and smart attorneys," she answered. "Up until Greer turned eighteen, I was terrified her wealth would be squandered by those closest to her. It would have been so easy to do. That's why I have the majority ownership. We pay Greer a salary and have locked her profits until she's twenty-one. Greer understands the value of this better than anyone. If she really wanted something, like a new van or a private university education, she could get it. But she's content. For now."

"What about your profits?" I asked. "I mean, you're not taking more than your fair share, I hope."

"Of course not," she said. "We audit every year, honey. You heard Greer yourself. She doesn't want charity. She wants an equal partnership. So, yes, I have invested in Greer Scott, Jack's daughter, and it's been the smartest investment I've ever made. And the most fun. I mean, seriously, how awesome is her website? All of her stuff is high quality, classic but trendy and fun. And she's just getting started. Her Delta Gamma dresses were sheer perfection. And I know you don't look at the cheerleaders," she winked, "but I think their uniforms are Greer's bravest work to date. The name Greer Scott will be as famous as

Vera Wang or Coco Chanel or Hubert de Givenchy one day. She's *that* good."

My mother was starting to remind me of Aunt Isabel.

"We shouldn't feel uncomfortable about it either," she said. "This is the way capitalism works. I've had the means to help Greer. She's done all the hard work. But I don't feel guilty about profiting. About helping you and your brothers buy new cars, or places to live, or supporting you in any way," she added. "I may not be working the hours that Greer does, but I've accepted the risks and liability surrounding a teenager-run business. One day, she will reap the fruits of her labor, too."

"You're telling me my car and my apartment here are from Scotty money?"

"They are," she said, nodding. "Your father isn't the only breadwinner in our family."

"Mom," I said. "She drives a van from a decade ago. My office at home is bigger than her bedroom!"

"Her van was Jack's," my mom said quietly. "And I don't want to know why you, Nico Camillo, were in her bedroom."

I blushed like Greer, from the top of my head to my toes. I needed to change the subject.

"I have to ask you why you were so afraid of me coming to this school," I said, "when you seem to really like Greer?"

"Because I didn't want *this* happening." She pointed to me and her. "I liked being anonymous, and if I'm honest, I didn't want anyone, including my son, threatening my partnership with Scotty Designs. It wasn't just because of the income. Creativity is a powerful drug, and even though I wasn't designing and making all of our wonderful products, it's always felt like I was doing just that. Greer always refers to Scotty Designs as 'us' or 'our' or 'we.' She's never made me feel like an outsider. Once my role's exposed, that ends for me."

"So, are you or aren't you still terrified of Sophia Scott?"

"Of course, I am scared of her!" she said. "It's complicated, Nico, and Caroline Scott is probably more dangerous at this point than Sophia. But I don't regret what I did. Filing another restraining order had to be done. And Greer is finally getting her help. Because of who I am, I've been very careful when advising her on her family. I could protect her assets, but I've had to let her figure out relationships for herself. Greer will never abandon her mother, and there is something very admirable about that. She has so much of Jack in her, it's remarkable."

I told my mother that I didn't think any of this footage was usable. She smiled and had to agree. So we talked more about the finer details of Scotty Designs. We went over the visuals I'd created, and each generation of the website. My mother was so proud of how Scotty had grown. She knew every product, too. Then she shared more of her thoughts on how to expand. While she liked my idea of buying a storefront closer to campus, she also thought blitzing college girls around the country with Greer's new game day dresses would be one of the easiest ways to grow.

"The infrastructure isn't ready for the volume of orders we'll receive," my mother said. "Starting out soft this year was smart. By next summer, we could increase sales by several thousand percent. It takes Greer minutes to make each one, and the fabric possibilities are endless. We just need four more Floreses on board." She smiled. "Scotty Designs was originally phone cases and backpacks. Greer has grown into a clothing designer. When I forced her to go to school, I originally thought she should go to a fashion institute. But she's taught herself everything. What she's really needed are the skills to run a business. She's trusting to a fault. I would never take advantage of her, but I feared that if something happened to me, someone else would. That's why I insisted on the entrepreneurship program here."

I nodded.

"But then you left Michigan," she said, "and picked *this* school above all others. Mostly for football, of course, but also for the same exact program I'd encouraged Greer to apply to. And my worlds started to collide."

"Do you think she should move Scotty?"

"That's a tough call," she answered. "Greer's going to withdraw from school if she moves. She has to in order to get the company up and running again. I fear she'll never reenroll." She shrugged. "It makes me sad to think about her and Sophia having to leave this town because of Caroline's actions. Greer is happy here. But, like I've said, I won't stop her. Her intentions are always good, Nico. Scotty Designs will succeed anywhere, and if in her heart she has to walk away from here, I know that she'll ultimately be okay."

My camera started to beep, and my mom glanced at her watch. She stood up and gathered her things. Her car was waiting outside. When I told her I'd drive her to the airport, she said she'd already anticipated that. "I have a driver waiting." She laughed. "You are exactly like your father. I knew you'd worry about me getting back to the airport. But I'll be fine. You can walk me to the car. Besides you have practice. And you're on curfew."

I packed up the camera and folded the tripod, tucking them with my laptop into my backpack. Our new deadline was this Friday morning, but I was already considering extending it. What I needed was additional time to think about my mother's involvement. You could argue strongly for keeping it from Greer. It might destroy her. But now I knew. If I kept it from her, and she found out about it, it would destroy us too.

My mom grabbed my arm, stopping me, as we exited the library. She nodded. Greer and Emma were about twenty yards away, walking in our direction, on the path that passed from the gymnasium to the commuter parking lot where Greer kept her van. They were both in athletic clothes, coming from phys ed. Emma and Greer were talking animatedly to each other, until they both started to laugh and playfully bump into each other. Greer's face was crinkling. Just two girlfriends enjoying a moment after class. Emma had a great sense of humor, and Greer was so relaxed around her. I'd never seen her smiling and laughing like this. My chest hurt watching the two of them because I now carried the equivalent of an explosive device on my camera.

Emma noticed me first. She shouted, "Hey Nico!" loud enough for this side of campus to hear her. Greer, still smiling, waved. They started to turn in our direction, but Greer stopped as soon as she noticed my mother. She pulled Emma with her back onto the path, but first said, "Bye Nico." Emma screamed, "Bye Seventeen!"

The moment was brief, barely a few seconds, yet illustrated how messed up our situation was.

"I'm so sorry, Nico," she said. "But put yourself in my shoes for a moment. I love Greer Scott like the daughter I've never had. It pains me that I can't show her how I feel about her."

34

GREER

November passed in a blur. The football team continued to win games but remained on what was essentially a lockdown. Female students began to come forward, not necessarily making allegations against Tripp Saunders. There were whispers about others in the organization, too. No players were named, but rumors swirled around the coaching staff. I assumed it was Coach Phillips, but Coach Evans swore he was not a bad guy. "He loves women and sometimes gets a little too touchy," she said, "but he would never hurt anyone. He's won so many offensive coaching awards, he's a legend."

This was over Thanksgiving dinner. Coach Evans invited my mother, Mark, Nancy and me to her house on the outskirts of town. A few of her neighbors, and some cheerleaders who did not go home for break, also came. It was laid-back and quiet but fun. Nico went home to Virginia but texted me that morning to wish me a happy Thanksgiving.

Ever since his mom came to visit him on campus, things were distant between us. I was convinced she'd talked him out of pursing a relationship between us. He still hadn't finished the documentary, but we'd presented on both of our Great Depression papers, and I hadn't tanked. I wasn't as skilled as Nico, but I never would be. He was so smooth and natural, and funny, behind a microphone. If he didn't make it to the NFL, any major company would be crazy not to hire him.

Saturday's home game against Texas was the last regular season game. Butler was favored heavily. For the first time ever, I would be attending the game. Coach Evans had nominated me for the phys ed award for my culminating report on the new cheerleader uniforms and, somehow, the department agreed with her. Even though I hadn't done what we were assigned to do, which was to create a curriculum, the committee had approved my project beforehand so it had to be considered. And due to how well the cheer squad and fan community received the uniforms, probably due to Nico's ridiculous shoutout after the Tech game, I was being honored along with other academic awards before kickoff.

My mother was still forbidden to come to the stadium, but Nancy promised to record it for her. It was unfortunate because she was instrumental in the design.

Nico's distance would help make moving easier, when the time came. My partner was dragging their feet, which was unusual. But, given schoolwork and Scotty, I didn't have time to investigate where we would actually live. And my mom and Mark refused to discuss a move. Mark couldn't leave. His practice was here, and it was successful. My mom was spending more and more time with him, too. At this point, I'd have to sign month-to-month at the studio to remain in business after January, and fly to California over Christmas break – with or without my mother – to settle on a location. It wasn't in my nature to procrastinate like this, but I also couldn't be hasty and make the wrong move.

Thankfully, Caroline hadn't gotten in touch with me. She

still talked to my mother, mostly to tell her how well everything was going with her. She'd even started dating a player for the Giants. Whenever I bumped into Lila or another Delta Gamma, their anger with her was still raw.

THE SATURDAY of the home game, my mother helped me to dress for the stadium. I wore a game day dress in Butler colors, and a cute pair of brown Frye harness boots that my mother found in the back of her closet from when we lived in Virginia. "Your dad bought me these," she smiled, "during my cowgirl phase. Coach Evans will *love* them!" Because it was cool and windy, I kept my hair straight. My mother added extra blush, some eye makeup, and a coating of pink lip gloss. It was way too much makeup, but she said I'd need it being on the big screen.

I walked over with Nancy, who was meeting her teacher friends at their tailgate spot. I stayed with her for a little while as they played corn hole and grilled hot dogs. I was too nervous to eat. I didn't tell Nico about the award because I knew he couldn't be there for it. I was meeting Coach Evans first. The ceremony took place about thirty minutes before kickoff, which meant Nico would be in the locker room.

As I was about to leave Nancy, Professor Simmons stopped by our site. She gave me a huge hug and twirled around in her new game day dress. It was the same fabric as mine, red, white, and black print, but hers was a shirt dress, midi length. She paired it with a grey blazer and white sneakers, which is exactly what I suggested she do, when Nico and I gave it to her. I might have squealed when I saw her. And before I even gave it a second thought, I had Nancy take our picture together – making sure she got our shoes – and texted it to Nico.

Then I left them to find Coach Evans. She was waiting at one of the stadium entrances for me, and we walked straight to her office. She unlocked it, told me to take off my jacket and close my eyes. She slipped something on my arms, and when I opened my eyes, I couldn't help but laugh. It was one of the new cheerleading jackets. White base, red sleeves, and black piping. I'd definitely sewed this.

"Oh my god, it's perfect," I said.

"I know. Today you're an honorary cheerleader," she said. "I love your boots by the way."

"My mom lent them to me," I grinned, "for you."

"I wish she could be here," she said. "You look so pretty today."

I followed her out through the maze of hallways and onto the tunnel leading to the field. Unlike the last time I was here, Tripp Saunders was no threat. And Coach Phillips would be too busy to notice me. There was a player waiting at the bottom of the tunnel, and I sucked in a breath when I read the jersey: number seventeen.

"Don't you look delightful," Nico called out as I got closer.

With his pads on, and his bright red jersey with crisp white embroidered numbers, he reminded me of a gladiator. But his face was relaxed and smiling, his cheeks red from exercise, and I fought the urge to wrap my arms around his neck and kiss him.

"Why didn't you tell me?" he asked quietly. When he spoke to me like this, I felt like I was his whole world, that the thousands of football fans surrounding us disappeared.

"I knew you'd be in the locker room. How did you know anyway?"

"Phillips told me. I'm proud of you Greer."

"It's almost time," Coach Evans said. "Good luck today, Nico."

"Oh," I paused as we left him, "I sent you a text if you have the chance to see it before the game. Someone special's here today for you."

"I'll try." He laughed.

The announcer went through all the academic awards swiftly. The stadium was about half full, but I couldn't find Nancy anywhere. I watched as Nico waited by the tunnel entrance. The Camillos were seated right at the fifty-yard line, on the home sidelines. They were among the best seats in the stadium that held close to one hundred thousand fans.

When it was my turn, all the cheerleaders went out on the field with me wearing their new home uniforms and white sequined booties. Whoever scripted the piece noted that no other student at this university ever collaborated with the cheerleading team, and the audience laughed. Coach Evans was, after all, notorious for being difficult to work with. Little did any of them know that she was a total sweetheart. They took a few pictures, and then all of the award winners were ushered off the field.

Nico jogged up to me and leaned his head into mine. "You belong here, Greer Scott," he said. Then he turned and ran into the tunnel to be with his team.

There were still about fifteen minutes before kickoff. I had a ticket for the game, but I needed to exit the stadium and walk back inside. I also had to retrieve my jacket from Coach Evans' office, which had my wallet, phone, and ticket inside. Emma and Blake were saving a seat for me in the student section. Since Coach Evans was needed on the field, she hugged me goodbye.

"You know where you're going, right?" she asked.

"I think I'll find it."

The security guard at the tunnel let me through even though she was waiting for the team to walk onto the field. I hurried up the concrete hill because I sensed about one hundred players were about to rush downhill. It was close since a set of double doors was open, the players corralled behind their coaches, who were shouting cheers to them. I passed by but didn't notice Nico, or anyone for that matter. Most had their helmets on.

I walked through the door Coach Evans and I had entered from. The hallways were empty, and I felt my skin crawl. This wasn't a smart move. Every hallway looked the same, most were darkened, and I felt my heart rate spike. I took deep breaths. Even though I worked late at night by myself in an office building, I knew security was always watching me. This was different. *Don't panic, Greer,* I told myself.

I heard voices up ahead and ran towards them. It was Coach Phillips and someone I didn't know. He was younger, dressed in a team windbreaker like Phillips. Obviously, an assistant coach or trainer.

Phillips gave me a creepy smile. "Well look who it is," he said. "The phys ed winner." He turned to his assistant. "I'm the one who oversaw her project." Then he turned back to me. "What are you doing here?"

"I'm looking for Coach Evans' office. I need to pick something up from her."

"I'll escort you." He spoke in what I'm sure his assistant thought was a kind voice but sent chills up my spine.

"That's really okay." I took a few steps backwards. "I'm sure I can find it if you tell me where it is."

"Take this to the field," he told his assistant, handing him a clipboard. "Tell them I'll be right there." Then to me, "It's not a problem at all. Coach Evans will ream me out if I don't help you."

Though my mind screamed, *Follow the assistant! Follow the assistant!,* my limbs were frozen. Part of me believed Coach Phillips wouldn't possibly waste time helping me. The game was about to start.

But he walked over to me as soon as the assistant was gone.

Then he placed his arm around my hips, pulled me to his side, and led me down the dark hallway.

Once we heard a heavy door click shut behind us, Coach Phillips started to palm my hip then my ass. I jumped away from him, but he pulled me back.

"You don't like that?" he said.

"No! Don't touch me."

"You're a little hard for me to resist, Greer Scott of Scotty Designs."

His eyes were dark and wild. He was as tall and bulky as Nico, so I knew he'd overpower me quickly. I didn't think I could reason with him, and my body needed to flee. Kicking him with these steel-toed boots might work, but my body was shaking all of the sudden. I pushed his chest as hard as I could and ran in the opposite direction. But he took a few steps, wrapped his arms around my waist, and pulled me back, laughing.

"Your cocktease sister and crazy mother aren't here to stop us," he whispered. "I know you want me. We have to be quick because the game's about to start."

I screamed.

NICO

The trainers were trying to pump us up before the game when Dylan brushed against my arm. "Is that Greer who just walked by?" I looked up and caught a glimpse of her black hair. The sequin logo also reflected off the tunnel lights.

"Yeah." I smiled. "She won the phys ed award."

"Oh really? That's awesome. You guys cool?"

"We're cool. It's still comp—"

"Complicated," he finished for me. "I know all about it. Lila hates this lockdown bullshit. I swear to God if I see Tripp Saunders again, I'm going to castrate the son of a bitch. Do the world a favor."

It wasn't funny because Tripp hurt a woman, but I laughed because Dylan always took God's name in vain whenever Tripp's name came up, breaking his pious persona. We ran out of the tunnel and onto the field. The cheerleaders were dancing and the band played. My parents waved to me in the stands, and somewhere out there Professor Simmons was wearing Greer's custom-made game day dress. Her text did make me laugh out loud.

Our opponent was Texas today, and we were expected to beat them pretty easily. Even though it was Thanksgiving weekend, the stadium was still sold out. This was why college football was so much fun. We won the coin toss and headed back to the sidelines for kickoff. We decided to receive the ball, start out with a bang.

"Where's Coach Phillips?" asked Owen.

I looked around but couldn't find him on the sidelines. When Owen started to worry since he wasn't sure of the first series of plays, I flagged down his assistant.

"Owen's looking for Coach Phillips," I said.

"He's not out yet?" He glanced around. "Weird. He was helping some cheerleader find Coach Evans' office. Let me talk to Owen."

I wasn't sure what made me stop him. "What did the cheerleader look like?" I asked him. "Black hair? Cowboy boots?"

"That sounds about right," he said. "She wasn't wearing one of those uniforms, that's all I know."

Coach Phillips was with Greer, and that wasn't sitting well with me. My skin broke out in a cold sweat. "Hey," I shouted to the assistant. "I've got to go to the locker room. Put in Ryan and Beau for the first series. I'll be right back."

"Nico!" he shouted. "You can't leave—"

I didn't wait for him to finish. I sprinted back to the tunnel and ran uphill, my cleats echoing off the concrete. I opened the door that led to the football offices and started to stalk the dim hallways. There was no one around. Coach Evans' office was on one of the older, unrenovated sections. This I knew from watching her leave Coach Phillips' office and head through the steel door. When I opened the door, I heard a faint crying. My blood raced, and I ran towards the sound.

I only saw Phillips' back and Greer's boots. She was pinned beneath him against the wall, and he had his hands and face all over her. She was fighting him and whimpering. My vision went black with instant rage, but I had the instinct and reflexes needed to pull him off her, slam him against the wall and throw him onto the hard floor, effectively knocking him out. Her hair was a mess, her face looked raw from him mauling her, and her dress was pulled up to her waist. It took her a moment to recognize me, but when she did, she screamed my name and reached for me, shaking and hysterical.

My adrenaline was so spiked that I was afraid of crushing her. But she needed to be held and soothed. So I patted her until she could talk, my eyes never leaving Coach Phillips. If he stirred, I'd have to let her go and deal with him again.

"Did he—"

"No!" she said. "But he would have if you didn't come."

The steel door opened, and one of the athletic trainers walked in.

"There you are," he started. "We need you on the field. Owen just got sacked and Texas scored."

"You can't leave me here, Nico!" Greer was immediately frantic, clasping my arms.

I cradled her face in my hands, looked in her eyes, and promised, "I'm not going to leave you." I turned to the trainer. "I'm not leaving her. You have to call 911."

The trainer noticed Coach Phillips on the floor. "Jesus! What happened?"

"What's it look like?" I screamed. "Call 911."

"I better check with Coach Hampton first." Then he disappeared.

"Do you have your cell phone?"

"It's in Coach Evans' office," she cried. "I don't know where that is."

I took my eyes from Phillips and looked over Greer. I pulled her dress down gently, then I held onto her and started to test all the doors in the hallway, making sure Phillips didn't stir. When we finally found a door that was open, Greer nodded and took her jacket from the coach's desk.

"Call 911 and tell them what happened," I said. "I'll help you. But if the head coach comes back he might try to cover this up, and that can't happen."

Greer did as I instructed. She started to cry on the phone. But she was able to get out exactly what Phillips did to her and where she was in the stadium. The operator kept her on the phone, assuring her there were cops on the way, not far from where we were. There were so many unanswered questions. But I didn't try to understand why this happened to her, just kept my arms around her or my hand entwined with hers.

The police arrived as the trainer returned with reinforcements. A couple of assistant coaches but not Coach Hampton. The cops woke up Phillips and sat him up. The sicko had his pants unbuttoned and his zipper down. He was planning to rape her, and the coaches had to hold me back again when I saw the evidence.

"You're done on this team, Nico Camillo," Phillips started shouting. "I gave you a chance, you piece of shit, and you come at me in a jealous rage. Greer Scott begged me for it. Just like all of them do."

"That's not true!" she shouted. And then she started to cry again, clinging to me like she did when I first arrived.

A female cop arrived and escorted Greer and me outside the hallway and into a different room. Within a few minutes, the hallways and offices were covered with staffers, campus security, and more police. It was mayhem. The cops had to separate Greer from me, but I refused to leave her alone. She needed someone here with her, who she could trust.

She called her mom. But her mom needed time to get here, and they were impatient to interview me. Then there was the football staff who wanted me back in the game. I had no choice but to call my parents and tell them where we were.

They were shell-shocked when they walked into the room, since they had to pass Coach Phillips being led away in handcuffs. Greer was sitting on a chair, and I was kneeling beside her, my hand holding hers. When the cop told me it was time to leave, I let her go and told my parents briefly what happened, and that Greer's mom was on her way.

"You can't leave her," I told them.

I turned to Greer. "You can trust them," I said to her. "I don't know how long this will take, or what will happen with the game, but I'll find you later, okay?"

She nodded. When my mom kneeled down and took Greer's hands in her own, I took a deep breath, hoping I did the right thing.

GREER

Three different cops, and a detective, interviewed me. Mrs. Camillo stayed by my side, holding my hand when they came to collect evidence. Each time they asked me exactly what Coach Phillips did, I had to repeat the story. It happened so fast, but his hands and mouth were everywhere. He pulled his pants down and was yanking down my panties when Nico arrived and pulled him off me.

"How did Nico know where you were?" they all asked.

"I have no idea," I stated each time. "But he found me and he saved me. I couldn't fight the coach."

Each time, they asked how he knew me. And I had to repeat my story about why we were introduced, through Nico, in order to meet Coach Evans. It was exhausting because it was a convoluted story. "Why didn't you just email the cheerleading coach directly with your project?" they'd ask. And I had to tell them about the cheerleading coach's reputation of being difficult.

"Why is this important to the story?" Mrs. Camillo finally asked. "He knew who she was. So do the thousands of fans in the stadium. Greer was on the big screen today. She received an award."

"He's a VIP," the detective admitted. "And she might not be his only victim. We need to be thorough."

"Oh my god," his mom said. "I thought he was a good man," she added, squeezing my hand. "I'm so sorry, Greer."

Then my mother walked into the room with Dr. Jane Forrester in tow. Nicholas Camillo was standing in a corner, Ana Camillo was holding my hand, while a detective was jotting down notes.

With the exception of the detective, we all held our breath.

"Nicky," she said. "You're here." Then she glanced my way. "Ana too. You came to help my Greer. That was nice. Thank you."

When the Camillos continued to stare at her, uncertain what to do, my mother spoke again. "Don't worry. I'm not going to hurt anyone. I'm just here for my daughter. And I brought my psychiatrist to vouch for me."

I wasn't sure why she thought to do that, but I started to giggle. It was probably just a release of trauma and nervous energy given the situation, but I was soon laughing. Then Dr. Forrester started to join in. I stood up, and my mom hugged me, and then my laughter turned to fresh tears as she herself started to cry and soothe me at the same time. The Camillos quietly exited the room.

It was amazing how much stronger I felt spending a few hours in the room, speaking with the police, Dr. Forrester, and my mother. Dr. Forrester was wonderful. I was so fortunate considering what would have happened had Nico not showed up when he did. I also lost the urge to cry. When I was finally allowed to leave, Coach Evans was being brought in for questioning.

"I had no idea, Greer." She shook her head, looking pained.

"The girls just told me that something terrible happened. And they all suspected Phillips. You were right to be afraid of him. What was I thinking all this time?"

"Serial abusers are master manipulators," Dr. Forrester explained. "Don't beat yourself up about it."

Nico never did return, but we left the stadium before the game ended.

TRUE TO HIS WORD, he did find me later. I'd showered, ate with my mom, Mark, and Nancy, and was about to go to bed for the night. He came up to my room to check on me but couldn't stay since his parents were waiting for him in the car outside.

Owen Ross somehow managed to win the game. Nico never played. He spent the afternoon with the police and then the football front office and university administrators. Apparently, he could lose his spot on the team because of Coach Phillips.

I was so much stronger, but when he told me that, I felt like I was back in the hallway. "That's not fair." I was angry. "You did nothing wrong."

"I know that. But Phillips is a giant in the NCAA. Who knows what will happen. All I care about is that you're safe."

"How did you know I needed you?" I asked.

"I can't explain it." He pulled me into his arms. "When the assistant coach mentioned cheerleader and Phillips, something wasn't right. I had to find you." He looked into my eyes. "But everything between you and me is on a whole different level. We belong together, Greer."

"Do you know what ran through my mind today," I whispered, "as everything was happening?"

"Tell me."

"How that monster could have been my first time—"

"I'd have kill—"

"Let me finish," I interrupted. "What I was thinking was how much I regretted *not* having dinner at your place." I smiled. "I know it's awkward with our families, but I love you, Nico. I think I always have."

He kissed me. "Let me get this straight. You've never hated me?"

"No." I laughed. "I never have."

"Good," he said. "Because I love you, Greer Scott. You said it first, but I knew when you walked into Professor Hawk's class, late, that you were the only one for me."

He kissed me again. And then we held each other.

"My parents are leaving after breakfast tomorrow," he said. "Why don't we have dinner at my place as soon as they're gone?"

NICO

When Greer came over the next morning, I made her watch a movie first. I couldn't finish the documentary because of the secret I carried inside. So we sat on the couch, I wrapped my arm around her, and I played my interview with my mother, her silent partner, for her.

Maybe it was because of the emotion of the day before, or the relief that the past few years finally made sense, but Greer did not cry or get angry like I thought she would. I didn't know what she was thinking, so when it was over, I turned to her.

"I meant it when I said you and I are on a different level," I started, "but I have no idea what's going through your mind right now."

She exhaled. "Is this why you've been avoiding me?"

"Yes!" I admitted. "I'm sorry."

"I should have figured it out," she said. "I was right that my partner was a woman."

"On the day of the interview, Dylan was waiting downstairs in case I needed to intimidate your partner. And then my mother walked in." I laughed. "I still haven't recovered."

"Was it the day Emma and I saw you?"

"Yes," I answered. "My mom loves you, Greer. She told me how painful it is to see you and not be able to show you that openly."

She nodded. "I don't know what to do with this." She pointed to my laptop.

"But this doesn't change us?" I asked. "You're not going to hold this against me?"

She looked at me funny.

"And my apartment. And my car," I added. "All funded by your sweatshop?"

"Oh!" Her brow creased. "Is that what you've been worried about?"

"Among other things," I said, "yes!"

She shrugged. "Maybe because that stuff has gotten my mom and Caroline into so much trouble I try not to get caught up. I always knew that if I needed anything, I could get it. I don't hold it against you though, if that's what you're afraid of."

"I don't know what I did to deserve you," I pulled her onto my lap, "but I'm never letting you go."

"Are you going to finally make me forget yesterday ever happened?" she asked, her lips hovering over mine.

"We don't have to rush this." My eyes met hers. There was nothing I wanted more than to make this girl mine, and I hoped she recognized that as her violet-grey eyes bored into me. But I wasn't stupid either. I stopped Coach Phillips from completing his sick and depraved mission, but he still assaulted Greer less than twenty-four hours ago. Her trauma was very real.

"Everyone is convinced that I'm going to have some sort of nervous breakdown." Her voice was quiet. "But for the first time since my mother and I came to Butler, I know I'm going to be okay. I'm not going to fall apart. It's because of you, Nico."

"But waiting is no big deal, Greer."

She clasped my hand, intertwining our fingers. "I never felt comfortable around Coach Phillips. This morning, the detectives stopped by to say that they've already had more victims coming forward. He's not getting out of jail." She studied me. "I don't know what I did to deserve *you*. Compared to those other girls, I'm so lucky. They weren't saved by Nico Camillo."

I hugged Greer to my chest then. Sleep was elusive last night. Images of Greer in the hallway, sheer terror on her face, flipped through my mind, and I told her this. What I didn't tell her was the panic I felt. What if I had been too late? What if I'd listened to the assistant coach and stayed on the field?

"Dr. Forrester came over this morning. And she was there when the detectives came. She asked me what happened when I closed my eyes last night. Was I afraid?" She lifted her face to mine and started to laugh. "I told her that I *only* saw you when I closed my eyes. I didn't tell her that I felt your hands all over my body, and your kisses on my lips. That I couldn't stop thinking about you all night."

"Now you know what's been dancing through my head since August," I teased her. "But given all that's happened, I don't want to hurt you."

"You won't hurt me. If you really want to wait, I will. But I don't want to have regrets either. Terrible things happen all the time, and we can't control them. I learned that when I was fourteen." She smiled at me. "You and I can control us though. I always feel safe when I'm with you, and I only want to be with you. Yesterday didn't change that. It's just strengthened my resolve to pick up where we left off weeks ago."

Greer leaned in, and her lips touched mine. I pulled away. "Promise me." I exhaled. "If this is too much for you, we stop."

She nodded. "Deal."

Once we started kissing, we both knew that this time, there was no turning back. I carried Greer into my bedroom and made love to her. She was not afraid despite all that she'd been through. I was still gentle even though my body had never been so fired up. Greer was magnificent. Every inch of her smooth skin tasted sweeter than I expected, and her scent drove me into a frenzy when I was loving her. She wanted to explore all of me too.

She tried, but she couldn't hide the pain I'd caused when I breached her. When I finally got all of me inside her, we both fought to breathe again. Her to adjust to the biggest erection I'd ever had, and me to not end this experience for both of us by erupting too soon. But her pussy was squeezing me so tight, I was right there. I had to start moving. She smiled and nodded when I told her, and then gripped me by the glutes inviting me to continue.

I pulled out and pressed my way back in. Gently I opened her thighs, saw Greer relax and felt her wet heat embrace me. So I picked up the pace, pumping into her like a piston. I watched her entire body blush as she got close. Her hands moved to the muscles of my arms and chest and back. Her caress felt worshipful, and I leaned down to capture her lips in a kiss. I couldn't get enough of her. While my tongue plundered her month, and my cock stretched her walls, my thumb circled her clit and softly pressed down.

She gasped, and her body clamped down on me. I swear I saw stars. She called out my name and then bit my shoulder as the contractions continued. I'd never felt an orgasm like this, and I pumped my way through it until I climaxed and her pussy squeezed every single drop of cum out of me.

After the first time, we showered together. It was her idea. I'd worn a condom but her skin was sticky because it was her first time. Seeing traces of blood unleashed a possessiveness in me I didn't know I had as I slowly cleaned her. When I saw her body coated with water and glistening with soap, her breasts still heavy with desire, my cock grew so thick Greer's eyes went wide. This wasn't about me though. I needed her to orgasm. I sucked her mouth, our tongues tangling, and then I moved to her nipples. She moaned each time I licked and pulled on them with my lips.

"Don't be scared," I said as wrapped her in a towel and brought her back to the bedroom. "I'm going to make you scream but I promise it won't hurt this time."

The sensitive skin of her neck and breasts was addicting. She pinked each time my mouth or tongue applied pressure, but her hands rubbing my back, her fingernails scratching at my skin told me she wanted more. My mouth finally trailed down to her core.

"What are you doing?" she asked, breathless.

"Trust me, okay?"

My hands were large and roughened, and Greer's thighs were smooth and firm underneath them. I rubbed my hands along them as I opened her up. The first swipe of my tongue along her clit made her gasp and close her legs. But I didn't let go, just gently pushed them open again. Greer was wet for me, and my tongue worked her clit and her folds until she was dripping. Her taste and scent drove me wild, my cock throbbed, and I continued to devour her with my tongue. Her fingers twisted my hair, and her voice mewed for me. I squeezed her full breasts, lightly pinching her rosy nipples with my calloused fingers. When I knew she was as wet as she'd ever be, I pushed a finger inside of her. My god she was still so tight and warm, and I almost came just at the memory of how good she felt when I moved inside of her.

Her voice started to change, her cries deepening. I knew she was close. "Come for me," I said. I pressed another finger into her and sucked on her clit until I felt her channel clamp down on my fingers. Then I heard my name on her lips. I didn't stop pumping my fingers into her and lapping her sweet cunt until her contractions subsided.

"Oh my god, Nico." She was blushing. "I'm so embarrassed you just did that."

"*That* was amazing," I said. "Don't ever be embarrassed. You are perfect, and I am the luckiest man alive. And we are just getting started."

"I guess this means I'm not moving." She smiled.

"Hold on," I said. "I know I said you belong *here* yesterday. But if I get kicked out of Butler, you can move Scotty and yourself wherever I go. Deal?"

Her face was still hazy, unfocused from the massive orgasm I gave her. But she nodded, and then hugged me to her chest.

38

GREER

e finished the documentary that afternoon as Nico finally made me a dinner I wouldn't forget. Aunt Isabel was right about his cooking. It came as naturally to him as public speaking. We didn't talk about Ana Camillo again that day. The truth was that when I saw her beautiful face on camera, her green eyes sparking against her pretty blue dress, I knew immediately that she was my partner.

She was always my button girl.

It was so obvious looking back, and I was disappointed in myself that I didn't realize it sooner.

But what if I had? Before Nico, I'd have been so stubborn I'd have severed ties with her. Now I had time to think. Nico suggested that I come home with him, back to Virginia, for a few days around the holidays. Provided, of course, that my mother would be okay here without me. I was considering it.

But I wanted to think about him first. And relive all of the moments from today. Nico's entire body was as sculpted and powerful as his chest and stomach were. Though parts of me were still sore from him penetrating me today, I knew I was addicted to him. I knew I wanted him again, as deep as he was willing to go.

He wanted to wait because he was convinced my body needed time to heal. And he had to focus on football. Coach Hampton didn't let him go. Coach Phillips was a bad guy. Dozens of students and women who'd graduated over the last decade, from all of the schools where he'd coached, came forward. Phillips never went to the NFL because he liked college girls. He controlled them, and football programs across the country protected him.

Because Butler cut him loose as soon as he was arrested, as they'd done to Tripp Saunders, our school was praised by the media and fans nationwide. Rather than vilify our players, people everywhere, outside of Butler, cheered for them. Even Nico Camillo. No longer was his name associated with Michigan College's bribery scandal. Now he was the guy who wasn't afraid to turn Phillips into the police.

Nico held a second dinner party the Sunday night before the conference championship. Curfew had been relaxed for one night only, and Dylan and Nico wanted to distract Owen from the stress of the highly anticipated rematch with Louisiana. If they could pull off a win, the team would train for the bowl game after Christmas and hopefully the national championship in January.

This time, I came over early to help him prepare. He'd made his mother's meatballs and gravy. His apartment smelled so amazing my stomach growled. He asked me to pick up ingredients for Italian bread, and making it that afternoon with him was, as Nico said, foreplay. He couldn't wait for the dinner party to be over. My body hummed with anticipation too.

Dylan and Lila were the last couple to leave. They'd already decided to move in together next semester. Lila still loved her sorority sisters, but she wanted to move past the drama. Unlike my sister, who thrived on it, Lila wanted peace.

When the front door closed on the two of them, Nico locked the knob and turned the deadbolt. "No one is interrupting us this time," he joked.

I loved it when his strong body stalked over to me, his gaze intense with need, and gripped my face. He didn't kiss me right away, but our foreheads touched and his green eyes burned into mine. "All day I've been fantasizing about you in my bed, totally naked, with your pink necklace on."

My heart raced for him. I ran my hands across his back and shoulders, loving how solid he was. Then I slipped my hands under his shirt and pulled him closer.

His kiss felt like fire. I wrapped my legs around him and he pressed me against the sliding door, just like he'd done weeks before. His erection grinded on me, and I felt emboldened. I unbuttoned his pants, slipped my hand below the waistband, and gripped his hard, smooth length. He hissed. "Greer," he said. "I'm not going to last long if you keep touching me."

But I didn't let go, even as we moved into his bedroom. Our clothes were soon shed, and he stared at me as I lay on his bed, naked, the diamond necklace I refused to take off even though my sister was no longer around to steal it. When his eyes smoldered, my breasts grew heavy and I felt my wetness dampen the sheets.

Was it possible to orgasm with just a look?

Nico stood above me, his erection so big I sucked in a breath. I wanted him inside me, stretching me. I have no idea where these thoughts came from, but soon I was sitting up, pulling him onto me. He started to kiss and lick his way from my neck to my breasts, my entire body so sensitive to his touch I cried out. When he rolled on the condom, he gently pressed against my entrance until the massive tip broke through the tightness and he drove himself inside.

"Oh my god," he said. "You feel so incredible, I don't know whether to move or come."

"Don't come yet," I commanded. My body needed him deeper, and I pulled his muscled chest against mine. Soon my legs were bend and spread, and he started to pound into me with controlled power, bracing his thick arms over my body so he didn't crush me. He filled me until I could not possibly stretch any more, and I kept getting wetter. His fingers found my center, and his thumb circled around my sensitive clit and pressed into it. I was moaning, fighting for sweet release.

"Come for me, baby," he whispered against my cheek then his mouth covered my nipple, pinching it with his teeth. His thumb was unrelenting as his slick rod pumped into me. And I shattered, calling out his name until his velvety tongue found mine and he sucked my cries down. I felt my body gripping his length, tightening around him in waves and he moved faster, making me shatter again as he found his own release.

Then our bodies, coated in sweat, held each other until we cooled down. When he withdrew from me, he held my face, and said, "That was not gentle sex. Are you okay?"

I smiled. "It felt amazing."

We showered together again. I got to touch and taste his erection as we washed each other off. We had sex once more before I went home. But this time, I was on top, controlling the tempo and letting him squeeze and suck on my breasts, nipping at my pebbled nipples. When he knew I was close, his fingers found my core and his thumb worked its magic. I loved how rough his fingertips were across my smooth and sensitive skin, and it wasn't long before I was seeing stars, my body clenching around Nico's, making him scream my name.

· · ·

MY MOTHER and I were lucky enough to get tickets for the conference championship in Atlanta. We sat with Emma and Blake in the nosebleeds, the entire Camillo family stories below us behind Butler around the fifty-yard line. If Butler advanced, Nico's goal was for the Scott and Camillo families to sit together at the bowl game.

It was a match for the storybooks. Owen trusted Nico more than his other receivers. Even though he was a tight end, he had more receptions than any of the wide receivers. Dylan was the players' MVP though. He didn't let Louisiana's defense inside to sack Owen Ross. And that was the difference in the final score. Owen got enough yardage to kick a field goal in overtime.

The four of us were hoarse when we made our way down the stadium steps. A plain clothes security guard stopped us at the bottom of the last escalator and asked us to follow him. It was bizarre considering we were four fans among thousands, all dressed in Butler colors.

We followed him down the steps and onto the lower level.

"Greer!" my mother shouted. "Look at the cheerleaders! I told you there was no such thing as too many sequins."

They were wearing their new championship game uniforms. In addition to their white sequined booties, the bralette sparkled too. I had to admit that they stood out among the confetti still flying around.

We were being escorted to the railing closest to the field. I held my mother's hand as we approached because Nico was standing next to the railing, his mother, father, brothers, and Isabella chatting with him on the other side. The pretty sidelines reporter, pregnant with her first child, was thanking him for his interview. Lila was on the field, her legs wrapped around Dylan.

Nico smiled when he saw me and waved us over. His green

eyes sparkled, and his cheeks were flush, his damp hair messy but away from his gorgeous face. When I leaned over to hug him, he stopped me and started laughing. I had a glittery seventeen tattoo on my cheek. "My mother has one too." I laughed with him. Then he hugged me and gave me a quick kiss. Emma and Blake mauled him, and then my mother leaned over, grabbed his face in her hands, and said, "Nico Camillo, you were amazing today," and kissed him on his forehead. "Congratulations, honey."

It was an appropriate greeting from the mother of your girl-friend, and I exhaled so hard I laughed. To any cameras filming this, Nico looked like he was being congratulated by a movie star. My mom wore tight ripped jeans and a tiny Butler T-shirt. Her heels were at least three inches, and her hair still held perfect loose waves. It shined under the bright lights. Her face, of course, was flawless. Somehow, I knew *this* was the image that would go viral. Not Dylan practically having sex with Lila on camera, or Nico sweetly kissing me.

Ana Camillo put her arm around me and squeezed. "That could have gone another way entirely," she said. "She's more like herself."

I was still so unsure what to say to her – thank her or tell her I love her – that I just embraced her, our heads resting on each other's shoulders for a moment. It was brief due to the chaos surrounding us, but enough. She smiled when we pulled away from each other and held my cheek tenderly.

My mother acted like nothing had ever passed between our families. She shook everyone's hand, told Ana how beautiful each of her sons was and how much they looked like both her and Nicky. Isabella, she said, was as cute as a button. As she spoke, she was holding onto me, so I knew this moment was hard for her. But I was glad she leaned on me for support. I squeezed her hand to let her know she was handling all of this well.

Then she said, "Jack would be so excited for Greer and Nico, don't you think?"

"Absolutely." Mr. Camillo wrapped his arm around Ana's shoulders. "Scotty would have loved it."

"Holy shit," Matteo muttered to Isabella. "What the hell is happening?"

EPILOGUE

NICHOLAS CAMILLO

Twenty-nine months later

Ana and I met Nico outside the stadium. It was May in Georgia and hot. This was the same weather we'd had the year before when Nico graduated. Today was Greer's turn, and Ana was more excited for her business partner than she'd been for her second, and arguably her favorite, son.

Greer wanted to finish in three years, and she'd done just that. We hadn't seen her yet, but Nico said she was standing with Dylan and Lila corralled in one of the tunnels, waiting to parade onto the field.

"Thanks for coming," Nico said to us.

We hugged our son and told him we wouldn't have missed it. He handed us our tickets, and we followed him inside. Nico would have been recognizable here no matter what given the school team's success the two seasons he played, but now that he was in the NFL, people everywhere called out to him. He was still seventeen, his lucky number.

Sophia and Mark Wilson smiled and waved to us when we

sat down next to Nico. They were on the opposite end of our row with their neighbor Nancy. Tucked in the middle was the Flores family, and they made a big fuss over us when we arrived. Especially over Ana. Now that my wife's role with Scotty Designs was out in the open, she was not shy about traveling down for a day or two and interacting with Greer and the growing staff. In another month, an apartment in Nico's building was ending its lease. Ana and I already decided to rent it so that it could be our home here. While Enzo had ruled against playing college football, he decided on a smaller school in Atlanta. So we had plenty of reasons to put down roots here.

Sam and Beatrice, Melanie's twins, rushed over to Nico the moment he sat down. They were having an argument over which one of them could run one hundred yards the fastest, and they needed him to settle the score. Nico listened, engrossed in what each seven-year-old told him, then gave his opinion on who he thought would win. In this case, it was Beatrice. Sam looked broken-hearted, until Nico gave his reasons.

"Beatrice weighs less than you, Sam, and her shoes have rubber soles." He pointed at her white tennis shoes. "But that's okay. You're bigger, and your muscles are stronger. You could definitely throw a football farther than her. You might have to work on your technique because she'll cover a lot of yards quickly." They both basked in his praise, then they argued about who was going to sit next to him until he sat Sam on one thigh and Beatrice on the other.

Aunt Isabel asked Nico about the Falcons. Nico and Greer couldn't believe how lucky they were that Nico got drafted to the local team. It made their risky purchase of Scotty's new studio, in the center of town, worth it. The storefront had become Melanie's domain. The way she saw it, she had the best of both worlds. She could still help sew when needed, but she preferred interacting with all the college kids, women, and young girls who shopped there. Ana had also convinced her to start college now that the twins were in elementary school.

In the back were Greer, Isabel, and whoever else was available to work. The Floreses' dry-cleaning, alterations, and tuxedo businesses supplied Scotty with seamstresses whenever they got behind. In the business world, it was a mutually beneficial relationship.

AFTER THE CEREMONY, when Greer found us, I had that familiar flutter in my heart but I didn't cry. Seeing her smile, with her dark hair and rosy cheeks, never failed to remind me of Jack Scott. She hugged Sam and Beatrice first. And then she laughed at whatever Nico said to her, her nose crinkling just like Scotty's, her violet-grey eyes merry, and I had to swallow my emotion down. Today wasn't a day for crying.

One thing Sophia and I shared, that Ana and no one else here did, was how easy it was to make Jack laugh. He was laid-back and kind, and he brought out the best in everyone. I wasn't funny unless Jack was around to laugh at my stupid jokes. Since we met in first grade, we were inseparable until Ana Romano moved to town. The irony of Sophia's fixation on me was that I ended it with her when I realized how much Jack liked her. We'd only been together a few weeks, and I saw Jack suffering.

Naturally, I chose him over Sophia. And then Ana enrolled in our twelfth-grade class, and I chose her over him.

But I never stopped loving Jack as the brother I never had. We still saw each other in our offices, or when we ran into each other in town, but it was never the same. I assumed one day Sophia would outgrow her imaginary love for me and we could go back to the way things were. But then my best friend dropped dead on Main Street, his lookalike daughter a witness, and I could not save him.

I still woke up in a cold sweat sometimes.

Having Greer in my life made mine better. She was the one for Nico. I knew it was inevitable the day he told me she was his partner for his capitalism class, but I had to be sure he never took her for granted. When he brought her back to Virginia that first Christmas, after Ana confessed to being Greer's investor, I knew my role as his father had shifted. He was his own man, desperately in love with a warm, strong and beautiful woman. I couldn't help but be reminded of myself when I found Ana.

But Nico had something extra. He had a piece of Scotty in his life.

Professor Simmons hurried over to Nico and Greer, practically tackling Nico she was so happy to see him. Then she unzipped her graduation gown, showing Greer and Nico her outfit.

"It's an original Greer Scott, Mr. Camillo." She twirled.

"Your shoes look perfect with that!" Greer exclaimed. "Can we photograph you for the website, Dr. Simmons?"

"I'd be honored," she answered her. "I was a model in my debutante days."

"Sounds like you found your cover girl, Gree," Nico said.

The professor, giggling, smacked Nico's shoulder.

Scotty Designs had started a new brand: Greer Scott. It was something Ana had been pushing for the last two years. She saw Greer as a dress designer and, like Professor Simmons, was wearing another one of Greer's originals. So was Beatrice. And Nancy. And Isabel and Melanie. And Lila. And Greer and Sophia. And many of the female graduates here, if Ana's numbers were right.

Greer and Ana, with the help of Nico, had become wildly successful. I stayed out of it for the most part, although I was pushing for a satellite store in our hometown in Virginia. I thought it belonged on Main Street. Isabella, Matteo's new wife, was contemplating running it.

"Miss Scott knows this already, but are you aware that your documentary still has the highest views *ever* by any other partnership in my history of capitalism class, Mr. Camillo?"

"That's because my mother made me cry, Dr. Simmons," Nico said, slinging his arm around Ana's shoulders. "I'll never live that down."

"Do you want to come over?" Greer asked her old teacher. "Nico and Dylan are cooking."

Sophia was hosting at her home in town. She and Mark had renovated and asked Nico and Dylan, who was drafted by the Dallas Cowboys, to christen their new kitchen. It was some kind of competition, and a bunch of football players and friends were expected to stop by. It wouldn't be the first time Ana and I were at their house, which was still so surreal. We'd helped them decide on a floor plan and architect. Sophia had asked for Ana's input, and I refused to let her go on her own. But Sophia was gracious, and kind, and even apologized for how unstable and crazed she was after Jack died.

In her words, she loved mothering Greer again, and she loved Nico as a son. The only painful thing for her was Caroline's continued self-exile from the Scott family.

Because we'd all learned to put aside our differences, Ana was pushing to bring Caroline back into the fold. To date, it wasn't going well. Caroline had found her own success as a reporter and influencer. Her social media following was huge. For now, she believed she was better off without Greer and Sophia in her life.

I found that so hard to believe. As I stood on the grass field under a bright sun, where Nico had fought for glory and the love of his life, my body and soul were content. And it wasn't just because I had Ana by my side. The people surrounding me had become my family. I watched with pride as Greer's and Nico's hands found one another, they smiled and kissed, and then returned to the rest of us. In less than ten seconds, without words, they spoke volumes about their love and support and pure joy with one another. Then, they went back to sharing their generous hearts with others.

Caroline could benefit from witnessing that. The power of true love. I had faith in her. She was Scotty's daughter after all, and Jack was as proud of her as he was Sophia and Greer.

One thing life continued to teach me was that it was never too late for redemption.

ACKNOWLEDGMENTS

My deepest love and gratitude for my husband and children for encouraging me to disappear and work on my stories when life slows down. You are my heroes.

xoxoxoxoxo

ABOUT THE AUTHOR

Clare Beck writes contemporary, new adult romances. Originally from Philadelphia, Clare and her husband are raising their family in Maryland. When Clare is not working, she enjoys adventuring with her family, hanging out with friends, and walking her shadow dog.

For more books and updates, visit:
CLAREBECK.COM